CW00524569

A Mersey Maiden

A Mersey Maiden

Mersey Murder Mysteries Book III

Brian L. Porter

Other Books by the Author

- A Study in Red - The Secret Journal of Jack the Ripper
- Legacy of the Ripper
- Requiem for the Ripper
- Pestilence
- Purple Death
- Behind Closed Doors
- Avenue of the Dead
- The Nemesis Cell
- Kiss of Life

The Mersey Mystery Series

- A Mersey Killing
- All Saints, Murder on the Mersey

- (Coming soon) – A Mersey Mariner

- (Coming soon) – A Very Mersey Murder

- (Coming soon) – Last Train to Lime Street

- (Coming soon) – A Mersey Ferry Tale

True Life

- SASHA – A very special Dog Tale of a very special Epi-Dog

Short Story Collection

- After Armageddon (Amazon bestseller)

Remembrance Poetry

- Lest We Forget (Amazon bestseller)

Children's books as Harry Porter

- Wolf (Amazon bestseller)

- Alistair the Alligator, (Illustrated by Sharon Lewis) (Amazon bestseller)

- Charlie the Caterpillar (Illustrated by Bonnie Pelton) (Amazon bestseller)

- **Coming soon**

  - Tilly's Tale
  - Dylan's Tale

- Hazel the Honeybee, Saving the World, (Illustrated by Bonnie Pelton)
- Percy the Pigeon, (Illustrated by Sharon Lewis)

As Juan Pablo Jalisco

- Of Aztecs and Conquistadors (Amazon bestseller)

Acknowledgements

A Mersey Maiden owes its existence primarily to the people of the city of Liverpool. Without them, and their influence on my younger life and without the family members, many of whom I have respectfully used as templates for many of the characters in my Mersey Mysteries I could never have begun the series. My thanks also go to my Beta reader, the indefatigable Debbie Poole in Liverpool, who painstakingly read every page of the book, correcting, suggesting and most of all; I'm pleased to say, enjoying this latest addition to the series. I send her my heartfelt gratitude.

I have to say thank you to Miika Hannila at Next Chapter Publishing for his encouragement and continued belief in the Mersey Mysteries and for helping in selecting the great cover designs for the books

My wife, Juliet is always there for me with words of support and earns my undying thanks for her faith in me and my writing.

I have to say a very BIG thank you to my friend and fellow author Mary Deal from the sunny Hawaiian

Islands for giving me permission to use her name for the trawler of that name featured in the book.

Finally, my thanks go to all my readers who continue to support my work by purchasing and reading my books. You are the most important people in the worldwide chain that links authors and readers and make the publishing world go round.

Introduction

Welcome to *A Mersey Maiden*, the third book in the Mersey Mystery series, following on from the success of *A Mersey Killing* and *All Saints, Murder on the Mersey*.

Once again Detective Inspector Andy Ross, Sergeant Izzie Drake and the rest of the Merseyside Police's Murder investigation team find themselves enmeshed in a complex and at times perplexing mystery.

When an American post-graduate student at Liverpool University is found murdered with his girlfriend sleeping by his side, it begins a case that takes Ross and his team back in time to the dark days of World War Two. A British Corvette and a German U-Boat are somehow inexplicably related to the murder of young Aaron Decker, who has quickly established himself as a star cricketer for the university team.

What links the talented young sportsman to the shipwrecks that lie deep beneath the waves of the English Channel? Very soon, Ross and Drake find themselves travelling to Falmouth in Cornwall where they link up with Detective Inspector Brian Jones and Detective Sergeant Carole St. Clair of the Devon and Cornwall Constabulary to investigate the sprawling international conglomerate, the Aegis Institute and its offshoot, Aegis Oceanographic.

Secrets abound and when a dead frogman is discovered, shackled to an undersea wreck, the case soon escalates to an international level. The Royal Navy becomes involved in investigating the wreckage and the web of secrets and intrigue takes the investigators back in time to the German submarine base at Kiel, in 1945, during the final days of Hitler's Third Reich. Aided by a respected German military historian, Ross begins to piece together an intricate jigsaw puzzle of fact and rumour, slowly unravelling the mystery that has brought the past very much into the present.

Unfortunately for Ross and Drake, the body count begins to mount as more facts from the past come to light. With their new Detective Chief Inspector, Oscar Agostini behind them, they formulate a daring plan to bring the perpetrators to justice. The plan revolves around a 'bent' detective and a hired killer.

Please read on to see how things pan out in this, the most thrilling yet in the Mersey Mystery series.

Author's note: For those not familiar with the very British game of cricket, it may be worth noting that an 'over' is a passage of play consisting of six 'balls' bowled by the bowler to the batsman. If the bowler succeeds in completing an over without

the batsman scoring a single run, this is known as a
'maiden over' and may give you a hint to the play on
words in the title of *A Mersey Maiden*.

A short glossary

Scouser/Scouse – A native of Liverpool (Scouse is also a local dish, a kind of stew made to an old Liverpudlian recipe)

Scally – a shortened version of the word 'scallywag' used extensively in Liverpool to describe a ne'er-do-well, a jack-the-lad, something of a wastrel

Made up – Another common Liverpudlian term, an expression of happiness, excitement or description of a pleasurable experience. e.g. "He'll be made up with the result of the game."

Uni – university

W.I. – The Women's Institute, a voluntary organisation that encourages women to take part in various activities within the community, originally formed in 1915 to encourage women to help in food production during World War One.

Chips - fries

Tom/prossie – a prostitute

Guvnor – short for governor, used extensively in the British police forces to describe one's boss or immediate superior.

Bent – 'A bent copper' is a term used to describe a corrupt police officer.

Dedicated to the memory of Leslie and Enid Porter
And to Juliet, my strength and number one fan

Chapter 1

Quintessentially British

"Oh, I say. Well hit sir!"

The time honoured cliché burst forth from the lips of an ageing, bespectacled gentleman, dressed in tweed jacket with leather reinforcements on the cuffs, white shirt and club tie and beige flannel trousers. Sitting in his deck chair, basking in the warmth of a sunny June afternoon, the old man could have been a contemporary of the great W.G. Grace himself, with his long, flowing beard adding to the appearance of a cricketing great from the past.

As applause rippled around the ground, the ball sailed gracefully over the boundary, the umpire duly raising both arms to signal another six runs to the university team. Nothing gave Andrew Montfort greater pleasure than spending an afternoon watching his beloved cricket; the sound of willow on cork as the batsmen amassed the best score they could be-ing almost like music to his ears.

This particular Sunday afternoon was a little spe-cial for Montfort, as the team from The University of Liverpool was engaged in the annual Montfort Tro-phy match against their fierce rivals from the Uni-versity of Manchester, the trophy being named for his grandfather, Sir Michael Montfort who had in-stituted the annual match soon after the end of the Great War in 1918.

Sir Michael had studied at the university before going on to become one of the leading industrialists of the early twentieth century. His business interests stretched from the city of Liverpool to Manchester and beyond, and the trophy was his way of encour-aging the post-war youth to enjoy his favourite sport whilst studying for their futures.

Having played cricket for the university he'd also later played for the local amateur club, Liverpool Cricket Club, an old established amateur club formed in 1807 and playing at the Aigburth Cricket Ground. The ground holds a singular claim to fame in that it possesses the oldest pavilion in the country at a first class cricket ground.

Now, the bowler completed his run up and another ball sped down the wicket towards the batsman who again made a solid contact, the thwack as bat con-nected with ball being greeted by yet more applause. This time, the ball was successfully fielded and the batsmen completed a single run.

A tall, mustached figure dressed in cricket whites walked up and stood beside Andrew Montfort's deck chair.

"He's quite a find, young Decker, don't you think, Mr. Montfort?" asked team captain, Simon Dewar.

"Indeed he is, Simon," Montfort replied. "Who'd have thought a Yank would become one of your best batsmen in years, eh?"

"Obviously, his experience playing baseball back home in the States gave him a good grounding, and don't forget his bowling prowess too," said Dewar, a tall, rangy student of accountancy and finance.

"Yes, I heard he was something of a star for his college team."

"It was our good luck when his father was transferred to the UK, and Aaron came over with his parents. Even more so that he chose us for his post-grad studies."

"A student of modern history, I believe, Simon?"

The team captain nodded as Montfort returned the conversation to his first love.

"How many centuries did he score last season, Simon? Was it seven, or eight?"

"Eight, sir, and got out in the nineties twice."

"It's a wonder the professional county cricket clubs haven't tried to tempt him."

"Oh, but they have, sir. Lancashire tried to coax him into joining them last summer, and Durham and Worcestershire made approaches, but he was adamant he wants to remain an amateur, free to play or not play as he chooses, and, as he rightly told them

3

all, if his father has to relocate again, he may have to leave the country at short notice."

"Well then Simon. We must make the most of young Aaron Decker while we have him, eh?"

"Definitely, sir, I couldn't agree more."

"Oh, yes, good shot, young Decker," Montfort suddenly exclaimed, applauding as he did so.

"I'd better go, sir. Soon be time to break for tea."

"Right you are, Simon. How many more do the university need to win? My damned eyes aren't what they were, even with the specs. Can't make out the scoreboard from here."

Simon Dewar glanced across at the scoreboard.

"We need fifty five to win, sir. If Aaron can stay at the wicket, we should cruise it after tea."

"Jolly good, Simon. Be nice to see the trophy stay at the old alma mater for another year. Been a while since you chaps won it two years running."

"Ten years since we achieved that honour, sir. I wouldn't have thought it mattered to you. You have as much influence in Manchester as you do here, don't you, as your grandfather did?"

"True, Simon, but I must admit, keep it under your hat mind; I always have a slight bias for you chaps. Probably because my wife hails from the area."

"Thanks a lot, Mr. Montfort. I shan't breathe a word," Simon smiled at the old man, and then wandered off towards the pavilion as another over ended. Simon Dewar retained a quiet air of confidence that the day would end with another triumph, thanks to Aaron Decker and his uncanny eye, which seemed to

4

guide his bat to make contact at the precise moment required to achieve maximum contact with the ball. American or not, he was a damn fine cricketer.

Following another single from Decker, and with Darren Oates now at the receiving end, the rest of the over played out without the addition of further runs, Darren being content to block the last two balls, after which the umpires signalled the tea interval and the players trooped off the field of play and into the pavilion, where refreshments awaited.

"It's going well, Aaron," Simon Dewar said as he handed Aaron Decker a refreshing glass of iced lemonade.

"Sure is, skipper," Decker replied. "Got to watch their fast bowlers though. They're not bad at all. The red-haired guy almost got me a couple of overs ago."

"Speaking of bowling, old Andrew Montfort has been watching you closely today. He was well impressed with your bowling figures earlier today. Six maiden overs from ten overs bowled is damn fine going."

"Hell, it was just good luck and poor batting," Aaron said, making light of his impressive bowling statistics. "Still, if it's giving the old guy a good afternoon, I'm real pleased."

Andrew Montfort chose that moment to walk up behind the two young men, and spent five minutes chatting to the pair, finally departing to speak to one of the lecturers he was friendly with, who'd just entered the pavilion.

thought he'd never leave you alone," said the eautiful long-haired blonde who walked up to the two men as Montfort walked away, wrapping her arms around Aaron's waist from behind, and reaching up to kiss the back of his neck. Dressed in a plain white, short-sleeved blouse with a fairly low cut v-neck and pale blue pleated mini skirt, her long legs bare, and with a pair of low-heeled white pumps on her feet, Sally Metcalfe exuded confidence, and Aaron spun round to take her in his arms and promptly kissed her on the lips before standing back to admire his girlfriend, who'd only just arrived at the ground, having spent the majority of the day at a family barbecue at her parents' home in Lancaster, some sixty miles north of Liverpool. Sally could have attended the university in her own town, but had chosen Liverpool in order to gain a degree of independence from her father, who she described as believing they still lived in the Victorian era.

"Hey, gorgeous," Aaron responded. "I was thinking you weren't gonna make it to see us lift that trophy again."

"I wouldn't have missed it for the world, Aaron. It's just, well you know how it is at home. I couldn't not go to the stupid barbecue; even if it was populated mostly by old farts and Daddy's cronies from the stupid transportation and pharmaceutical industries with their boring trophy wives, or worse still, their hired tarts."

"Ah, so young and yet so cynical," Aaron laughed. "I'm sure they were all perfectly charming as you English folks like to say."

"As charming as a nest of vipers, perhaps, and old man Roper, the local undertaker tried to grope my bottom too, the weasel-faced little pervert." Sally smiled back at him. "So, anyway, are we winning, darling?"

"Well, we need less than fifty to win after the interval. Roper the groper eh? Want me to go up there and challenge him to a duel?"

Sally giggled.

"You really would, I think, wouldn't you?"

"Sure thing," said Aaron. "A lady's honour and all that, eh?"

His attempt at an upper-crust British accent gave Sally another fit of the giggles. She then returned to the game.

"You're still batting?"

He grinned in the affirmative.

"Oh well, in that case they might as well start engraving Liverpool's name on the trophy now then. You're bound to win."

"Hey, this is sport, honey. Anything can happen out there, you know. I'm not invincible, not by a long chalk."

"No, but you're the very best player we have, my darling and I'm sure Simon has every faith in you to see out the game, don't you Simon?" Sally grabbed hold of Dewar's arm and pulled him close, so close he could actually see down the front of her blouse to

7

her cleavage. Embarrassed, Simon Dewar politely extricated himself from Sally's grip as he replied, "Let's say I very much hope Aaron will do the job for us, Sally."

"Oh, I say," Sally giggled. "I've got faith, Simon's got hope, but I hope you won't show their bowlers any charity when you get started again, Aaron, darling. Get it? Faith, hope and charity?"

"Very clever, darling, and very witty. Did you also know that during the German's siege of Malta during World War Two, the RAF used three old Gloster Gladiator biplanes to defend the island against massed attacks by the Luftwaffe and they named those airplanes Faith, Hope and Charity too?"

"Oh, really, how interesting," said Sally, who despite caring deeply for Aaron, couldn't care less about his other great passion, history. Aaron thought the world of Sally, but sometimes wished she'd realise that a working knowledge of history is, as he thought, our passport to building a better future. Still, she was great in almost every other aspect, even turning up regularly to watch him play cricket, a game he knew she barely understood, a fact that applied to most people outside the game. Trying to explain the intricacies of being 'in' or 'out' or the various fielding positions, including the odd sounding 'silly mid-on' or 'off,' square leg, long leg and so on, could be a baffling task, not to mention attempting to instruct someone in the difference between 'the wicket' and 'wickets' and just what the heck L.B.W. stood for, or what 'leg before wicket' actually meant was hard enough for a native, but when Aaron had tried to get the rules across to his father, Jerome Decker the third, it had turned into a session of much mirth as the elder Decker felt he was suddenly in the presence of an alien being, speaking an unknown language, rather than listening to his own son. All he said, having become totally lost as Aaron had tried to explain what the meaning of a 'maiden over' was, "Heck, son, don't tell me any more, just you go out there and enjoy yourself and show these Brits how to play their own game."

Aaron himself had known little about the game himself upon his arrival in Liverpool just over a year ago, but when team captain, Simon Dewar heard that the new American student had been something of a college star at baseball back home, he'd persuaded Aaron to try his hand at the quintessentially British game, with startling results. Aaron was a natural at both batting and bowling, and once he'd received a crash course in the rules of the game, he'd become an instant hit with players and spectators alike.

* * *

With the tea interval over, the match was resumed and with able support from Darren Oates, who was caught out with twelve to his name, and Miles Perry, Aaron was still there at the end, striking the ball cleanly for another boundary, a 'four' this time to take Liverpool past the Manchester total. Miles had added eight runs and Aaron ended with a total of fifty-five, out of the team's total of 211 for the loss of seven wickets, the last boundary taking them two runs past the opposition's quite respectable 209 all out.

The Montfort Trophy was duly presented to the winning captain by guest of honour, Andrew Montfort, and in his victory speech, Simon Dewar paid high praise to the team's star player, their superbly talented 'American cousin,' Aaron Decker, who received the man of the match award, a small silver salver, engraved with his name and the year of the award, and decorated with two crossed cricket bats overlaying a set of wickets.

As the applause died down and the crowd slowly departed, some by car, others on foot or bicycle, the two teams enjoyed a half hour of socialising in the pavilion before the coach carrying the Manchester team departed and at last, Aaron Decker relaxed as Sally sat on his knee, her crossed legs showing them off to perfection.

"Thank God that's over," Aaron whispered into her ear.

"I thought you loved it, Aaron," Sally said in quiet surprise at his comment.

"I do, honey, I do," he replied, "but I had some bad news earlier this morning and it's been on my mind all day."

"Oh, no, sweetie, what is it? Can I help?"

"Heck, no, Sally. It's just some news I'd rather not have heard. I don't really want to talk about it, if you don't mind."

"Sure, okay Aaron. Whatever you want. Listen, why don't we go to the pub, have a couple of drinks and then go back to my place?"

Aaron seemed to be deep in thought for a few seconds and then snapped out of it and replied, "Yes, why not? Sounds good to me."

"You can stay the night if you like? If we're quiet, no one will know." Sally whispered, tantalisingly. She was lucky in that her father's money had paid for her to jointly rent a house in the city with a friend and was currently considering buying her an apartment in one of the new building complexes along Liverpool's renovated waterfront. Aaron, despite his father's position at the U.S Embassy in London, had preferred to throw himself into university life in every way and currently shared a house in Wavertree with two other students. He and Sally often spent the night together, usually at his place, though he preferred the privacy of staying at her place where they couldn't be heard enjoying themselves through the walls. This was despite her landlord, prudishly in Aaron's opinion, frowning on overnight visitors of the opposite sex.

"You're on," Aaron smiled as he spoke, his earlier depression seeming to have lifted. Sally hopped from his lap and he grasped her hand firmly and led her from the pavilion, to a chorus of congratulations and 'cheerio' and 'lucky bastard' from the other remaining team members.

"Hey, don't forget this," shouted wicket-keeper Alex Dobson, as he tossed Aaron's man-of-the-match plaque across the room towards him, confident that Aaron would make the catch. He did, mouthed a thank you to Dobson as he and Sally disappeared through the pavilion door, a few drinks and a night of passion ahead of them.

Chapter 2

Wedding Day

Pedestrians passing by St. George's Hall in Liverpool's city centre might have been forgiven for thinking the police were attending a bomb threat or some other crime within the building. The presence of three police patrol cars, two rather obvious unmarked police vehicles and a dozen uniformed officers seemingly guarding the entrance to the building certainly backed up the wholly erroneous theory.

Within the famous old building, in the Sefton Room, Detective Sergeant Clarissa (Izzie) Drake and Senior Mortuary Receptionist Peter Foster gazed lovingly into each others eyes as the registrar pronounced them man and wife. Standing beside the groom, Doctor William Nugent, the city's senior pathologist and medical examiner was actually smiling for once, having been surprised but delighted when invited by Foster to be the best man at his wedding. Peter had told the rotund, overweight physician that he considered it a great honour to have him as his best man, not just as a mark of respect for the doctor, but because he was a genuinely nice man to work for.

In addition to Izzie's parents and younger sister, Astrid, also in attendance were the groom's parents, and most of the members of the city's specialist Murder Investigation team, including Detective Inspector Andy Ross and his wife, Maria, a local General Practitioner, and Detective Constables Samantha Gable, who was proud to be Izzie's maid of honour, Paul Ferris, with his wife Kareen and young son, Aaron, looking healthier than he'd ever done since a successful kidney transplant, Derek McLennan and Tony Curtis, who'd all done their sergeant proud by turning out in their best suits for the occasion. Back at police headquarters, the squad room was being manned in their absence by Detective Constable Nick Dodds, who, having worked with the squad on an ad hoc basis over the last two years, had now been assigned permanently to the team, together with their new boss, Detective Chief Inspector Oscar Agostini, who had recently replaced the outgoing and retiring D.C.I. Harry Porteous, who was present in the Sefton Room with his wife as special guests of the bride and groom. Also there from Peter's workplace was Francis Lees; Doctor Nugent's slim, pale and cadaverous but totally efficient assistant, looking cheerful for the first time in Ross's memory.

Agostini, an old friend and colleague of Ross's prior to his promotion, had offered to man the squad room with Dodds for a couple of hours, with Ross and his colleagues promising to return after the ceremony concluded. Ross had excluded Ferris from that promise, believing his senior D.C and family should represent the team at the small reception the happy couple's parents had clubbed together to pay for at the nearby Marriott Hotel. The ceremony over, the couple signed the register and left the room to the strains of the old romantic song, *No Arms Can Ever Hold You*, by the Bachelors. Izzie had fallen in love with the music of the 1960s while working on the case involving Brendan Kane and the Planets, and a missing young woman, Brendan's girlfriend Marie Doyle some four years previously. She could think of no song more romantic than this one to accompany her wedding service.

As they walked out of the building, the dozen uniformed officers who'd waited patiently outside formed a guard of honour with truncheons raised to form an arch and a beaming Izzie Drake looked towards her boss and mouthed a 'thank you' to Andy Ross for she knew it had to have been Ross who had arranged this final touch to make the ceremony complete and memorable for her.

A wedding photographer, a friend of Francis Lees, himself an expert with a camera in his hands, quickly arranged the wedding group and a series of photographs were taken in the morning sunshine, a perfect reminder of the happy day, after which he would follow the couple and guests to the reception.

Photographs over, everyone began to make a move towards transferring the celebrations to the hotel, and Ross quickly made his way to have a quiet word with his sergeant before taking his leave of the wedding party.

Pulling her to one side, Ross hugged Izzie fondly and placed a fatherly kiss on her cheek.

"Congratulations, Sergeant Drake," he said, with mock formality.

"Thanks for everything," Izzie replied. "You arranged the guard of honour didn't you?"

"But of course. No way was the best sergeant in the city getting away without a proper send off. Seriously, Izzie, I hope you and Peter have a long and happy future ahead of you."

"Thanks, sir. I appreciate that. At least, Peter's under no illusions about what I do for a living or the extra hours I have to spend at work on occasions."

"That's true," said Ross. "And you see him quite a lot when we have to visit the morgue too."

"Yes, well, we try to keep that contact to a professional level, as you well know, sir."

"I know you do. I meant to ask, are you going to continue to be D.S Drake from now on, or are you changing it to Foster?"

"Peter and I agreed it's best if I carry on as Drake at work, sir. I'll get plenty of time to be Mrs. Foster in my off duty hours."

"Right, that's good to know, Izzie. At least the rest of the force won't think I've got a new sergeant working for me."

"Right, well, I'm glad we've sorted that out, sir. Oh, look, sorry, but I'm wanted."

Peter was waving to Izzie. It was time they left for the reception.

"Off you go then," said Ross, "and enjoy the honeymoon," he continued, referring to the long weekend she and her new husband had booked in London. Ross had urged them to take at least a week off work, but Izzie had insisted four days was long enough for him to survive without her and Peter had actually agreed with her, knowing just how much she loved her job and the buzz she got from working with Ross.

As the happy couple were whisked away in a gleaming silver Bentley for the short journey to the Marriott, Ross rejoined his wife and the other guests, his own detectives amongst them, who'd remained to see them off, others having already made their way to the hotel to greet them as they arrived for the reception.

Ross said goodbye to Maria, who, like him, was heading back to work at her surgery, and suddenly, standing there outside the magnificent old building on St. George's Place, he felt really alone. For the first time in as long as he could remember, Izzie wasn't there to drive him back to headquarters, or to the next case. He and his sergeant had worked together for so long they almost thought as a single entity, being able on occasions to virtually read each other's thoughts, anticipate the other's next move in a case and so on.

"Sir?" came a voice from behind him. He turned to find D.C. Sam Gable standing there, having somehow changed from her wedding finery into her usual work outfit of plain white blouse, short black jacket and matching trousers.

"Hello, Sam. Been a good day so far, eh?"

"Yes, it has sir. Sergeant Drake looked beautiful didn't she?"

"She was positively radiant, Sam, definitely. What can I do for you?"

"More the other way round, sir. Sergeant Drake said I was to look out for you while she's away, so I thought I'd get changed in the ladies room back in the hall and then come down and give you a ride to headquarters. Izzie said your wife would probably take your car to her surgery and you'd end up stranded and having to cadge a lift with the uniform lads."

Ross couldn't help himself. He laughed out loud as he said, "Well, bloody hell, talk about a mother hen. Doesn't she think I can cope without her for a few days?"

Sam Gable cocked her head on one side, smiled a lop-sided grin at her boss and replied, "Sergeant Drake said you'd say something like that, sir, and, with all due respect, she told me to say, '*Do you really want me to answer that?*'"

Andy Ross laughed again, said, "Women, can't live with 'em, can't live without 'em," and in reply to the odd look on Gable's face, said, "Just ignore me Sam. I'm getting old, I think."

"You sir? No, not a chance," Gable replied. "Much too soon for you to be pushing up daisies or maybe retiring with pipe and slippers and a nice line in gardening tools."

"My God, Samantha, you're almost as bad as my bloody sergeant. Go and fetch my chariot, wench, before I change my mind and walk all the way back to headquarters."

Sam laughed with her boss as she almost ran round to the car park and soon had D.I. Ross seated next to her in the passenger seat of her car as she drove the short distance back to police headquarters.

Detective Chief Inspector Agostini was waiting expectantly for the team to return and was pleased to hear the wedding had gone off without a hitch. A couple of the Detective Constables had taken photos using their mobile phones and were quick to show them to Agostini and Nick Dodds.

As he sat at his desk in his office, Ross allowed himself to relax a little and take advantage of the fact that the last few days had been relatively peaceful and crime free, allowing him to catch up on the mountain of paperwork that seemed to grow exponentially with each case the squad handled. Even his team had welcomed a little peace and quiet as they also sat typing reports or preparing for forthcoming court appearances at various trials and so on.

As with all such times in the lives of the officers of law enforcement, this short lull would prove to be nothing more than the calm before a storm, and when the next storm hit, it would prove to be a damn big one!

Chapter 3

The Storm Clouds Gather

A hearty breakfast with Maria, followed by a smooth drive to headquarters through unusually quiet streets during his short commute from Prescot put Andy Ross in a good mood and the early morning sunshine gave the city a hint of the long hot summer that lay in wait for the inhabitants of the great sea port.

Ross made his way to the fourth floor, using the stairs as a means of exercise, and walked across the squad room, receiving morning greetings from Ferris, Gable and Dodds, already at their desks awaiting the day's developments. Placing his hand on the handle to open his office door, Ross sensed rather than saw D.C.I. Oscar Agostini enter the squad room, making his way through the mini-maze of desks to reach Ross before he'd made it into his office.

"I'm guessing you're not here to simply wish me a good morning, sir." Ross declared as he saw the look on Agostini's face, his furrowed brow a sure sign of a major problem looming for Ross and his team.

"Let's talk inside, Andy," Agostini responded, as he followed Ross in to the small office.

Ross sat at his desk as Agostini seated himself in the visitor's chair.

"I take it we have a new case?" Ross surmised.

"We do, Andy, and it might prove to be something of a hot potato."

"Come on, Oscar, it's not like you to beat about the bush. Let's have it," said Ross. Having worked together years earlier and being good friends outside of work, the two men would invariably revert to first names in private, Ross acknowledging the D.C.I.'s seniority in front of the team or in public.

"How much do you know about the United States Department of State, Andy?"

"Only that it's usually referred to as the State Department for short, and it has something to do with the USA's international political machinery."

"Right, well, we have a death on our hands that could get messy. The body of a young man was found in his bedroom in a shared house in Wavertree, yesterday. Because of his age and lack of external means of determining cause of death, pressure was apparently applied by his father for an immediate autopsy to be carried out."

"Hold on," said Ross. "Back-pedal a bit. Who is the father?"

"His name is Jerome Decker the third, and he works for the U.S Department of State, based at the

U.S Embassy in London. His son Aaron was studying at the University of Liverpool and was also a bloody top class cricketer, apparently. He is reported to have gone to bed some time after ten on the night before his death, with his girlfriend and was found dead by his house-mates, the girlfriend asleep next to him when he failed to appear for breakfast yesterday morning."

"Ah," said Ross. "This sounds a bit messy. I'm presuming we're certain it's murder?"

"We are now, Andy. The friends woke the girlfriend, Sally, and she reportedly went into fits of hysterics when she realised she'd been sleeping next to her dead boyfriend without realising anything was wrong. The lads from Wavertree were on the ball, thankfully. It didn't add up to them, so they asked the paramedics to leave the body in place while they got the forensics people and medical examiner in to take a look. Doctor Strauss attended, together with Booker's team and it didn't take long for the doc to ascertain that young Decker had been suffocated. Obviously the boys from Wavertree thought right away of the girlfriend, but, seeing the state of disorientation of the girl, Vicky Strauss examined her on the spot and she's convinced the girl was drugged, probably to make sure she was well out of it while Aaron Decker was murdered."

"And we've been called in because the case looks like being high profile and the Chief Super wants his favourite sacrificial lambs on the job, just in case it all goes pear-shaped."

Ross's words were more a statement than a question, and Agostini had to agree with him.

"You're right, of course, Andy. If the U.S. embassy can exert pressure on the Chief Constable and he shovels the pressure down the chain of command, then sooner or later it has to reach a point where' the buck stops here," and that, unfortunately will probably be right here, Andy. You're the best we have at this sort of case and the Chief knows it, but heaven help us if we screw up."

Andy Ross fell silent for a few seconds, apparently lost in thought.

"Everything okay, Andy?" Agostini asked.

"Mmm, yes," said Ross, thoughtfully. "Just a thought, but I have a contact at the American embassy. I might be able to find out something about this Decker character. He must carry some diplomatic weight if he's got the chief jumping through hoops already."

"Really? Tell all, Andy. It's not like you spend much of your life down South in the capital is it? Who's this contact of yours?"

"Name's Ethan Tiffen, works in Immigration. He was helpful in a case four years ago, and we've remained in sporadic contact ever since, exchanging Christmas and birthday cards and so on and Maria and I spent a weekend in London as his guests two years ago. I owe him a return of the favour to be honest. You might remember the case? We had a body found in an old disused dock and it led to a murder

24

investigation and the case of woman missing for over thirty years."

"Brendan Kane, and Marie Doyle, right?"

"Good memory, Oscar. Yes, that was the case. I had to contact the U.S. Immigration service in the course of the investigation. Ethan Tiffen was the guy who did his best to help us out, and even came up here for the eventual joint funeral of the couple."

"That was one great piece of police work," said Agostini. "You managed to solve a thirty something year old murder and the disappearance of the woman in one felled swoop, if I remember."

"Yes, we did, so I'm thinking maybe Ethan Tiffen can fill me in on this Decker character."

"Okay, good idea, talk to him, Andy. First though, we have to take over the case. Detective Sergeant Meadows at Wavertree is waiting in my office. I asked him to come over and bring their file with him. You need to get moving on this as fast as you can, Andy."

"Right, let's go talk to Meadows," said Ross and he and Agostini quickly made their way to the D.C.I's office. As they walked through the squad room, Ross called to his team as they sat at their desks or at the coffee machine, "No one leaves the office, people. I'll be back shortly. We've got a new case, and it could be a big one."

Leaving the small team of detectives to gossip and conjecture between themselves, Ross and Agostini were soon being fully briefed by D.S. Ray Meadows on the strange case that was about to be dropped in their laps.

"As far as we can ascertain, the young guy was something of a local hero," Meadows informed them. "Went from being a star college baseball player back home to becoming a star varsity cricketer over here. Seems he almost single-handedly won the Montfort Trophy, whatever that is, for the University of Liverpool in a match with Manchester last week."

"So why would someone want to kill him?" Agostini mused.

"And why do it in such a haphazard fashion?" Ross added, "leaving the girlfriend as an obvious suspect, yet leaving her in such a state she'd be immediately eliminated from our inquiries?"

"Already asked myself that one, sir," said Meadows. "And I can't say as I'm not happy to hand the case over to you, that's for sure. Once my gaffer got the whiff of the politicos being involved, he couldn't offload it fast enough."

"Wow, thanks, Sergeant," Ross said, wryly.

"You're only too welcome," Meadows continued as he passed the thick folder containing the notes made on the case so far to D.C.I Agostini who in turn handed the file to Andy Ross.

After the sergeant had departed, Agostini said very little. Ross had read through the file and given it back to the boss to glance at. There was nothing in it that might help them in formulating a theory for the murder of Aaron Decker.

"Would someone mind telling me, just where the hell I'm supposed to start with a case that's already over twenty four hours old?" Ross asked of nobody in particular.

Chapter 4

Autopsy Room Two

The drive to the city mortuary building had been a strange one for Andy Ross. It had been ages since he'd driven himself there, with Izzie Drake normally doing the driving, and visiting the place without his trusted assistant felt somehow wrong, out of place, especially as he knew her husband, Peter Foster, a familiar face on entering the mortuary building, would also be absent, and another, unknown receptionist would be on duty, ready to admit him to the antiseptic and formaldehyde-scented inner sanctum of the world of the pathologists.

Ross parked the car and waited for D.C. Paul Ferris to arrive in his own vehicle which he did a couple of minutes later. Ross's resident computer 'genius' and team collator Ferris had an incisive mind and Ross wanted him to view the body of Aaron Decker to get his 'feel' on the case. It was unusual for the team to be called into a case after the body had been removed from the murder site, so Ross felt they were playing catch-up. The old theory that the first twenty four hours of a murder investigation were the most important had definitely gone out the window on this one.

"Bet it feels strange without Sergeant Drake, sir?" said Ferris.

"I admit it does, Paul," he replied. "Still, only another couple of days and she'll be back on the job."

"Meant to ask you, is she still Sergeant Drake or Sergeant Foster now, sir?"

"Drake at work, Foster at home," Ross replied.

"Makes sense, I suppose," Ferris said as Ross pressed the buzzer beside the door that allowed entry to the mortuary building. A female voice answered, asking who required entry to the premises. After identifying himself and Ferris a click sounded and Ross pushed the door open. At the reception area usually manned by newly-wed Peter Foster, Ross was greeted by a petite brunette whose name badge gave her name as Michelle Hill.

"Inspector Ross, nice to meet you," Michelle said, after the two men had produced their warrant cards. "Peter speaks of you often."

"He does?"

"Of course. As his wife's boss your name comes up quite often in conversation."

"Hmm, I see," said Ross, wondering what Peter Foster really thought of him, but that was for another time.

"You're here to see Doctor Strauss, I presume?"

"Yes, please," Ross replied.

"Autopsy Room Two," said Michelle, "Doctor Nugent is with her I think."

"Oh, that should be fun," Ross smiled, as he thought of Doctor William Nugent, the overweight but brilliant Scottish Chief Medical Officer, not a man renowned for his sense of humour. Two minutes later, Ross and Ferris were to receive their first view of the mortal remains of Aaron Decker, just twenty two years old at the time of his death.

"Come in, Inspector Ross, come in," Nugent said in a hale and hearty voice as he and Ferris entered the autopsy room after a brief knock and wait. William Nugent stood beside Doctor Vicky Strauss, who Ross had not dealt with since her brief involvement in the horrific graveyard murders of the previous year. Ross noticed that the petite pathologist had had her brunette hair cut in a fashionable bob since the last time he'd seen her. He thought it added to her look of vulnerability, though he knew she was quite superb at her job. Anything less and she wouldn't have lasted a day working under William Nugent.

"Hello, Doctor Nugent, Doctor Strauss," Ross said as the two detectives walked slowly across the room towards the stainless steel autopsy table where the remains of Aaron Decker were already laid out, his chest cavity opened up and the majority of the internal organs already removed and weighed.

"Ah, D.C. Ferris," Nugent observed on seeing Paul Ferris at Ross's side. "I see the inspector has let you out of the office for a breath of fresh air in the absence of the newly-wed Sergeant Drake."

"Hello, Doctor," said Ferris. "Not that I'd necessarily class a visit to the mortuary as a breath of fresh air, but yes, it's good to see you again, you too, Doctor Strauss."

"Detectives," said Strauss by way of greeting. "Sorry to have to meet like this. Such a shame, tragic when we see them this young on the table," she added as the body on the table loomed larger in the view of Ross and Ferris, as they arrived at Vicky Strauss's side.

"No Lees this morning?" Ross asked, referring to Nugent's erstwhile assistant. Seeing Nugent without Lees was akin to how Ross probably appeared to those used to seeing him with Izzie Drake.

"Ah, poor Francis," Nugent replied. "Had such a good time at the wedding the other day, seems he was a little worse for the drink, and slipped on the stairs when he got home. Spent three hours at A & E, only to be diagnosed with a severely sprained wrist. He's nae good to me in that state, all wrapped up and fingers useless with the strapping, so I've told him to stay at home until he can work his hand again."

"The dangers of the demon drink, eh Doc?" Ross grinned.

"In Francis's case, aye. Silly wee boy isn't used to all that hard liquor. Seems the punch at the reception was a wee tad over-imbued with vodka, and Francis was literally bundled into a taxi by a couple of guests when he was found slumped on a staircase singing *I belong to Glasgow.*"

"But he's from Fazakerley, isn't he?" Ferris observed.

"Aye, that he is," Nugent laughed. "Must have spent too much time working with me. Ma Glaswegian roots seem to have rubbed off on him and tainted the man's perception after a couple of drinks."

"Right, well, can we get to work, please Doctors? Seems this young man's father is on his way up from London. He's something to do with the U.S. State Department so the case could have political implications. The Chief Constable has apparently already been applying pressure to the Chief Super who in turn put the squeeze on D.C.I Agostini..."

"Who in turn, is putting pressure on you, I presume," Strauss observed, logically.

"Quite right Doctor Strauss. As I wasn't involved in the case until this morning, I have little to go on so far except the report from the Detective Sergeant who responded to the original emergency call, and the crime scene photos that were taken by Miles Booker's forensic team."

"Right, well, Inspector Ross, I can tell you that Sergeant Meadows was very thorough and carried out a very professional examination of the scene," said Strauss.

"I'm glad to hear it," Ross replied. "I have his report here," he added, holding up the file he'd brought from headquarters.

"Yes, in fact it was Sergeant Meadows who first suggested to me that something might be wrong with Sally Metcalfe."

"That's the girlfriend, right?"

"Yes, I was examining Mr. Decker of course, and then the sergeant asked if I'd take a look at the young lady. He thought she might be on something at first, but from her state of disorientation, he suspected she'd been deliberately drugged. I broke off from my examination of the body for a few minutes and it was clear to me that Miss Metcalfe had been drugged in some way. Her reactions didn't suggest she'd deliberately taken any kind of recreational drug, and the symptoms she displayed made me believe she'd been given something to anaesthetize her for a period of time. On close examination, I found a small needle mark on her arm that could be the site of an injection having been administered. I took blood samples at the scene, and sent them for a tox screen. We should get the results later today."

"That was good thinking, Doctor Strauss. Now, what can you tell me about this poor fellow?" Ross said as he looked at the body of Aaron Decker. Sadness showed on Ross's face, the sadness he felt at the lost life of a young man who, it appeared, had everything to live for before being cut down by the hand of a killer.

"This is where things get interesting," Strauss said, and Ross could almost swear she said it in exactly the same tone of voice that her boss, Doctor Nugent had used with him over the years. "Of course, the first thing I did was look for signs of a natural death. Even young men of Aaron's age have been known to keel over from heart failure, for example, but then, I noticed a few scraps of lint-like fibres in the nasal passages, petechial haemorrhaging around the eyes and signs of cyanosis in the face. I compared the lint fibres with the pillow cases on the bed and they provided me with a visual match. Tests are ongoing to confirm my thoughts. I made a quick examination of the body as it lay on the bed and lo and behold, I found a similar pin prick on Aaron's upper left arm. I had enough to warrant a determination of a suspicious death, and that's why we're here today."

"Seems to me you've got it all worked out, Doctor," said Ross. "I'm surprised you're going through the whole business of the autopsy if you think you've already determined cause of death."

"Ah, procedures, rules and regulations, Inspector," Nugent chimed in. "As ye well know, in cases of suspicious death we have tae carry out a full post-mortem examination, and so that's what we're about today."

"Yes, of course. I know that Doc, just seems a waste of time sometimes."

"Aye, well, I'll not disagree with you on that one, Inspector, but anyway, we were just finishing up anyway, when you and D.C. Ferris arrived."

"Okay, so, what's your verdict, Doctor Strauss?"

Ross directed the question to the younger pathologist as, strictly speaking, it was her case, despite Nugent being her supervisor.

"Death was caused by asphyxia, Inspector. But, it's possible the victim was drugged first in order to render him unconscious and therefore eliminate any chances of him struggling while he was being suffocated. It looks very much as if his girlfriend was also drugged to pacify her while the murder was being carried out."

"There is another option that you may have missed here, Doctor, if you don't mind me saying so," said the quick thinking Paul Ferris.

"Go on, please, D.C. Ferris," Strauss replied.

Ross smiled, thinking he already knew what Ferris was about to add, and as the young detective spoke he confirmed Ross's own thoughts.

"Well, what if the murderer was actually intending to kill both Aaron and Sally? He successfully knocks them both out somehow with a drug of some description, manages to complete the murder of Decker, and then before he can kill the young woman, something disturbs him, a knock on the door, a noise at the window, I don't know. It could have been anything, I'm just theorising here, but it's surely possible. The girl could still be a target."

"You're quite right, Paul," Ross agreed.

"Yes, I suppose you are," said Strauss.

After a moment's hesitation, Ross added another option to Ferris's initial supposition.

"Your theory is good, Paul, but it also opens up another possible scenario."

"Sir?"

"Yes, it's equally possible the girlfriend is a very clever and devious killer. She could have injected Decker, suffocated him while he was unconscious and then injected herself with enough of whatever the knockout drug was, just enough to make sure she was still out of it when someone came to find them in the morning. She was bound to know the housemates would come looking for Aaron when he didn't show up at breakfast time."

"I see what you mean, sir. So, Sally Metcalfe could be a potential victim or she could be the murderer. Looks like we either have to protect her, or investigate her in detail."

"Exactly," said Ross.

Having listened to the two detectives thinking 'on the hoof' Doctor William Nugent turned to his female colleague and observed,

"Aye well, that's why they're the police and we're just the old sawbones, Vicky," Nugent concluded. "It's their job to look one step beyond our findings, in order to catch the criminals. Am I correct, Inspector?"

"I suppose you are, Doctor. Yes, we rely heavily on what you can discover from the dead, but we have to take what you give us and try to build a case around the simple facts of what actually caused a person's death."

"Well, I wish you luck with this one. Such a shame, and him so young," said Nugent. "I'll have our full report on your desk as soon as humanly possible."

"Thanks to you both," said Ross, at which time the doors to the autopsy room flew open and a well-dressed figure of a man burst into the room closely followed by a red-faced and flustered-looking Michelle Hill.

Chapter 5

Jerome Decker III

No one in Autopsy Room 2 needed to look further than the face of the tall man who blustered into the room to know he was the father of the young man who lay on the stainless steel autopsy table in front of them. The facial resemblance was clear for all to see. With swift presence of mind, Paul Ferris stepped quickly towards the advancing man and despite being considerably shorter and of a lesser physique, stood his ground directly in front of him, his arms spread out to form a physical barrier.

"Sir, you really don't want to some any closer. Please, just wait here a minute."

"That's my son," the man shouted, the anguish clear in his voice. "I want to see my son."

Ross quickly joined Ferris and the two of them managed to force Jerome Decker to back-pedal until he was standing with his back against the wall beside the double doors.

"Mr. Decker, I'm Detective Inspector Ross, and this is Detective Constable Ferris. You do not want to see your son at this moment, I assure you. Please allow the doctors to complete their work and then I'm sure Doctor Nugent will arrange for you to see your son."

"Aye, of course I will, Mr. Decker," said Nugent, "but the inspector is quite right about not seeing him just now. The inspector will talk to you while we finish here. Inspector Ross, you can use my office if you like. You know the way, of course."

"Yes, thank you, Doctor," Ross replied, gratefully. "Please, sir, come with me. I know you're upset and grieving, but we really do need to talk to you."

Somehow, Ross and Ferris managed to shepherd Decker senior from the room and along the corridor. Ferris opened the door to Nugent's office and Ross guided the father into the room, Ferris closing the door as he followed them inside. As soon as the door closed, without invitation, Jerome Decker slumped into one of the visitors' chairs in the office and held his head in his hands, his grief palpable as his shoulders shook and tears began to fall from his red-rimmed eyes.

"Take your time, Mr. Decker," said Ross, passing a box of tissues across the desk, obviously kept there by Nugent for just such occasions, which Ferris handed to the distraught man. Decker looked up, saw the box and took out a single tissue which he used to dab at his eyes.

"Thank you. I'm real sorry for bursting in like that. I was just ... hell, I don't know what I was doing."

"You're upset, you want to lash out, and you want answers, am I correct, Mr. Decker?"

"Well, yes, you're right, Inspector. This news has devastated my wife and me, I can tell you."

"Where is your wife, sir?"

"She's still in London. I didn't want her to come here just yet, not until things are clearer. Do you have any idea exactly what happened to my son, Inspector...?"

"Ross, sir. Andrew Ross is my name."

Ross turned to Ferris and asked him to organise tea and coffee for them all. "Maybe young Michelle can help," he said as Ferris rose to leave,

With Ferris gone, Ross leaned forward and looked into the eyes of the grieving father. He decided the out and out truth was his best option in dealing with the American.

"Mr. Decker, I won't hide anything from you. All the evidence we have so far points to the fact that your son was murdered."

"Murdered? My God, we were told he'd been found dead, but nobody at the embassy said anything about murder. Please, tell me what happened. Aaron was so popular; I just can't believe anyone hated him enough to murder him."

"Your son was found dead in his bed by one of the young men who shared the house in Wavertree with him. His girlfriend, Sally Metcalfe, was still asleep beside him apparently, and when woken up, she became hysterical on finding Aaron had died in the night. We've since discovered that both Aaron and Sally were given some sort of drug intravenously to knock then both out, after which Aaron was asphyxiated with his own pillow. Toxicology tests are being carried out as we speak to determine the drug that was used to knock them out. That's about it, so far, Mr. Decker. My team were only called into this investigation this morning, though we have the file from the officers who first responded to the emergency call."

Decker looked stunned. Maybe he thought his son had died from an accident or natural causes. To be told your child has been murdered must be a terribly traumatic experience, Ross thought, glad at that moment that he and Maria had no children of their own,

"You have no suspects?" Decker asked.

"Not as yet, no sir. It's early days, yet. Tell me, do you know of anyone who might have wished Aaron harm?"

"Not a soul, Inspector Ross. Like I said, Aaron was popular, gregarious and easy to get along with. This is a nightmare, a real nightmare. What the hell am I going to tell his mother?"

"I'm sorry. I know this isn't easy for you, for we have to know as much as we can about your son if we're to find his killer."

"I understand. Ask away, Inspector Ross."

"Do you have any enemies, Mr. Decker? Could someone have tried to get at you through your son? Could killing Aaron have been meant to send you some kind of message? I understand you're something in the U.S. State Department?"

"I'm nothing special, Inspector, just a simple Cultural Attaché."

"And what exactly does that entail, Mr. Decker?"

"Nothing sensitive, I assure you," said Decker. "My job simply involves furthering positive relations between my country and yours, and any others who happen to come into contact with our embassy in London."

"So you don't have any kind of political agenda that might have made someone think that hurting Aaron could influence you in some way?"

"No, Inspector Ross, definitely not. You need to look elsewhere. What about the guys he was rooming with, or house sharing or whatever you call it over here?"

"You never met them?"

"Hell, yes, once or twice, I think, when Aaron first moved in up here. We came up to help him get settled and met the two other guys then. I never got to know them. It was just a few minutes here and there. Aaron said they were both studying at the university too, and I thought that was good enough as a recommendation."

"Okay, and the girlfriend, Sally Metcalfe?"

"Met her a few times. Seemed a nice enough girl, a little stuck-up maybe, but nice enough. Aaron said she was studying Marine Biology, and I thought that a bit odd for a girl like her, but he said she wanted to help preserve the oceans for the future, so maybe not so odd after all, huh?"

"I'd have to agree with you," said Ross. "Would Sally have any reason to harm Aaron?"

"Oh, come on, Inspector Ross. Now you're clutching at straws. You said she was knocked out too, so how could she have killed my son? And as far as I know, she adored him. Why would she hurt him? And what possible motive could she have? She came to visit us in London at least a dozen times, with Aaron. No way would that girl have hurt him."

"Okay, so, thank you for your patience, Mr. Decker," said Ross, as Ferris entered the room, carrying a tray, followed by Michelle the receptionist with a second tray. Between them, they'd made tea and coffee, and now brought them in to the inspector and the diplomat.

* * *

Ross allowed a lull in the questioning as they sipped their tea or coffee, and in those few quiet minutes, Decker seemed to relax slightly, the tension of earlier releasing itself a little.

Sensing a good moment, Ross began again.

"Do you have any other children, Mr. Decker?"

"Yes, Peter and Kelly. Peter is twenty seven and Kelly's just eighteen. She's at home with her Mom, in a totally distraught state."

"And Peter?"

"Back home in the States, Inspector. Peter's in a rock band, not quite the career choice I'd have picked for him after his years at Harvard, but then, what can we parents do nowadays, huh?"

"So, he doesn't know about Aaron yet?"

"Oh, he knows alright. I caught him between gigs when his band stopped over in Seattle last night. They've cancelled the rest of their tour and Peter is on a flight across the Atlantic right now. He's gonna check in with his Mom in London and then grab a flight up to your John Lennon airport to join me here."

"You do realise, Mr. Decker, that there's little you can do up here, unless you have information that can help the investigation? Don't you think you'd be better staying in London with your family while we do our jobs and find your son's killer?"

Decker's face seemed to change in that moment, displaying a hardness that hadn't been evident a few minutes earlier.

"Inspector Ross, if you think I'm leaving Liverpool before my son's killer is found, then you sure as hell don't know me. When Peter arrives he'll be bringing his Mom and sister up here with him and we'll be here for the duration. Any way we can help, we will, but I do promise not to get in the way of your investigation."

"I see," Ross replied. "It's a free country, Mr. Decker and you and your family will be welcome here in Liverpool. I just hope it doesn't distress your wife too much, and your daughter of course."

"They'll be fine, Inspector, just fine. Now, is there anything else I can do for you right now? I'd like to see my son, and carry out the formal identification you require, if that's okay."

"Go and see if they're ready for Mr. Decker, would you, Paul?" Ross asked Paul Ferris who went to check on the status of the remains, returning a minute later with Doctor Strauss in tow.

"We're ready for you now, Mr. Decker," Strauss said, as Decker rose from his seat, following her from the room, with Ross and Ferris close behind.

Nugent and Strauss had worked quickly to make Aaron Decker's remains suitable for viewing by his father, the Y incision having been quickly closed and the skin and hair on the skull replaced so the elder Decker wouldn't see that his son's brain had been removed for autopsy purposes.

Decker stood stoically at the viewing screen window with Straus and the two police officers as William Nugent himself performed the ritual display of the body, covered in a discreet white sheet, and Ross could almost feel the grief emanating from every pore of Decker's body as he nodded and almost in a whisper, confirmed that the body was that of his son, Aaron.

"What happens now?" Decker virtually whispered as his voice faltered.

Ross placed a hand on Decker's shoulder, slowly managing to turn him away from the viewing window as the curtains on the other side automatically slid across to block the view into the room, Ross having pressed a small button beside the glass that lit up an indicator in the laying-out room, letting the attendant know identification was complete.

"Well, for now, I think you should go back to your hotel. You've told us what you know about your son's housemates and his life over here, unless there's anything else you can add."

There were three burgundy upholstered upright chairs in the room, placed against the back wall, and Decker suddenly sat down heavily onto one of them, his face appearing even more ashen than before, having looked at the dead face of his youngest son.

"He was a good son, Inspector Ross."

"I'm sure he was," Ross replied sympathetically.

"He made friends easily, but I never knew him make any enemies."

"Well, we understand from his girlfriend's original statement to Detective Sergeant Meadows that he received some news that day that had upset him slightly. Would you have any idea what that was?"

"No idea at all, I'm sorry. Heck, it might just have been something to do with his cricketing for all I know."

"Tell me, Mr. Decker, whereabouts in the USA do you and your family live?"

"What? Oh, we live in Washington D.C. Aaron was at Georgetown University before we transferred over here. He was quite a rising star for the college baseball team and they sorely missed him when we moved, I can tell you."

"I've heard he didn't take long to make a name for himself with the University cricket team when he got here too, Mr. Decker?"

"So he did, though I can't for the hell of it figure out that crazy game of yours, Inspector."

"Neither can a lot of us, please believe me, sir."

Decker seemed to have calmed down and Ross was glad he'd been able to turn his thoughts away from the cold, lifeless cadaver in the next room with talk of his son's achievements on the sports field. He needed to press on with the investigation and for now, Jerome Decker III needed to go to his hotel, eat something and try to relax, maybe phone his wife, do anything to give Ross the chance to get on with the job of finding his son's killer.

Thankfully, Ross was able to convince Decker to return to his hotel soon after, hoping that the imminent arrival of his family might keep him occupied for a little while, and Ross had Michelle arrange for a taxi to collect Decker and ferry him to his hotel.

Ross and Decker parted with a firm handshake and soon afterwards, Ross and Ferris made their way back to headquarters, where Ross intended to step up the pace of the investigation. Something was eating away at the back of Ross's mind and he believed he knew just the man to answer his questions.

Chapter 6

Old Buddies

"Andy Ross, well I'll be," the distinctive New York accent of U.S. Immigration Officer Ethan Tiffen bellowed into the phone when his secretary informed him who was waiting on the line to speak with him. "How are you, old buddy?"

"I'm good, Ethan, thanks. How about you and the lovely Sophie?"

"We're fine, Andy, just fine. But, I'm guessing this isn't a social call?"

"You guess correctly, Ethan. I'm looking for information about one of your compatriots, and fellow embassy employees."

"Really? Can I ask why?"

"We've got a suspicious death on our hands, a young man found dead in his bed, and his father is one of your cultural attachés."

"Got a name?"

"Decker."

"As in Jerome Decker III?"

"You know him?"

"Let's say I know of him, Andy. You say his son is dead?"

"Murdered, Ethan. Suffocated with a pillow."

"Jesus H. Christ. That's bad, real bad, Andy. I take it Decker is in Liverpool?"

"He is, and says he won't be leaving until we find Aaron's killer. I need to know if there's anything I should know about him. Seems he had the power to demand an immediate autopsy to find out what killed his son and there's some heavy pressure coming down from above for us to effect a fast resolution of the case."

Tiffen fell silent for a few seconds, and Ross could almost sense his friend being locked in thought. Ross broke the silence.

"Ethan?"

"U huh, yeah, sorry, Andy, just thinking there for a minute."

"Thinking what, Ethan? Come on my friend, I know you want to tell me something. I promise if it's of a sensitive nature, I'll keep it jut between the two of us. Just what is it about this cultural attaché of yours?"

"Look Andy, I could get canned for this, so listen up. I ain't gonna repeat it okay?"

"I'm listening, Ethan. What's going on, my friend? Just who is Decker?"

"Andy, you're not familiar with the way diplomatic missions and embassies are set up are you?"

"Never had much need of that kind of information, Ethan, but I'm guessing you're about to educate me?"

"Just a little my friend. You're obviously not aware that in diplomatic circles, a 'cultural attaché' is kind of a catch-all description for a number of different disciplines."

Ross interrupted, his initial vague suspicions already vindicated.

"He's a spook, isn't he Ethan? Some kind of spy."

"Not a spy, Andy. That would be going too far. Let's just say Jerome Decker is on the side of the angels, and looks after certain matters of our country's international security."

"C.I.A." said Ross, not a question this time, but a statement of conclusion.

"You didn't hear it from me. I never said it, Andy, you did."

"How high up is he?"

"Deputy Head of London Station, that high up, Andy."

"Right, that explains the pressure from above. Thanks Ethan."

"We never had this conversation, Andy, right?"

"What conversation?"

"Thanks, friend."

"Thanks to you, Ethan. Better go, got lots to do."

"Me too. Say hello to Maria okay?"

"Okay."

The line went dead.

Chapter 7

Manor Court, Liverpool

As D.I. Ross was allowing the information Ethan Tiffen had given him to assimilate itself into his thought processes in relation to the case, Detective Constables Sam Gable and Derek McLennan were seated in the lounge of the house that Aaron Decker had shared with his two friends, both of whom sat on the sofa resembling a pair of bookends, as Gable and McLennan took up the two matching armchairs.

Tim Knight and Martin Lewis did indeed give the two detectives a book-end feeling as they sat facing the detectives, both looking nervous and apprehensive, this being almost certainly the first time their lives had been affected by such violent tragedy. McLennan expected no less and as always, was prepared to make allowances for any hesitancy, although he was aware that the two men in front of him were at present the best suspects they possessed for the murder.

The two young men were very different in appearance. Tim Knight was tall and rangy in build, with dark brown hair cut very short, and a handsome, almost aristocratic look about the face. Lewis on the other hand, was shorter, built rather more powerfully, his legs thicker around the thighs, and his chest threatening to break out of the thin t-shirt that covered his torso. His collar-length hair was pure Nordic blonde.

Of the two, Tim Knight appeared slightly more self-assured, not surprisingly as far as Sam Gable was concerned. She'd already read the initial report from Sergeant Meadows and knew that Tim was the eldest of the three house mates at twenty-five, so was perhaps a little more mature than his friend Martin Lewis, at twenty-two, the same age as the unfortunate Aaron Decker. It had been Lewis who had first found the body of Aaron, another reason for him to be in a rather greater state of shock than Knight. What privately amused Gable was that both men wore virtually the same clothing, white T-shirts, faded denim jeans and white trainers, of differing brands to be fair. *So much for the young and their aversion to uniformity*, she thought, adding to herself, *a student is a student is a student.*

"So, Martin," said Derek McLennan, "You knocked on the bedroom door and then what?"

"Well, I knew Sally had stayed over, you know? But Aaron was a real early riser, and he always said breakfast was an imperative part of the day, so when they didn't come down when they smelled the breakfast, I thought I'd better go and give 'em a shout, like. Tim was cooking, grilling bacon, tomatoes, and fried eggs with hash browns, and I left him to it, went and knocked on Aaron's bedroom door, and got no answer. I knocked again, a bit louder, and then opened the door a crack and peeped in, just in case they were... you know, doing it, like. They both looked fast asleep so I shouted, "*Hey you two, breakfast's ready. Come on, get up, it'll go cold.*" Nobody moved, and I thought it odd, because Aaron is, sorry was, a very light sleeper. I moved a bit closer and something sort of spooked me. They didn't look right. I walked up to Aaron and gave him a nudge, but he just didn't react. Then I noticed his left hand was just dangling from the side of the bed. I felt his neck, like in the movies, you know, and his skin was cold as ice. I just knew he was dead. I shouted at Sally, thinking maybe she was dead too, but she moved a bit and moaned, so I went round to her side of the bed and started shaking her. After a minute or so, she began to come round a bit more and I virtually screamed at her, "For fuck's sake, wake up, Sally. I think Aaron's dead."

That got through to her and she sat bolt upright, and the duvet slipped down, and I could see was naked, so I grabbed Aaron's dressing gown from behind the door and wrapped it round her shoulders. As I did, she looked at Aaron and it was like she suddenly realised what I'd said and she started to scream. Boy, did she scream? She went from semi-conscious to hysterical in a few seconds and I ended up slapping her face to try and calm her down. When she eventually shut up, I asked her if she and Aaron had been using anything, which was a stupid question, because Aaron hated anything to do with drugs. He'd have chucked me or Tim out of he ever thought we were using anything, even a bit of weed."

Martin finally fell silent, as though he was all talked out, and had finally come up for air.

"Thanks, Martin," said Gable. "That was very precise, if you don't mind me saying so."

Breathing heavily, Martin went on, "Thanks, it's not something you forget in a hurry, finding your mate dead in his bed like that. I forgot to say, when Sally started her screaming, Tim came running up the stairs like an express train and when I sort of gasped out what I'd found, he was the one who ran downstairs to the phone and dialled 999. The police and an ambulance were here within fifteen minutes, I think. One of the paramedics confirmed Aaron was dead and the police sergeant told me and Tim to wait downstairs while he called for the Scenes of Crime people, and looked around the bedroom. We went to the kitchen, tried to eat breakfast but couldn't face it, so we just made fresh coffee and sat at the kitchen table until the sergeant came to talk to us."

Derek McLennan now joined the conversation, seeking additional background on the two housemates.

"Where are you both from originally, and what are you both studying? Tim, you sound fairly local, but your accent is definitely not Liverpudlian, Martin."

Tim Knight, the eldest of the two was the first to answer, having said little so far.

"Well spotted, detective. I'm from West Derby, originally. We moved down to Chester when I was twelve, and I thought I'd lost most of my accent over the years. Looks like I was wrong about that. I'm in the last year of doing my post doc in Molecular Biology. I could have gone to a bigger university but Liverpool is close to home, plus the labs here are great and we're lucky to have Professor Joseph Freund here, a real expert in his field."

"Thanks," said McLennan. "Your accent's not that strong, but you know what they say, you can take the lad out of Liverpool, but..."

"Yeah, right, I know," said Tim with a wry grin.

"And how about you, Martin?" McLennan asked.

"I'm from Grimsby," the younger man replied. "I'm in my second year of a post doc in English Literature."

"And how will Aaron's death affect you two with regards to the house, I mean? I presume the three of you shared the rent?"

"No problems, there," Tim Knight replied to the question. "The house is actually owned by Aaron's father. He's already been in touch to say we can stay on, same rent, as long as we find another post doctoral student to share with us."

"Isn't that unusual?" Sam Gable asked. "How come Aaron's Dad, an American embassy official, owns a house in Liverpool?"

"Oh, nothing sinister, I assure you. When we met, Aaron was looking for a place to live; he was in a hotel up until then. When we invited him to move in with us after Charlie Stone got his doctorate and moved out, Mr. Decker came up one weekend, met the two of us and the next thing we knew, he'd contacted the landlord, made him an offer he couldn't refuse, and bought the place. He said it would be a good idea for the future to have a good place for post grad students to live while they're here."

"Very altruistic of him, I must say," said McLennan.

"And did either of you share Aaron's love for cricket?" Gable asked next.

"That's how I met him," said Tim Knight. "I was the one who kind of got him hooked on the game. I was already playing for the uni team and I invited him to come and watch a game one weekend. He was fascinated by the game so I got him to come to practice one evening.

He initially thought it was a bit of a 'quaint' game but soon changed his mind after he'd been struck a couple of times on the neck and shoulder by our fast bowlers, and when he got his fingers stung trying to catch a well hit ball. Anyway, Aaron was a natural at the game and when we found out he'd played college baseball in the States, we could see why he had such great hand and eye coordination. The team captain invited him to join us and he soon learned the game and never looked back. The team's going to miss him, that's for sure."

Gable looked towards Martin Lewis, a questioning look on her face. The young man realised she was waiting for his response to the same question.

"No, sorry, I'm not a cricket player. Rugby's my game, wing three-quarter."

"Yes, I can see you're built for speed," said Gable appreciating the muscles easily discernible under the young man's T-shirt. Lewis actually blushed as he caught Sam eyeing his physique.

"I see, and did either of you mix socially with Aaron?"

"We both did," said Tim. "We were mates, for God's sake, of course we did."

"And during your nights out and so on, did you ever see Aaron get mixed up in any trouble?"

"Hell no. He was definitely a turn-around and walk the other way sort of bloke if anything started in a pub or club. Trouble just wasn't Aaron's thing, believe me, right Martin?"

"Right," Lewis confirmed. "Aaron was a real gent. He always saw himself as a guest in our country and treated everyone with great respect. He was a great guy."

"So neither of you know of anyone who may have wanted to harm him?" Derek McLennan asked the pair.

"No way," Tim replied forcefully. "He had no enemies, detective. Aaron was an all-round popular chap."

"Well," McLennan spoke in a deadpan tone, "I think it's safe to assume he had at least one, don't you?"

The two young men fell silent. There was little they could say in response to McLennan's observation, the answer being all too obvious.

Chapter 8

Sally's Story

Andy Ross still found it a little strange walking into the office of the D.C.I. After seeing Detective Chief Inspector Harry Porteous ensconced behind the expansive desk for so many years, somehow, his old friend and Porteous's replacement, Oscar Agostini appeared somewhat incongruous in the boss's familiar leather chair.

"Still find it a bit weird seeing you in that chair, Oscar," he said as Agostini invited him to sit down.

"You'll get used to it in time, Andy," Agostini replied. "I still feel odd myself, to tell the truth, having this bloody great office all to myself. Something we both need to come to terms with. Still never mind all that. Where do we stand on the Decker case?"

Unlike Porteous, Agostini made it a point to talk to Ross immediately after the morning team briefing, in order to ensure he was always up to date with whatever his team were up to. Ross found it a good idea which took no more than ten minutes and meant he didn't have to go looking for the new boss to bring him up to speed on current cases.

"Remember I told you I had a contact at the U.S. embassy?" Ross opened the update.

"Sure I do. I take it you found something?"

"I certainly did. Our grieving father, Jerome Decker III is only the bloody Deputy Head of Station for the C.I.A. in London."

"Bloody hell, a spook," Agostini exclaimed. "Do you think it might be significant in the case?"

"At this point, Oscar, I don't know, but it does explain why he was able to bring some pressure to bear on the top brass. Whether the murder of his son has any connection to his intelligence work, I can't say, but we can't discount the possibility."

"So, this could get very messy, Andy. If there's a political motive or anything to do with the damn C.I.A's covert activities we could find ourselves chasing shadows and getting nowhere if the powers that be put the blocks up."

"I know," said Ross. "I propose to talk to Decker, let him know I'm aware of the true nature of his work, and see how he reacts."

"That's a good idea, but won't it place your source in jeopardy of exposure?"

"Hmm, you're right," Ross agreed as he contemplated ways of revealing his knowledge without compromising his friend, Ethan Tiffen.

"I don't want to go into this investigation with one hand tied behind my back, and I need to know if Decker is keeping anything from us."

"I agree. Let me make a couple of calls, see what I can do. If I can find a way to protect your source, I will. What are your immediate plans?"

"I'm going to talk to Sally Metcalfe, the girlfriend, this morning. I've given her time to grieve a little before interviewing her. She should be ready to talk to us now."

"Okay, do it and I'll see if there's a way we can 'out' our friend Decker. Izzie Drake's back at work tomorrow, isn't she?"

"Yes, and I must say I've missed having her around."

"Good sergeants are hard to find, Andy. You've worked together a long time now. You make a good team."

"I think so too."

"Well, it'll be good to have the squad back at full strength tomorrow. I'm sure you'll value her input into this one, for sure."

"I will indeed. She can be very insightful."

"So I've heard," said Agostini.

The D.C.I was well aware of the almost telepathic relationship that Ross and Drake enjoyed, and knew it was one of his team's biggest assets.

"You'd better be off then," he said, as Ross rose to leave. "Who are you taking with you?"

"I've got Ferris working with me at present. He's intelligent and also has a good insight into difficult problems. And, it's good to get him out into the field and away from his computers for once."

"Right, off you go, and check back with me when you get back and we'll compare notes."

* * *

Ross and Ferris sat opposite Sally Metcalfe, who was dressed in a 'Save the Whales' sweatshirt and a pair of expensive beige coloured jeans in the tiny living room in the small house she shared with her fellow student Megan Rose. The two-bedroomed terraced house was not far from Aaron Decker's home in Wavertree, on a street of old back-to-backs that had mostly been converted into student accommodation. The house clearly showed itself as being the domain of two young women. For one thing, Ross immediately noticed, it was clean, with the scent of air freshener hinting at housework having been completed before the arrival of the two police officers. The old fashioned sash window was slightly open, allowing fresh air into the room and there wasn't a speck of dust to be seen on the top of the television, the mantle-piece, or the glass topped coffee table positioned in the middle of the room. Ross guessed the two women probably used it as a dining table for fast food dinners or sandwiches in an evening.

The walls were decorated with old-fashioned anaglypta wallpaper, painted in a neutral magnolia finish, an obvious landlord's choice. The picture above the fireplace however, Ross surmised was purely Sally's choice, based on his knowledge of her studies in the field of marine biology. It was a superb print of an oil painting, depicting what he assumed to be a pod of dolphins leaping from the waves of, he assumed, the Antarctic Ocean, given the dramatic backdrop of what he presumed to be an ice shelf. He'd seen enough David Attenborough nature documentaries and was sufficiently well-read to feel able to comment on the dramatic scene.

"Yes, Detective Inspector," Sally confirmed. "It is Antarctica. That's the Ross Ice Shelf in the background. It could have been named for you, couldn't it?"

"Nice thought, Miss Metcalfe. Who was it actually named after, as a matter of interest?"

"It's named after Captain James Clark Ross, who discovered it in 1841. It's the largest ice-shelf in the world, and has often been used as the place to locate base camps for many Antarctic expeditions, due to it being so flat, apart from the massive coastal cliffs and ridges of course. The cliffs can reach as high as 70 metres, around 230 feet, and they are really a magnificent sight."

"You've actually been there?" Ross asked, incredulously.

"Last year," said Sally. "My parents paid for me to go on an Antarctic cruise. I flew from Punta Arenas to St George Island and then boarded an Antarctic cruise liner called the *Sea Sentinel* from there. Those Antarctic cruise ships are incredible, Inspector Ross, built to withstand the ice and the freezing temperatures while keeping the passengers warm and comfortable as long as you're not out on deck of course. For two weeks, I felt like I could be on an alien world. All the photos and TV documentaries in the world can't prepare you for the real thing, honestly"

"I'm sure they must be, that is, the ships, well protected against the ice and so on," Ross agreed, pleased that the short diversion from the true reason for his visit had seemingly put Sally Metcalfe at her ease in his company.

"My friend Megan loved the print too so she had no problem with me making it the centrepiece of the room, but you haven't come to talk to me about my Antarctic adventures, have you?"

"I'm afraid not, Miss Metcalfe."

"Call me Sally, please."

"Okay, Sally it is. Detective Constable Ferris and I have a few questions we need to ask you. I know you're possibly still in shock and grieving for Aaron, but whatever help you can give us may help us to find his killer, and the person who drugged you both."

"Ask anything you want to, Inspector. I can't believe anyone could have hated Aaron enough to want to kill him. It gave me the biggest shock of my life when Martin woke me up and I realised poor Aaron was lying dead beside me."

With those words, the realisation of the event took hold of the young woman, and tears appeared in her eyes. Ross and Ferris could see her fighting to control her emotions and both men felt a huge wave of sympathy for her.

"Wait, did you say we were *both* drugged?" Sally suddenly asked.

"Yes, it looks that way," Ferris replied. "We're awaiting the toxicology results from Aaron's autopsy and the results of your blood tests to find out what drug was used, but we think you were both drugged, and the killer then suffocated Aaron in his sleep."

"But, drugged, how?"

"Doctor Strauss found a pin prick on Aaron's arm, and there was one on you too when she examined you," Ross explained.

"But how can we have been given injections without us knowing about it?"

"You and Aaron had a few drinks before you went to bed, right?"

"Yes, why?"

"It's possible the killer gave you time to fall asleep naturally then entered the room and administered the injections as you slept. If you'd both had a few drinks you'd have been in a deep sleep in minutes."

"But wasn't that a big chance to take? I mean, what if one of us had woken up while he was doing it?"

"That's a question we've yet to answer, Sally. What were you both drinking?" Ross asked.

"Aaron had a bottle of vodka and we had maybe two or three vodka martinis. Him being American and all, he loved making exotic drinks for us."

Paul Ferris had followed Ross's reasoning perfectly.

"You think it's possible someone may have drugged the vodka to make sure they both fell asleep quickly, sir?"

"Yes, it could have happened like that," Ross replied. "How well do you know Aaron's house-mates, Sally?"

"Quite well, Inspector. You can't think one of them had anything to do with it, surely?"

"I'm not eliminating anyone from our enquiries yet," he said. "They were both perfectly placed to have spiked the vodka, and would have known exactly when you went to bed and so could have calculated how long it would take for you both to be safely asleep."

"I still don't believe Tim or Martin could be involved," Sally protested. "They were both Aaron's friends, Tim especially, being on the cricket team with him and all. Before Aaron and I got together I'd gone on a couple of dates with Tim, nothing serious or anything, but I can tell you he's a very gentle and kind person, and was really happy for me and Aaron when we did become a couple."

Ross didn't press the point, feeling sure that Sally and the two men would doubtless be in touch with other and it wouldn't be prudent to give away too much at this point. Instead he rolled out the old cliché, "Do you know of anyone who may have wanted to harm Aaron or you?"

"Well no. I'd say Aaron was universally liked. As for me, I don't have any enemies that I know about either. Why do you ask if someone might have wanted to hurt me, Inspector?"

"Because Sally, and I hate to say this to you, but it is a vague possibility that whoever killed Aaron may have wanted you dead too, and that something happened to prevent them carrying out the full extent of their plan."

A look of pure shock appeared on Sally's face and she threw her right hand up to cover her mouth as she gasped, "No, surely not. Why would anyone want to harm me, Inspector?"

It was Paul Ferris who provided the answer as he said, "Why would anyone have wanted to harm Aaron Decker?"

Sally fell silent, at a loss for words.

Ross picked up the interview once again.

"You're studying marine biology, I believe, Sally?"

"Yes, that's right. You don't think this has anything to do with my studies, surely?"

"Like I said, nothing's being discounted at present. Do your studies include anything of a sensitive nature?"

"Meaning what, exactly?"

"Well, anything that might be of value to someone outside of the university?"

"Oh God, no, nothing like that. I'm currently working on a paper relating to the effect of global warming on the southern ocean and its ecology. Nothing secretive or sensitive about it, I assure you."

"And Aaron?"

"What, his historical research? Again, nothing to get anyone wound up about."

"You're sure of that?" Ferris asked.

"Honestly. He was writing a paper on the Allied invasion and liberation of Greece during World War Two. I doubt anyone could find a reason in there to want to murder him. But, listen can we get back to my question? Do you really think someone might have wanted us both dead?"

Ross replied. "Yes, Sally. We have to take it as a possibility at this time. For that reason, I'm going to assign a police officer to keep an eye on you for the next few days, to make sure you're safe."

Ross didn't say it, but such a move would also enable them to keep an eye on Sally Metcalfe's movements, just in case she was involved in the murder of her boyfriend.

"That's really going to look good, isn't it? I mean, walking around campus and going to the pub with a policeman trailing around after me like a puppy dog."

"Don't worry, Sally. The officer will be female and in plain clothes. We'll make sure she fits in with your student life as far as appearance goes, and anyone seeing her with you will just see her as another student."

Still not totally convinced, Sally acquiesced to Ross's suggestion, privately acknowledging to herself that she'd probably feel safer with a police shadow, just in case she was on a killer's hit list.

Ross nodded to Ferris who moved on to the next part of the interview.

"Tell me about your family, please Sally."

"My family? What do you want to know about them?"

"Well, just some basic background information. It helps us build a better picture of everyone involved in a case like this. We know your father is a reasonably wealthy businessman in Lancaster. What about your Mum, any brothers and sisters?"

"Okay, so you know my Dad owns a road haulage company. He started the company with one beaten up old truck and built it up to what it is today. Mum is the company secretary. She didn't have to work but hates sitting around doing nothing. My two brothers are really supportive of me even though they thought I was mad going to university."

"Why was that, Sally?" Ferris asked.

"They both went to university. Trevor, he's twenty-nine now, went to Oxford, got a degree in Applied Physics, and wanted to be a research chemist, but when he left uni, just couldn't get a job in his chosen field. Seems lots of kids got their A levels, bypassed university and got jobs with the big companies who paid for them to go to college one or two days a week. By the time Trevor left Oxford all the available jobs had gone. He got a job in a supermarket in Lancaster, stuck at it and now he's a branch manager in Sheffield, but it's not quite what he was aiming for. Ian's twenty six, and went to uni in Exeter, got his degree in biological sciences and hit the same brick wall as Trevor. There are more than two hundred people chasing every decent job for graduates, and the chances of finding what you are looking for are slim. I'm lucky, because I have a sponsor and when I leave uni, as long as I have my degree, I'm guaranteed a placement at an oceanographic institute in the U.S.A. thanks to a couple of contacts my Dad made through his business dealings."

"Lucky girl," said Ferris, and Ross couldn't help wondering if there was a connection between Sally's sponsor and Aaron's C.I.A father. He had to ask.

"Yes, very lucky. Mind if I ask who your sponsor is, Sally?"

"It's a company called Aegis Oceanographic. They're well known in the field of oceanographic exploration and it was a real surprise when I got their offer."

Ross flashed a look at Ferris that the detective constable correctly understood to mean, *Check out Aegis Oceanographic as soon as we get back to headquarters.*

"Where are they from, Sally?"

"Oh, I think their main offices are somewhere in Maine, at The Aegis Oceanographic Institute, which is where the letter offering my sponsorship came from, but of course they own various survey ships and their people work all around the world, often working for different countries on ecological or environmental projects."

Ross was even more interested in Aegis by now.

"Does this company often sponsor students like you, Sally?"

"I should think so," she replied. "A lot of big companies work like that nowadays. I suppose it's how they target their future employees."

"Yes, I'm sure, and you say your Dad helped you get this sponsorship?"

"That's right. His company doesn't do work in the U.S.A. of course, but Aegis have a European division based in Spain and smaller research facilities all over Europe including one in Falmouth and apparently Dad had a contract to haul a load of stuff for them from the U.K. to their Spanish facility. Dad mentioned to one of their executives that I was looking to study ocean sciences and next thing I knew I received the offer from them a few weeks later. Dad said it was a gesture from Aegis because they were so pleased with the efficiency of Metcalfe Logistics. Some of the loads Dad's company carries for them are quite delicate and need special handling and he's never had any damages reported so their European director, who Dad plays golf with as well, is well pleased with the service."

"Is this European director American, Sally?"

"As far as I know, yes, but why all this interest in Aegis and my sponsorship, Inspector? What has any of this to do with what happened to me and Aaron?"

Ross hesitated for a second, unsure for a moment just what to say to Sally without tipping his hand to the way his mind was working.

"Well, with them being an American company, and Aaron being an American too, and his Dad working at the embassy in London, I just wondered if anyone from Aegis might have some connection with the Decker family, that's all, and I must say I'm fascinated by how this whole sponsorship thing works. I'm just a simple policeman, Sally; you must forgive me if I'm not quite on the ball when it comes to the academic world."

As answers go it was as bland and non-committal as Ross could have made it, but it seemed to do the trick in placating Sally Metcalfe, whose grief at the death of Aaron Decker remained the number one priority in her mind. Just as Ross was thinking of bringing the interview to a close, Ferris, who'd been unusually quite during most of the interview, intervened with a new question.

"Sally, you said Aegis have a U.K. office. Do they have any other working facilities in this country that you're aware of?"

"I think, when I looked them up after receiving the offer, I read that they have the facility in Devon, but that's the only one I seem to remember. I'm sure the webpage I read said something about Aegis being involved in some kind of research into the long-term environmental effects of decomposing shipwrecks on the marine life in the English Channel. I remember mentioning it to Aaron, who thought it was a great project, but then he would, being so interested in history. He'd have loved to go down and investigate the shipwrecks I'm sure, just for the fun of it."

"Yes, I'm sure," said Ferris. "He didn't do anything about that though, did he? And Falmouth's in Cornwall, not Devon, Sally."

"Sorry, my geography is awful isn't it? Oh no, I'm sure he didn't do anything, of course not, but he did get all excited for a couple of weeks."

"About what? Do you remember?" Ferris was on a roll.

"Yes, he said I'd inspired him to take a break from the paper he was working on and he was investigating the known shipwrecks in the Channel. He was amazed by how many recorded wrecks there are down there, a lot from the Second World War, he said, but also quite a few dating back over a hundred years or more in many cases. He seemed to have quite a bee in his bonnet about it for a few weeks, then he just stopped talking about it."

"And when was it that all this took place, Sally?"

"Oh, round about the time I was preparing for my Antarctic discovery cruise. In fact, he was still going at it when I left for the cruise but never mentioned it again after I returned. I never gave it much thought at the time. I just assumed it was one of those things he researched out of general curiosity and then lost interest after a while if it didn't give him anything that would further his post-doc studies."

"I see, thanks Sally," said Ferris as he finished jotting down her reply in his notebook. It was a good job he could read his own private shorthand which he'd developed over the last couple of years, when trying to make fast but accurate notes of witness statements and so on, because it was sure as hell that no one else would have been able to make sense of the apparent squiggles and scrawls that covered the pages of his

73

notebook. Ross had a feeling that Paul Ferris might have hit on a new theory and would look forward to hearing his thoughts as soon as they left Sally Metcalfe's neat and tidy student accommodation.

Ross had one last question.

"Your friend, Megan. Did she know Aaron?"

"Yes, but only through me, Inspector. She's attending lectures at present but if you need to speak to her, I can ask her to call you and arrange it."

"That would be good, yes please, Sally. We just need to speak to as many people who knew Aaron, no matter how well, to dot the 'I's' and cross the 't's' so to speak."

Ross made a mental note to arrange for Sam Gable to visit Megan Rose and see if Sally's housemate could give them anything useful, and he and Ferris were soon motoring back to headquarters, where Ross called Ferris into his office for a quick two-man conference.

Chapter 9

Nautical Theories

"Tell me where your thoughts are leading you, Paul," Ross said after he and Ferris had closed the door to his office, armed with mugs of hot coffee and Ferris's all important notebook.

"Well sir, it just seems to me that everything we have so far seems to be pointing across the Atlantic, so to speak. Aaron Decker was American, his father, as you told me is a fairly senior officer in the C.I.A, and then we find that Aaron's girlfriend is sponsored by an American company that could, and I stress *could*, sir, be involved in work for any number of countries around the world and so open to some kind of industrial espionage, at the very least. I thought it odd that Aaron would find it interesting when he heard about the work Aegis are doing in the English channel and then seemed to have forgotten or dismissed it in the time it took Sally Metcalfe to complete her Antarctic cruise. And didn't someone, somewhere down the line say something had upset Aaron in the days before his death, but he never told anyone what it was that had caused that upset? It all adds up to a whole load of conjecture, I know, but maybe Aaron's murder is a bit more complicated than we thought at first."

"Well done Paul, that's exactly the way I've been thinking too," Ross smiled at his detective constable. "The question is however, just what kind of complications. Any thoughts?"

Ferris went into deep thought for a few seconds, and Ross would swear he could almost hear the D.C's brain moving up a gear as he sorted through a jumble of thoughts before finally speaking.

"Suppose for a minute that Aaron Decker was digging into the past. History was his subject, so he'd know how to research a subject thoroughly. I know that some of the wrecks around our coastline are designated war graves. What if he found that Aegis, in the course of their explorations, were disturbing or desecrating those sites? Not a great motive for murder, but worth considering. Or, maybe he found something with more tangible value to Aegis, something they would kill to protect."

"Such as? Go on, Paul, I'm fascinated by your thinking on this."

"Okay, weeell," said Ferris, drawing out the word *well*, "What if Aegis discovered one of those wrecks was carrying something when it sank, something with either significant monetary value, or maybe even military value?"

"Right," said Ross. "Now you're thinking, Paul. It would certainly interest the C.I.A. if he stumbled upon some long-lost experimental weapon or even something of substantially greater potential. A lot of work on the Atom bomb during the Second World War was shared, and maybe Decker discovered some secret he shouldn't have, or of course, as you say, maybe a previously secret cache of gold on board one of the wrecks, worth a fortune by today's standards, and it definitely wouldn't be the first time gold has served as a motive for murder."

Ferris allowed himself to take a breather and then looked almost forlornly at his boss.

"What's wrong Paul? Suddenly I get the feeling you're not totally convinced by your own theory."

"Sorry sir, don't mean to be defeatist. But if Decker did discover something and then told his father about it, surely the C.I.A would have moved on the case and Decker senior would have been a more logical target if Aegis wanted to stop any investigation into their operations. Plus, I haven't looked them up yet, but are we really going to suppose that a large company like that would resort to murder to cover up their activities?"

"If they were illegal activities, yes, they probably would and it's not necessarily Aegis as a whole that's involved here, it could just be a local thing, someone in their European division with an eye to making big money without the company being aware of it. Also,

Decker would want to be certain of his information, and maybe he approached Aegis with his theory and spoke to the wrong man, from his point of view, before going to his father. That could have been what got him killed."

"Yes, that makes sense, sir, like a sort of rogue operation within the Aegis group, Decker stumbles on it, tries to check it out before telling his father, has the bad luck to speak to someone who is involved in whatever's going on, and they have to silence him before he tells his Dad, and the shit hits the fan, so to speak, pardon my French sir."

"I know it may sound a bit fanciful, Paul, but it's possible and you know what Sherlock Holmes said, don't you?"

"What's that sir, bearing in mind he was a fictional charac...oh, wait, yes, I see what you mean," Ferris smiled and went on, "When everything else has been eliminated, whatever is left, no matter how fanciful it may be, has to be the truth, or something like that, anyway."

"Exactly," said Ross. "Now, all we need to do is find out if young Decker went diving anywhere off the South coast while his girlfriend was freezing her boobs off in the Antarctic, If he did, we may just have a starting point for this case, Ferris."

Ferris saluted, sailor like as he replied, "Aye, aye sir," just as the phone on Ross's desk began to ring. Ross snatched the phone from its cradle

"Ross," he spoke into the receiver, then, "Oh hello, Doctor Strauss."

Ferris moved to rise from his chair to leave the office but Ross motioned for him to stay put, as he listened to the young pathologist's words.

"Right, I see, thank you. And there's no doubt about that?"

Ferris could hear Strauss speaking again at the other end of the line and then Ross thanked her again and slowly placed the phone back on its cradle, turning to speak to Ferris once again.

"They got the toxicology results back, Paul. It was Ketamine."

"Ketamine?" Ferris repeated. "Don't they use that on horses, sir?"

"Yes, and in other veterinary uses, though it can be used as an anaesthetic in humans too according to Dr. Strauss. The thing is, only a small dose was used on Sally Metcalfe, enough to keep her asleep for a good while, but the dose used on Aaron Decker was enough to have killed him without resorting to suffocation."

"So why the overkill, sir? Why suffocate a dying man, for God's sake?"

"That, D.C Ferris, is the burning question. Answer that one and we may just have found the key to solving the case, but do you know what I think?"

"Do tell, sir," said Ferris.

"I think the killing of Aaron Decker was personal. Yes, there may have been a greater motive that needed him out of the way, but whoever carried out the actual murder really wanted that young man dead,"

As Paul Ferris left the office to begin his on-line search and investigation into the Aegis Oceanographic Institute, Ross leaned back in his chair, scratched his head and said a small prayer of thanks that his team would return to full strength the next day with the return of his sergeant, Izzie Drake, the new Mrs. Foster. He had a feeling he was going to need her skills before this case was solved.

Chapter 10

Drake's Return

Like many police officers, Andy Ross harboured something of the eternal optimist deep within his soul. A new day would always dawn with the possibility that this would be the day when they would crack their big case, or at least unearth the vital clue that might help bring a criminal to justice.

Today, though, Ross felt real cause for the optimism that had seen him whistling to himself while washing and shaving before work, (two shaving cuts as a result), and why he arrived at headquarters fifteen minutes before his usual time, thanks in no small part to his wife, Maria ensuring he quickly changed one of the odd socks he'd contrived to pull on while dressing, and who fully understood his enthusiasm for getting to the office. "Go on, get along now," she'd chided him as she kissed him at the door on his way out, "and be sure to ask her all about the honeymoon."

Without mentioning her name, they both knew the reason for Ross's enthusiasm. Izzie was returning to work. The night before, Ross had confessed to Maria that he sorely missed his long-time assistant, even though it had only been four days working without her. The pair were held in almost legendary regard by their fellow officers in the Merseyside Constabulary as being so tuned in to each other's thoughts and methods that they could communicate without words at times, which, though not quite true, did sum up the way their thought processes seemed to run along parallel lines at times, the two often being able to finish each other's sentences, so alike were their working mantras.

Seated behind his desk, a mug of coffee steaming on his desk, Ross heard the sound of footsteps walking across the polished squad room floor towards his office. A single polite knock on his door was followed by a small squeak of one hinge as the door creaked on opening, followed by the smiling face of Detective Sergeant Izzie Drake, or the new Mrs. Peter Foster, whichever way you wanted to look at it.

"I heard a rumour you were looking for a good detective sergeant," Izzie said by way of greeting to her boss.

"Quite right," said Ross. "Any idea where I can find one?"

"Sadistic sod," Izzie countered. "I don't have to work here you know. I could go and get a job on the drug squad."

"Of course you could, but then where else would you find a boss who brings you coffee first thing in the morning?" and he rose and carried the mug of coffee from his desk to his sergeant and handed it to her with a broad grin. "Welcome back, Sergeant Drake."

"Thank you, Inspector Ross. Aren't you having one?"

"Oh, mine's over here," Ross replied as he walked back to his desk and extricated a second, previously hidden mug of coffee from the well under his desk.

"Neat hiding place," Izzie grinned as he almost banged his head as he straightened up with the coffee mug in his hand, slopping a few drops on the office carpet.

"Only place I could think of. I knew you'd be early so thought I'd give you a treat on your first day back."

"Great," said the sergeant, taking a seat in the familiar visitor's chair.

"So, how's married life?"

"Excellent, thank you, sir. Details later. What's been happening while I've been gone?"

Ross spent the next ten minutes giving Drake a detailed summary of the Decker case, after which she whistled through her teeth before replying.

"Bloody hell. We've got a real nightmare case on our hands by the sound of it, sir. Any thoughts as to viable suspects yet?"

"Let's face it, Izzie. The two housemates are the only real prime suspects we have in the frame so far. They were both in the house at the time, and both had the opportunity to visit the couple in Aaron's bedroom at some time in the night to carry out the murders. Plus, if it wasn't one or both of them, how did the killer get in without either of them hearing anything?"

"Sounds like a slam dunk as the Yanks would say, then, doesn't it? But it also sounds too damn simple as well. Would two intelligent men, or even just one of them, commit a murder where it's bloody obvious they're going to come under immediate suspicion?"

"Precisely the way I see it, Izzie. Listen, we'd better go do the morning briefing, then when everyone's busy with their own assignments, I want you to come with me. I want another chat with Mr. Jerome Decker the bloody third, C.I.A. or not."

"What about Paul Ferris? Surely he should go with you again as he was at the first interview?"

"Paul's done a great job, but you know he's not going to take it the wrong way, you stepping in at this point. Besides, he's doing a very important job, trying to get the lowdown on this Aegis Institute. No one can work the computers like he can, and he's probably suffering from severe computer withdrawal syndrome, if such a thing exists. If there's anything dirty in their background, Paul will find it, I'm certain."

"Good point," Drake conceded. She followed with a question.

"Was Aaron Decker a diver, sir?"

"Eh, a diver? I don't know. Why?"

"Just thinking aloud here," Drake mused, "but, if as you surmise, he maybe discovered something about the activities of this Aegis lot, surely he wouldn't have simply confined his research to online searches or library records. If he thought there was something fishy, excuse the pun, about one or more of those wrecks in the Channel, it would have made sense if he'd gone to take a look for himself, or at least got someone to do it for him. Sounds as if he could afford to hire a boat and a diver if he couldn't do it himself."

"Very good point, Izzie. Ferris wondered if Aaron might have gone to Cornwall and done some diving. It's worth looking into. I'm glad to see that all the excitement of the wedding and the physical stress of the honeymoon haven't blunted your incisive thought processes."

Ross sat back, a grin on his face.

"Physical stress? What do you...oh, right. You dirty minded bugger, Inspector Ross. I'll have you know I'm a good girl, I am."

"Not what I've been hearing," he laughed as his sergeant picked up a pad of yellow post-its from his desk and playfully hurled them in his direction. Ross deftly caught the pad in his right hand, placed it back on his desk and said, "Better go or the team will think you're being unfaithful with the boss after less than week of wedded bliss."

"Yeah, right," Izzie laughed.

Glad to be working together again, Ross and Drake left the office and made their way to the briefing room, where the team was ready and waiting for the morning briefing.

A quick ripple of applause and a few risqué and ribald comments greeted the return of the newly married sergeant, and then Ross brought the meeting to order. Standing at the back of the room were six uniformed constables, assigned by Agostini to assist with the inquiry. He knew there'd be a lot of people to talk to and many statements to be taken and with the pressure from above, it was best to leave nothing to chance. The extra manpower was essential in his opinion. At Ross's request, the five men and one woman introduced themselves to the rest of the team, and Ross got to work. It was time to get serious.

* * *

"So there you have it," Ross said, bringing the update on the case to a close. As you all know, we have absolutely nothing so far. Apart from the two young men who shared the house with Decker, there are no other viable suspects at present, and up to now there doesn't appear to be any motive for either of them to have wanted him dead, and as everyone keeps pointing out, it's a bit obvious to think one or both of them would do this in their own home where they'd be bound to come under close scrutiny. I want them both brought in individually in the next day or so and we'll see how their stories hold up when they're interviewed separately. Sam," he said, looking at D.C. Gable, "I want you to track down Sally Metcalfe's housemate, Megan Rose. Get her on her own and find out what she thought about the relationship between

Aaron and Sally. Any arguments or rifts between the couple, we need to know about them."

"Okay, sir," Gable replied, rapidly writing in her notebook.

Ross next turned to D.C.s Nick Dodds and Tony Curtis.

"I want you two to hit the university. Speak to Aaron's and the housemates' professors, tutors, however they style themselves these days. Then try to talk to as many of their friends as you can pin down while you're there, and that goes for friends of the girlfriend too. I know it's a big ask and there's likely to be a lot of ground to cover and most of them will know nothing, but make use of the constables the boss has assigned to help us out with the legwork on this one. I understand from D.C.I. Agostini that you all volunteered to help with this inquiry?"

He looked at the six officers standing nervously by the wall, a couple of whom nodded in the affirmative to his question.

"That's great," he said smiling to try and put them at their ease. "I know it's probably the first time you've worked on such a big case, but don't be put off by this lot of reprobates," he laughingly motioned with his arms to encompass the rest of his team. "They're detectives, not aliens from Mars, and like me, they're grateful for your help, so work with them and do your best. It might be boring most of the time, but whatever you're asked to do will, I assure you, be pertinent to this inquiry and will help us build up a bigger picture of what and who we're dealing with. Got that?"

As the rest of them hesitated, the tallest of the men spoke up.

"Yes, sir, and thank you for having us along. We'll try not to let you down," said P.C. Will Sutton.

"You won't," Ross replied confidently, and then turned his attention to the team's collator.

"Paul, I want you to concentrate on Aegis, find out exactly who they are, what they do and how far their influence in the field of oceanographic research reaches around the world."

Ferris nodded.

"Whatever you need to help with that inquiry, just ask. It's vital we know who and what we may be dealing with. It might turn out that Aegis is in the clear, no skeletons in their corporate cupboards, but that's fine too. It's just as important to eliminate potential suspects as it is to bring new ones on board in a case like this. Like I said, dig deep, and let me know immediately if you find the slightest hint of anything that doesn't look or sound right about them. The way they approached Sally Metcalfe was a bit odd to me and I wonder if they knew she was in a relationship with the son of a C.I.A officer before they made her that offer of sponsorship."

"I'll leave no stone unturned sir and no seashell either," Ferris replied.

"Oh no," Ross groaned. "Don't you start with the funnies too. Don't you think I've got enough to do just coping with my sergeant's little witticisms?"

Ferris smiled at the boss, and just laughed as he said, "Sorry sir, something of the sergeant's style must have rubbed off on me while I've been riding with you the last few days."

"Well, rub it off yourself, Ferris," Ross spoke light-heartedly. "I can't cope with all this frivolity and jocularity."

The rest of the team giggled like schoolboys and even Sam Gable joined in.

"Oh, and Tony, Nick, find out if Aaron went diving, you know, as in skin diving, aqualungs and so on. Sergeant Drake's had an idea."

"Good to know marriage hasn't blocked the old thought processes Sarge," D.C. Curtis quipped.

"Takes more than a wedding to put me off my stride, Tony," she replied, smiling at the young detective.

"Right," said Ross in a firm and commanding tone, "It's time to hit the streets. Sergeant Drake and I are going to talk to the father again, and probably the mother and brother too if they've arrived in town. Let's go find ourselves a murderer, people, and let's do it soon!"

Chapter 11

Secret Missions?

Jerome Decker III seemed to have aged ten years since Ross had first met him two days ago. Still immaculately dressed, his face looked drawn and haggard and his hair had a greasy sheen to it. The grief and stress that went with the loss of his youngest son was having an obvious effect on the man. Decker however, had been as charming as he could be on being introduced to Izzie Drake as she and Ross were admitted to Decker's suite at the hotel where he and his family were now firmly entrenched. Liverpool's Hilton may not have quite rivalled London's equivalent but was still one of the best hotels the city could offer. Decker explained that he and his wife had a suite of their own, while Peter and Kelly were sharing a second. Kelly adored her eldest brother and the pair had no qualms about sharing a suite so they could catch up with each other's news as well as share in their grief for their brother.

Ross's first surprise of the morning had been meeting Decker's wife for the first time. Elaine Decker was a beautiful woman, of that there was no doubt, but after doing a quick double-take, the inspector recognised her as being a well known former actress, known for her roles on both stage and screen. He realised that like millions of others, he'd never thought of her stage name as being just another tinsel town fabrication.

"I'm pleased to meet you, Mrs. Decker, though I wish the circumstances could have been happier. I'm so very sorry for the loss of your son and I assure you we're doing all we can to find the person who did this to Aaron."

"Thank you, Inspector. I'm sure you are, and I at least have faith in the great British police to handle the investigation thoroughly."

Those words led Ross to surmise that Elaine Decker and her husband had disagreed on how the investigation should proceed, with Elaine urging Jerome to stay out of it and leave it to the locals. *Good for her*, he thought.

"Thank you," Ross replied and he and Drake then found themselves being introduced to the two remaining Decker siblings. Peter looked so much like Aaron that the two could have been twins, despite the difference in ages. Facially, they were almost identical, much like the father and son resemblance Ross had noted on his first meeting with Decker senior.

Peter, however, differed markedly from his younger brother by sporting what Ross thought of as the trademark long hair of a rock guitarist and his clothes though looking unkempt and faded were clearly expensive and specially tailored to produce such an appearance. His handshake had been firm and his demeanour polite and respectful, and Ross found himself liking Peter Decker almost instantly.

Kelly, the Decker's eighteen year-old daughter was another kettle of fish entirely. The girl was obviously still distraught at the loss of her brother, her eyes red and puffy from crying. Dressed in a simple roll-neck sweater and jeans, she could hardly look Ross or Drake in the eye, and obviously wanted to be anywhere other than in the same room as the detectives, or Ross thought, her parents. Here was a young girl who clearly wanted to be alone, to grieve privately for her dead brother. Ross vowed to keep it as short as possible when it came to Kelly Decker, who lacked the composure her more mature brother had succeeded in maintaining through his own grief.

"So you're no nearer to finding my son's killer, Inspector Ross?" Decker said, as though he was expressing his dissatisfaction with what Ross had reported to him so far.

"Mr. Decker, no we are not," Ross spoke firmly, "though we might have moved a little faster had you been a little more forthcoming with us in the first place."

Ross had cleverly turned the heat in the other direction.

"I really don't know what you mean," Decker countered.

"Oh, come on, Mr. Decker. You're the C.I.A.'s Deputy Head of Station, London. Did you really think we wouldn't find out? If you did you've seriously underestimated the intelligence and efficiency of the British Police."

"See, Jerome, what did I tell you?" Elaine Decker interjected.

"Right, okay Honey," Decker tried to calm his wife. "You were right, and yes, Inspector, perhaps I should have told you right away instead of leaving you to find out by whatever means you have found out, but I didn't see it had any relevance to Aaron's death."

"No relevance?" Ross was astounded. "I think you should leave the detecting to me, Mr. Decker. I don't know how the C.I.A. actually works, but I'm sure as hell you're not trained as police detectives. For all you know, your son's death could well be connected to you and your position in the C.I.A. Speaking of which, was Aaron a diver?"

"A diver? Like deep sea diving? What's that got to do with me or Aaron's death?"

"I don't know if it has any connection yet, but please, answer the question."

"He was a very accomplished diver, Inspector Ross," Peter Decker answered. "Not deep sea stuff, but with an aqualung maybe in a few fathoms, he was fine. He loved being under the water, always said it was like being in another world."

"Thank you Peter," Ross smiled at the rock singer. He explained his question now.

"We have reason to believe that Aaron was researching a particular project that the company that is sponsoring his girlfriend, Sally through university is involved in. If he found something he shouldn't have found it's possible they took action to prevent him revealing that information."

"What project?" Decker senior asked.

"Aegis Oceanographic are apparently conducting a survey to discover the effects of the wreckage of ships in the English Channel on marine life and the environment."

"Aegis is sponsoring Sally Metcalfe?"

"Yes. I take it you didn't know, Mr. Decker. You've obviously heard of them?"

"You're correct that I didn't know, about the sponsorship and yes, I know of Aegis. They're a large organisation, with many worldwide interests in various areas of marine and oceanographic research. You think they may be involved in something shady?"

"At this stage I don't know anything," said Ross. "It's a theory we're looking into. Maybe you, with your contacts would know more about an American company than we do."

"Trust me, Inspector Ross, if there's anything going on at Aegis, I have no knowledge of it, and Aaron never said anything to me about any suspicions he may have had about them. But, by God, if there is anything illegal going on within Aegis Oceanographic, or the Aegis Institute, I'm damned sure I'll find out about it and I will let you know right away."

"I hoped you'd say that," said Ross, "but please, remember you're in England, Mr. Decker. You have no authority to take any kind of action over here, covert or otherwise, so don't even think of going off half-cocked and trying to deal with things by yourself. You and your people, if you discover anything, no matter how small, about Aegis, you ring it through to me, or I'll have no choice other than to arrest you for obstructing an investigation and I don't think your family would be too happy about that."

"You hear him, Jerome?" said Elaine Decker. "Do what the man says, you got that?"

"As long as I don't hear about it, you can investigate as much as you like," Ross grinned at the C.I.A. man. "Now, I think my sergeant has some questions she'd like to ask," Ross went on.

"Okay, okay, I've got it," Decker said, holding both hands up in surrender. "I promise, no rogue operations on UK soil, Inspector. But we will be investigating Aegis in our own way."

Decker looked at Izzie, unsure how to take this young woman, dressed in her smart skirt suit, her shoulder length hair perfectly in place and her eyes bright and intelligent. He waited as she looked around the room, taking in everything in sight, before beginning her questions. Izzie had been 'people watching' as Ross had spoken to the head of the family and now she looked directly at Kelly Decker, who she was certain had something to tell them. One of Drake's greatest attributes was her ability to read people's body language.

"Kelly, I think you have something to say."

"Me?"

"Yes, it's okay, please just tell us. If might help us in finding your brother's killer."

Kelly hesitated for no more than a second and then replied.

"Well, when Sally went away to the Antarctic last year, Aaron did go down South, to a place in Cornwall or Devon, I think it was. I don't know the name. I'm not that good on English geography yet, still finding my way around London, you know?"

"Sure, that's okay. It wasn't a big secret though, was it?"

"No, not a secret, but he said he was on a 'secret mission' as he called it, and he told me it might make him a lot of money, but I should keep quiet about his little trip. He didn't want me to say anything to Mom and Dad because Mom always worries when he goes diving and if she'd known he was diving on wrecks, well, her hair would have turned purple at the thought of it."

"Kelly!" her mother said.

"Sorry Mom, but that was what he said. "He also said Dad would tell him to keep his nose out of other people's business so it was best to say nothing to him either."

Decker senior scowled, a look not lost on Ross or Drake.

"Right," said Drake, "and did he tell you anything else about this 'secret mission' of his?"

"Not really, but he did send me some great photos that he'd taken with his underwater camera. He loved using it. Me and Peter had bought it for him two Christmases ago and he sent me copies of the digital photos he'd taken. I've still got them on my computer at home."

"Why didn't you tell us anything about this before?" Kelly's father asked, his voice filled with accusation.

"Dad, I...well, I never thought of it until now and how was I supposed to know they might be important or have anything to do with Aaron's death?"

Drake could see that Kelly was on the verge of tears and quickly stepped in to diffuse the developing situation.

"Mr. Decker, I think Kelly is quite right. She couldn't have known this had anything to do with Aaron's death and it may not have, but it is important we see those photos, Kelly. Did you print any of those photos?"

"Sure did. I've got half a dozen in my backpack in my room. I'll go get them if you like?"

"Fantastic," said Drake, and the smile on Kelly's face showed she enjoyed being appreciated, something that maybe didn't happen a lot in her life.

A couple of uncomfortable minutes passed as Ross and Drake waited for Kelly to return. Her father obviously felt she'd been keeping secrets from him and her mother looked perplexed and worried. Ross breathed a sigh of relief as the girl re-entered the suite, and quickly held out her hand, passing a small collection of seven by five inch colour prints into his hand.

"There you go, Inspector," she said. "There's a few more at home on the computer, but these were the best quality so they're the ones I printed out."

"Thank you, Kelly. These might be a big help," Ross said as he looked at the photographs one by one, passing each one to Drake after he'd perused them.

"These are very good quality prints," Drake observed.

"It's a really cool camera," Kelly enthused. "Ain't that right, Peter?"

"Yes, it is," her brother agreed. "We bought the best we could afford."

"What's this?" said Ross, peering at one photo in particular. "It looks like a warship of some kind, but look at the old gun turret. It's small, looks like it would only have held one gun, probably rotted away by now, but what kind of warship could be so small and only have a tiny little gun turret like that?"

"May I see, Inspector?" asked Decker, and Ross passed him the photograph.

"A corvette, if you ask me," the American said. "Small ships used during the war to provide convoy escorts or coastal protection duties. Some of them weren't much bigger than a trawler, but they did good work, Inspector Ross."

"Thanks, I take it you know something of the history of World War Two, Mr. Decker?"

"Something of a pet subject of mine, Inspector. What else we got there? I like to think that's how Aaron first found his love of history."

Ross passed the entire collection to Decker who mused over them for a few seconds.

"Wouldn't surprise me if that little corvette went down during the Dunkirk evacuation, or maybe later, perhaps it hit a mine or was sunk by a German E-Boat on a hit and run raid in the Channel. Some of these are interesting. If you have a maritime museum here in the city you may find someone who can give you more help than me."

"There's the maritime museum at the old Albert Dock, sir," said Drake.

"Yes, maybe we can find some help there," Ross agreed.

"Hmm," said Decker, thoughtfully. "This is really old, look."

He pointed to what appeared to be nothing more than a gathering of old wooden beams and a few pieces of twisted metal but his trained eye saw something more.

"It's an old wooden hulled ship, Inspector, and if I'm not mistaken those are the circular metal hoops that would have been parts of barrels the ship was carrying. Fascinating! Wait a minute. Look at this."

Something had excited the C.I.A. man and he held one of the photos up to the light near the expansive window of the suite. "My God, it really is what I thought."

"What is it, Mr. Decker" Ross wondered what he'd missed when he'd looked at the prints.

"Look closely at this one, Inspector. Tell me what you see."

Ross did as Decker asked. It was another photo of the corvette, taken from another angle, and was of the other side of the ship to the first photo. Ross looked closer, and then, as he focused his vision on the slightly blurred section at the bottom of the photo he saw what Decker was so excited about.

"Is that what I think it is?" Ross asked.

"What is it? What didn't we see?" Drake added.

"If you think you're seeing the business end, the bow and torpedo tubes of an old time submarine somehow embedded under the keel of that corvette, then you're right on the button, Inspector. By God, my son was one hell of an undersea photographer."

The sudden pride in Decker's voice was tinged with a hint of sadness as he remembered why they were gathered here in his hotel suite.

"But what does it mean? Is there some significance to that submarine being there?" Drake asked the obvious question.

"I don't know," Decker replied, "But my guess is that that is a German U-Boat, possibly sunk by the corvette. Maybe she was depth-charged or the little warship rammed her after the sub had torpedoed her or damaged her with fire from its deck gun. Hell, I don't know but your naval historians might be able to throw some light on the two ships being out there, locked together; embracing one another in death, as it were."

"That's all well and good," Ross was now playing Devil's advocate. "But can this have anything to do with Aaron's death? What possible connection can this have to his murder? Aegis is legitimately working with these old wrecks, after all. The whole purpose of their remit is apparently to study just how these wrecks have affected the environment around them."

"Wait sir," Drake butted in. "Kelly, you said Aaron told you that what he found could make him a lot of money, right?"

"Yes, that's what he said," Kelly agreed.

"So maybe it's not the corvette and submarine we should be looking at. What about the old wooden hulled ship?"

Decker and Ross both looked again at the photo of what appeared to be an old wooden ship, but couldn't make out any defining images from the photograph.

"At this point, anything's possible," Ross replied. So far, the only thing he knew for certain was that they knew virtually nothing. Andy Ross felt a frisson of excitement at what they'd just discovered, but the frustration he felt at a total lack of real progress pervaded his thoughts like a disease. He was sensible enough to acknowledge when he needed help or when he was out of his depth, he thought, ironically.

It would take an expert to try to identify what they were looking at, in terms of the wooden hulk. Another of the photos again showed the corvette, this one taken from what would have been the bow, and Ross could clearly see damage of some sort to the warship.

"Maybe the corvette was hit by a torpedo but had enough power or steerage way or whatever they call it in nautical terms left to ram the U-Boat," he theorised.

"But, what does any of this have to do with the murder of a young man?" Izzie Drake spoke up. "Okay, so these ships are war graves, but nothing about them would give anyone a motive for murder, surely. I'll bet Aegis have all the necessary permissions to dive on the wrecks in order to carry out their research."

"Maybe it's not a matter of who, but what?" said Decker.

"Pardon?" said Ross.

"The corvette wouldn't be involved, but it's possible the U-Boat may have been carrying something valuable. I know for a fact that the Germans often attempted to smuggle secret and expensive cargoes to countries sympathetic to their cause towards the end of the war. I think you need to identify that submarine, Inspector."

"I think you're right, Mr. Decker," Ross agreed.

"Can I make a point here, sir?"

"Go ahead, Sergeant," said Ross in response to Drake's question.

"The maritime museum at Albert Dock mostly relates to Liverpool's own seafaring history, and that was mostly based on the big liners that sailed from here, like Lusitania and Titanic. If we want to find out about warships then I think we need to direct our inquiry to the Royal Navy."

"A good point," Ross agreed. "We'll get on to that as soon as we return to headquarters. Meanwhile, give Ferris a ring, and ask him to find me the number for the Royal Naval Museum, which will probably be in Portsmouth unless I'm very much mistaken."

"Will do sir," and Drake moved to the far side of the room to make the call to Paul Ferris.

"What's this?" said Peter Decker, who'd picked up the photos from the table where his father had laid them. He was indicating one of the other photos that seemed to show a large seal swimming across the camera lens."

"That's a seal, Peter," said Kelly, derisorily.

"Not the seal, lunkhead," Peter laughed. "Look in the background."

Kelly did, and then passed the photo to Ross, pointing at the object Peter had noticed.

"Well, I'll be a monkey's uncle," said Ross.

"Okay, I'm hooked," said Decker senior. "What have you got?"

"I wish we had a magnifying glass here," Ross said gravely, "but I'm pretty sure that what your son Aaron accidentally photographed in the background, if you look very closely, is the dead body of a frogman. Aaron wasn't the only one interested in the wreck of the corvette and the U-Boat, obviously."

Jerome Decker took the photo from Ross, held it close to his eyes and squinted in deep concentration as he focused on the image. With an effort he could see what Peter and Ross had noticed. There, probably trapped by part of the wreck debris, the body floated, seemingly twisting slowly and gracefully with the movements of the current, in a macabre dance of death.

"Goddammit, Aaron," he finally exclaimed. "What the hell did you get yourself into?"

Chapter 12

Family Connections

Paul Ferris had been busy. While Ross and Drake were enjoying the luxury of the Decker's hotel suite, the detective constable had been slaving away over a hot keyboard, as he laughingly thought it, immersed in his research into the enormous, though previously unheard of, worldwide conglomerate that was Aegis Oceanographic. Ferris had found himself fascinated by much of the information he'd unearthed. Known as The Aegis Institute, or Aegis Oceanographic, or Aegis Maritime, depending on the discipline being undertaken, the company seemed to be almost octopus-like in having arms or branches in numerous countries around the world.

The Aegis Institute for example, took in the company's corporate headquarters near Boston, Massachusetts, another major office in New York and the actual research institute, based close to the waterfront in the city of Portland, Maine, with various smaller facilities on both the Eastern and Western Seaboards of the USA. Ferris digressed from his main research for a few minutes, fascinated by the history of Portland, with its regenerated Old Port District, similar in some ways to Liverpool's newly regenerated docklands area, and possessing the oldest lighthouse in continuous use in the USA. The city even has a number of pubs more akin to the English equivalent than the traditional American 'bars' and was the home of the famed poet, Longfellow.

Bringing himself back to the matter in hand, Ferris dug further and found that Aegis had various facilities in Europe, based in England, Spain and Italy, and further but smaller locations in Asia and the Far East, including a new state of the art research unit in Japan. The English facility was of obvious interest, and Ferris spent ten minutes looking into the publicly reported activities of Aegis (UK) Limited, based not far from Falmouth in Cornwall, well off the beaten-track for such a dynamic company, Ferris thought. Apart from the research they were aware of into the effects of the rotting Channel wrecks on the environment, it seemed the UK division was doing little else at present, at least nothing that had been made known to the local press.

Ferris now had a moment of inspiration as his initiative kicked in. He remembered that his wife had a cousin who was a police officer down in Cornwall. Kareen, although raised in Liverpool from the age of four, had been born in England's southernmost county, her father having been skipper of a trawler sailing out of the village of St. Keverne, not far from Falmouth. The family had moved north when Sam Tremayne was offered the chance to skipper a new, larger deep sea trawler operating from the then vibrant port of Fleetwood on the Lancashire coast. Kareen's father had sailed and fished some of the most inhospitable waters in the northern hemisphere, but the eventual decline of the fishing industry saw him finally giving up the sea, and the family moved once again, settling in Liverpool where Sam found work on the famous Mersey Ferries. The thing that gave Paul Ferris his inspiration was the memory of the fact that Sam Tremayne had a younger brother who was a police officer in the Cornish Constabulary. As far as Ferris could recall, Reginald (Reg) Tremayne had been a constable in Redruth, located not too far from Falmouth. Although Kareen hadn't stayed in close contact with her uncle over the years, Ferris thought that the family connection might come in useful if Reg was still on the force, and still based in Redruth.

A quick phone call to the Redruth police brought Ferris a slice of information he thought almost too good to be true. A Sergeant Grant, to whom he was put through to at Redruth police station, informed Ferris that Reg, now Sergeant Tremayne was still on the force, but was no longer at Redruth. Ferris's initial disappointment turned to unexpected excitement when Grant told him that Reg Tremayne had transferred to Falmouth three years ago.

Reg was surprised and delighted to hear from Paul Ferris. Ferris had to take a minute or two to get used to hearing the rather slow drawling Cornish accent in order to accurately follow Reg's words. Kareen of course, had no trace of a Cornish accent, having lived in Liverpool almost all her life, and her father had lost most of his accent over the years, but Ferris soon came to terms with Reg's speech, and Reg likewise joked about trying to keep up with Paul's Scouse accent.

Reg was full of questions about Sam and his niece, Paul's wife and apologised for not keeping in closer touch through the years, though the disjointed family had continued to exchange cards at Christmas and birthdays. Ferris soon had to curb 'Uncle' Reg's enthusiasm for family news as he quickly explained the professional nature of his call.

"Bloody hell, Paul," Reg exclaimed after Ferris has outlined the nature of the case he was working on. "You be the third person to be making inquiries about that lot from Aegis in recent times."

"Really?" said a surprised Paul Ferris. "Who were the first and second?"

"Well now. First of all I strongly suspect it was yon young feller whose murder you be investigatin'."

"And when was this, Reg?"

"Well, it were last summer, like. I were on duty one day when this good lookin' young chap walks into the station when I was on the front desk and starts askin' me if I knows anything about the folks who work at the Aegis place just out of town."

Ferris smiled to himself. When Reg had mentioned 'recent times', he'd assumed he meant within a few weeks or a couple of months, not a year ago, but then he thought to himself, life certainly moves at a much slower pace down in Cornwall. But, at least he could be on to something.

"Were you able to tell him anything, Reg?"

"Well now Paul, it were a bit weird. I told him as how they were a pretty secretive bunch, and that they didn't take too kindly to strangers hangin' around their place, or getting' too close to their ship. He just laughed and said as how they wouldn't know he was there and that he was after findin' out if they were doin' anything illegal out at sea, where they were supposed to be investigatin' old wrecks, as he told me. I told him if he thought anything untoward was happenin' he should tell the police and coast guard, but he just said the police couldn't do anythin' about what they was up to and that he'd sort it out himself. To be honest I thought he were a young lad who were just full of hot air, like, and tried to tell him to stay away from private property. From what you're tellin' me, seems he didn't take too kindly to my warning."

"I think you're right, Reg, but listen, I'm probably asking you the same questions he did. Why don't the people at Aegis want anyone near their property, and what's this about them having a ship of their own down there?"

"Your guess is as good as mine, Paul. Their place is protected by a ten foot high fence, electrified, and floodlights at night light the place up like daytime.

I don't know what they do in there, but it is private property and they are entitled to their privacy I suppose. As for the ship, it's apparently a research vessel, called *Poseidon*. A real modern vessel it is too. Only about three hundred feet, but carries lots of cranes, gantries and looks like it carries more than one submersible or ROVs on or below decks."

Ferris deferred to Reg Tremayne's nautical knowledge. He was after all from a family that had lived its life on or near the sea for many years, but he did have a question.

"Submersibles I'm familiar with, Reg, but explain ROV please."

"Them's remotely operated underwater vehicles, Paul. You know, like those things you might have seen in the movie, *Titanic*. They can go down real deep and send live pictures up to the mother ship on the surface."

"Right, I understand that, Reg. Thing is, none of that sounds out of order for a maritime research company does it?"

"I've got to agree with you, Paul. No, it doesn't."

"Then why did you use the word 'weird' earlier?"

"Ah, yes, well, that brings me to nosey parker number two, so to speak," said Tremayne.

"Do tell, please Reg," said Ferris, likening getting information from Kareen's uncle to pulling teeth from an unwilling patient.

"He were a German feller, this other chap. Turned up about a month after the last time I'd seen the young chap. Told me he were some sort of Naval Historian, looking into German naval activity in the English Channel and specially around the Channel Islands during World War Two. I presume you know the Germans occupied the Channel Islands during the war, young Paul?"

"Yes, I knew that," Ferris replied, trying to force the conversation forward. "So what did this German want? Did he give you his name?"

"Aye, that he did, Paul. Hold on a minute, whilst I check back in me notebook." Ferris heard a slight 'clunk' as Tremayne placed the phone down on his desk. A minute passed and Reg came back on the line.

"You still there, Paul?"

"Yes, Reg. Go ahead."

"He gave his name as Klaus Haller, from Hamburg he said, and before you ask why I never got the young man's name, that were because he just came making general enquiries at the front desk, but this Haller chap came and we had a long talk in a more formal way, as him turning up so soon after the young man sort of got my interest roused, if you know what I mean."

"Yes, I understand, Reg. I think I'd have done the same. So what was the upshot of your meeting with Haller?"

"Not much really. I told him I knew nothing about Aegis or what they were doing in the Channel. All I knew was that they had permission to be out there exploring the wrecks for some sort of environmental research project. For some reason he seemed to think we, meaning the police, had some sort of control over their activities. I told him things don't work like that in England. He did mention though that he'd been invited over by a young university student who thought he'd find something interesting in the work Aegis were doing. Again, I presumed it were the young chap who you're looking into. He also asked if I knew what area of the Channel Aegis were operating in, and I had to tell him again I knew nothin' at all about what or where they were working. I told him he'd have to maybe hire a boat and follow their research vessel out to sea if he were so interested in them. He said he'd do that and that were the last I saw of him."

"Thanks, Reg, that's all very helpful," Ferris said, not sure if it was or not. He felt there was little else Reg Tremayne could tell him at that point, but it was interesting that young Decker had perhaps invited Haller to England to look into the activities of the Aegis group. Ferris was unaware at this point of the gruesome discovery that Ross and Drake had uncovered as a result of their interview with Decker's family. He said his goodbyes to Reg Tremayne with a promise to ask Sam to call his brother in the near future and with Reg's message of love to Kareen and the Ferris's son, Aaron the last words from the slow-speaking Cornish police sergeant, the call ended.

Ferris returned to his computer, sure now that something about the Aegis organisation wasn't quite as it might appear to be on the surface. He needed to dig deeper if he was to discover exactly what they might be up to. And who the hell was Klaus Haller? Maybe the internet could help him.

Chapter 13

The party was in full swing. Even though the Officers Mess stood some 200 metres from the guardhouse, the naval ratings on guard duty could hear the raucous sounds as they shivered in the cool night-time air. Most knew the war was going badly and the fact that their officers could still find cause for celebration and enjoyment escaped them.

"Hey, Max, come here. A drink for you, my friend."

Korvettankapitän Max Ritter forced his way through the small throng of bodies and found a beer being thrust into his hand by *Kapitän zur See*, Heinz Schmidt.

"To the future, Max," Schmidt shouted as Ritter took a swig from the beer glass.

"Sure, the future," Ritter replied, knowing only too well what the future of Germany would be over the coming weeks.

"The admiral would have been here himself to see you off in the morning, but, well, you know how busy he is," said Schmidt.

"Of course," said Ritter, knowing full well that the admiral never had any intention of coming to Kiel to see *U3000*, recently redesignated *U966* slip her moorings in the morning. He'd most likely be curled up with his latest mistress, so much more preferable than standing on a cold wet dockside as Ritter and his crew left Germany for what the U-Boat commander knew in his heart would probably be the last time.

"Come, Max, enjoy yourself. See, there are plenty of young ladies eager to make your acquaintance." The captain, a former U-Boat skipper himself, now aide to Admiral Werner Stein, called across the room, over the sound of the piano and the group of officers gathered around it, singing and swaying, and two young blonde women rose from a couch and walked through the throng on the small dance floor to reach them.

"Ladies, see, here is the hero, home from the sea," said Schmidt as the two women sidled up to Ritter, both immediately seeing and recognising the Knight's Cross with Oak Leaves worn around the young U-Boat commander's neck.

It had been a while since Ritter had been with a woman, and the availability of one, or perhaps both of the young blondes was sorely tempting. Ritter knew they were part of that strange group of young women who had allowed themselves to become 'whores for Hitler,' many of them actually sent by their proud and willing mothers to become nothing more than 'comfort women,' prostituting themselves to provide sexual comfort for the officers of the Third Reich.

Ritter gazed around the room. On one couch nearby a young brunette lay on her back, her skirt hoisted up around her waist, legs spread, as a young *Lieutnant* pleasured himself between her thighs.

Looking at the two smiling girls standing one on each of his arms, Ritter looked at the girl on his right, and asked her name.

"Claudia, Herr Kapitän," she replied.

Dressed in a low-cut, diaphanous white blouse, and a black pencil skirt that accentuated the girl's hips and rear as she walked on what to Ritter seemed painfully high heels, Claudia still retained something of an air of innocence about her, despite wearing a little too much make-up that added a red lustre to her lips and a dark sensuousness to her blue eyes. He guessed her age at no more than eighteen or nineteen. Looking at her obvious charms, barely hidden by the thin material of her blouse, he felt himself becoming aroused.

"Come with me," Ritter ordered, taking her by the hand. "I'll see you later, sir?" he said to Schmidt.

"Sure, have fun Max," Schmidt replied, as Ritter led the young blonde towards the stairs and the private rooms upstairs. "Don't be late."

"I'll be back on board by midnight," Ritter called over his shoulder as Claudia led the way upstairs, her young hips swaying as he followed her, her legs looking long and inviting from behind.

As Max and Claudia disappeared from his sight, Schmidt turned to the second girl. "How old are you, girl?"

"Seventeen, sir," she replied in a small voice.

"How long have you been here?"

"Almost three months."

"Good, come with me," he ordered and the girl followed obediently as Schmidt led her up the same stairs Ritter had trod a minute ago.

* * *

Three hours later, Ritter stood on the conning tower of *U3000*, a prototype of one of Germany's latest 'breed' of U-Boats, his second-in-command *Leutnant zur See* Heinrich Engel by his side. The two men were aware of the importance of their mission and as the truck carrying their cargo pulled up on the dock alongside the boat, Ritter simply tapped Engel on the shoulder and the young first officer saluted and dropped through the hatch into the submarine's control room loading, emerging again a minute later from the forward deck hatch. Ritter looked on as Engel supervised a number of wooden boxes as they were first deposited on the dock, before being manhandled through the deck hatch by half a dozen members of *U3000's* crew.

In the submarine's control room, a pair of boiler-suited dock workers were completing a task that had mystified the two officers, and Ritter felt uncomfortable and unsure of the reasons for their actions which had been sanctioned by a written order signed by no other than Grand Admiral Doenitz himself. Their work done in less than ten minutes the two men, who in reality were not civilian dock workers but members of Germany's military intelligence service, the *Abwehr*, headed by Admiral Wilhelm Canaris, departed the submarine without a word to anyone, and disappeared into the night.

Once their cargo was safely secured and the hatch battened down, Engel reported back to Ritter.

"All is secure, Kapitän. The boat is secured and ready for sea, but this subterfuge, those two men, I wonder...?"

"Excellent Heini, now we wait for Schmidt to finish screwing his whore. Once we receive our sealed orders we can get underway. Perhaps they will answer your question, mine too. It may be a long time before we see our homes and families again, my friend."

"We must do what we can for the Fatherland, my Kapitän," Engel replied, but Ritter simply nodded as he said,

"The Fatherland is all but defeated, Heini. What we do now, we do because we are officers of the Kriegsmarine and it is our duty to follow the orders of our senior officers, whether we think them right or wrong."

Engel looked askance at Ritter, the first time he'd heard his Captain speak in such a way. Engel knew

Ritter well. He'd first found fame during the 'happy time' when the German U-Boat 'Wolf Packs' roamed the North Atlantic at will, sinking allied merchant shipping virtually unopposed after the outbreak of war. His first command came almost by accident during a surface battle with an armed merchantman, the *S.S. Cressida*, whose captain refused to surrender. The merchant ship opened fire on the U-Boat, a lucky shot hitting the conning tower and killing the sub's commander, Ritter's friend, Gunther Adel. As first officer, Ritter assumed command and withdrew from the surface fight, laying off far enough to send two torpedoes into the enemy vessel, sinking her with all hands. Three further merchant vessels plus a convoy escort were sunk under Ritter's command during the voyage and on return to base the young first officer was awarded his first Knight's Cross, promoted to *Oberleutnant zur See* and given command of his own U-Boat. He received the Oak Leaves to his Knight's Cross when saving the lives of two crewmen from the damaged rear torpedo room of his boat after a collision with a convoy escort destroyer in the North Atlantic, refusing to seal off the compartment and leaving them to drown, after which he'd single-mindedly stalked the destroyer despite the damage to his boat, eventually sinking his opponent with two well placed torpedoes.

For Engel to hear his skipper talk of Germany losing the war was a shock to the young first officer, who for the first time began to doubt much of the propaganda that tried to convince the German people of eventual victory over the allies. If Ritter thought the war was lost, Engel believed him.

Just after midnight, as the middle watch replaced those on the last, (second) dog watch, a black Mercedes car pulled up on the dock beside the still silent U-Boat. The driver climbed out of the car, opening the rear door to allow *Kapitän zur See* Schmidt to exit the car. The driver saluted smartly, his salute being barely acknowledged by Schmidt who stood looking up at the submarine's conning tower. Seeing Ritter looking down at him, he marched smartly up the gangplank that led to the narrow deck of the U-Boat, where he was briefly held at bay by the two seamen on armed guard at the base of the conning tower, before being admitted to the interior of the boat. By the time he'd been escorted to the control room, Ritter was already there, waiting for him, Ritter escorted him to the so-called 'Captain's cabin,' in fact little more than a small cubicle with a dark red curtain draped across the entrance to provide a modicum of privacy to the boat's commander.

Ritter poured them both a measure of Schnapps from a bottle beside his bunk as Schmidt seated himself on a small stool beside Ritter's chart table.

"To your health and the success of your mission, Max," Schmidt said, raising his glass to the U-Boat skipper.

"I'd drink to that a little easier if I knew exactly what our mission is," Ritter replied, at which point Schmidt reached into the black leather briefcase he'd carried on board and removed a large, sealed envelope from within, which he passed across to Ritter, who sat on his bunk awaiting some explanation of the forthcoming mission.

"You are to sail before first light, Max," Ritter began, "and you may open your sealed orders as soon as you have cleared the harbour and have reached the open sea. There can be no risks of anyone leaking the nature of this voyage, and once opened, you may divulge the true nature of your voyage to your first officer, and your engineering officer only. What you tell the rest of the crew is up to you, Max, but do not underestimate the importance of this mission. Is that understood?"

"Perfectly," Ritter replied, "but first, can you tell me why my boat's maker's plate has been changed? This is *U3000*, and yet now the plate identifies us *U966*. What is going on, Kapitän? Can you personally tell me nothing of what lies ahead for me and my crew?"

"I'm sorry, Max. My orders are as specific as yours. I was to deliver the sealed orders to you with your instructions, and no more. I can tell you however, that the change in your boat's designation was authorised at the highest level. From this moment, you are in command of *U966*. *U3000* no longer exists. The admiral was quite explicit in his orders."

"I'm sure he was," said Ritter sarcastically, unsure precisely which admiral. Stein or Doenitz, Schmidt referred to. "And what of the real *U966*?"

"No longer in service, lost in '43. Due to the nature of your cargo and the other... erm, special features of your boat, you are now a ghost ship, Max. Everything that could identify you as *U3000* has been systematically obliterated during the recent maintenance work on your boat."

Ritter knew he'd learn nothing more on the subject from Schmidt but wanted the answer to one more important question.

"Are you aware that while I was away from the boat earlier today, a dockyard crew under the command of an S.S. colonel, of all people, came on board and stripped out almost all my torpedoes? The rear torpedo compartment is bare of armaments and I've been left with the four torpedoes in the forward tubes and the rest have been similarly removed. We've been left almost defenceless."

"All will be revealed when you read your orders, Max, and now, I must go. You have a voyage to prepare for."

Schmidt stood, drained his glass and gave Ritter a perfect Nazi salute.

"Heil Hitler," he said, and then, "Good luck, Max. I hope we meet again when this is all over."

Ritter casually returned the salute. He'd always been a sailor, not a Nazi, and he had little regard for Hitler and what he saw as the fawning band of sycophants that surrounded him, but he'd sensibly kept such thoughts to himself through the hard years of war. In Nazi Germany, you never knew who was listening, ready to report supposed 'treasonous' activities to the Gestapo. More than one U-Boat commander of Max's acquaintance had been summoned to Kriegsmarine headquarters in the past, never to be seen again. A waste of good men, Max knew, but such was the way of life in the Fatherland.

Just before first light, the newly designated *U966* slipped her moorings, and under the power of her virtually silent, gently throbbing diesel motors, she slowly eased her way out of the submarine base and into the open sea, destination unknown.

Chapter 14

Megan Rose

Sam Gable sat opposite Megan Rose in the same room Ross and Ferris had occupied when they'd interviewed Sally Metcalfe. A petite auburn-haired young woman of twenty-three, Megan had made tea for them both and expressed surprise that the police needed to speak with her about the death of Aaron Decker.

"There's nothing to be nervous about, Megan," said Gable. "We just need to speak to as many people who knew Aaron as possible so we can build up a better picture of what he was like and perhaps why someone might want to hurt him."

"I see, I think," Megan replied, "but I didn't know him very well, I'm afraid."

"Okay, so how often did you see him Megan?"

"Well, he'd often come round here to collect Sally if they were going out, and sometimes, Sally would cook a meal and they'd spend the evening here, but on those occasions I'd usually go out with friends, or even on my own to the cinema sometimes, not wanting to cramp their style, you know?"

"Yes, I understand. So, when he came to collect Sally, did you and he talk much?"

"Just small talk, you know? Like, how's things? Maybe I'd ask how his research was coming along, that kind of thing."

"You mean for his post-doc, right?"

"Yes, but he was never very forthcoming, so I steered clear of the subject. I'd talk about the weather, or his cricket or other sports. He liked to talk about that stuff. I think despite being a nice guy, Aaron was a bit full of himself at times, liked to blow his own trumpet a bit."

"You mean a bit of a big head?"

"Yes, no, not really. I think it was because he was American. They tend to be a bit more direct and out-spoken, or at least that's how I've found the few who I've come into contact with at the university."

"I think I know what you mean, Megan. So you'd leave them to it if he came here, but did he ever spend the night with Sally, here I mean, not at his place?"

"No, he didn't. Well, he wasn't supposed to, but now and then, he'd stay really late, you know...? Part of the terms of our student rental is that no overnight visitors of the opposite sex are allowed and we're both well aware of it. This is a nice house, and we don't want to risk losing it."

"I can understand that. I'm not here to get you in trouble with the landlord if Aaron overstayed a bit later than he should have done now and then. Sally has already told us he stayed over now and then. Do you have a boyfriend, Megan?"

"Not at present, no. I went out with a lad from Huyton a while ago but it only lasted a couple of months. He said I was too wrapped up in my studies and didn't spend enough time with him. I think the truth of the matter was really that I wouldn't drop my knickers for him. He was one of those guys who thinks all students are an easy lay, if you know what I mean"

"Oh yes, I know exactly what you mean. Better off without him then, eh?"

"Definitely."

"So, did you ever meet any of Aaron's friends?"

"Only once or twice, when I went to the pub and him and Sally would ask me over for a drink. There were sometimes a few of his mates there, but I never got to know any of them."

"What about the two men he shared his house with?"

"Oh yes, Tim and er, Martin is it? I never met Martin but Tim was in the pub a couple of times when I saw them there. I always thought he leered at Sally a bit. She told me they went out a couple of times, ages ago before she met Aaron but Tim wasn't her type."

"Did she say why?"

"No, not really. I don't think it was anything specific, just that they didn't have much in common as far as I could make out. Anyway, they'd finished long before Aaron came on the scene. Sally is the one you need to talk to about that."

"Yes, of course and I'm sure we'll be doing that. So, you don't know of anyone who might have wanted to harm Aaron or Sally, or both of them, maybe?"

"No, of course not. It's just unbelievable, what's happened to Aaron. Sally's so upset and she told me that someone had drugged her too with a powerful anaesthetic. Is that right?"

"I can't go into details of the case, Megan, but yes, Sally was attacked too."

"That's just awful. Are you close to catching whoever did it yet?"

"We're following a number of leads at present," Gable lied, not wanting to let Megan know the police were so far baffled by the killing.

"So, is that it? Do you want to know anything else from me?"

"Just about Sally. Did you know her before you both moved in here together?"

"Not really. We met at a party when we were both looking for digs and we hit it off and started going out together, then the idea came up to look for a place to rent, to share the expenses, and we got lucky finding this place."

"So you don't know much about her background?"

"Not really. I know she's fanatical about her Marine biology research and anything to so with the environment, not that she's what you'd call an activist or anything like that. Just passionate about her work is how I'd describe her."

"And you wouldn't know if she had any enemies, or just anyone who dislikes her enough to want to hurt her through Aaron?"

"No way. Sally's always been popular with everyone. The only person I know who she's ever had 'words' with is Tim Knight."

"Really? In what way?"

"Well, like I said, they dated a couple of times, long before she got together with Aaron. But one day, when we were in the pub, I heard Tim saying something like *I was never good enough for you, was I Sally?*" or words to that effect, and Sally told him to stop being a prat, and that he'd had too much to drink. I think Tim might have been feeling sorry for himself because he'd just broken up with Fiona Gregg, his girlfriend at that time, plus he'd had a few pints, you know?"

"Yes, that's probably all it was," Gable agreed while at the same time filing that little piece of information away in her mind and in her notebook. It was probably nothing, as Megan Rose said, but as Sam knew, you never took anything for granted or at face value in police work, especially in a murder investigation.

Sam left the house after thanking the young woman. On the whole, she hadn't learned anything of value, though she'd learned at least that Aaron Decker had definitely possessed a high opinion of himself, but, was that sufficient to provoke someone to commit murder? Stranger things had happened in the past, she reminded herself.

Chapter 15

A Meeting of Minds

Andy Ross and Izzie Drake returned to headquarters with their minds buzzing, having been shocked to see the dead frogman captured on Aaron Decker's underwater photograph. Ross was certain now that the wrecks of the Corvette and the submarine must in some way be connected to the death of young Decker. Drake agreed and also put forward her supposition that the Aegis Institute or whatever name they were using in the UK must have a part to play in the growing scenario.

As they walked in to the squad room, still unaware of Ferris's conversation with Reg Tremayne they found the rest of the team all in one place at the same time, something of a rare occurrence nowadays.

"Nothing to do, people?" Ross half-joked as he and Drake walked towards the large whiteboard that Paul Ferris, as team collator, always used to display any and all information or photographs pertaining to their current case.

Sam Gable was first to reply.

"Just back from talking to Megan Rose, sir, Sally Metcalfe's room mate, house sharer or whatever we want to call her. Not a lot to be gained there, I'm afraid, apart from the fact that Tim Knight and Sally had a small altercation soon after she and Decker got together."

"What kind of altercation?" Ross asked her.

"Oh, just a drunken moan I think, sir. Knight had drunk too much, had just split with his girlfriend at that time, and accused Sally of seeing him as not good enough for her. As he and Sally had dated all of twice, Megan thought it was just a case of Knight feeling sorry for himself and lashing out verbally at Sally for no good reason. I must say, I tend to agree with her assessment of the event."

"Yes, sounds about right for a testosterone filled young stud of Knight's age group," Izzie Drake said.

Ross smiled.

"Of course, Sergeant Drake would know all about that, eh, Sergeant?"

A small ripple of laughter rolled around the squad room.

"Oh, come on," said Izzie. "Anyone would think I was the only person who ever got married round here."

"You are," laughed Derek McLennan. "At least, the only one who's got married while being an active member of the team. Paul and the boss were both married before the team was formed, and the rest of us are single, so yeah, you are the only one."

"Alright, let's get serious," Ross ordered, as he brought the impromptu team meeting back on track. "I agree too, Sam. I don't think a two-date relationship constitutes a major cause of unrequited love leading to murder. How about you two?" he asked next, looking at Dodds and McLennan, who'd been assigned the task of conducting the initial interviews at the university.

Derek McLennan replied first.

"Again, not a lot to be gleaned there either, sir. One chap, a Professor Tilkowski, the 'w' is pronounced as a 'v' by the way, told us that Aaron Decker was one of the most single-minded students he'd ever encountered. Everything came second to his work and studies, even the cricket, the prof said."

"Yes," Nick Dodds chimed in. "Apparently a couple of the big professional County Cricket clubs had approached Decker about him turning professional with them, but he'd rejected their offers, saying he was happy being an amateur and that cricket was just a pastime, not a profession as far as he was concerned."

Ross pulled a face, as he imagined how the stuffed shirt brigades at some of the old established County Cricket clubs would have taken to being dismissed in such a cavalier fashion by young Aaron Decker.

McLennan took over again.

"We spoke to a few students who knew Decker. As it was explained to us more than once, as a post doctoral student, it wasn't as if Aaron was involved in loads of organised lectures or tutorials like the younger students just setting out on their degree courses. We felt a bit thick, to be truthful, sir, not knowing quite how university education and the various degrees, post-doc studies as they were referred to and other various study courses were organised. In the end no one could tell us anything of any significance, apart from talking about his sporting prowess. Seems he was a pretty good tennis player too."

Ross was beginning to think the two young detectives were fast turning into a well-versed double act, a thought reinforced as Nick Dodds spoke up once again.

"There was one other thing, sir. A young chap by the name of Robert Allen told us that Decker had recently taken up playing snooker as well. He must have been a pretty mean pool player back in the States, because he'd become a first class player in no time."

"A real life pool shark, eh?" Ross commented.

"Yeah, apparently Allen and some other guys from the university ran a kind of gaming society at the 147 Club over on Fleet Street and Decker was known to have won quite a bit of cash from some of the players."

Ross knew of the 147 Snooker and Pool Club, to give it its full title. Well placed to attract customers in the city centre of Liverpool, the club had really reached its heyday back in the eighties when snooker had enjoyed massive popularity thanks to television coverage of the major tournaments, but word around town was that the place was struggling and the management probably welcomed the potentially raucous but well-heeled young men from the university who doubtless spent a good deal over the bar, in addition to losing money to people like Aaron Decker.

"So there may have been one or two potential bad losers in the pack who may have had it in for him," Drake observed.

"Yeah, but not enough to kill him, surely," said Dodds.

"That might depend how much he won, and if anyone might not have had the money to pay up on the spot when they lost, and owed him money. Nick, see if you can visit the place. Have a word with the management and staff and see if they know what kind of stakes they were playing for. This may not be much, but if it had gone from a few simple friendly frames of snooker to some form of big money gambling, it could cast a new light on things."

"Right boss," Dodds acknowledged.

"Okay everyone," Ross now said, calling for the team's attention. As he spoke he attached the underwater photograph from Decker's camera to the whiteboard.

"Paul, can you stop what you're doing for a minute?" he called across the room to Ferris who had continued to search the internet for more information about Aegis while Ross had received everyone else's updates.

"Sure boss," said Ferris as he turned round in his swivel computer chair. "Still looking for the dirt on Aegis, if there is any."

"Oh, I think you'll find some, somewhere," said Ross as everyone's attention was drawn to the small photograph he'd just displayed.

Ferris walked right up to the board, took one look and said,

"Is that a body?"

"First prize for observation goes to Detective Constable Paul Ferris," Drake said, smiling.

"Too right it is," said Ross as the others gathered closer to get a good look.

"It's a bloody frogman," said Tony Curtis who'd been quiet until now.

"A dead frogman," McLennan concurred.

"And that's a bit of a submarine, if I'm not mistaken, crushed under the ship," Dodds added.

"A ship, a dead frogman and a submarine. What's it all mean, sir?" Sam Gable asked.

"Good question, D.C. Gable," Ross replied. "Ferris, take the photo, get it blown up and let's see if we can find anything else. This was taken by Aaron Decker during a trip he made last year to check out something Aegis was involved in. That's why I think you'll find something in the course of your probing into their affairs, Paul."

"It could also be a pointer as to what got him killed," Drake added.

"Er, sir," said Ferris.

"Yes, Paul, what's up?"

Ferris went on to relate the conversation he'd had with Reg Tremayne after finding the Cornish connection to Aegis in the UK.

As soon as he'd finished speaking, Drake said,

"Why do I suddenly think that dead frogman is none other than this Haller chap?"

"And why do I think you're absolutely right?" said Ross, who now made a quick decision.

"Paul, get that photo blown up right away. I'm going to go and talk to D.C.I. Agostini. It's clear we need to bring the Cornwall police in on this now, and maybe the Coast Guard too. The biggest problem we have is that we don't actually know where the wrecks are. The English Channel is a bloody big body of water. The next thing on the agenda is to contact the Royal Navy museum. They might be able to identify the corvette in the photo or at least the type of ship. If we can find out where this ship or this type of ship operated we might be able to get a rough idea where to look."

"We could always ask Aegis Oceanographic, sir," Curtis joked, receiving a stern look of rebuke from Ross.

"Not very funny, Tony, not funny at all."

"Sorry sir."

"Right. For that, you can get a copy of the enlarged photo when Paul's done it, and then make it your priority task to get in touch with the Royal Navy. I want to know everything they can tell us about that shipwreck, and while you're at it, ask them about that bloody submarine too."

"Right sir. I'll get on to it right away, well, soon as Paul enlarges the photo." They turned to find Paul Ferris was already walking away with the photo in his hand. They knew he wouldn't be long.

"Okay, Sergeant Drake and me are going to bring D.C.I. Agostini up to date. He'll need to be the one to make an approach to the police down south, and if needs be, to get the Coast Guard involved too. It's beginning to look as if poor Aaron Decker found something he shouldn't have found, got this Haller chap involved and it somehow cost them both their lives. We need to find out what that something was and how Aegis is involved. Everyone tread carefully on this one, until we have a better idea of what we're dealing with. Direct your inquiries towards finding out if any strangers were seen or heard from by either Sally or Aaron in the weeks leading up to his death."

"One question, sir," said McLennan.

"Yes, Derek?"

"Well, if Aaron Decker took this photo around a year ago, and if, as Paul says, this German chap turned up soon after Decker was seen making his inquiries, then doesn't it make more sense to think the frogman must have been down there when Decker made his initial dives and that would mean it can't be Haller?"

Ross scratched his head for a minute, and then realised McLennan could be right.

"Well done Derek. That makes sense, unless of course, the photos we have were taken later, after Haller's death. It's possible Aaron took some earlier photos, sent them to Haller and when the German came over here and disappeared, Decker went back, found the body, photographed it and tried to blackmail someone at Aegis with his knowledge. We need to find out if the Deckers have or can locate any other memory cards from Aaron's camera that may contain earlier photos."

"I hadn't thought of that, sir but you're right. It could have happened that way, too."

"Well, we obviously have a lot of digging to do before we find our answer," Ross said as he and Drake moved to leave the room, ready to give D.C.I Agostini the latest news on the extremely tangled web they were gradually revealing that seemed to surround the death of Aaron Decker.

Chapter 16

Two days out from Kiel, and already the interior of what was now officially *U966* was taking on the atmosphere of a submarine at war. The air was heavy with the smell of diesel fumes, mingled with the scent of the sweat of those who crewed the boat. Most of the young men who served in *U966* had stopped shaving as soon as they'd left their home base just two days ago, and soon the lack of proper sanitation, a deprivation standard to U-Boat crews would increase the heady atmosphere within the boat, which would only be relieved when Ritter ordered the submarine to surface to recharge its batteries, and the hatches could be opened.

As soon as the boat had cleared Kiel and headed north towards the coast of Denmark, Ritter had called Engel to his tiny berth where he solemnly opened the sealed orders handed to him by Schmidt. Ritter read through the orders, then silently handed the two sheets of paper and an accompanying map to his first officer.

Engel took the orders, read them slowly, his eyes widening as he did so.

"This is madness, Max," Engel said.

"Those are our orders, Heini," Ritter replied. "We are officers of the Kriegsmarine and we are honour bound to obey them."

"We are virtually unarmed and we are supposed to make this crazy voyage?"

"The torpedoes were removed to lessen the weight of the boat, obviously, and to compensate for the weight of our cargo. There is no going back, my friend. To do so would be to invite summary execution for us all. You've read the orders and seen the signature at the bottom. They come directly from the Fuehrer himself."

"I can see that Max. But why us? Why *U966*? Come to that, why the change from *U3000*?"

"I can't answer that, Heini. Maybe my reputation for seeing my commands through tough voyages brought me to Hitler's attention. Maybe we just drew the short straw. There aren't many of us left. The days of the wolf packs are long gone; you know that as well as I do."

Ritter took a bottle of schnapps from under his bunk, together with two tin mugs, into which he poured a liberal measure for each of them.

"Come Heini, let us drink to what may be our last voyage together. We have a long way to go and if we are lucky, then who knows? We may see Berlin again after all."

"See Berlin again? I've never been there at all. Until I joined the Kriegsmarine I'd never left Bremen in my life."

"I never knew that. Well, if we do make it, and one day return to Germany I will personally take you to the finest restaurant in the city and then we will find a top class brothel and enjoy ourselves as never before, eh, Heini?"

Engel looked at his captain, and smiled in resignation. Like Ritter he knew their chances of pulling off this mission were slim, but they would do as Ritter said. They would obey their orders as any naval officer would.

Ritter held his mug up and Engel reached across, tapped the rim of his own against Ritter's and the two men drank a toast, not to the mission, or to the Fuehrer, not even to *U966*, but instead, they drank to life, long or short, and to each other.

* * *

"Attention, this is your Kapitän speaking."

The sound of Ritter's voice, calm and commanding sounded throughout *U966* as the tannoy system carried his voice to every man on board.

In the control room, as elsewhere on *U966* the crew fell silent. Ritter had earlier informed the crew that they were sailing under top secret sealed orders and that news of their mission would be communicated to them when he deemed it necessary. *Oberfänrich zue See*, (sub-lieutenant), Wilhelm (Willi) Becker, at nineteen years old, the sub's youngest officer, currently in command of the boat while Ritter and Engel were in conference stood beside the periscope, a cigarette dangling from his lips, hands in pockets, trying not to betray his nerves as Ritter spoke. Around the boat, the rest of the crew listened attentively, some with excitement, others with trepidation, as the nature of their mission became clear.

"We are now sailing to the north of Denmark, and before long we will head into the north sea, after which we will adopt a new course that will take us south, along the east coast of Scotland and then England until we turn to the west and make a run through the English Channel, breaking out into the Atlantic after which we face a long and arduous voyage across the ocean, until we reach our final destination, which for the moment must remain secret. Some of you will have seen that our boat's maker's plate has been changed to identify us as *U966*. Henceforth we are no longer *U3000*. Do not ask why. It is part of the mission that we adopt the new designation. The cargo some of you may have seen being loaded into our boat is of vital importance to the Third Reich, and the orders we sail under have been signed by none other than the Fuehrer himself. Some of you will have noticed that the majority of our torpedoes have been removed prior to leaving Kiel. This was done to lighten the boat, enabling us to run silent and deep for longer periods, and to compensate for the weight of the boxes loaded on board at Kiel. We will surface only when necessary to recharge our batteries, so the air might become a little rank in here at times."

This brought a few quiet ripples of laughter from a few of the men.

"I make no apologies for the possible hardships we face on this voyage. Remember, we are not on a search and destroy mission. We are under orders not to engage the enemy unless it is absolutely necessary, so we must use stealth as our watchword at all times. The most dangerous part of our outward voyage will be the dash through the English Channel which is heavily patrolled by the Royal Navy, as we all know. Silence will be strictly maintained as we navigate through those waters. For now, I can add little more. We sail on a mission of the greatest importance, and I know I can count on every man aboard to do his duty to The Fatherland. That is all."

Ritter flicked the 'off' button on the microphone, omitting the usual *Heil Hitler* at the end of his address to the crew, a mark of his dislike for the man he considered unfit to lead his country. Only then did he notice his hand was shaking. This damned voyage was getting to him already.

"That was some of the finest and most resounding bullshit I've ever heard in my life," Engel said quietly as Ritter placed the microphone back on the hook beside his bunk. "You almost had me cheering you and believing that codswallop about the importance of the mission, and doing it for The Fatherland."

"What did you want me say, Heini? Should I have told them the British, if they detect us, will hunt us down remorselessly and destroy us without giving us a second thought?"

"Why not?" said Heini. "After all, this is a U-Boat and the British would try to sink any U-Boat they came across anyway."

"True, but I need the crew to be on my side, to believe we can do this. It's a long, long voyage, Heini and we need the men with us, not grumbling and becoming discontented and rebellious."

Engel smiled.

"Okay, I'm convinced. Shall we get back to work my brave and silver-tongued Kapitän?"

"A good idea, Heini, a very good idea. Let's go and relieve poor Willi at the con. He's probably having kittens by now, poor kid."

"They get younger all the time, the ones they send us now," said Heini, ruefully, forgetting he was barely twenty-two himself, though after surviving five years in the service, he could be considered an old man by many.

"They're getting younger because we are running out of men to recruit," Ritter replied. "Come, my friend, we have a course change to calculate," and the two men left the relative privacy of Ritter's cabin, relieved Becker, much to his relief, in the control room and were soon bent over the chart table, plotting the next stage of their voyage.

"Take her down to fifty metres," Ritter ordered.

"Fifty metres, aye sir," the voice of *Bootsmanns-maat* (Coxwain) Boris Nagel, the helmsman replied as the nose of the submarine tipped downwards and the boat began a shallow descent to the required depth, almost two hundred feet below the surface of the sea. It would be some time before they reached the dangerous waters of the North Sea and eventually the English Channel.

In *U966's* engine room, surrounded by the quiet hum of the boat's twin AEG electric motors, the submarine's resident doom and gloom merchant, Joseph Ziegler, bare chested and with three day's growth on his chin, turned to fellow seaman Karl Meister, eighteen and still struggling to grow any semblance of facial hair and said, as he sat sipping from a tin mug of ersatz coffee,

"No good'll come of it, this voyage, young Meister, I can feel it in my water."

"Really, Joseph?" the young and impressionable teenager replied. "Why do you say such things? Hasn't the Herr Kapitän always seen us safely home after every trip?"

"How many trips have you completed?" was Ziegler's reply.

"Six now, Joseph."

"Ha, I've done twelve in this sardine can, and twenty six before that in other boats. Don't you think I should know when things are different?"

"Different?"

"For the love of God, Meister. Look around you. We've been stripped of our main armaments, for a

145

start. We normally carry fourteen fucking torpedoes, and they leave us with four up the spout in the for'ard tubes, enough for maybe one, two attempts to sink an enemy, if we're lucky. They load us up with a deck full of wooden crates carrying God knows what and then, our dear Fuehrer, old 'Adolf, head in the clouds' orders us to sail halfway round the fucking world to deliver them to God knows where. These boats weren't made for voyages of that length, and d'you know why we've got to stay submerged for so long?"

"Why, Joseph?" young Meister asked the seasoned hand.

"Diesel fuel, young Meister, that's why. These boats have limited fuel capacity. Unless we are intended to meet up with a refuelling tender somewhere in mid-fucking Atlantic, we barely carry enough diesel fuel to see us halfway there under normal conditions. Do you have any sodding idea how foul it's going to get in here if we have to run underwater almost all the way?"

"But we'll be surfacing to recharge the batteries won't we, Joseph?"

"That's what I mean," said Ziegler. "We'll surface to recharge the batteries and while we're up top we have to run on the diesels and the fuel will be getting lower and lower all the time."

"But, the kapitän would not take us into danger deliberately, would he?"

"No, Meister, but I tell you, this whole mission stinks, and I don't just mean the fucking air in this tin can."

"Stop trying to scare the lad, Ziegler, and get on with your job."

The sharp voice of the U-Boat's engineering officer, the blonde-haired, blue-eyed Aryan stereotype, Heinz Muller cut in to the conversation. Although he would have made a perfect advertisement for Hitler's Aryan superiority theme, Muller was a fierce anti-Nazi, though he managed to keep those thoughts to himself. He was first and foremost an engineer, in love with the pristine examples of German engineering that had been placed in his devoted care, and secondly, he considered himself a professional officer of the Kriegsmarine, a naval officer above thoughts of politics and race. He served the navy, and through the navy, he served his captain and his ship, which meant that for the time being, Heinz was madly in love with, and married to the engines that propelled the *U966*.

Ziegler grudgingly complied with Muller's order, sluicing away the dregs of his ersatz coffee, and turning back to his task of maintaining the efficient running of *U966s* engines. Muller wiped the sweat from his face with the oily rag that never seemed to leave his hand, the result leaving his face looking even dirtier than he'd appeared a few seconds earlier.

* * *

As *U966* silently crept around the northern coast of Denmark, the Royal Navel Dockyard at Portland in Dorset was as usual, a hive of activity. In one small corner of the docks, two 'Cathedral' Class corvettes stood, berthed side by side, being readied for sea. *H.M.S. Norwich* and *H.M.S. Ripon* were sister ships, small, poorly armed escort vessels normally assigned to convoy escort duties despite their apparent unsuitability for the task. Smaller than many of the ships they were ordered to protect, they carried a single 4 inch turret forward of the bridge, together with a number of ack-ack (anti-aircraft) guns positioned along the port and starboard sides of the ship, two depth charge launchers on each side, with twin torpedo launchers at the stern. For the crews of these two little ships, their current assignment on channel patrol was like being sent on a well needed holiday after their last stint of Atlantic convoy duty. Constantly cold and wet, unable to sleep in the rolling, pitching waves, and subject to repeated alerts and hours at battle stations, the Atlantic convoy routes were unforgiving on those whose duty it was to protect the merchant vessels that carried the goods and materials essential to Britain's war effort.

For the moment, both ships were engaged in regular patrols in the English Channel, on the lookout for raids by German E-Boats, that had recently been attacking lone trawlers and small merchant vessels that plied their trade close to the coast. The Royal Navy simply didn't have enough Motor Torpedo Boats (M.T.B.s) in home waters to counter the threat, hence the current assignment.

On board the *Norwich* her captain, Lieutenant Commander Giles Clarkson, stood on the bridge, watching the activity taking place both on board and on the dockside. The *Norwich* might not be a battle-ship or cruiser, not even a destroyer, but she was his ship, his first command and he was proud of her and her crew, who had served with distinction on their last voyage which had seen five of their number fail to return to port. Clarkson had spent an afternoon writing letters of condolence to the relatives of his fallen crewmen and now, with darkness falling, he needed to wind down, to relax, and as was his usual routine, he did so by keeping a close watch on every-thing that happened around the dockyard, always a fascinating scene for the twenty eight year old officer. A sound from his left signalled the arrival of a duf-fel coated figure who stepped over the side coaming onto the bridge to join him.

"Permission to join you sir?" asked Lieutenant Pe-ter Hicks, his first officer.

"Of course Number One," he replied. "Everything alright below?"

"Totally ship-shape, sir. The stores will soon be fully loaded, armaments already done. The coaler will be coming alongside as soon as they've finished with *Ripon* and she's moved away to grant them ac-cess.

"Excellent. Well done, and well done to the men too. How's morale, Peter?"

"Still good, sir. Despite the losses on the last trip, they know we did a good job. It was a shame we just missed nailing that damn sub, though"

"True, but you never know, we may just get a chance to find some action on our next patrol."

"We still have four men to return tomorrow, sir. They were allowed compassionate leave, you recall, family losses in the bombings in London and Liverpool."

"Yes, of course, poor buggers. They go through bloody hell for weeks at a time at sea, and then come home to find their homes, families, kids all gone. God, Peter, I hate this damned war."

"As we all do, sir. But don't worry, the men will be ready for sea by tomorrow night, as scheduled."

"Good. Bloody awkward having to cast off after dusk but those damned E-Boats like to dash across the channel and hit our fishing vessels as they're returning to port, the cowardly bastards."

"Yes indeed, sir. So let's hope we can nail one or two of them this time, eh?"

"Definitely, Number One. It would be great for morale too if we could sink one of those bastards."

The sound of someone in clumping heavy sea boots sounded on the short bridge ladder and was quickly followed by the appearance of the smiling face of Chief Petty Officer Albert (Nobby) Clark, the ship's bosun. Clark's toothy grin seemed fixed in place, and even through the fiercest North Atlantic gale, the experienced and stalwart senior N.C.O. on board the *Norwich* always had a kind word or found the right thing to say to often fearful young ratings, many of whom had never served aboard a ship in their lives. As kindly as he was, however, Clark was a fierce taskmaster and didn't suffer fools gladly. Twenty years in the Navy had honed his skills as a manager of men to a fine art and Clarkson had often wondered how such a man had ended up on the *Norwich* when he could have served with distinction on a battleship or cruiser or one of the new breed of submarine hunting destroyers that helped turn the tide of the war at sea against Germany's underwater marauders. In a conversation with the Captain (D), in command of the destroyer squadron assigned to Portland, he'd eventually discovered that despite his previously excellent war record, Clark had been sent to the Corvette squadron as a kind of punishment for a breach of King's Regulations. Whilst serving on *H.M.S. Forester*, a cruiser of the Mediterranean fleet, Clark had countermanded the orders of a young Lieutenant who had ordered two men to release an anti aircraft gun mounting that had locked in place during an engagement with a small Italian cruiser. Clark knew there was no hope of them succeeding in the task and he'd seen the approach of two Italian *Macchi C200* fighter aircraft off the starboard beam, heading straight for the *Forester*. The two ratings would have been horribly exposed to the inevitable canon fire from the fighters and Clark had belayed the Lieutenant's order and commanded them to take cover instead. Seconds later a burst of shellfire from the leading fighter plane raked the ship's starboard side, totally destroying the anti-aircraft gun and its mounting, where the two men would have been working if they'd followed the inexperienced officer's order.

Rather than commend Clark for his foresight in anticipating the attack on the anti-aircraft guns, saving the lives of the two ratings, the Lieutenant instead placed Clark on report for inciting the men to disobey an order. The captain of the cruiser, knowing in his heart that Clark was the hero of the hour, had little choice but to follow regulations, especially as Clark admitted to the charge and did the best he could by reprimanding the C.P.O. and arranging his transfer to another vessel. Hence, the *Forester's* loss was *Norwich's* gain. As for the Lieutenant who had been so pernickety in his observance of the letter of the law, he was lost soon afterwards when the *Forester* was torpedoed off the coast of Greece and went down in less than ten minutes with only twenty survivors from a crew of nine hundred men. The captain was one of those who survived, miraculously blown off his bridge and into the sea by the force of one of the explosions that tore his ship apart. In a touch of supreme irony, the captain, stunned and floating helplessly, close to his sinking ship and almost certain to be pulled under by the undertow when the ship went down, was pulled to safety by two young seamen in a collapsible life raft, the same two ratings saved by Clark's action a few weeks earlier.

Now, Clark saluted and stood before the captain of the *Norwich*, his usual smile fixed in place as though he hadn't a care in the world.

"Hello Bosun," said Clarkson. "To what do we owe this honour? It's a rare thing indeed to see our beloved bosun up here while we're preparing for sea."

"Evenin' sir," Clark replied. "Just thought as how you'd like to know the men have completed the repairs to that cracked boiler we was worried about. The dockyard people said as it would take at least three days of work, a deal of welding and what have you to get the job done. But our lads completed the job in just over twenty four hours. The ship will be ready to sail as ordered tomorrow, sir, that's definite. Like I said, just thought you'd want to know."

Clarkson knew the smile on Nobby Clark's face was not only genuine but was one of pride. In a few short weeks, the bosun had succeeded in doing his own spot of welding, having welded together a bunch of disparate personalities that included twenty ratings straight from training establishments, into a truly efficient fighting crew that possessed a fierce pride in their ship. The *Norwich* might be small and outgunned by almost every ship in the German navy, but she was their ship, and the pride Clark had instilled in them gave them an added edge when it came to going into action. Clarkson knew this only too well and was grateful he had the experience of the bosun to rely on when the *Norwich* was called into action once again.

Clarkson returned the bosun's smile.

"Thank you bosun. I had every faith in you and the men. When you told me you could do it I had no hesitation in telling Captain Hennessy we'd sail on time tomorrow."

Clark's smile grew a little broader.

"Thanks sir. They're good boys, most of 'em. A few's a bit raw, but they'll do. The couple of moaning minnies we inherited with the ship are learning they can't take liberties any more, not as long as I live and breathe, at any rate."

"I'm sure they are," Clarkson replied. "Why don't you go and get some sleep now, Chief? There's no need for you to burn the midnight oil tonight. We'll have plenty to do tomorrow and I do know you've worked without a break for over twelve hours."

"Well, if you say it's alright sir, I think I might do as you suggest. Couple of hours sleep sounds pretty good to me."

"Then go, rest a little. And Bosun?"

"Sir?"

"Tell the men well done from me, won't you?"

"I'll do that for certain, sir. Thanks."

With that, Clark disappeared as quickly as he'd arrived and Clarkson turned to Hicks and said, "Thank God for people like Clark, Number One. I think he could single handedly force this bloody ship to sea with the strength of his will if he had to."

"You might be right, sir," Hicks replied. "I think though, if I might make a suggestion, you should turn in too, as you've told Clark to. You need to rest too. I've got the watch for the next four hours. Nothing's going to happen to us while we're here and I can supervise the loading of the coal when the old *Farimond* arrives."

Clarkson yawned, clapped his first officer on the shoulder and said.

"You're right of course, Number One. I'll be off then. Goodnight."

"Goodnight sir," Hicks replied as Clarkson departed the bridge, leaving the first officer alone with his thoughts and the sounds of the ship at anchor as she and her crew settled down for the night.

Chapter 17

A Passage to Wrexham?

Andy Ross and Izzie Drake sat opposite D.C.I. Oscar Agostini in his office. They'd spent an hour going through the entire case so far with the boss, and Agostini looked thoughtful as he contemplated all they'd learned so far.

"This is turning into a far more complex case than we first envisaged," Agostini mused. "The thing we need to do is go back to the beginning, Andy. First of all, where did the killer obtain the Ketamine? There can't be that many places where it can be easily obtained without a pharmaceutical licence. Next, how did the killer get into the house and young Decker's bedroom without the two other housemates hearing anything? Okay, it appears the front door was locked but the back door wasn't so there's a possibility, a strong one, the killer entered there and crept silently up the stairs. We just don't know yet. Third, we really need to find the motive for the crime. So far you have some tenuous links to this American Company, Aegis, who suddenly came along and offered some kind of sponsorship to Decker's girlfriend, with the offer of a job at the end of her university studies. We know young Decker felt there was something 'off' about them, hence his trip to dive on the wrecks in The Channel, but listen, how did he know exactly where to dive? There's a possibility someone on the inside was helping him.

You then have the frogman's body. Who is it? Could it be this German man, Klaus Haller? We need to find him. If he's alive and well, it makes identifying the body at the wreck site even harder. Then we have to take into consideration the fact that Decker's father is a senior officer in the bloody C.I.A. of all things. Is there some connection between the father's occupation and the murder of his son, or is it purely coincidental? And we need to try the Royal Navy for help in identifying the ship you saw in the photos, and maybe the submarine too. So tell me, Andy, where are you going next with all this?"

Ross leaned back in his chair, and thought long and hard for a minute before replying.

"Well sir, Ferris is still looking into the Aegis Institute and its various operations around the world. It's obvious we need to look very carefully at them if we're to push the case forward, but I can't just go blundering down to Cornwall and encroaching on another force's turf."

"Leave that to me," Agostini interrupted. "I'll speak to my counterpart at the Devon and Cornwall Constabulary, and elicit their help. You may have to make a trip down there and it might need a few days. I know you've just got married, Sergeant," he said to Drake, "so how will your husband feel if you go swanning off with D.I. Ross to the wilds of Cornwall?"

"Peter understands what my job entails, sir. It won't be a problem," she replied.

"Good, now, make it a priority to find out if this Haller chap is still alive, and if he is, where he is and what he's got to do with all this. It seems we have a real mystery on our hands, and I agree that the Aegis Institute is definitely connected to it in some way. You mentioned that young Decker said he felt whatever he'd discovered could be worth something. We need to find out what he meant by that. Did he mean financially or academically? You have a difficult path to follow I think, Andy. Try taking one step at a time."

"Yes, sir," Ross replied. "If there's nothing else for now, we'll get back to it, then."

"Yes, off you go, and I'll let you know as soon as I've spoken with the force down in Cornwall."

"Right, sir, thanks," said Ross and he and Drake made their way out of the D.C.I's office and back to the squad room.

As they walked in, Paul Ferris saw them and immediately beckoned the pair across to where he was sitting at his computer terminal.

"Please tell me you have something for me, Paul," Ross said, a hint of desperation in his voice.

"Perhaps, sir," Ferris responded. "It appears the Aegis Institute was set up fifty years ago by a wealthy philanthropist called Silas Wren, who all those years ago felt that the human race was slowly polluting and destroying the ecological balance of the world's oceans. Wren died twenty years ago and the institute suddenly blossomed into a true international conglomerate, controlled by a board of directors in Boston, U.S.A. Despite that they seem to work mostly out of massive office facilities in New York. They spread their influence rapidly around the world, their facilities becoming bigger and better year on year. They own a fleet of ships, mostly research vessels and a massive number of submersibles, able to probe the deepest parts of the world's oceans. Now, if they were purely concerned with academic research and projects to protect the ecology of the oceans, there'd be nothing fishy, excuse the term, to find, but I found that Aegis has taken to doing a lot of what can only be called underwater archaeology, locating, investigating and in some cases downright plundering many of the sites they've worked on. There've been drowned cities, ancient and modern shipwrecks, some of which they've raised, amassing a small fortune in salvage fees in some cases, like a supertanker they raised with state of the art recovery technology. It seems as if the current Aegis Institute is more interested in making money that in being a kind of multinational Greenpeace type organisation."

"Very good, Paul. So you think they may be hiding a treasure hunting operation behind the veneer of oceanographic conservation, is that it?"

"That's exactly what I think, sir. The biggest problem we're going to have is proving it, and then proving that they're acting illegally."

"I have a feeling that's just what Aaron Decker did find out, Paul, and it cost that young man his life, because someone in that organisation is prepared to kill to protect whatever secrets they're hiding." Ross concluded.

"What about Klaus Haller?" Izzie Drake asked. "Did you have a chance to look him up, maybe find out if he's still alive?"

"I didn't have to," Ferris replied, much to their surprise. "Klaus Haller is alive and well and living in Wrexham."

"He lives in Wales?" Ross asked, astounded.

"Yes, sir. Derek McLennan did a simple search of his name on his computer, and located him in about ten minutes."

"I thought he told your wife's uncle he was from Hamburg," Izzie Drake said.

"He is from Hamburg, originally, but he's lived over here for the last five years. He's a genuine naval historian alright, in fact he's written three books on the subject of naval warfare. He probably told Reg he was from Hamburg from a sense of security if he was looking into the activities of Aegis. Anyway, Derek spoke to him and then took off in his car with Sam Gable. Wrexham isn't far so he phoned the guy and arranged to go and see him. They'll probably be there already."

"Well, that's initiative for you," said Ross, pleased that McLennan had taken it upon himself to go right away to interview a potentially important witness.

"Hold on though, let's rewind a minute," Izzie Drake said. "If Haller is in Wrexham, then who the hell is the frogman?"

"Precisely one of the points the D.C.I. brought up," Ross replied. "We have yet another layer to add to our growing mystery, it seems."

At that point in the conversation Curtis and Dodds strolled in to the squad room.

"Well, look who's back," said Izzie Drake. "It's the pool hall wizards."

"*Snooker and* pool hall, actually, Sarge," Curtis replied.

"Yes, but that doesn't fit with the song," Drake joked, referring to the old record, *Pinball Wizard* by The Who.

"Okay, okay, come on then, you two, what have you found out, if anything?"

"Well sir," Curtis began, "The manager at the 147 remembers Aaron Decker very well. He referred to him as 'The Yank' and said he took a lot of money off the other guys who he played with regularly. He didn't really know them by name, but he did say that more than one or two of them often got more than a little mad at the amount of money Decker won from them. Seems there were some heated arguments sometimes, when players lost to Decker and didn't have enough cash on them to pay up. Once, he heard someone refer to him as a hustler, but Decker just laughed."

"That's right," said Nick Dodds. "He also said that Decker played pool there as well, with similar results, though that was mostly against the local lads. They ended up refusing to play against him, he was that good."

"So young Aaron wasn't quite the paragon of virtue everyone holds him up to be," said Ross.

"Exactly, sir," said Dodds. "Seems he might have racked up a fair few enemies at the 147 club."

"Yes, but would any of them dislike him enough to murder him?" Ross mused.

* * *

Although located in North Wales, Wrexham is only 35 to 40 miles from Liverpool, depending on the route taken, so Derek McLennan and Sam Gable had arrived at the home of Klaus Haller about an hour after leaving the headquarters car park.

Haller lived in a small village on the outskirts of town, in a well kept period cottage, one of a small terrace of three that looked to have been built some-time during the nineteenth century. With its small windows, a front door at which anyone over five feet tall had to bend down to navigate entry into the home and its overhanging roof, it could have come straight out of a Dickens novel.

McLennan and Gable were seated opposite the German, on a chintz covered two seater sofa, the largest item of furniture in the small, cosy living room, which Gable thought might be best described as 'the parlour'. Haller was seated in the room's sole matching armchair, the only other items of note in the room being a small table in one corner holding a twenty four inch screen television, with a combined Video and DVD player seated on the shelf that ran along the underside of the table.

A compact portable CD player was precariously positioned on the window sill and a glass fronted cabinet against one wall held a number of model ships, a link to the resident's preoccupation in life. A small three-shelf oak bookcase finished off the room's furnishings. The carpet was thick and plush and on the bare stone interior walls, painted a subtle shade of cream, a couple of good quality prints of world war two warships took pride of place. Derek McLennan thought he recognised one of the ships as *Bismark*, having seen the film about the sinking of the great battleship some years ago.

Haller hadn't seemed surprised to have heard from McLennan, and having made his visitors a cup of the finest coffee McLennan had ever tasted, Haller sat back and waited for the two officers to begin their questions. Sam Gable would initially leave it to McLennan, who had done the work in locating Haller in the first place. She contented herself with studying the man they'd come to see as Derek began his questioning. Haller was of medium height, around five feet six or seven, and looked to be in his late fifties, maybe early sixties. His hair was almost pure white, and his clothes, though of good quality, betrayed the lack of female influence in Haller's life, Sam thought. The thing that caught her attention more than anything were the German's almost penetrating blue eyes, which despite the man's age, sparkled with life and vitality. Klaus Haller must have been an incredibly handsome man in his younger days, she concluded. Despite his height, Haller gave off the air of a much smaller man, appearing diminutive in stature, something Sam found odd, but put it down to the man's age and overall bearing and the architecture of their surroundings which made everything in the cottage appear miniaturised.

"Oh yes," Haller said in response to Derek McLennan's questioning, "young Aaron Decker came to me with his suspicions about Aegis Oceanographic's motives surrounding their Channel Project."

"But, why you, Herr Haller?"

"Ah, you see, Constable, Aaron and I had met a year previous to his seeking me out last year. I am regarded as something of an authority on the history of the war at sea during World War Two," and he reached one arm out from his chair towards the bookcase which stood close enough for him to pull a book from the top shelf, which he passed across to the detective. McLennan read the title, *A History of Naval Warfare in the Hitler Years*, and waited for Haller to explain.

In excellent English, Haller went on, "He was writing a paper about the events leading up to the sinking of the *Deutschland class* heavy cruiser, what you British called a 'pocket battleship' *Admiral Graf Spee*, under the command of Hans Langsdorff, sunk by the British off Montevideo in the Battle of the River Plate in December 1939."

Haller pointed to one of the prints on the wall.

"That's her in her glory days, during a review at Spithead in 1937, when she paid a visit to England."

The detectives followed Haller's pointing finger. McLennan could see the difference in size between the *Graf Spee* and the *Bismark*. Despite being smaller, *Graf Spee* seemed to simply bristle with gun turrets, large and small, giving her the appearance of a veritable floating arsenal. Now McLennan recalled seeing another old black and white movie, *The Battle of the River Plate*, which had told the story of her sinking by three British cruisers, the *Exeter*, the *Ajax* and the *Achilles*. McLennan mentioned this to Haller who smiled.

"Yes, a very stirring film, D.C. McLennan, and surprisingly accurate in the details considering when it was made, showing Langsdorff to be a real humanitarian in his treatment of prisoners. It was sad he felt he had to take his own life after scuttling his ship."

Klaus Haller sighed a sad sigh at the thought, and then continued.

"So, anyway, I had been of some use to Aaron in his research so when he had some doubts about the work the company that his girlfriend had contracted to work for, I suppose it was natural for him to contact me again."

"And you were living here in Wrexham at that time, Herr Haller?"

"Yes. I rent this charming cottage of course, it is not mine to own. I move around the world a lot in my work Detective Constable. Before this, I lived in the United States for four years, researching various aspects of the beginnings of the fledgling United States Navy, before that, in Norway, looking into the voyages made by the earliest Viking navigators, and so on. While here, I have been engaged in discovering much about the ships lost around the coast of Britain in the last two hundred years. For a relatively small island, Great Britain has some very treacherous coastal waters that have led to many shipwrecks over the years, I assure you."

"I see," said McLennan. "So you thought there may be something in what he told you?"

"I was not sure, to tell you the truth, but as I had great respect for the young man's dedication to his subject and his diligence in wishing to protect his lady friend, I thought it could do no harm to at least make some inquiries to see if he might be correct in his thoughts and assumptions."

"Please tell us what you discovered," said Sam Gable, now joining in the conversation.

"Well, it was all a little strange. I first of all contacted the man called William Evans, an American who was listed as the Research Director at the Aegis facility near Falmouth. I wrote to him and introduced myself as an author and historian and explained I wished to investigate certain aspects of the small engagements that occurred in the English Channel during World War Two. I told him I had been informed by a colleague that his company was currently working on an environmental project that included locating the wrecks of various ships on the sea bed and asked if he would be prepared to share the locations of such wrecks with me. He told me his company's work was confidential and that he was unable to furnish me with the information I required. This seemed odd to me. I have worked with many businesses over the years, involved in such work and could not understand his position. Surely, I thought, there is nothing of a confidential nature about the environmental effects of shipwrecks. I wondered if perhaps Aaron could be right so, my suspicions aroused, I travelled to Cornwall and sought out the local police at first to ask if they had any information on the activities of the Aegis people in their town. A sergeant told me that Aegis were very secretive and protective of their facility and did not encourage visitors. Undeterred, I paid a visit to Aegis but was turned away at the gatehouse to their private dock and told they did not allow unauthorised access to the site. Next, I asked if they at least had any information leaflets that I could take that gave any information on the company. Again I was rebuffed."

"You certainly tried hard, Herr Haller," said Gable.

"Ah, but I was not yet finished," Haller said, excitedly. "I returned to my hotel, where I placed a transatlantic call to the Aegis Institute in the USA. That was when I became convinced something was indeed not quite right about the situation."

"In what way, Herr Haller?" McLennan asked.

"After I introduced myself as an international author and well-known historian, I was put through to the publicity department where a lady called Hannah Ryker was very helpful and arranged to send me a dossier on the work of Aegis around the world, including the many historical sites they have helped to unearth beneath the oceans of the world. This seemed at odds with the words of Mr. William Evans, and I said so to Ms. Ryker. She was unaware of any secrecy surrounding any Aegis projects and said she would put me through to one of their research directors.

Mr. Francis Kelly spoke next to me. He told me that there was no real secrecy about their work in the English Channel, but the fact that the wrecks they had found were designated war graves meant they wished to ensure privacy as they had been subjected to protests from some people who thought they were desecrating the sites. Now, the thing is, constable, to be designated a war grave, a sunken ship must first be identified and all such wrecks are catalogued and their positions are common knowledge to anyone who knows where to look them up. So, I asked which ship or ships Aegis were currently working on, and Mr. Kelly became evasive. He said he was not privy to that information and as far as he knew the Aegis operation in the English Channel was currently centred on up to three un-named wrecks they had located. That made no sense but I did not challenge his words. It was obvious he was not going to tell me any more, so I thanked him and hung up."

"Wow," said Sam Gable, "you are quite a tiger when you get going, eh, Herr Haller?"

"One does not become an expert in any field in life without being tenacious, young lady," Haller smiled as he spoke.

"So, you then reported back to Aaron Decker, I presume?" said McLennan.

"Oh no," Haller sounded offended that the D.C. assumed he'd given up. "I hired a boat."

"You hired a boat?" McLennan was incredulous. "What for?"

"To follow their research vessel of course. How else would I find out where they were working?"

"You're amazing," Sam Gable spoke to Haller with a hint of admiration in her voice.

"It was only a small boat of course, but I am an experienced sailor. I served in the German navy in the nineteen sixties, and was not put off by going to sea in a small craft. It was during my military service that I developed my love of naval history you see. Anyway, I found a vantage point from which I could see into the Aegis facility and when their vessel *Poseidon* was obviously preparing to leave port two days after my phone calls, I quickly drove down to the harbour, boarded my boat and took to sea, taking up a position from which I could see their vessel as it left port and headed out to sea. I simply followed them from a distance, my boat being small enough not to be seen by any lookouts they might have posted on deck. I assumed they would have radar, sonar and so on but didn't believe they would be looking for anyone tracking them, and it appeared I was right."

"Are you telling us you know where they were working, Herr Haller?" Gable asked.

"But of course," Haller said, "and upon my return to Falmouth, I immediately called Aaron and told him what I'd discovered. He had already been to Falmouth once, you see, but had been unable to find anything. He thanked me and said he would take it from there, and would come down to Falmouth again and arrange to dive on the wreck and see what they were doing. I am not a diver, and had no intention of joining him in his venture, but asked him to tell me if he found anything of historical significance, which he agreed to do."

"I see," said McLennan, "and did Aaron ever contact you again?"

"Yes, he did, a few weeks later, to tell me he'd been down to the wreck and that it was a badly decomposed merchant vessel of no significance and that he was sorry to have wasted my time, and that there was nothing to be concerned about. I never heard from him again and soon decided that whatever Aegis was up to was no longer any of my business."

"That's what he told you?"

"That's what he told me. I'm not an idiot, Constable. I thought he might have been holding out on me and when I saw the news the other day about his death, I realised that Aaron had lied to me. He did lie to me, didn't he?" Haller said with a note of sadness in his voice.

"Yes he did," Herr Haller," said Gable. "But tell me, do you still have the co-ordinates of the location of the wreck he dived on?"

"But of course." Haller stood and walked to the bookcase where he picked up a briefcase that lay on its side on the bottom shelf. Opening the case, he took out a small black book, flicked through the pages and finding the page he was looking for, simply tore it out and passed it to her.

"A good historian never loses anything that might be of help, Constable. Please take it. It is of no use to me any longer but if there is anything interesting from a historical point of view down there, I would appreciate hearing about it in due course."

"I'm sure my boss will be only too pleased to inform you of any historical information we discover," a smiling Sam Gable said.

"Thank you," said Haller. "It is sad that Aaron felt he had to be evasive with me. Perhaps he just did not want to share in whatever it was he had discovered, but still, a shame."

"Yes, I'm sorry too, had he done so perhaps things may have turned out differently. And thank you too, Herr Haller, you've been a great help," McLennan spoke, rising from the sofa and shaking the historian's hand.

The two detectives were soon on the road back to Liverpool, both aware that they may just be holding the key to unlocking the case and solving the murder of Aaron Decker on a small sheet of paper in Derek McLennan's jacket pocket.

Chapter 18

A sleepless night

"You're sure you don't mind me disappearing like this for a couple of days?" Izzie asked her husband of just over a week. The couple were sat together on the sofa in the lounge of their home, Izzie leaning back into Peter's chest with her knees curled up beneath her as the original *Star Wars* movie played quietly to itself on the TV.

"Mind? Of course I mind, but in the nicest possible way," Peter replied. "I knew what your job entailed before we married, so it's okay, really. It's just a shame that this comes so soon after the wedding."

"It'll only be for a couple of days, my darling, three at the most, I think, and I will of course make it up to you in the best possible way when I get back," Izzie said, flashing him an impish, highly suggestive smile."

"Oh yes?" he replied. "So how about a little bit of that making up right now, just to keep me going, as it where?"

"But what about *Star Wars*, Paul? It's one of your favourites."

"I've only seen it about fifty times so far," he jokingly replied. "I don't think the ending is about to change because we're up in the bedroom do you?"

"Well, what are we waiting for?" said Izzie as she slid off the sofa, stood up and took his hand, leading him out of the room and up the stairs to the bedroom, where their passion soon banished thoughts of Izzie's imminent departure for Cornwall in the company of D.I. Ross.

* * *

Andy and Maria Ross had also enjoyed the pleasures of an early night and now lay together in bed, Maria resting with her head on Andy's shoulder.

"It's really getting to you, isn't it darling, this case?" she said softly, almost reading his thoughts.

"Yes, it is," he confessed. "We seem to have very little in the way of concrete evidence so far, just lots of conjecture and suppositions, Maria, and you can't build a case of murder against a suspect based on those, not that we have a real suspect either."

"But I thought you said you were sure someone at this Aegis company must be involved?"

"Involved, maybe, but even if Aegis are behind it, we still don't know who actually carried out the murders. I can't get away from the thought that one or both of Aaron Decker's housemates must be implicated somehow. I think we need to dig deeper into their past lives to see if there's anything that would leave them open to persuasion to commit such an act."

"So, do you think this visit to Falmouth will help?"

"I hope so. Oscar has fixed it for us to meet with a D.I. Pascoe who knows the waters of the Channel very well apparently, being something of a weekend sailor himself, so Oscar was informed by his counterpart down there. The chap I spoke to at the Ministry of Defence was helpful too and some chap from the Admiralty is going to meet up with us too. Seems the Royal Navy has a special department dealing with wrecks and war graves that also happen to be former Royal Naval ships. That photo I told you about really does seem to have stirred up a hornet's nest of activity."

"What about the father, Andy? Do you still think this has anything to do with him being in the C.I.A?"

"I don't think so. That was just a dreadful and unfortunate coincidence I think."

"Well, if I'm going to be deprived of my husband for a few days, the least you can do is give me something to help me drop off to sleep," Maria said softly as she reached up, kissed her husband and then allowed her hand to wander down his chest, finally finding its target as Andy Ross groaned softly. He turned, kissed her hard on the lips in return, and then pushed his wife onto her back, Maria moaning softly in turn as his own hand found her wet and ready for him.

Later, as Maria slept peacefully beside him, Andy Ross lay awake until the small hours of the morning. He couldn't get the case out of his mind. The whole thing reeked of some form of corporate cover up by the Aegis Institute, but just what, he wondered for the hundredth time could they possibly be hiding? He'd been assured that the police inspector he was meeting knew the seas down there as well as anyone he could hope to encounter, and the local Coastguard station had also been informed of his visit and would send someone to meet him when he'd made contact with D.C.I. Trevelyan.

As the figures on the digital bedside clock read four o'clock in the morning, Maria stirred and turned to face him.

"You're awake aren't you, Andy?"

"Mmm," he replied. "Can't sleep. Sorry if I woke you."

"You didn't. It's this bloody case, isn't it?"

"U-huh. I have a feeling we're missing something. I'm just not sure what the hell it could be."

"I thought of something just before I fell asleep."

"What is it?"

"The two men who shared the house with your victim. You say they are technically the best suspects, but if I recall, you said they had a few drinks downstairs, probably fell asleep watching TV, and heard nothing, right?"

"That's right, so, what of it?"

"Just suppose, Andy, that someone spiked their drinks too, like the dead man and his girlfriend, just enough to make them drowsy enough to not realise someone had crept into the house. They could be totally innocent."

Ross could see the logic in Maria's words. As always, his wife's intuition had given his thought processes a nudge in a different direction. Her analytical medical mind had often come up with incisive thoughts and theories that had assisted him in solving tricky cases in the past.

"I'll hold that thought," he replied. "You may have a point my darling, though it's too late now to test any cans or bottles they may have drunk from and any knock out potion will have been purged from their systems by now."

"Ooh, I love it when you talk medical terminology at me," Maria giggled. "It gets me all turned on."

"Oh yes," Ross said, in a serious tone. "Then what, dear Doctor Ross, do you intend to do about it?"

As the first shafts of early morning sunshine forced their way through the tiny crack in the bedroom curtains, Maria rolled onto her back, and pulled her husband on top of her as she opened herself to him.

"How's this for starters?" she said in a husky, very sexy voice.

"Who am I to argue with the doctor?" Ross laughed as they made love once again before rising earlier than usual, as dawn broke over the city and all thoughts of tiredness were temporarily banished from his mind. An early breakfast was followed by Ross taking his time to pack a suitcase for his trip to Cornwall, helped by Maria who made sure he had enough pairs of matching socks, to last at least three days, plus one extra pair, just in case, as she put it.

"You always forget to pack enough socks, even when we go on holiday," she chastised him. "And what about underwear?"

"I've packed four pairs, *Mummy*," he playfully goaded her.

Maria laughed and equally playfully slapped her husband's bottom and he feigned pain and put his hands over his eyes, pretending to cry.

"You cruel, husband-beating woman," he pretended to sob.

"So, go call a policeman and have me arrested."

"Help, police," Ross shouted as Maria took him in her arms, held him close and kissed him into silence. Five minutes later he was in his car, Maria waving to him from the front door-step as he headed into town to headquarters. He'd a telephone conference arranged with a specialist at the Admiralty in order to pick the man's brains on potential ships that fit the description of the assumed corvette on the sea bed of the Channel. If he could identify the wreck, and get an idea where it went down, he might just know where the search for the dead frogman should be directed. He was as yet unaware of the information McLennan and Gable had discovered the previous day, the pair having arrived back in Liverpool after Ross had left for home.

With luck he and Izzie Drake would be able to set off on their journey south by lunchtime. D.C.I. Trevelyan would be calling him as well with details of the accommodation arranged for them in Falmouth. Bearing in mind the length of the journey, some three hundred and fifty miles, Ross thought it best if he and Drake settled in to their hotel on their arrival in Falmouth and began their investigation first thing the next morning.

Chapter 19

The English Channel, 1945, and the Mary Deal

"Everything alright, Number One?" Lieutenant Commander Giles Clarkson asked his first officer, Peter Hicks, as he stepped over the coaming on the bridge of *H.M.S. Norwich*. Clarkson had managed a couple of hours sleep as the *Norwich* completed her latest sweep around the Eastern approaches to the Channel with Hicks in charge on the bridge as officer of the watch.

"All quiet, sir," Hicks confirmed. "Radar reports no contacts and we've maintained constant Asdic scans as ordered. Not that I can envisage any U-Boats trying to make it through the Channel when they can take the easy route around Scotland and into the Atlantic that way. Lieutenant Bailey has plotted the course for a zig-zag run from east to west as ordered as soon as you give the order."

"Hello Bailey," said Clarkson as he looked across the bridge to the young navigator. Bailey was a member of the Royal Naval Volunteer Reserve, the so-called 'Wavy Navy' christened as such owing to the wave shaped stripes worn on the officer's sleeves. Before the war, Bailey had been training as a doctor and it was a continuing mystery to Clarkson how the young man had forsaken his medical career to join the war as a volunteer naval officer. Bailey had told no-one aboard *Norwich*, his first ship, of the early dawn when he'd left the training hospital after a long night on the wards only to find his home had been completely obliterated when an unexploded bomb, buried underground and left over from the days of the Blitz, had exploded almost immediately outside the front door, not only destroying the house, but taking the lives of his mother, father and two sisters. With nothing left to live for, so he felt, Bailey lost no time in giving up his medical studies and arranging to join the RNVR.

"Hello sir," Bailey replied to his captain, his face as always serious-looking and totally focused on the job in hand.

"You've settled in well, Bailey," Clarkson said, encouragingly. "You'll be a fine officer if you keep up your current performance."

"Thank you, sir," Bailey replied, but still no hint of a smile crossed the young officer's face.

Clarkson turned to his first officer once more.

"What's the latest weather report Number One?"

"We have a report of fog rolling in from the west, sir. We'll probably hit it somewhere in the region of Exeter or Plymouth if we maintain our current course and speed."

"Okay. Well, at least the fog should hamper the Jerries as much as it does us. Maintain course and speed and continue the zig-zag manoeuvre. If there are any E-Boats out here, we don't want to present ourselves as a sitting duck for them."

"Aye aye, sir," said Hicks, acknowledging Clarkson's orders.

"And Number one?"

"Sir?"

"Keep me posted on those weather reports. If that fog starts to roll in faster, I want to know about it."

"Of course sir."

"How many of our own ships do we have on the plot at present?"

Hicks drew Clarkson to one side, where he pointed to the chart table positioned under cover at the rear of the bridge. He quickly pointed to half a dozen red pins in various locations of the map.

"These three are trawlers, heading for home and already relatively safe. This one is our friend, the *Ripon*, giving close escort to a small tanker which was damaged in an attack on the convoy she was in, originally headed for Liverpool. She was ordered to break off and head for the safety of Portland. One of the convoy escorts shadowed her as far as the Scilly Isles and *Ripon* took over from there."

"And the other two?" Clarkson asked, indicating the remaining pins on the chart.

"This one is one of our submarines, the *Altair*, sir," Hicks pointed to the closest pin. "She's running on the surface, making for Portland too. She was damaged in a surprise attack by a *Condor* long-range patrol aircraft. Her ballast tanks are damaged and she can't submerge, apparently. The last pin is the *Paragon*. We were warned we might encounter her before we left port, sir."

"Yes, of course. The cruiser heading to reinforce the Mediterranean fleet. She's fast, Number One. I should think she'll disappear off our plot by morning."

"I agree sir. So, nothing untowards as far as we can make out. Lookouts are posted as well though and we'll remain at action stations as per your order"

"Good, I'm going below then. I'll relieve you in two hours."

"Thank you sir," Hicks replied as Leading Seaman Charlie Knox appeared, smiling and handing Hicks and Bailey two steaming hot mugs of extra-thick cocoa in tin mugs, both precariously carried in one hand as he used his other hand to balance himself against the rolling motion of the ship in the undulating waves.

"Oh, sorry sir," he said to Clarkson. "I didn't know as you was up here."

"That's okay, Knox," Clarkson replied, smiling whilst inwardly groaning at Knox's awful grammar.

"I shouldn't be here. Just popped up to see the first officer."

"Oh, right, sir. You'll not be wantin' a cup then?"

"No thank you, Knox. I'm going below now."

"I can bring you one to your cabin if you like, sir," the smiling young rating offered. Charlie Knox, twenty three, from the Spitalfields area of London's East End, was a perpetual optimist and his smiling face never failed to make others feel a little better when he was around. Clarkson was grateful to have the hard-working, cheerful young rating aboard his ship.

"Alright, that would be very nice, thank you, Knox."

If anything, Knox's smile grew even broader at the captain's reply.

"Right you are sir. Give me ten minutes to get back to the galley and mix you a brew."

"No hurry Knox, and, thank you."

"It's my pleasure, sir, honest it is," said Bailey, and Clarkson knew the young man actually meant it. As he sat on his bunk awaiting the arrival of Charlie Knox and his mug of almost sludge-like cocoa, Clarkson contemplated his command. The *Norwich*, though small, had proved to be an efficient ship, with its crew a mixture of disparate individuals from varying parts of Britain, and from equally varied social backgrounds, from elite public schools to middle-class grammars and back street secondary-moderns all working together in harmony to produce a vessel Clarkson was rightly proud of. Knox soon arrived with the cocoa that Clarkson had accepted more from politeness and not wishing to hurt the man's feelings than from want, but he accepted it gratefully. Before Knox departed for the galley once more, Clarkson said,

"Can I ask you a question, Knox?"

Knox stopped in his tracks, had he done something wrong?

"Of course, sir," he replied.

"Why the hell are you always so damned cheerful? We're in the middle of this bloody god-awful war, people are being killed around us, and at home, and here on the ship we're mostly cold, wet and miserable twenty four hours a day and yet you always have a smile on your face, and a good word for everyone."

"Well, sir, that's thanks to me dear old Mum, that is. When I were a nipper, there were six of us kids at home, me, three bruvvers and two sisters. Dad were a bus driver, and we was never well off but we always 'ad food to eat and shoes on our feet. Mum always said as there was always folks in this world far worse of then us an' we should always be 'appy that we 'ad our 'ealth and strength and was loved and cared for at 'ome. I never forgot that, sir, even when me two eldest bruvvers was killed, one at Dunkirk, and the other on the old *H.M.S Hood*. Our 'ouse was bombed in the blitz, but no one got 'urt, so we 'ave a lot to be thankful for. I've made some great mates on this ship too. She ain't no battleship, that's a fact, sir, but, well, she's a good ship, and she's my 'ome until either the war's over or the Admirals send me on to another ship."

Knox fell silent, his story over. Clarkson felt quite humbled by this young man from one of the poorest areas of London, who'd lost two brothers, seen his home all but destroyed and yet maintained the most positive outlook he'd ever encountered.

"Thanks for telling me, Knox. You're a credit to the ship, just thought you should know that."

Knox's face lit up again, his smile so infectious that Clarkson beamed back at him.

"Thank you, sir," Charlie Knox said, pulling himself up to his full height and saluting his captain, ignoring the fact he wasn't wearing his headgear. "And I'm proud to serve under you, too sir. I shan't ever let you down."

Clarkson returned the salute and then Knox was gone, and he was alone again, with the sounds of the ship at night his sole companions as he sipped at the turgid brew, then put it down on his small bedside cabinet and, keeping his sea boots on in case of emergencies, Clarkson stretched out on his bunk, closing his eyes, but not for one minute did he fall asleep. The *Norwich* sailed on; the rhythmic sound of her engines the captain's constant companion in his small and at times very lonely cabin.

* * *

U966 continued her clandestine crawl through the English Channel, her sleek black shape hidden well below the surface, though her crew were no less anxious for that fact after Ritter told them where they were. He'd successfully brought his boat through the Straits of Dover, the shallowest part of the Channel at just under 150 feet, and past the channel ports and major cities of Dover, Portsmouth, Southampton and Weymouth, with the nearby Portland Naval Base and their attendant defensive minefields, laid to take care of just such incursions as Ritter was doing his best to avoid. His was a passive passage through the Channel, though the British wouldn't see it that way of course.

Ritter could feel the tension emanating from his crew, an almost palpable sensation. He still wondered privately why he'd been instructed to adopt this course, though he felt it was probably an attempt to take a day or two off the total journey time of his voyage.

Heini Engel stood quietly watching his captain as he quietly passed on his orders to the members of the control room crew with calm self-assurance. Engel admired Ritter more than he cared to admit. If ever there was a U-Boat captain he wished he could emulate it was the man who now gave the order to bring the *U966* up to periscope depth. Apart from his skills as a commander, Ritter possessed one vital quality missing from many officers in Hitler's much vaunted Third Reich, that of a sense of humanity. Not only did he care for those who served under him, but Ritter took no great delight in the deaths of those who died as a result of the actions of his boat. He had a job to do, a dirty job as a rule, that involved the sinking of enemy ships, both merchantmen and warships, and he carried out his task with a grim professionalism, but Engel knew, from his many conversations he'd had with his captain, that Ritter always felt a private sense of grief for those who died as a result of his successes. To Ritter they were sailors, as he was, and no matter their nationality, all sailors shared a bond that those who lived and worked on the land could never truly understand.

Heini knew this was a potentially dangerous moment, but equally, he understood Ritter's decision. They had almost successfully negotiated the dangerous passage through the narrow body of water separating England and France and would soon be passing the Scilly Isles and heading out in to the Atlantic, where they would need to remain submerged for the majority of their crossing. Engel knew what was in his captain's mind. If it was safe to do so, Ritter would surface and recharge the submarine's batteries, allowing him to stay below the Atlantic waves away from the prying radars and echo location devices employed by the British and American convoy escorts and patrolling warships they might encounter as they made their run towards their eventual destination.

The scope raised, Ritter swivelled his cap round, placing the peak to the rear of his head as he lowered the twin handles used to rotate the periscope, leaning both forearms laconically over the shining steel handles and peering into the scope's viewer.

"Fog," Ritter exclaimed almost immediately. "Thick fog, Heini. What the British call a 'pea souper' I think. I can't see a bloody thing up there, and you know what that means, my friends?" He spoke as though addressing the entire control room crew.

"What, sir?" Engel asked, feeling that Ritter's comment called for a reply from someone.

"It means the gods are smiling upon us, Heini," Ritter smiled. "If we can't see anything, then neither can the British. If we silence the boat, we can surface and recharge the batteries and be submerged again before anyone knows we were here."

"But the British will have their direction finding equipment, that damned Asdic working for them. We know they can locate us even in fog."

"Maybe so, Heini, but Asdic only works when we're submerged and in this fog, they'll find it difficult to pinpoint our exact position if they do detect us with their *verdammt* radar and we should have plenty of time to dive and be out of their range before they know what's happening. Plus, they won't expect us to be in this area and with luck may mistake us for one of their own submarines just long enough to breed a little confusion in any warship's captain, again giving us time to slip away safely."

"You may be right, Herr Kapitän," Engel replied, hoping his captain was right in his estimation of the British ability to locate and track them if they did identify them as a hostile craft. German technology lagged somewhat behind the British in its echolocation devices. The U-Boats depended on a less than totally convincing passive sonar system that required the boat to turn through a full one hundred and eighty degrees in order to scan the entire horizon, not perfect in a precarious and potentially deadly situation. Ritter ordered his hydrophone operators to be on full alert as he ordered *U966* to the surface.

Throughout the sub, despite any lurking danger above the waves, Ritter's crew looked forward to the chance to breathe some fresh air, certain that Ritter would go 'up top' to the conning tower once the sub surfaced. If all was well, they hoped to have a few minutes at least to open the hatches and let the interior of *U966* 'breathe' as well, a natural fumigation that would clear the submarine of some, if not all of the smell of unwashed bodies and poor sanitation.

The sea was as calm as the proverbial millpond as *U966* broke through the gently rolling waves nose first, with Ritter being the first to the top of the ladder leading to the conning tower hatch. As the submarine settled itself in the all-enveloping fog, he was followed by Engel and the two men gratefully breathed in the cool night air. Two lookouts joined them, armed with powerful binoculars, rendered useless by the enveloping fog.

The smell of the ocean acted as a panacea to both men, and Ritter quietly called down through the hatch for the forward deck hatch to be opened and the men allowed up top in small groups to take their first breaths of fresh air since leaving Kiel. Meanwhile, the U-Boat's chief engineer, Heinz Muller began the process of recharging the batteries that would need to be operating at their best if *U966* was to successfully complete her Atlantic crossing.

Meanwhile, out of earshot of Muller, Joseph Ziegler moaned about having to wait his turn to go up top and young Karl Meister worked beside him, as always hanging on the every word of the older and he thought, wiser man.

* * *

Five hours earlier, approximately two miles west of *U966's* current position, the trawler *Mary Deal* had run into a spot of bother on her return voyage to her home port of Mevagissey, a small fishing village some five miles south of St. Austell. Her skipper, Andrew Douglas, fifty five, had fished these waters all his life and had decided to try one last trawl while daylight allowed. Unfortunately for Douglas, the *Mary Deal's* radio had begun playing up on the outward leg of their current trip, and failed to hear the fog warning that had been broadcast to all shipping in the area. Consequently, the incoming bank of thick, grey fog appeared ghost-like from astern of the trawler, seemingly hell-bent on catching up with the small vessel and wrapping her in its impenetrable cocoon.

"Fog coming in fast, skipper," came a shout from Johnny Baldwin, the skipper's nephew and senior crewman, having sailed with his uncle for nearly ten years.

"Damn, where the hell did that come from?" Douglas neither expected nor received a reply to his rhetorical question.

"What do you want to do?" Johnny asked his uncle.

"We'd better haul the nets in and make a run for home," Douglas replied. As an experienced seaman, the skipper had no intention of being caught at sea in thick fog.

Together with sixteen year old Peter Evans and Davy Billings, Johnny Baldwin began the task of hauling in the *Mary Deal's* nets. Andrew Douglas cursed silently. An extra haul would have gone some way towards making this trip worthwhile. Recent catches had been poor, and earnings reduced as a result. Still, no need to take unnecessary risks, he knew. There was always tomorrow.

Suddenly a shout from Johnny brought the whole job to a halt.

"Bloody hell, skipper, there's a mine in the net."

"What?"

"A bloody great mine, Uncle Andrew," Johnny repeated with fear in his voice.

"Ain't no minefields in these parts, though," Douglas replied, keeping as calm as he possibly could. No sense in making the lads panic, which would only increase the chances of disaster.

"What should we do?" asked a terrified Peter Evans.

Douglas thought for less than two seconds before making the only decision he could.

"We'll have to cut the nets loose. The damn thing must have come adrift from its mooring in one of our own bloody minefields. Damn the Royal bloody Navy. Can't even set a bloody minefield properly without endangering their own bloody fishermen."

"That's hardly fair, Uncle," said Johnny.

"Maybe not, but it's going to cost us dear, lad, having to cast adrift the net and whatever it holds. Now, set to it lads. Get that damned thing cut free and we'll have to report it when we get back home. Damn that bloody radio."

It was an unfortunate fact that occasionally, a mine would indeed break free from its moorings and float to the surface, presenting a dangerous hazard to shipping both friendly and enemy. Usually, a call to the appropriate authorities would result in the Royal Navy despatching a mine sweeper to the area to clear the offending floating ordnance and ensure the safety of our own vessels. Without his radio it would be at least a couple of hours before the *Mary Deal* could make port and allow Douglas to make a report on the floating mine.

"God knows how long it'll take the Navy to get a mine sweeper out here," he grumbled. "We'd best find new grounds to fish tomorrow."

"Let's hope nobody else runs into that bloody thing before the Navy can get a mine sweeper to clear it," said Johnny Baldwin as the *Mary Deal's* net together with its precious catch finally floated away from the trawler, the mine firmly enmeshed in it. The crew of the trawler breathed a collective sigh of relief as the mine disappeared from their view, where it was soon enveloped in the almost impenetrable shroud of fog that rolled inexorably into the English Chanel from the Atlantic.

Unknown to Johnny Baldwin, the young trawlerman's sadly prophetic words would soon herald a series of tragic and unforeseen events.

Chapter 20

The Hope and Anchor

Ross intended to keep the morning briefing as short as possible. In under an hour he expected the scheduled call from a Captain Anthony Prendergast, whom the Royal Navy had informed Agostini was the man in the know as far as the history of the war in the English Channel was concerned. Agostini had made sure the Navy had all the details, including a copy of the photo that showed the dead frogman, in order to ensure their fullest co-operation. It had worked. The Naval historical branch at the Ministry of Defence had pledged their help in any way they could, not only to identify a possible 'lost' shipwreck, but to help the police in their search for a murderer.

"Okay everyone," Ross began as the room fell silent. "You all know Sergeant Drake and I will be gone for a couple of days, but I need you all to keep searching for clues at this end. Ferris, keep digging into Aegis and their various offshoots. I want you to speak with Jerome Decker. See if you can get him to use his C.I.A. position to do some further probing into their affairs. If he hesitates, remind him it's his son's murder we're investigating."

"Got that, sir, no problem," Paul Ferris replied.

"Next, on the basis that they're our only two viable suspects in terms of having the opportunity to commit the murder, I want both the housemates looked into closely, and when I say closely I mean *very* closely."

"Tony, I want you to take Tim Knight, and Derek, take Martin Lewis. Find out everything there is to know about these men, and I mean *everything*. Could one or both of them have been coerced or blackmailed into participating in the killing? Find out. If either or both of them had any reason, no matter how small, to have a grudge against young Aaron Decker, find it. Leave no stone unturned. I don't care if you have to tread on a few toes along the way. If there's anything in either man's past that gives you cause for concern, I want to know about it. Got it?"

Curtis and McLennan both nodded their understanding as Ross turned finally to Nick Dodds and Sam Gable.

"Nick, Sam, go and see Haller. Try to get him to open up about the historical side of things. Let's remember there was a submarine involved in this affair according to that photograph. I strongly suspect it may have been a German U-Boat. Take a blow up of the photograph. If we can find out what kind of sub it was we might be able to come up with a possible date for when this all took place. That's a long shot I know, but if he can say with any degree of certainty it's a model that entered the war after, say 1944, we can knock out the first four years of the war for starters."

"There's not a lot of the submarine showing sir. There might not be enough for him to identify it with any certainty. Maybe your Royal Navy chap will know when he sees it."

"And maybe he won't, Nick. We're getting nowhere fast at present so let's use every asset we can until we've exhausted all possibilities, Okay?"

"Okay sir, whatever you say."

"Good, and all of you, remember to keep Paul updated with whatever you discover. He's still our collator so Paul, if you log anything onto the board that you think I should know, you call me right away on my mobile, and if you can't get me, try Sergeant Drake."

"Will do, sir."

"Right everyone, off you go. I'll be checking in regularly with D.C Ferris and calling daily updates in to D.C.I. Agostini while we're away, so let's try and make some progress. If you need anything, go and talk to the D.C.I. He won't bite and he's promised to be available for any help or advice you need in my absence."

With that, Ross brought the briefing to a close and while Drake went to get them fresh coffee and waited in his office, he paid Oscar Agostini a very quick visit, brought him up to date on who was doing what while he was away, and then returned to join Izzie, and the pair could only wait for the call for the man from the Royal Navy. The Navy, being very security conscious had insisted on their man calling Ross, rather than the other way round. That way, they were certain they'd be going through the police switchboard and talking to a bona fide police officer.

Ross was pleased when Captain Prendergast phoned him two minutes ahead of the scheduled time. At least the man was prompt. Ross soon came to like the man he was speaking with on the telephone, and quickly lost his preconceptions of a stiff upper-lipped, stuffed shirt type of naval officer. Prendergast was affable, easy to talk to and sounded keen to help Ross however he could. After listening to everything Ross had to say the line was silent for no more than five seconds.

"Well, I have to say, Inspector Ross, you and your people have done pretty well so far. I've taken a long hard look at the photo you sent us, and I've had our own people blow it up even larger. You were quite right in your assumption that the ship you saw is a corvette, though at present I can't give you a positive identification. You have to understand that during the war we used various types of corvettes, some purpose built, some bought or leased from the U.S.A. and a few were even converted merchant ships, though the one in the photograph does look like a true warship, I have to admit, possibly built later in the war. The raked bow tends to give it away."

"So do you think you will be able to identify her for us?" Ross asked, hoping for a positive reply.

"We stand a good chance, Inspector. It may be necessary to send divers down, but that shouldn't be a problem. Your Mr. Haller seems to have given you an accurate position for the wreck, and if it is a Royal Naval vessel previously uncharted, it is highly likely to be a war grave situation so we would want to check it out and clarify it."

"Captain Prendergast, you've just made my day. Thank you, sir," Ross said, feeling like punching the air with delight. If the Royal Navy became involved there was no way Aegis or anyone else could prevent them diving on the wreck and they just might have a chance of identifying the poor devil whose body was floating down there, somehow caught up in the wreckage.

"I really hope we can help you, Inspector Ross, and please call me Anthony, no need to be too formal, don't you agree?"

"Of course, thanks, Anthony, and do please call me Andy."

"Excellent," said Prendergast. "I understand you're heading down to Falmouth today, so how about I meet you there tomorrow at your hotel?"

"You're coming down yourself?" Ross sounded surprised, and Prendergast registered that surprise.

"But of course, Andy. I love to have an opportunity to get out of the office and I'd like to take a personal interest in this one. The chances of finding an unknown World War Two wreck after all these years are few and far between. I think it calls for a personal involvement."

"I must say I'm delighted to have your help, Anthony."

"Don't mention it. You might be interested to know the local Coast Guard commander down there is ex-R.N. too. He served with me in fact on the old *H.M.S. Lupus* back in the early eighties. We were much younger back then of course, but we've kept in touch over the years."

"You're kidding me?"

"Not at all, Andy. His name's George Baldacre, and I promise you he'll be all for diving in himself to help you out. Actually he was the diving officer on the old *Lupus*."

"Oh, so the *Lupus* was..."

"A submarine, Andy, quite right. She was a deep diving attack boat, but she was decommissioned soon after I left sea duty. I was the weapons officer at that time, otherwise known to all and sundry as "Weps.""

"Well, I'll be glad to have you both along," said Ross, impressed even more by Prendergast who he'd thought at first was probably a career desk officer rather then a former warship officer, much less one who'd served on a nuclear submarine, and now it appeared they were getting two for the price of one, so to speak. For the first time in this God-awful case, Andy Ross began to feel a hint of confidence creeping into his investigation. In fact, as he and Izzie were motoring along the M5 four hours later, having left the M6 behind where it linked up with the M5 near

West Bromwich, another thought came to Ross as Izzie drove, the car eating up the miles as they headed towards the south coast.

"I've had an idea, Izzie," he suddenly said, as a light bulb seemed to illuminate in his brain.

"I thought I could hear the old brain cogs grinding in there," Izzie joked. "Come on, sir. What have you come up with?"

"Marriage hasn't done anything for your sense of humour, Sergeant," Ross quipped.

"Did you expect it to?" Drake giggled.

"Of course not."

"Well that's alright then," Drake grinned. "Now, what's this new idea of yours, boss?"

"Well, I'm glad you've remembered who's in charge. But seriously, Izzie, if Ferris comes up with anything that casts any doubt on Aegis and their activities over here, we might be able to make use of Miss Sally Metcalfe to draw them out."

"That's different," said Drake. "In what way, sir?"

"I'm pretty sure she's in the clear, so it's safe to assume she'll want to help us find Aaron's killer. So, we know she already has a job offer from Aegis after she finishes at the university, so what do you think might happen if she suddenly decides she wants to turn their offer down?"

"I think someone at Aegis might be a little pissed at her if she did that after they've invested in her already with the sponsorship."

"More than a little pissed, Izzie, if you ask me. So what might they do, do you think?"

"If it was me, I'd want to talk to her, try to get her to change her mind, sir."

"Right, my thoughts exactly. I'm hoping the head man at the Falmouth base will be ordered to invite her down there to talk things through, and if he does, we can prime Miss Metcalfe with a few prime questions and also get her to keep her eyes and ears open for anything in their set up that doesn't sit right with her. She's a marine biologist after all. She should know if something is out of place. I know it's along shot, but…"

"But it might bring dividends, I agree, sir. But won't we be putting her at risk?"

"Not if she is properly prepared with a few genuine concerns and I'm sure she can think of a few things that would qualify in that respect." "But what if she doesn't want to help, sir?"

"We'll cross that bridge when we come to it. For now, I could use a coffee. There's a Service Area in a mile. Let's pull over, have a drink and a rest and I'll take over the driving for a while when we get back on the road."

* * *

The strangely named Hope and Anchor Hotel stood in its own grounds, set back from the road, about five miles outside Falmouth. With Ross now taking a turn at the wheel, Izzie Drake had displayed her map reading skills in directing them to their destination without a single wrong turn along the way, a feat Ross wasn't sure he'd have accomplished. Map reading had never been his speciality, something to do with trying to translate the tiny squiggles and signs on a map into the real world, so he thought.

The receptionist had them booked in within a couple of minutes of their arrival, and before they were shown to their rooms, a large, rather corpulent and extremely jolly looking man with swept back grey hair came bustling into the reception area from what was clearly an office to the rear of the reception desk.

"Hello, hello," the man spoke as though welcoming two old friends. "You must be Detective Inspector Ross and Detective Sergeant Drake, am I right?"

"Yes, we are, and you are?" Ross replied.

"Thomas Severn, owner of the Hope and Anchor, at your service."

Severn held out his hand and Ross reflexively shook hands with the newcomer, who proceeded to follow the same routine with Izzie Drake.

"I wanted to be here to meet you, Inspector," Severn went on. "We tend to be used for visitors or guests of the local constabulary so wanted to be sure you were comfortable with your rooms."

"That's very welcoming of you, I'm sure," said Ross, feeling a little overwhelmed by the man's effusive nature. Not so, Izzie Drake, who immediately asked the proprietor of the hotel the question she knew Ross would also like the answer to.

"It's a rather unusual name, the Hope and Anchor, Mr. Severn.

How did that come about?"

"Oh, no secret there, Sergeant," Severn replied. "This used to be an old coaching inn, and until I purchased it, it went by the name of The Coach and Four. It was looking a bit tired when I took over so we gave the place a makeover, and added the new wing out back. A new name seemed appropriate. Hope is my wife's first name and I added the anchor part as I used to be in the Navy, until I was invalided out." He tapped his right leg, which made a hollow sound as his hand connected with it. "Lost the leg in a shipboard accident. No way I could carry on in the Navy after that. I got a massive pay-off from the M.O.D. though, enough to secure the down-payment on this place. It's virtually doubled in value in the ten years I've owned it so it seems I made a bloody wise investment."

Severn gave no further explanation and Drake didn't press the point. She didn't feel it right to question their host on something so personal. For Ross, it perhaps explained why the local police were happy to book their visitors and guests into the Hope and Anchor. Severn seemed a totally reliable and friendly sort of character with what appeared to be an impeccable background.

Severn called for one of his staff, a young man called Lewis, who helped load their cases onto a small trolley and the owner led the way to their rooms, which were on the ground floor to the rear of the hotel, away from any road noise, and, as Severn put it, "Sound proofed from any noise from the lounge bar and dining room, so you won't be disturbed."

He left them to unpack and get settled with instructions to call upon him or his staff if they needed anything at all. Ross informed him they'd be having visitors the following morning and asked if Severn could make a room available to them for the purposes of a small meeting. Severn assured them there was no problem and he'd have a room ready for them when ever they needed it. He was impressed when Ross told him the visitors would be a Royal Naval Captain and the local Coast Guard commander. He apparently knew George Baldacre well and spoke highly of the Coast Guard man, telling Ross he knew the local waters better then anyone he knew.

Time was passing quickly, so Ross and Drake both took the opportunity to shower and change and then met in the lounge bar for a drink before dinner. Their rooms were at the rear of the hotel in the newer part of the building, and were decorated in a modern style, both had en-suite facilities and tea and coffee making facilities and were clean and warm, so passed muster with both detectives. Ross was pleased to find that the dining room was situated in the original coaching inn part of the establishment and was possessed of great charm and olde-worlde character. Pictures of sailing ships adorned the walls, and the tables were a dark oak in colour, to match the window frames and doors. Word of who the pair were must have got around, he thought, as none of the waiting staff took them for a courting couple and none of the other guests gave them disapproving stares, thinking of him as an older man carrying on an affair with a good looking younger woman.

"I don't know whether to be disappointed or not," he said to Izzie after making the point about the other guests especially.

"Well, what's to stop you corrupting a junior officer?" she joked. "We could always act a bit flirtatious, give 'em something to talk about, sir."

"Are you kidding?" he looked aghast. "The old biddy with the blue rinse over in the far corner would probably get up and come across and stab me with a knitting needle if I so much as wink at you. Have you seen the looks she's been giving me? If those aren't daggers in her eyes, I don't deserve to be a D.I."

"Oh, well, what do we do now?" Izzie asked, at the same time dropping her voice, smiling coquettishly and leaning forward across the table conspiratorially. To the elderly lady in the far corner of the room, seated with her ageing and decrepit looking husband, it would appear as if Drake was whispering to Ross, perhaps inviting him to enjoy a spot of after dinner enjoyment in her room. Andy Ross knew exactly what she was doing.

"Are you trying to incite that little old lady to commit grievous bodily harm against a police officer, Sergeant Drake? Because, if you are, be aware that the old biddy over there is now on the verge of throwing those aforementioned daggers at me. I warn you, if she comes and throws a bowl of soup over me, you can be the one to make the arrest. Should make for an interesting arrest report, for sure."

Drake grinned at him, the inviting smile was back again as she spoke in hushed tones. "Well, sir, I'm only asking you what we do next, after all. It's not as if I'm publicly inviting you to some illicit tryst, or shouting at you to rip my knickers off in front of the locals is it?"

"Izzie Drake, if you don't put a sock in it, I swear I'll have you demoted as soon as we return to Liverpool."

Izzie couldn't help herself. Her voice rose to its normal volume.

"Oh no, please, don't. I'll do what you say, sir. Please don't do that. What would my poor old Mum say? She'd think it was my fault."

Ross groaned in anguish. Izzie's twisted sense of humour had got the old lady in the corner well and truly fired up but instead of coming across the room to physically or verbally berate him, he heard her say loudly to her poor, and obviously long-suffering husband, "Walter, come along. We're finished here. We're going back to our room."

"But, my coffee…"

"Forget the coffee, Walter. We're leaving."

The poor man forced himself to rise and follow his overbearing wife as she stomped from the room, casting a disapproving glance in Ross's direction as she flounced out of the dining room doors, Walter trailing obediently at least five paces behind her.

As the two detectives collapsed in a fit of stupid giggles and laughter, a grinning Thomas Severn stepped towards them from behind one of the columns that rose from floor to ceiling of the dining room, clapping slowly but happily.

"Oh, I say, that's the most fun I've had in ages, priceless. A superb performance, Sergeant. You had old Mrs. Twining almost wetting herself, poor dear. I think she had you squirming a little too, Inspector Ross," Severn laughed.

"My sergeant has, shall we say, a certain sense of humour, Mr. Severn?" said Ross, grinning.

"I can see that, much like many of the lads from Liverpool I met during my time in the Navy."

"I presume at some point you'll tell the old lady we were only kidding?" Drake asked.

"Oh no," Severn exclaimed. "You'll be the highlight of her week, and the talk of Cheltenham when she returns home. I can see her telling her friends at the W.I. or whatever she belongs to about the brazen hussy and the exploitative policeman she met on her holiday. She'll probably embellish the whole thing until she virtually has the pair of you making love across the dining table in full view of the guests."

Now Ross was laughing, and Izzie joined in too.

"Now, what would you like to eat?" Severn asked.

Ross selected a simple Sirloin steak with chips and peas, while Izzie went for the grilled Sea Bass with new potatoes and seasonal vegetables. Both agreed the food was superb and Ross asked Thomas Severn to give their compliments to the chef.

"My wife will be delighted, thank you," Severn replied.

"Your wife's the chef?"

"She certainly is," Severn grinned. "Hope was trained as a chef in the Navy. We served together, you see, Inspector."

"Well, you certainly have a real diamond there, Mr. Severn. The food really was excellent."

After dinner, Ross and Drake retired to their rooms, where each phoned home to their respective partners. Ross related the story of the old lady at dinner to Maria, who, knowing Izzie only too well, found it highly amusing. Later, they met once more in the lounge bar where they enjoyed a nightcap before turning in for the night. Ross hoped for great things from tomorrow's meeting. Surely, the combined efforts of the Merseyside Police, the Royal Navy and the Coast Guard would help to move this case towards a conclusion. He slept surprisingly well, another compliment for the hotel he thought. On the rare occasions he'd stayed away from home in the past, sleep had proved elusive, usually because of uncomfortable hotel beds, but not so at the Hope and Anchor. The mattress simply moulded to his body and he slept like a baby, waking at six a.m. as usual. After showering and dressing, he made his way to the dining room where Izzie Drake was already seated, sipping coffee.

Knowing they had a potentially long and demanding day ahead of them, both availed themselves of the Hope and Anchor's full English breakfast, Bacon, eggs, sausage, mushrooms and beans, with fried bread. Again, the food was excellent, and this time, they were able to meet Hope Severn and compliment her in person.

"Thank you," she said when Ross told her how much he and Drake had enjoyed her cooking. "My husband told me something of why you're here. I was sad to hear of that poor young boy's murder."

"You knew him?" Ross sounded surprised.

"Oh no, not the young man, but I did meet the man who was helping him."

"You mean Herr Haller, the German historian?"

"No, no, the other man."

Ross was suddenly on full alert.

"What other man, Mrs. Severn? We weren't aware of anyone else working with Aaron Decker down here."

"Oh, I see. He was a youngish man, about twenty four to thirty, I'd say. He came here looking for the young man. I said we'd never heard of him, which was true, and the man said he knew his friend was staying in a hotel somewhere in Falmouth, but he didn't know which one."

"Can you describe him for us, Mrs. Severn? Apart from his age of course." said Drake.

"Brown hair, cut in an old fashioned short back and sides, a fisherman's sweater, blue with a red design of some sort I think, and jeans, and oh, yes, he had a local accent . It was over a year ago, Inspector, Sergeant. That's the best I can do."

"You've been a great help," Ross replied. "Do you know where he went after leaving here?"

"Sorry, no idea," said Hope.

Ross thanked her for her time and her information and as he and Drake finished their third cup of coffee, he looked into his sergeant's eyes, and voiced the thoughts he felt they both shared.

"If I'm not much mistaken, Izzie, we have a possible third diver here. If that man wasn't Haller, of course, and I'm sure Mrs. Severn knows the difference between a middle aged German, a local man and a twenty-something American. Do you know what I'm thinking?"

"That the man who came here looking for Aaron was working with him in his research into what ever Aegis was up to, and if I'm not mistaken, you also think that man is in all probability the poor sod in a wet-suit who's floating around at the bottom of the English Channel."

"Bingo," said Ross. "You've got it in one, Sergeant Drake."

Chapter 21

A Meeting of Minds

Captain Anthony Prendergast, R.N. (Retired) arrived a good ten minutes before their pre-arranged meeting time. Ross was luckily positioned in the reception area anyway so couldn't fail to witness his arrival, though Ross mentally kicked himself for expecting the man to be dressed in uniform, only realising as Prendergast walked through the doors of the Hope and anchor that as a retired officer, he'd be dressed in civvies. Prendergast still managed to stand out however, dressed in his black blazer with the submariner's blazer badge and shining brass buttons, crisp white shirt and tie that also bore the logo of the submarine service, and sharply pressed grey flannel trousers. His black shoes were polished to a resplendent finish, every inch an ex-military man.

He equally had no difficulty in recognising Ross and walked straight across the floor of the hotel lobby and greeted the detective, who shook hands and quickly led the captain along the corridor to the room Hope Severn had prepared for their use, where he was introduced to Izzie Drake.

"Very pleased indeed to meet you, Sergeant Drake."

"Pleased to meet you too, Captain Prendergast," she replied, and Ross could have sworn he detected a slight blush crept up Izzie's cheeks as Prendergast held gently on to her hand a second or two longer than necessary,

"Please call me Anthony," he said in a soft, yet gravelly voice that had probably charmed more then a few young ladies into his bed during his younger years. It amused Ross to think the old seadog appeared to have retained every ounce of his charm.

A knock on the door was followed by the smiling face of Hope Severn who announced that the final member of their quartet, the Coast Guard officer, George Baldacre, had arrived. Ross immediately left the room, returning barely a minute later with the latest arrival.

Baldacre was somewhat younger than Prendergast, Ross correctly recalling that Prendergast had told him they'd served together. Obviously, Ross realised, Baldacre had entered the service some years after the older man. As head of the local Coast Guard unit, Baldacre obviously was still fit enough for sea duty and indeed, he was often to be found at sea on any of the local Coast Guard vessels, usually observing the crews at work. Ross had found out that the

Coast Guard unit covered a large section of coastline along the Cornish coast, and was not simply restricted to Falmouth. That made sense as anything else would have meant the UK Coast Guard Service would have needed a navy of its own.

Prendergast greeted the former diving control officer of *H.M.S Lupus* with enthusiasm, the two men engaging in a bear hug of mammoth proportions. Baldacre was easily six foot tall, and built like the proverbial battleship. He was dressed in the uniform of H.M. Coast Guard Service. His hair was all but gone; just a few wisps of grey seemed to be fighting a losing battle to remain in place across the top of his balding pate when he removed his peaked cap.

"George, you old renegade," said Prendergast as he pumped the younger man's hand. "How the devil are you?"

"I'm well, thank you, sir," Baldacre replied, confirming Ross's thought that Prendergast had been the other man's senior officer.

"Forget that old sir malarkey, those days are long gone. It's Anthony as you well know."

"Right, Anthony it is then," said Baldacre.

"Forgive us please, Inspector," Prendergast apologised to Ross. "It's been a few years since we met up. Too many years in fact."

"That's quite alright," Ross smiled at the pair, wondering at the same time how someone the size of Baldacre had managed in the confines of a nuclear submarine. Perhaps, he thought, the man had been smaller in those days, though his height would surely have been the same. His question would have to remain unanswered however, as they had pressing matters to attend to.

After all four had helped themselves to coffee from the large pot supplied by Hope Severn, they arranged themselves around the large table in the centre of the room, on which Anthony Prendergast spread a large map of the English Channel that he'd removed from his briefcase, carefully unfolding it to its full size.

Using his pen as a pointer he gave the others a quick resumé of what lay before them on the table.

"As you can see, this map indicates all of the known wreck sites pertaining to ships of the Royal Navy and others in the Channel. These blue dots are our ships, nothing more recent than the Second World War, and not many either. The black dots indicate the known remains of ships of the German Kriegsmarine from World War Two, we have no records from World War One of any such wrecks. The green dots indicate the few known wrecks of civilian ships, mostly the odd trawler and one or two cargo vessels that were lost in deeper waters."

"That's quite impressive," Ross interjected. "I never realised there'd be such an accurate and comprehensive record of the wrecks on the sea bed."

"Normally you'd be correct, of course," Prendergast replied, "but the English Channel is one of the busiest waterways in the world and it's important from a safety angle that any wreck that might at some time present any hazard to shipping, no matter how remote, is known about and charted."

"Of course, yes, I understand," Ross nodded.

"Now, that's what makes this case of yours interesting, Andy, because the co-ordinates given to you by Klaus Haller do not correspond to any of these known wreck sites. Either the man has deliberately misled you, or, his coordinates are incorrect, or..." Prendergast hesitated.

"Or what?" Ross asked, eager for the final part of the reply.

"I think what he's saying," Baldacre joined in the conversation, "is that the only other conclusion that we might come to here, and it's not one the Navy would really be too happy with, is that Herr Haller, or, more precisely, these people from the Aegis institute, appear to have stumbled on an unknown wreck site. That means in effect, that somewhere along the line the Navy has managed to lose a ship somewhere, right, Anthony?"

"Right," Prendergast confirmed.

"I'm not sure I'm following this exactly," said Ross. "When you say they've lost a ship..."

"Let me explain," Prendergast stopped him in mid-sentence. "When a Royal Navy vessel is in trouble, Andy, standard procedure is for the Captain to transmit its position, enabling search and rescue units to locate it and carry out their tasks. The same holds true now as it did during the war. As long as we know where the ship went down, we can co-ordinate the search for survivors, wreckage and so on. However, if the ship, for whatever reason, transmits incorrect co-ordinates, or, worst of all, doesn't send out a distress call, we have no way of knowing where that ship is in reality. If the wrong position is transmitted the rescue craft could be searching miles away from where the ship went down."

"And if no distress call goes out?" Drake now asked the question.

"Well, Sergeant. In that case we would in effect have 'lost' a ship as George so succinctly put it. If we don't know it's been sunk, how the heck do we know we've got a missing ship until such times as it fails to report in or doesn't return from a patrol for example?"

"But surely," Drake said, "the Royal Navy knows when one of its ships is missing, presumed sunk, Captain? They must have records of such things."

"Anthony, please," Prendergast corrected her. "It's not always as simple as that, Sergeant."

"Izzie," she interrupted.

"Okay, Izzie, let me explain a little. You see, when World War Two was in progress, we obviously had ships at sea in virtually every ocean of the world. Now, say for the sake of argument the ship Aegis has discovered was part of a convoy escort, sailing from, let's say Halifax, Nova Scotia, to Liverpool, your home town..."

"But that's nowhere near the Channel," Drake persisted.

"No, but what if the convoy had been attacked by U-Boats, or perhaps a roving *Condor*, that was a German long range maritime patrol aircraft, by the way, and one or two merchant ships had been damaged but not sunk. If the ship, or ships were not too badly damaged and the commander of the convoy escort screen, normally the senior captain of the destroyers that often sailed as cover, together with perhaps two or three corvettes decided they stood a chance of making port, but not necessarily the original port of destination, he had the authority to detach those ships from the convoy, and send them to a closer port of safety and would usually send one of his escort vessels to accompany the stragglers to port. Depending on where the attack too place, it might have seemed sensible for him to direct the escorting vessel to see them safely to a port on the south coast, perhaps Plymouth, or Portsmouth, where they could have picked up Naval protection as they neared home waters."

"I'm getting the picture," Drake said. "I think you're saying that if a ship was lost after being detached from the convoy and didn't have a chance to send a distress signal, you, that is the Royal Navy, I mean wouldn't have a clue were it went down."

"Precisely. Now you're beginning to understand the problem. It's clear from the photograph young Decker took that the ship is in all probability a Royal Naval vessel, and we've already guessed it looks likely to be a corvette. So far, so good. However, since I was asked to look into the matter, and as I already explained, there are no records of any naval vessel going down at that position in the channel. So, we now need to look at any ships that may have mysteriously disappeared in the Channel or its approaches in the later years of the war. We know it had to be around that time by the design of the ship's bow. Earlier corvettes were built to a pretty dated design and had what you might call a 'sit up and beg' bow, fairly straight rather than the raked bow on later, more modern designs."

"And have your initial inquiries come up with anything, Anthony?" Ross asked, expecting the Captain to perhaps come up with a long list, knowing how many ships were lost during the war.

"As a matter of fact, they have, Andy" Prendergast smiled. "I have a list here..." Ross groaned, "of three possibilities." Ross perked up immediately.

"Only three?" he asked. "Are you sure?"

Prendergast smiled sympathetically, knowing Ross to be a little in the dark on this subject.

"The Royal Navy isn't now, and never has been in the business of totally losing track of long lists of our warships, Andy."

"I'm sorry, Anthony. No offence intended."

"None taken. It's a tricky thing to get your head round, I know."

"So, just three ships possible then," Ross repeated.

"That's all, Andy, and one is a definite favourite for your wreck"

"I'm all ears," Ross said as Prendergast pulled another sheet of paper from a compartment in his briefcase.

"Okay, first of all the three names. We have *H.M.S. Denbigh, H.M.S Violet* and *H.M.S. Norwich*, all reported missing without trace during 1945. Of the three, my money is on the *Norwich*.

Ross held a hand up to stop Prendergast.

"Hold on a minute, Anthony. I think we'd better have a coffee refill before you tell us this part."

Five agonising minutes passed, Ross wanted to hear Prendergast's theory as much as Izzie Drake, but he knew they'd all feel better for a little refreshment to go with it.

Finally they all sat round the table once more, and as Anthony Prendergast passed copies of a grainy black and white photograph of a small and insignificant looking warship to each of them, he began to relate, in as much detail as he could the tragic story surrounding the mysterious loss of *H.M.S. Norwich*.

Chapter 22

The English Channel, 1945

Four hours after her encounter with the drifting mine, the *Mary Deal* was almost home. As the trawler crept through the fog, Andrew Douglas eventually breathed a minor sigh of relief as the ubiquitous sound of the foghorn positioned at the end of the small quay in the harbour of the tiny fishing village of his home at Mevagissey managed to claw its way through the all enveloping grey cloud finally reached his ears. He knew they were within reach of safety at last, and he called to his nephew, Johnny Baldwin to join him in the little trawler's wheelhouse.

"Listen lad, as soon as we tie up I want you to hop off and run as fast as you can to P.C. Pryde's house and tell him about that there mine."

"Right you are, Uncle Andrew," Johnny replied.

Douglas thrust a piece of paper into Johnny's hand.

"This 'ere piece o' paper's got the position of the mine written down on it, at least, where it were when we met up with it. Daresay it might have drifted a bit since then, but at least it'll give the Navy boys an idea where to look for the damned thing."

Young Baldwin nodded and fell silent as he watched his uncle guide the little trawler closer to safety, the sound of the foghorn growing louder as the *Mary Deal* crept along at little more than three knots. Then, like an angel beckoning them to Heaven the glow of the harbour light, complete with a spectrum-filled halo produced by the fog that shrouded the boat's approach broke through the dense cloying cloud. Andrew Douglas reduced power to the engine, which growled its acceptance of his touch on the throttle and the *Mary Deal* almost came to a stop but maintained enough steerage way under the command of her experienced skipper to slowly edge her way into the tiny harbour, where Douglas soon had her starboard side bumping up to the harbour wall, the thick tyres hanging along her side preventing damage to her hull.

Douglas instantly threw the engine into reverse, bringing the craft to an almost instant halt as Johnny Baldwin leapt upward onto the steps that led up from her berth to the top of the harbour wall. The young man quickly disappeared into the fog on his errand to report the mine to the authorities. Douglas switched off the engine and called for his remaining crew members to help him secure the boat and seal the hold. The few boxes containing the day's meagre catch could wait in the cold of the hold until morning as they were too late to offload and sell the catch thanks to the fog. Douglas cursed inwardly, fully expecting some of the catch, despite being packed in ice, to be useless by morning.

* * *

As Andrew Douglas threw the switch that turned off the *Mary Deal's* engine, the trawler shuddered for a moment from the last throb of the diesel motor, and then all was silent aboard the boat, apart from the lapping of the rippling harbour waves against the hull and the gentle creaking of the deck planking as she settled at her moorings.

Peter Evans and Davy Billings offered to stay with Douglas to await the return of Johnny Baldwin, but Douglas thanked the two younger men and told them to go home to their families.

"Your Mum will be worried about you, Peter," he said to Evans. "We're late enough coming back as it is. Go and put her mind to rest lad."

Left alone with his thoughts as he waited for his nephew to report back to him, Andrew Douglas sat in the *Mary Deal's* wheelhouse and took a small hip flask from his heavy seaman's duffle coat pocket. The flask contained the last of the trawlerman's supply of rum, a gift from a grateful destroyer captain when Douglas had presented him with a box of freshly caught fish when the two had met at sea some months earlier.

Sipping the amber liquid that sent an instant warmth down his throat and into his stomach, Douglas allowed himself to be lulled for a few seconds by the gentle movement of the *Mary Deal* as she swayed in time to the movement of the barely perceptible swell within the little harbour.

"I'm getting too old for this lark," he spoke aloud, his only audience being his boat, the ocean and the stars that he knew illuminated the night sky somewhere beyond the bank of fog that now seemed to be slowly clearing, with minor improvement to the overall visibility from his perch in the wheelhouse. "Perhaps Stella was right. Maybe it's time to pack it in, Andrew, me laddo, leave the sea to the young 'uns."

"Talking to yourself now, are you, Andrew?"

The deep voice of the local police constable, Sebastian Pryde, known to all as Seb, broke into his reverie. The muffling effect of the fog had prevented Douglas from hearing the approach of the policeman.

"Seb Pryde, you be careful, creepin' up on a man like that. You could have given me a heart attack. And where's that nephew o' mine?"

"Right here, Uncle Andrew," Johnny replied as he appeared almost wraith-like from behind the constable, an apparition materialising from the fog bank.

"I came to see you personally, Andrew," Pryde said, "and let you know I've telephoned the Royal Navy base at Portland. They said to say thank you for reportin' the mine and they'll be sendin' a mine sweeper along as soon as possible to clear it and make the shippin' lane safe again."

"Hmph," Douglas grumbled. "I doubt they apologised for allowin' the damn thing to drift away in the first place, puttin' my boat in jeopardy like that, did they?"

"Course not," said Pryde. "But at least they'll see to it, though I must say you were damn lucky you saw it rather than hittin' it. You and the *Mary Deal* and crew might never have been seen again if you had."

"That's what I was thinkin' afore you crept up on me," Douglas admitted. "Perhaps it's time to hang up me sea boots. How do you fancy skipperin' the *Mary Deal*, young Johnny?"

"Are you serious, Uncle?" an astounded Johnny Baldwin asked, his face a mask of total surprise.

"Aye lad, I am. You're aunty has been a' naggin' at me to give up the sea and I'm thinkin' tonight's just about done it for me. We'll talk with your father tomorrow and see about fixin' a decent wage for you, and the *Mary Deal* will have a new skipper the next time she puts to sea."

"I don't know what to say," said Johnny, and the policeman clapped him on the shoulder and congratulated him on his good fortune. Before leaving the two seamen, Pryde gave them a cautionary warning.

"Just be sure you and your crew don't go spreading it about that you almost hit one of our own mines, you hear me, Andrew?"

"I hear you, Seb. We'll call on the others on the way home and warn them off from sayin' anything, though they'll have told their families, I'm sure."

"Just make sure it goes no further," Pryde warned him. "It wouldn't be good for morale among the population if they thought our own ships were at risk from our own mines. That's why the Admiralty provide us with charts so our people don't end up in our minefields."

As Douglas and Baldwin followed P.C. Pryde as he led the way back towards the village, each man felt satisfied that he'd done his duty satisfactorily, the *Mary Deal* was left at her moorings, her deck silent and her engine making an occasional clicking sound as the metal machinery parts cooled in the night. She and her crew had played their part in what would become one of wartime's cameos of circumstance, a part none of the other participants would ever be aware of.

* * *

"Damn this fog," Engel cursed as he and Ritter stood together on the conning tower of *U966*, peering into the murk that surrounded them. Five hours had passed since the *Mary Deal* had passed this self-same position as she headed back towards Megavissey. Ritter and Engel of course, had never heard of the little trawler, nor would they in the time they had remaining to them.

Ritter placed a hand on his first officer's shoulder.

"What we can't see, neither can the enemy, Heini. We're as safe as we can be at present. Won't be long before we submerge and break out into the Atlantic."

"I'll feel a lot safer when we do," Engel moaned at his skipper who merely shook his head and said, "Don't be an old woman, Heini. Do you want to live forever?"

"Not forever, mein Kapitän, but at least until we see the coast of South America would be good for now."

"Then come, Heini, she should be ready now. Let's take a last deep breath of fresh air and go below. We'll submerge and make a dash for it. Perhaps you're right. Best not to push our luck too far, eh?"

"Yes, and by the way, did Kraus tell you some of the crates we were loaded with had come loose this afternoon? We had to tie them down again?"

Jurgen Kraus was in effect the bosun of the U-Boat, the senior non-commissioned officer on board. He was responsible for all aspects of shipboard discipline and other more mundane tasks at present, like overseeing the safety of the mysterious cargo.

"No, he didn't. Knowing Kraus he'll have seen to it without feeling any need of disturbing me with such matters of routine."

"It's just that, apart from cursing those blasted SS types who loaded them on board and wouldn't let the crew near them, Krauss told me he could hardly believe the weight of six of the crates. It took four men to manhandle them into the correct position so they could be lashed to the bulkheads properly this time. What the hell is in those things? The ones in the rear torpedo compartment and up for'ard are nowhere near as heavy, according to Kraus."

"Speculation is futile, my friend," Ritter replied as he and Engel dropped down the ladder into the control room. Looking back over his shoulder he said, "We sail on orders from the Fuehrer. What choice do we have?" Engel didn't reply.

"Secure the hatch," Ritter ordered and as soon as his order had been complied with he gave the order to dive. *U966* levelled out at ten metres below the surface and before Max Ritter could say another word a shout from Gerhard Shenke, from his position on the hydrophones brought everyone in the control room to attention.

"Kapitän, engines, I'm detecting engines in the water."

"Shit," Ritter exclaimed. "Location, course and speed, Shenke."

"Two kilometres to the west, sir, course two two zero, speed approximately twelve knots."

"What do you think, Shenke?"

Shenke was an experienced operator who could often identify the type of enemy quickly from the sound of her engines.

"I don't know, sir. If it was a destroyer it would be moving faster. Could be a merchantman, maybe a straggler from a convoy."

"I don't know either," said Ritter, removing his cap and scratching his head. "Even twelve knots is pretty good for most of the old rust buckets they send out in the convoys nowadays. I wish we'd remained on the surface for a few more minutes, and maybe got a look at it."

"But we probably wouldn't have been able to see it anyway with that bloody fog up there," Engel countered.

"True, Heini, very true."

Shenke spoke again, urgency in his voice.

"Whatever she is, she's got Asdic, sir. She's scanning. Maybe she heard us."

"Damn," said Ritter.

"What now?" Engel asked.

* * *

Having completed the outward leg of her patrol area, *H.M.S. Norwich* had turned for home twenty minutes earlier and was on a heading that Clarkson couldn't know would take her directly towards *U966*. As luck would have it, the fog had begun to lift in patches and *Norwich* had been blessed with a clear window for the last five miles of her passage. Even so, there was no way her lookouts could have seen the *U966* on the surface as she recharged her batteries. The submarine was still shrouded by fog. Unfortunately for *U966* however, when the crew had re-secured the mystery crates after they'd worked loose, a careless rating had left a wrench propped on a steam pipe that ran along the top of the passageway where the heaviest crates were stored. As the U-Boat slipped below the waves following Ritter's order to submerge, the wrench had slid from its place atop the pipe and clattered to the deck, the sound loud enough to be heard by the ever alert crewmen of the corvette.

"It's a U-Boat, sir, I'm sure of it," said petty officer Sykes as Clarkson stood beside him, the pinging echo of the Asdic resounding in the enclosed space, Sykes continually turning the control wheel as he followed the track of the target.

Clarkson ordered the *Norwich* to full speed ahead and in seconds, their routine patrol had turned into a deadly game of cat and mouse.

Peter Hicks had joined Giles Clarkson on the bridge, together with the young navigator Lieutenant Bailey, who stood beside the voice pipe ready to convey the skipper's orders to the engine room. Leading Seaman Charlie Knox, still smiling, was at the helm, and two young ratings, Adam Phelps and Albert Taylor stood, one on each wing of the bridge, binoculars in hand, surveying the surrounding waters, which were suddenly becoming more visible as a break in the fog seemed to be a heaven-sent gift to the hunters of the submerged submarine.

Below the waves, Max Ritter cursed his ill-fortune. Another ten minutes and he'd have been clear of the area, and secondly, if he'd remained up top, he'd have possibly escaped detection altogether, sheltered in the haven provided by the fog.

"Bring her up to periscope depth," he ordered with a hint of angst in his voice.

"But sir…"Engel began to protest.

"Now, Heini," he reiterated.

"Jawohl, Herr Kapitän," Engel replied, repeating the order to the helmsman.

"Up scope," Ritter snapped and quickly scanned the surrounding sea, surprised to see the fog dissipating by the second as the view became clearer. His eyes quickly picked out the approaching warship, its bow wave indicating she was probably at full speed, on a course that would put them right where *U966* was in less then a minute.

"It's a corvette, probably a convoy escort," he said as he calculated his best course of action, at the same time remembering his orders not to engage the enemy unless absolutely necessary.

"Damn Hitler's bloody 'special cargo'," he cursed.

"Your orders, Kapitän?" Heini spoke with respect, professionalism overtaking the bond of friendship that existed between the two men.

Ritter knew he had only seconds to make a decision; stay and fight, use his limited supply of torpedoes to attempt to sink the small warship, or save them for bigger prey that they may encounter on the voyage, or attempt to evade the corvette, which, by nature of its purpose as he well knew, would be armed with enough anti-submarine weapons, depth-charges and torpedoes of its own, to damage his boat, perhaps fatally.

As the sound of the *Norwich's* propellers filled the ears of the crew within the sleek but sealed interior of *U966*, growing louder by the second, Max Ritter, faithful to his orders, made his decision.

"Crash dive," he ordered. "Take her down, now. Helm hard right."

Almost immediately, the bow of *U966* noticeably dipped as the submarine made its attempt to reach the sea bed, out of range of any depth charges the warship might be about to release. Simultaneously, the sub began to turn to starboard, Ritter's ploy being to confuse the surface ship as to his true intent. He wanted the corvette's captain to believe he was trying to escape by turning to starboard and making an emergency course change. If he could make his adversary wary of the possibility he may be preparing to launch torpedoes against his ship, he might pause to think and in those precious seconds, *U966* would slip under the corvette and be on the sea bed in less than two minutes.

Aboard the *Norwich* the sense of excitement was palpable as the constant pinging of the Asdic penetrated almost every compartment of the corvette. On the bridge, Clarkson held on to the bridge railing with one hand, while holding his binoculars in the other. Turning to his yeoman of signals, Seaman Hurst, he said in a calm voice, betraying not a hint of emotion, "Send the following signal immediately, adding our position at the end."

He passed a slip of paper to Hurst with the ship's position clearly written upon it.

TO CAPTAIN (D) COMMANDING DESTROYER SQUADRON PORTLAND stop FROM CAPTAIN, H.M.S. NORWICH stop AM ENGAGING UBOAT stop CURRENT POSITION…

It was at that moment when all the laws of probability, happenstance and sheer bad luck overrode the best intentions of both Lieutenant Commander Giles Clarkson and Korvettankapitän Max Ritter and the vagaries of the sea took control of the battle between the *Norwich* and *U966*.

The madness took everyone by surprise. The excited shout of "Instantaneous echo" from the Asdic operator was followed immediately by Clarkson's order to fire a salvo of depth charges. The death-dealing, amatol-filled barrels of explosives arced away from the *Norwich's* port side as she raced over the position of the German submarine.

Aboard *U966* Ritter actually heard the sound of the depth-charges as they hit the surface of the sea. He hoped his ploy had gained him enough seconds for his boat to gain the depth he needed.

It worked. As the charges exploded, the concussion from the exploding amatol caused momentary panic on *U966* as the sub lurched almost onto its port side, the lights went out, various pipes burst and small leaks caused jets of freezing water into various compartments, steam into others, but after a few seconds the lights came back on, repair crews dashed to repair the leaks and the submarine stabilised and continued its controlled dive to the bottom, reaching safety a few seconds later. Ritter ordered full stop to the engine room and allied his order with the command for total silence aboard the boat. The corvette's captain would, he hoped, either think the *U966* had escaped to the South, or alternatively, might believe the sub to be fatally damaged and sunk, crippled to the bottom of the sea.

Just as Clarkson was about to order a turn to starboard, and as the ship's wireless operator was about to send the Captain's message to Portland the mine that had drifted some ten miles since its encounter with the *Mary Deal* entered the equation.

The *Norwich's* starboard lookout just had time to shout "Mine" before the ship's port side came into contact with the deadly prongs of the mine and an almighty explosion rocked the corvette. The explosion literally ripped the guts from the warship, the engine room and the magazine being holed and flooded in seconds, everyone in those areas killed almost instantly.

The corvette, almost cut in half by the exploding mine and her own armaments, began to sink immediately. The explosions had by then left the bridge a tangled mess of metal and human tragedy. Clarkson lay dazed beside the binnacle housing the ships compass. Peter Hicks was dead, his shocked, staring eyes peering upwards and unseeing. The helmsman, yeoman, and all but one other man on the bridge had also perished. A hand came to rest on Clarkson's arm.

"Come on, sir, please. Let me help you."

"Is that you, Knox?" Clarkson asked breathlessly, the wind having been knocked from him by his fall against the binnacle.

"Aye sir, it is. Let's get you out of 'ere, eh? Don't seem too 'ealthy to me up 'ere any more," said the ever smiling Leading Seaman.

"You're a bloody sight for sore eyes, Knox, that's what you are. What about the others?"

"Dead sir, sorry to 'ave to report. Mr 'icks is over there and poor Mr. Bailey copped it too, and 'urst and the others."

Clarkson tried to focus his sight on the devastation on the bridge. Sure enough, the body of the young, depressed navigator lay slumped in one corner, his head cleanly taken off by a shard of flying metal. The rest of the bridge crew lay dead around him and he felt the urgency in Charlie Knox's words.

"Sir, we need to get out of 'ere. She'll go under any minute."

Another voice seemed to appear from nowhere.

"He's right sir. Come on, let me help you get him to his feet, Knox," said Chief Petty Officer Nobby Clark.

"Chief," Clarkson gasped the word, "I might have known you'd turn up too."

Clark smiled at his captain, but looked with grief as he turned to Charlie Knox. The two men saw the blood as Clarkson coughed. Knox gently opened the captain's blood-soaked duffel coat and the two men saw the wound. A large piece of shrapnel had penetrated Clarkson's left lung and stuck out grotesquely from his torn and shattered body. Clark and Knox knew enough to realise that attempting to remove it would only hasten their captain's death.

Clarkson seemed to know what was in their minds, and through his pain, and through gritted teeth he gave his last order to the two men.

"Leave me," he gasped. "Try and save yourselves."

Knox looked at Clark and pulled him to one side.

"I ain't leavin' 'im, Chiefy. 'E's a good man, and I can't leave 'im to die alone."

"You're a good man too, Charlie Knox," said the C.P.O. "We'll stay together, eh lad?"

Still smiling, Charlie Knox just nodded and turned back to his skipper. He eased himself onto the deck of the shattered bridge, gently placed an arm round Giles Clarkson and placed the captain's head on his own shoulder. Chief Petty Officer Nobby Clark took up a position on the other side and took the captain's hand in his own. Only then did Knox see that the Chief's left hand was missing, the end of his arm wrapped in an assortment of rags and pieces of other unknown materials. Blood dripped slowly through the makeshift dressing.

"Caught a bit of a packet yourself, eh Chiefy?" he said, not needing an answer, though Clark smiled back at him and replied,

"Anyone ever tell you you've got a great talent for stating the bleedin' obvious, Charlie boy?"

"Oh yeah, me Mum says that all the time, she does."

At that moment, for the first time since he'd known him, Nobby Clark saw the smile disappear from the face of Charlie Knox, only for a second, as he realised he wouldn't be seeing his mother again, and then it was back.

"We'll be alright though. We'll go together, eh Chiefy?"

Clark nodded, astounded at the cool bravery and stoicism of young Charlie Knox.

Clarkson looked up at the two men, and tried to smile at them.

"You're both bloody fools, you know that don't you? Stupid, idiotic, insubordinate bloody fools, and the two bravest men I've ever known. Thank you, thank you both"

"Don't mention it, Skipper," said Knox, smiling benignly at Clarkson, as the captain gripped Clark's hand in one final gesture of thanks, and his head lolled to one side on Knox's shoulder.

The two men looked at one another, no words necessary as they gently lowered Clarkson's lifeless body to the deck.

"What now then, Chiefy?" asked Knox.

"Can't do much, can we, Charlie?" Clark replied, supporting his wounded arm with the other as he looked at the devastation around him.

An ominous rumbling sound emanated from the bowels of the *Norwich* as the ship began to slide beneath the waves. Almost broken in two, but with her keel remaining intact enough to hold the bow and stern sections together.

"Does it 'urt much?" said Knox, indicating Clark's hand.

"Not for much longer, Charlie," Clark replied with a wry smile. The *Norwich* lurched suddenly as her forward compartments flooded beyond the point of no return and as she slipped below the waves,

Nobby Clark held tightly onto the arm of young Charlie Knox and said, "Been nice knowing you, Charlie Knox"

"Same here, Chiefy," Charlie replied, and the young man put an

arm round the Chief Petty Officer, and smiled.

* * *

"What was that?" Engel said as the sound of the explosion filtered down through the waves to reach the *U966*.

"Sounded like our hunter blew herself up."

"But what, how?"

"I don't know, Heini. Maybe another U-Boat found her, perhaps she hit a mine, or her boilers exploded. I don't know."

"But there are no minefields in this area, surely?"

"Agreed, but maybe it was a drifting mine, broken loose from one of the Britishers' own minefields."

"So, what do we do?"

"We wait, Heini. We need to be sure there are no other warships in the area."

"But there may be men in the water," Engel said, his humanity for fellow sailors in trouble taking over."

"I'm sorry," said Ritter. "Our mission comes first. We must remain unseen and unknown."

Engel nodded his understanding.

Unfortunately for the men of *U966*, they couldn't know that the *Norwich* was now sinking fast, and heading straight for the position on the sea bed where the submarine lay in hiding.

As the crew of *U966* held their breath, wondering what Ritter would do next, none of them, Ritter included, could have known that the *Norwich*, her descent slowed by the waters of the Channel, was now headed inexorably for the stern section of the submarine. The sinking corvette now appeared to twist in a macabre death spiral as the current played with her dying shell.

For a few seconds, her spiralling motion made it appear as though she would narrowly miss the U-Boat but then, in a disastrous and cruel twist of fate the current tugged her back towards the submarine. Still, there was a chance of a narrow miss and the *Norwich's* stern settled on the sea bed, less than ten yards from where *U966* sat helplessly, unknowing. The stern quickly dug itself into the soft sea bed at an angle of about 45 degrees, leaving the bow section pointing up towards the surface, like an accusing finger. What remained of the ship's funnel now collapsed towards the stern and the sound as it was torn from its mounting by its weight and the action of the current transferred itself to the interior of *U966*, and a tremor of fear spread throughout the still and silent submarine.

"What the hell's happening out there?" Engel asked as he looked at Ritter, more in hope than expectation of a logical reply.

Ritter however, had a very good idea of what was taking place just yards from his boat.

"Sounds to me as if the warship just hit bottom quite close to us, Heini. That sound we heard was probably her funnel being torn from its mooring points."

"Bloody hell, Max, that was fucking close then. It must be our lucky day."

"I think you're right, Heini. It's time we weren't here, my friend. Let's get the hell out of here while we can."

"What if there are any other ships up there?" Engel asked.

"That's a chance we have to take," Ritter said, and a shudder ran through his body, a premonition, a warning, quite what it was he couldn't say. Pulling himself together, he grabbed the microphone that hung from the control room ceiling.

"This is the captain speaking. I know you're all wondering what's been happening. All I can tell you is that we encountered a British corvette which was making an attack run on us when it suddenly exploded after releasing a single spread of depth charges which failed to do any real damage. I do not know why. The loud noise we heard was the ship as it struck the sea bed not far from us. We appear to have had a narrow escape. We will now prepare to get under way and continue our mission. That is all."

Unfortunately for Ritter and his crew, the *Norwich* now began to move again as the bow section began to settle in a downward motion that saw the first twenty feet of the corvette's keel come to rest with a grinding sound across the stern section of *U966*. In a few horrendous seconds, the U-Boat found itself trapped, pinned to the sea floor by the weight of the *Norwich*. Somehow, the submarine's pressure hull withstood the impact. Instead of imploding and killing all on board, instead the deck buckled where the *Norwich* impacted upon it, and various leaks sprang around the rear compartments, but *U966* stood firm.

Sadly, Ritter, Engel and all those on board would soon realise that the initial reprieve would turn into something far worse than instant death. Pinned to the sea bed, the submarine was now incapable of movement, despite Ritter ordering full ahead, and then full astern, all in vain. Max knew that *U966* had become his tomb, and that of his crew. He knew the air in the boat would gradually grow fouler and fouler as they breathed in what remained of their good air and that slowly and inexorably, he and his crew would die a slow and agonising death by suffocation.

He made his grin announcement to the crew, keeping nothing from them. He felt it fair they should know the truth, enabling them to make their peace with whatever God some of them may follow.

"Shit, shit, shit," Joseph Ziegler had said to his young protégé Karl Meister as the news sank in to everyone's minds.

"Joseph? What is it?"

"Oh, nothing, young Meister. It's just that I always wanted to die in a Berlin brothel from a heart attack, lying on top of a buxom whore, not in this stinking rat trap of a sardine can."

Heinz Muller, the submarine's engineering officer took a tour around the engine room, stroking and polishing his beloved engines. Finally satisfied that all was as it should be, Muller sat down on the little stool that the crew had always called his perch, closed his eyes, and fell asleep. He would not wake up again.

Young Willi Becker succumbed early to the effects of oxygen deprivation. Ritter was glad, for the simple reason he had seen the white faced fear and panic in the young man's eyes. It was good, thought Ritter that Willi hadn't suffered for long.

As the hours passed, some of the men spent what time they had left praying, others slumped on their bunks looking at photographs of wives, sweethearts, children until the pictures blurred before their eyes, eventually slipping from their lifeless fingers.

Heini Engel stayed close to his captain, his hero, right to the very end. Both men felt the onset of that final unconsciousness around the same time, and somehow, found enough strength to reach out to each other and shake hands. Max Ritter leaned back against a bulkhead, sighed once, and everything turned black. Heini Engel lasted only seconds longer, his last thoughts being of Ritter's promise to take him to Berlin after the war, sad it would never happen. Then he too was gone.

Soon, all was quiet aboard *U966*. The only occasional sounds were those of the metal of her hull as it groaned against the pressure exerted by the warship nestled on her stern. No distress signal had been sent from the submarine, nor from the corvette, that had blown up before her radio had sent the report of the engagement with the u-boat. Together with their crews and Hitler's mystery cargo, *H.M.S Norwich* and

U966 finally settled deeper into the mud of the sea bed, lost and forgotten, missing, position unknown to the Admiralty or the Kriegsmarine.

Chapter 23

Hands Across the Sea

Detective Constable Paul Ferris was happily typing search instructions into his computer when D.C.I. Agostini walked in to the squad room. The Chief Inspector placed a hand on Ferris's shoulder and the D.C almost jumped out of his skin.

"Wow, sorry about that, Ferris," the boss said with a smile. "You were miles away there, lost in your work I'm pleased to see."

Relaxing slightly, Ferris stood up as he replied.

"I was, sir. It can really pull you in once you get started searching the internet for information. I'm finding some very interesting stuff about Aegis, but nothing specifically illegal so far."

"I see, but it sounds as though you suspect there could be something there if you dig deeper, am I correct?"

"You are indeed, sir. I just get the feeling that they're too good to be true."

As Agostini was about to ask Ferris why he felt that way the phone on Ferris's desk rang.

"Excuse me a moment, sir," he said as Agostini nodded.

Ferris listened for a few second and then replied to the desk sergeant who'd called his extension, "Can you get someone to bring him up please Sarge? I'm with D.C.I. Agostini at present."

Replacing the phone on its cradle, he turned to the Chief Inspector.

"You might want to stay for a few minutes sir. Could be something interesting."

"Really?"

"Yes sir, Sergeant Cross on the front desk is sending Jerome Decker the third up. It seems Aaron Decker's father has something to tell us. As D.I. Ross and Sergeant Drake are away, you may want to hear what he says first hand."

"Interesting, and yes, Ferris, I'd love to hear what he has to say."

Two minutes later, Decker was shown into the squad room by a young woman in plain clothes, and Ferris greeted the C.I.A. man and introduced him to Agostini.

"Good to meet you, Detective Chief Inspector," said Decker as the two men shook hands."

"I believe you have some information for us Mr. Decker," Agostini wasted no time in saying.

"Yes, I do. Detective Inspector Ross asked me to use, shall we say, my connections to look a little more into Aegis from the U.S end and see if I could find anything that might be helpful to you. In short I asked one of our analysts to do some serious infiltration of the company without them being aware of it."

"You hacked them," Ferris said immediately.

"You said that, Mr. Ferris, not me," Decker smiled at the D.C.

"So, what did your analyst find, Mr. Decker?" Agostini asked.

"Okay, well there's something odd about the way the company is set up in some ways. No disrespect, Mr. Ferris, I know you're very good at what you do, but our people knew what to look for, whereas you're shooting pretty much in the dark."

"I don't mind if it helps the case," Ferris replied.

"So, the thing we've discovered is that the personnel Aegis employ varies greatly depending on where they're employed. We found that wherever they are involved in instances of underwater archaeology around any historic location, the head of the local operation is in fact a specialist in marine salvage. I can assure you that is not normal. That is the case with every one of Aegis's operations around Europe and in the Far East, Chief Inspector. So the immediate question that springs to mind is why they need a salvage expert in charge of what are supposed to be either historical or environmental investigations?"

"Because," Agostini surmised, "Aegis, or someone high up on their payroll, is plundering historical sites and lining their own pockets."

"That's exactly what my people think, Chief Inspector," Decker replied.

Both Ferris and Agostini could tell that Decker was now acting not as the bereaved father of young Aaron, but as a senior operative of the Central Intelligence Agency. There was a hint of steel in his voice, a determination to help them find out just what was going on within the Aegis operation on a worldwide basis.

"But how can they be getting away with this under the noses of the top people at Aegis?" Ferris asked, quite logically.

"Let's just say it depends how high up in the company this goes, Detective Ferris," Decker replied.

"A good point," Agostini agreed, and then introduced a note of caution to the conversation.

"Mr. Decker, we really appreciate you calling on your...professional resources to help us, but are you sure this isn't going to cause problems with your superiors, using C.I.A. resources to carry out these checks and passing information to us?"

"Chief Inspector. My son has been murdered and sure as hell, I want his killers brought to justice. The C.I.A's remit is to protect U.S. interests abroad. If an American company such as Aegis is carrying out clandestine operations to desecrate and or steal national treasures or valuable items belonging to friendly nations then it's totally within our purview

247

to investigate. Further, if they are carrying out such actions against nations not overly friendly to Washington, it could lead to an international incident if discovered."

"Right," said Agostini. "So, is there any way to find out if any of the executives at Aegis might be dirty?"

"Bank accounts," said Ferris before Decker could reply. "If we could ascertain whether any of the people at the top have suddenly become richer than they should be, according to their status and salary, we might be on to something."

"Listen," said Decker. "Things are a little different in the States. Yes, it's possible someone might have a grossly inflated bank balance, but that would be too easy for the authorities to track. We have strict rules at home governing the amounts of money that can be paid into or withdrawn from domestic accounts. As it happens, I have a few friends at the F.B.I. who might help us look into the finances of the Aegis executives, but it's highly likely, if there are very large sums involved that the money they're making will be squirreled away in an offshore bank account, maybe in the Caymans or even in Switzerland. That would be almost impossible to trace."

"Lifestyle," Agostini said.

"Eh?" asked Decker.

"Lifestyle," the D.C.I. repeated. "If we have one or more bad guys at Aegis in the States, it's likely they are living an inflated lifestyle compared with the time before they started all this. Maybe a house they shouldn't really be able to afford, new cars for the kids, who knows?"

"Yes, I see what you mean," Decker agreed. "Looks like I need to speak with my friends at the Federal building."

"We appreciate this, Mr. Decker, and you may wish to start with a man named Francis Kelly, who spoke to Klaus Haller when he phoned Aegis in the States last year. Haller told us the man seemed evasive in his replies to his questions." said Agostini. "Meanwhile, I'll make sure D.I. Ross knows what's going on at our end when I speak with him later."

"Do you have any idea if he's made any progress on the coast yet?" Decker asked.

"He's meeting with representatives from the Royal Navy and the Coast Guard as we speak. I'm hoping for a report from him later this afternoon."

"He seems a good man, your D.I. Ross," Decker said before taking his leave of the Chief Inspector and D.C. Ferris.

"One of the best, Mr Decker, one of the best," Agostini agreed.

After Decker had departed, Agostini stood beside Ferris's desk for a minute, and then had an idea.

"Ferris, I want you to try and find out as much as you can about the man who heads up the Aegis facility in Falmouth, his name according to Haller is William Evans. It's all very well thinking as we now do that there's a worldwide web of corruption emanating from somewhere within Aegis, but it's here in England that we're going to find young Aaron

Decker's killer or killers. If we can find something we can use to put pressure on the local head of the operation, you're the man to find it."

"Thank you for the confidence sir. I'll do what I can."

"Good man. It looks as if the Aegis thing is a large multi-pronged operation, like a many-headed Medusa. If we can find a way to cut off the head of the local snake-in-charge, we might actually discover how to take them all down."

"Wow, that would be bloody impressive, sir."

"Wouldn't it just, Ferris?" Agostini smiled and rubbed his hands together in anticipation. "Maybe we can teach the highly vaunted C.I.A. a thing or two eh?"

"Maybe we can, sir. I'll get right to it."

"Good man. And Ferris?"

"Sir?"

"This is between you and me at present, and D.I. Ross when I speak to him, got it? Let him be the one to tell the rest of the team what we're doing."

"Sure, sir. Mum's the word."

"The fewer people who know we're investigating Aegis, the less chance there is that they'll find out we're on to them, understood?"

"Of course sir. I understand."

"D.I. Ross will tell the others what we're up to, I'm sure, but I mean it, Ferris, keep your search as low-key as possible but leave no stone unturned, right?"

"Right sir," Ferris agreed as Agostini left him to peer at his computer screen as he began to type in a set of new search parameters.

Chapter 24

Holmes and Watson?

Andy Ross had to admit to being impressed with the level of cooperation he was receiving from the Royal Navy and the Coast Guard. His next step was to arrange liaison with the Devon and Cornwall Police. Thanks to D.C.I. Agostini, the local force had been made aware that he and Drake were 'on their patch' and were expecting his call. He'd delayed contacting them until he'd spoken with the Navy and Coast Guard representatives. Now he was sure of their support he felt he could move to involve the locals. Agostini had furnished him with the name of the local Detective Inspector who'd been tasked with working with him and he placed a call to the local station and was put through to D.I. Brian Jones.

"Jones here. I've been expecting your call, D.I. Ross."

"It's Andy," Ross replied. "Thanks for agreeing to be my chaperone while I'm here."

"My pleasure, Andy. I'm Brian. From what your boss told my boss, and he told me, it sounds as if you have something quite interesting on your hands."

"That's one way to put it," said Ross. "Don't mind me saying this, but I was expecting to be working with a D.I. Pascoe."

"Sudden change of plan, Andy. Tommy Pascoe fell downstairs at home and broke his leg yesterday. He's in hospital, well and truly plastered at present, so you're stuck with me, I'm afraid."

"I'm sure you're every bit as good at your job Brian. I'm glad to have the chance to work with you."

"Same here," Jones replied. "Let's catch some bad guys eh?"

* * *

Two hours later, Ross and Drake walked into the small office occupied by D.I. Brian Jones at Falmouth Police Station. The pair were greeted cordially by Jones who introduced them to his own assistant, Sergeant Carole St. Clair. Drake was delighted to have the opportunity to work with another woman, and St. Clair seemed equally pleased when she also realised there'd be another woman on the team.

"So, how exactly can we help?" Jones asked, after the foursome had settled themselves in chairs around his desk, supplied with steaming mugs of coffee by a young constable who closed the door quietly on his way out.

"I'm not entirely sure, and that's being honest," Ross replied. "I think we need your local knowledge more than anything. It wouldn't do for me and Sergeant Drake to go blundering around on your patch without having the foggiest notion where we are or where we're going."

"True," said Jones, "though it sounds like you need a pair of babysitters more than anything else."

"I doubt that, sir," Drake piped up. "We could be up against some very nasty characters here and your knowledge of the area and the people will be invaluable to us."

"Very true," Ross agreed, "and after I've filled you in fully with all we know, you might see that there could be a little danger along the way."

"Now you're talking," Jones clapped his hands together. "Isn't he Carole?" he asked his sergeant, rhetorically, as it was clear the D.I needed no reply.

"Of course sir," she replied anyway, then, "Sorry about my gaffer sir," she said to Ross. "He loves a bit of excitement now and then and sometimes lets his enthusiasm run away with him."

Jones laughed and Ross was pleased to see the D.I. and his sergeant appeared to enjoy a similar easy going relationship to him and Izzie.

"Been together long?" he asked.

"Afraid so," Jones smiled as he spoke. "I've had this one round my neck for three years now. Can't seem to get rid of her."

"Ha, more like you wouldn't know what to do without me," St Clair replied, grinning at her boss.

"Well, looks like we're in for a good time down here, Izzie," Ross said and Izzie Drake nodded in agreement.

Jones suddenly turned serious and said to St. Clair.

"Better tell our new friends here what we've found out so far, Carole."

"Right you are sir," she replied.

Carole St Clair was thirty, but looked younger, her short blonde hair and slim figure belying her quick mind and her black belt in judo, as many criminals had discovered to their cost over the years.

She lifted a pale brown folder from Jones's desk, opened it and began to read from a fact sheet she'd already prepared for the newcomers.

"Aegis International, as they're known round here are extremely secretive about their operations. The people who work there are, for the most part, brought in by the company either from their U.S operation of from other facilities around the world. Nothing wrong with that of course, but it had been thought they'd have given the local economy a boost by providing a number of jobs when they got the go-ahead to build their own docking facility close to the existing harbour. As far as we can tell, they only employ a small number of locals, mostly in low-grade jobs such as security guards, cooks for their staff dining room and a few cleaners. All of them are sworn to secrecy and will not reveal anything of what takes place at the facility, though from the jobs they do, I'd seriously doubt they'd know anything, anyway. The really odd thing is that the people Aegis has brought in never appear to socialise in the town. Aegis must have built an accommodation block or something on-site because none of their imported staff are ever seen in town, at the pubs or shops for example so it's assumed they live and work within the confines of the facility."

"That's more than a little strange," said Ross.

"That's what we thought too, Andy," Jones agreed. "There's something fishy about that place, and I'd love to know what it is they're trying to hide."

"Fishy? In Falmouth?" St Clair said, and laughter erupted between the pair again.

"You two are really corny, do you know that?" Ross said, joining in the momentary hilarity.

"Corn? Not in Falmouth, Andy," Jones quipped again, and this time, even Izzie Drake groaned.

"Okay, thanks," Ross said, trying to get back on track. "Joking aside, we really can't do much until we can get out to the wreck and see exactly what it was that young Aaron Decker was so fired up about."

"I understand the Navy and Coast Guard are willing to help you out on this one," said Jones.

"Yes, and we're going out on one of their ships tomorrow to the position Herr Haller gave us to see what all the fuss is about. I'd like you and Sergeant St Clair to join us."

"We can hardly refuse an offer like that, can we, Carole? A nice sea cruise and the wind in your hair. A fine day out if the weather holds, eh?"

"I'm not a very good sailor, sir, actually," Carole St Clair replied with a worried look on her face.

"Oh, I forgot. You get sea sick watching your rubber duck bobbing about in the bath don't you?"

"Ha, ha, very funny," she responded.

"You'll be fine, Carole," Izzie Drake leaped to her defence. "I'll get you some of those special anti-sea sickness pills on our way back to our hotel."

"Thanks," St Clair replied.

"Yeah, don't worry Carole. My daughter has some of those wrist bands that are supposed to counter motion sickness too. I'll bring 'em along in the morning," Jones said, more serious now.

"Hope they work," said St Clair.

"I'm sure they will," said Drake, feeling a little sorry for her Cornish counterpart.

* * *

Following a good night's sleep, preceded by another splendid meal provided by the redoubtable Hope Severn, Ross and Drake set off at a brisk walk, intending to time their arrival for 9 a.m. the time agreed for them to meet up with Captain Prendergast, Coast Guard George Baldacre and the two Falmouth detectives. Thankfully for the pair, most of the walk was downhill as the distance turned out to be a little further than they anticipated.

As they arrived at Falmouth's picturesque harbour, Ross and Drake could hardly believe their eyes as they easily recognised their ride for the morning.

When Anthony Prendergast had told them the Royal Navy would be providing a ship to ferry them out to the wreck location, Andy Ross had expected a small launch or maybe something the size of a tug boat at most. Instead, tied up to the harbour wall, the two detectives saw a sleek, grey warship, which Prendergast would soon explain was in fact *H.M.S. Wyvern*, one of the Royal Navy's latest submarine hunting frigates.

"Impressive, isn't she?"

Prendergast's voice had taken the pair by surprise as he arrived from their rear, having walked across from the dockmaster's office.

"I should say so," Ross exclaimed. "I was expecting something a little…erm…smaller."

Prendergast laughed.

"I'm sorry if you're disappointed, Andy," he said, grinning.

"Oh, no, I didn't mean…"

"I know, I know, just pulling your leg," said the retired naval officer.

Within minutes, they were joined by George Baldacre, D.I Brian Jones and Sergeant Carole St Clair, the latter looking distinctly nervous as she looked up at the ship that appeared to tower above them.

"Well, ladies and gentlemen, shall we go aboard?"

Prendergast led them up the gangway, where they were met by a pair of Royal Marines who'd been expecting their arrival, and who, having examined their credentials, escorted them to the bridge where a tall, superbly groomed officer, with razor sharp creases in his uniform turned at the sound of their arrival.

"Welcome aboard the *Wyvern*, ladies and gentlemen," said Captain Charles Howell, commanding officer of the frigate.

Prendergast shook hands with the captain and introduced his companions, and then communicated Ross's surprise at the frigate being assigned to this particular mission. Howell smiled and then replied.

"Never let it be said that the Royal Navy ever gives up on its own, Detective Inspector. If one of our corvettes from World War Two is lying on the seabed, lost since the forties, it's time we found her and gave her crew the respect they deserve. The *Wyvern* is by design a submarine hunter, but that also makes her perfect for this job. We have the latest state-of-the-art technology on board that will help us in an underwater search. I won't bore you with the technical names or descriptions of everything we can put to use in the search but believe me, if there is a wreck down there, we will find it, that I can promise you."

"We're grateful, Captain," said Ross, "though a little surprised that the Navy has sent such a magnificent ship to assist us."

Charles Howell smiled as he replied, "Inspector, we go where their Lordships of the Admiralty send us, and you're in our backyard really, us being based at Portsmouth. Of course, it also helps that we're the best equipped vessel in the area to look for and find one of our own ships, even if it has been missing for over half a century. Now, let me introduce you to Lieutenant Ridley."

The tall figure who until now had remained standing ramrod-straight behind Howell now stepped forward, his outstretched hand reaching for Ross, who took it and winced at the sheer power he felt in a quick handshake with the lieutenant.

"Pleased to meet you, Inspector Ross," said the man. "I'm Gareth Ridley, Royal Marines."

Howell spoke again.

"Lieutenant Ridley and a team of twelve Royal Marines will be accompanying us on our little trip, Inspector Ross, just to ensure we have added security in case your killers come calling when they find we're diving on the wreck site."

"I'm delighted you're with us," Ross said to Ridley, who bowed graciously in the direction of Sergeants Izzie Drake and Carole St Clair.

"You two ladies must be Drake and St Clair," he said politely, a typical officer and gentleman, Ross surmised, but not one he'd care to take on in a fist fight, if his handshake was anything to go by.

Both sergeants smiled back at Ridley and D.I. Brian Jones politely coughed in the background and stepped forward.

"D.I. Brian Jones, Lieutenant," he said, introducing himself and offering his hand.

"Of course, my apologies," said Ridley as he almost mashed Jones's fingers to a friendly pulp.

"I don't know about the rest of you, but I find all this formality rather grim with so many of you police officers around," Howell interjected.

"I'm Charles, and Gareth won't mind you using his name so I suggest we dispense with all this Detective Inspector this, and Detective Inspector that, and the same for the two sergeants as well if that's agreeable."

"It would certainly save some time and breath," Ross smiled. "I'm Andy, Sergeant Drake is Izzie, and our friends from Falmouth are Brian and Carole."

"Righty-o," said Charles Howell, "glad we've sorted that out. We must of course maintain our ranks in front of the men, I hope you understand but for now, if you will show our friends to the wardroom, Lieutenant, I have work to do. I want to be under way in less than an hour."

Ross thanked Captain Howell and allowed himself and the others to be led from the bridge by the strapping marine officer, who escorted them to the wardroom or 'officers mess' of the ship, where tea and coffee was supplied along with a selection of biscuits, all very civilised and exactly as Ross imagined it would have been in those rare off-duty moments for the officers of the corvette they were seeking in those long ago, dark days of World War Two, before they and their ship met with their as yet unknown fate.

Carole St Clair thought the sea-sickness pills she'd taken before boarding the *Wyvern* must have worked. She felt okay, so far, though she soon realised the gentle motion of the ship at anchor would be totally different to the way the ship would behave once they left harbour and were exposed to the waves that would be waiting for them in the Channel. Her right hand subconsciously reached across and touched her left wrist, checking the 'sea band; was in place. Satisfied, she repeated the procedure with the other hand, making sure the so-called 'magic,' magnetic motion sickness bracelets were in the correct places on her wrists.

Izzie Drake saw her and reached a hand out and touched St Clair on the arm.

"You'll be fine, Carole. I heard the Captain say it's like a millpond out there today."

"Yes, but he probably feels at home in a force ten gale. What he calls a millpond might be pretty rough seas for someone like me."

"I say, er...Carole," Ridley interrupted. "I couldn't help overhearing your conversation. Am I correct in assuming you suffer from a touch of the old *mal de mere*?"

"I'm afraid so," St Clair replied a little shamefacedly.

"Not to worry," Ridley smiled and shouted for the wardroom steward who magically appeared as if from nowhere at his side.

"The sergeant here gets queasy at sea. Fix her up with a 'special' would you, there's a good chap?"

"Of course, sir. Won't take long, miss, er, sorry, Sergeant," the steward replied.

In reply to St Clair's puzzled look, Ridley explained, "Believe it or not, even seasoned sailors can often feel a bit under the weather at sea. There isn't a wardroom steward in the Navy who doesn't have a guaranteed antidote for the old wobbly tummy."

"I see," said Carole St Clair. "Thank you."

"Don't thank me, thank Leading Seaman Bowles. Ah, here he comes," said Ridley as the steward appeared, carrying a mug of something that resembled a mixture of ground charcoal and diesel fuel.

"Get that down you, Sergeant," he grinned and in response to her worried look, he went on, "and don't worry, it tastes better than it looks, honest."

It did, much to St Clair's relief.

"Mmm, not bad," she said. "Do I detect a touch of honey in there?"

"Indeed you do," Bowles smiled at her, "but don't ask what else is in it. That's top secret that is."

"He wouldn't reveal his secret recipe under torture, Carole," Ridley said, so straight-faced she actually believed him.

Very soon, there was a distinct feeling of anticipation in the air as they heard the sounds of running feet, the shouting of orders and felt a distinct increase in vibration from the deck, the engines increasing in the engines' revolutions as the *Wyvern* cast off and began to manoeuvre her way out of the harbour towards the open sea.

"Perhaps we should join the skipper on the bridge now," Ridley suggested. "He asked me to escort you back up there once we'd cleared our moorings."

"Right, thanks," Ross replied and he and the others followed the marine officer as he led them back to the

bridge. In contrast to their earlier visit, the bridge of
H.M.S Wyvern was now a hive of activity.

Ross and Jones in particular found themselves
fascinated by the machinery, if it could be so described, that they'd failed to notice on their earlier visit. Unlike the controls of wartime warships
they'd probably both seen in old action movies, the
Wyvern's bridge was clean and uncluttered, with
computer screens and controls arranged in banks at
strategic points around the bridge. Even the steer-
ing could be controlled by computer although there
was a wheel, which Ross somehow found comforting, though it was gleaming steel and smaller than
the multi-pronged wooden ones he'd seen in those
old films.

"Welcome back," said Howell as he acknowledged
their return. "This is my first officer, Mike Sutherland," he said as he introduced them to his second-in-
command. "Mike will be in overall command of the
dive when we reach the wreck site. We'll be sending down two ship's divers, plus two of the marines
who are also qualified to work in the submersibles we
carry. Let me explain, 'ship's divers' are specifically
trained to carry out any and all activities relating to
underwater work. They are specialists and one will
accompany each marine as they take a first look at
the wreck you've located. Once we know what we're
dealing with down there we can formulate a plan of
action. I'm assuming you'll want to know as much as
possible about the corvette and the submarine that

you say is buried beneath her, and of course, there was some mention of a body?"

"Yes, a frogman, or at least a man n a wetsuit as far as we could make out," said Ross, who pulled a copy of the underwater photograph taken by Aaron Decker from his inside jacket pocket and handed it to Sutherland.

"Hmm, yes, I see. Under normal circumstances, a body would be carried away for miles by the current but it seems this poor chap was trapped, possibly by a cable or something similar,"

"Or maybe his killer anchored him to the wreck," Drake suggested, "maybe hoping he'd just decompose and disappear."

"He didn't know a lot then, did he?" said Ridley. "The wetsuit would afford a degree of protection against decomposition and the body would slowly break down within the suit but certainly wouldn't disappear. After all the bloody suit's made of neoprene and rubber," he went on.

"You seem well versed in such things, Gareth," Brian Jones said.

"I've dealt with a few recoveries of bodies from the sea," Ridley replied. "One gets used to the effects of the ocean on the human body after a few of those, I can tell you."

"Yes, Unfortunately, I suppose you do," said the Falmouth Detective.

Clearing the breakwater, *H.M.S Wyvern* headed out into the English Channel and Carole St Clair stood staring straight ahead through the bridge viewscreen, as the gently rolling waves lifted the sharp prow of the ship and then just as gently lowered it into its equally placid troughs. Amazingly, she felt fine, but deferred from moving from her position or looking around for fear the movement might bring on a bout of sea-sickness.

A voice spoke from beside her.

"How are you holding up, Carole?"

It was Gareth Ridley.

"Oh, fine so far, thank you. Your steward seems to know what he's doing with that concoction of his."

"I'm pleased to hear it. By the way, he's not 'my' steward. I don't usually serve aboard the *Wyvern*. I only met him when I came aboard last night."

"But than how did you know he could...?

"I told you in the wardroom. Every wardroom steward worth his salt has a recipe for something similar. It wouldn't do for the ordinary seamen to see one of their officers looking green around the gills with sea-sickness, so they all seem to come up with a sure-fire cure to keep their officers on their feet and fully operational."

"Well, I'm grateful to him, anyway," St Clair replied. "What was his name again?"

"Bowles, Leading Seaman Bowles."

"Well, I hope I get the chance to thank him before we leave the ship."

"I'm sure you'll get the opportunity," Ridley said, smiling at the attractive sergeant.

Izzie Drake couldn't help but notice the attention the handsome marine lieutenant was paying to the attractive Cornish detective and smiled to herself, suspecting a budding romance being born before her eyes.

For now though, they were heading further away from Falmouth with each passing minute and she moved to stand beside Andy Ross as they watched with interest as the bridge crew managed the running of the ship.

Ross felt comforted by the sight of the gun mounted on the deck ahead of the bridge. Though equipped with only one barrel as opposed to those massive three barrelled turrets he remembered from the battleships in the movies, this was a modern, computer controlled weapon that packed a deadly punch. No one would stand in their way as they explored the wreck, of that he was sure. Whatever fate had befallen the poor soul who remained floating above the wreck, nothing similar would happen today.

* * *

Ninety minutes later, the deck of the *Wyvern* was a veritable hive of activity as her crew prepared the equipment necessary for the forthcoming exploration of the sea bed. An air of quiet expectancy pervaded the ship, no more so than on the bridge, where Ross and the other police officers stood watching the myriad activities taking place around them, whilst feeling a little helpless not to be directly involved in this stage of the operation.

Together, they watched as the submersible being used for the dive was made ready for sea. Bright yellow, with twin Perspex bubbles that formed the viewing windows for the two man crew, the strange-looking craft possessed a series of mechanical 'arms' with various configurations at the end that could be used for underwater retrieval purposes, and what appeared to be powerful headlights mounted, front and rear, that would illuminate the depths around the craft.

Two men appeared on the bridge, and reported first to Captain Howell. They were the two man crew of the submersible, Lieutenant Dave Cox, and Chief Petty Officer Bob Lomax, affectionately known to the rest of the *Wyvern's* crew as *The X-Men* due to the matching letters at the end of their surnames.

"All ready, chaps?" Howell asked the pair.

"We are, sir," Cox replied for them both. "Any last instructions?"

"Better ask Detective Inspector Ross, Lieutenant. He might have something to add to your earlier briefing."

"Sir?" Cox asked, looking at Ross.

"I've nothing to add, Lieutenant Cox," Ross said. "Please remember that as far as we, that is the police are concerned, it's important to try and identify that body. So again, please do the best you can to recover it intact, if you can."

Cox snapped a quick salute at Ross.

"You can count on us sir, don't you worry."

"Better be on your way then," Howell said as the pair quickly left the bridge and made their way to their craft.

Five minutes later, the deck crew had lowered the submersible to the sea's surface and amid a large stream of bubbles, it slowly disappeared beneath the waves.

"It's a weird looking vehicle," Izzie Drake commented as she watched it dive under the waves.

"Looks can be deceptive, Sergeant," Howell replied. "It's American designed but built over here under licence. It can go where divers can't, can lift a payload ten times its own weight, and yet, in the right hands, its arms can pick up a seashell from the ocean bed without crushing it. If anyone can find anything to help you in your investigation, it's Cox and Lomax, and the *Watson*."

"Watson?" Brian Jones asked.

"Ah yes," Howell replied. "As I told you earlier, we have two submersibles on board and rather than refer to them by their identification numbers, which seemed a tad impersonal, the dive crews christened them *Holmes* and *Watson*. Seemed appropriate really, as they are used mostly for underwater investigative purposes."

"Good choice of names, Captain," the Cornish D.I. answered, approvingly.

"How long till they reach the wreck, Captain?" Carole St Clair asked, all her earlier seasickness having disappeared completely.

"Not long," said Lieutenant Commander Mike Sutherland, the *Wyvern's* first officer who was tracking the submersible's dive on a computer screen off to one side of the bridge. "I reckon she'll reach the bottom in another minute or so."

Sure enough, the cameras onboard the submersible were soon enabling them to see the sea bed. Cox and Lomax had stated that for safety's sake they would aim to arrive at the bottom some thirty yards or so west of the wreckage, then take a slow look around to ascertain there were no visible impediments to a close inspection of the wreck.

Ross, Drake and the two Falmouth police officers all gathered around the viewing monitor, watched in total fascination for the next twenty minutes as Cox and Lomax carried out their initial survey of the wreck. Next they swung the *Watson* round to approach the gently swaying body of the frogman.

Cox's voice came over the radio, loud and clear.

"It's a body alright, confirmed. Tell the inspector it definitely looks like murder. We're going in closer but we can see from here the body is attached to the wreck with a length of chain, and it's evident the poor bastard's air hose was cut."

Ross merely nodded. He could think of nothing to say for a moment, his thoughts focused on the horrible death the victim had endured. He'd drowned, his air piece cut though and his leg chained to the wreck, left to struggle as his air ran out and his lungs filled with seawater.

It was Izzie Drake who spoke first.

"Are you able to release the body and bring it up, Lieutenant Cox?"

"Yes, we are," Cox replied from the submersible. "It's evident from here however that there won't be much left. What hasn't decomposed has been picked off by the fishes as far as we can see."

"Inside a wet-suit?" St Clair added.

"Yes, sergeant," Cox answered. "The wet suit might look intact in the photos you showed us but there are numerous tears and rips in it which would have let our finny friends in."

"Damn," said Ross at last. "I suppose that buggers up our chances of identifying the poor guy."

"Not necessarily," came the voice of C.P.O. Lomax, speaking for the first time since the submersible had arrived over the wreck. "It's possible, if he used his own equipment, that you can trace him through the serial numbers on his air tanks."

"We can?" Ross asked.

"Yes, Inspector," said Lomax, "believe me, it can be done."

"Thanks, Lomax," said Ross.

They all watched fascinated as Cox and Lomax gently manoeuvred *Watson*, and using the mechanical arms, carefully cut the floating body free and lowered it into a metal cradle at the side of the submersible, which was then covered with a metal lid to ensure the contents couldn't float away.

"Moving on to inspect the rest of the wreckage now," said Cox as *Watson* slowly moved up and over what would have been the forward deck of the corvette.

The next hour saw *Watson* cover every inch of the wreck, and then move on to the remains of the submarine trapped under what remained of the corvette's keel. In close up, through the submersible's cameras, those watching were left in no doubt that they were seeing the shattered remains of a second world war German U-boat.

Cox and Lomax kept up a steady stream of comments and observations, and Ross noticed a young rating standing close to the captain, making copious notes of the submersible crew's words. Marine Lieutenant, Gareth Ridley noticed Ross and Drake looking quizzically at one another and stepped across to explain.

"That seaman is what's known as a 'Ship's Writer' and is obviously qualified in shorthand. He's taking down every word they're saying and will transcribe it when they come to the surface so we'll have a full record of everything that's happened down there. Normally, we'd just have the recordings taken during a dive but the captain thought, as this is a police case, you'd want the equivalent of a written statement of everything that transpires down there."

"That's really helpful," said Ross. "I'll remember to thank Captain Howell later."

Ross could see that Howell was busily engaged in a lively conversation with Captain Prendergast. The retired captain had become extremely animated from the moment the submersible had begun transmitting pictures of the wreck to the *Wyvern*. As the man responsible for looking into the case of the sunken corvette on behalf of the Navy's historical branch, Prendergast was now in his element. More than once, Ross heard him mention the name *Norwich* and he felt reasonably sure that the ship down on the sea bed was indeed the one Prendergast had hypothesised it to be.

An hour after it had first sunk beneath the waves, the submersible *Watson* returned to the surface, and was soon retrieved from the sea, and secured on deck. The hatches opened and Cox and Lomax exited the craft, stretching their cramped limbs as their feet came to rest on the *Wyvern's* deck once more.

The two men looked up towards the bridge, Cox giving a thumbs-up signal to those watching their disembarkation from *Watson*. The deck crew was already at work extricating the frogman's remains from *Watson's* cradle. It would soon be undergoing an examination by the ship's senior medical officer.

Captain Howell turned to the watching band of police officers and coast guard officer, and said, "We'll give them a half-hour to change and get some refreshment and then we'll hold the debriefing. From what we've heard already, it should be very interesting."

Ross agreed, and at Howell's invitation, the party of visitors, accompanied by Lieutenant Ridley, left the bridge, went below to the wardroom and were served fresh coffee and hot croissants as they waited somewhat impatiently for the arrival of Cox and Lomax, when they would learn in full the results of their preliminary inspection of the wrecks on the sea bed.

Chapter 25

Plots and Plans

William Evans was not a happy man. As head of Aegis's UK facility, life had been good to him so far. His wife loved England, they had a beautiful house overlooking the sea, and his kids had not only settled well into the local school, but they actually preferred British TV to that at home. Okay, so the coffee was crap, but what the hell, you couldn't have everything. Ten minutes earlier however, news reached him of a disquieting nature following a knock on his office door.

The door had opened to admit Ryan Newton, Deputy Director of the facility.

"Hello Ryan, what can I do for you?" he'd asked as Newton walked into the office.

"You wanted to know what the Royal Navy were doing here, William?"

"You've found out?"

"Yes, it was easy enough. I just asked the dock superintendant, in a very casual manner as I took a walk along the quayside."

"Okay, okay, and what did the man tell you?"

"Apparently, one of the crew told him they were here to search for a World War Two warship that was reported missing but never found. Seems they have an idea it might have sunk somewhere in our vicinity."

"I see," Evans had answered. "Did this man tell the superintendant anything else?"

"Only that for some reason, a delegation of police officers and the coastguard were sailing with them."

"I see, well, thanks Ryan. I don't suppose they will be interfering with us if they're on a glorified salvage mission,"

"Just what I thought too," Newton had replied. "Will there be anything else?"

"No, thanks for coming in to let me know, Ryan. As you say, nothing to concern us."

As soon as Ryan Newton closed the door on his way out, Evans's face darkened and his bunched up fist thumped into his desk top, the resulting vibration making pens and pencils dance off the edge of the desk and fall clattering to the floor.

"Damn, damn, damn," Evans cursed to himself.

In point of fact, there was much for Evans to worry about, despite his outward calm in front of his deputy. As soon as he was sure he had total privacy, the director picked up his phone, pressed the number

9 to give himself an outside line and dialled a number that was answered on the third ring.

"Finch," was the one word reply as the recipient of the call picked up at the other end.

"It's me," said Evans, knowing the other man would immediately recognise his voice."

"What's wrong," the man named Finch asked, instantly sensing the tension in Evans's voice. "You do realise what time it is here, don't you? Do we have a problem?"

"Yes I do and yes, we may have," Evans replied. "The bloody Royal Navy has turned up with a bloody great frigate, or salvage tug, I don't know what they call it. Some damned police officers from Liverpool and a couple of locals are with them. They sailed from Falmouth this morning. Our contact says they're searching for a missing ship from the war years."

"And you think it's our ship, right?"

"Oh, come on Finch, what do you think? It's too much of a coincidence them turning up like this, especially with coppers from Liverpool. It can't be any other ship, can it? They must have pieced some of it together. I said it was a fucking mistake getting rid of that kid who was nosing around."

"So what do you think we should have done? He'd already got Knowles involved and that German historian who was nosing around last year could have been in league with the kid too for all we know. Maybe we should have done him as well."

"Don't say that, Finch. You know as well as I do that Haller was too high profile, a respected expert in his field. Another disappearance would definitely have drawn attention to us. As it is they could well be on to us now."

"And maybe they're not. Stop panicking until you know more. Okay, the kid might have said something to someone and they know there's a ship down there, but they can't know for sure that Aegis has anything to do with it, or with the death of Decker."

"But what about Knowles? Those stupid goons we paid to get rid of him left him chained to the bloody wreck, for God's sake. They'll probably find his body and then they really will have something to be suspicious about."

"After over a year? I doubt there's anything left down there by now. The fishes will have feasted on Mr. Knowles long ago, I'm sure."

"Listen, Finch, whatever you say, as far as I'm concerned the whole operation's at risk now. We've almost finished our work on the wreck site as it is, but we need at least two more dives to complete the salvage operation. If only Aaron Decker had backed off and taken the money we offered him, everything would have been okay."

"But he didn't, did he, Billy Boy? Now, we have to make the best of the current circumstances."

Evans hated it when Finch called him that name. His over - familiarity grated on Evans. Just who the hell did Finch think he was talking to? William Evans was no two-bit lackey, for Christ's sake.

"So what do you suggest we do?" he asked, doing his best to control his temper.

"We wait, Billy Boy, that's what we do. We wait until the Navy comes back to port and you use your contacts, or bribe some new ones, to find out just what they've found and more to the point what they intend to do next. Just remember, the police have no idea what they're looking for down there, and with a bit of luck, they never will. Call me again when you have something real to report, and for Christ's sake, remember the time, Billy Boy."

The line went dead before William Evans could say another word. He banged the phone down on its cradle, more incensed by Finch's use of the name 'Billy Boy' than anything else the man had said. He knew only too well that what Finch had said made sense, but he couldn't help but feel that things were slowly slipping out of control here on the south coast of England and wished he could be back in Greece, where things had run much more smoothly on his last 'exploration'.

Back in the States, the man known as Finch now made a phone call, this time to Francis Kelly.

"Mr. Kelly," he said as soon as the other man replied. "William Evans sounds as if he's on the verge of panic in England."

"That's not like Evans," said Kelly.

"He thinks the police are on to something. They've got the Royal Navy searching for the *Norwich* as we speak."

"Ah," said Kelly, "perhaps I was remiss in saying too much to that German, Haller, last year. I should never have told him we were searching for three wrecks that could be undesignated war graves. At the time, I thought it would deflect him from our operations if he believed we were carrying out legitimate and authorised work and that he would take it no further. Looks like I was wrong. Damn these people. Why can't the historians and the police keep their noses out of other people's business? Are we anywhere near completion in the English channel, Finch?"

"Yes, sir, we are. Evans estimated another two dives and we'd have everything we can possibly expect to lift from the submarine, but as you know, we have had to leave a respectable time between our dives on the wreck, just in case anyone gets suspicious, and now that the Royal Navy is on site we look like missing out on those last two dives. Looks like we're left holding a busted flush, Mr. Kelly."

"Sadly, Mr. Finch, I do believe you're right. It may be time to cut our losses as far as the U.K. is concerned, if you follow my meaning."

Finch simply nodded his head as he understood exactly what Kelly was referring to.

"No loose ends I take it, sir?"

"You've got it, Mr. Finch, no loose ends. Time for you to visit your old homeland I believe.

* * *

With the dive crew changed into fresh clothes and rejuvenated by mugs of hot coffee, Cox and Lomax now sat opposite the gathered assembly of police officers, plus Prendergast and Baldacre, in the *Wyvern's* wardroom.

With Captain Howell, and Lieutenant Commander Mike Sutherland seated either side of the submersible crew, and Gareth Ridley and two of his marines guarding the door, Lieutenant Cox was the first to speak after Charles Howell asked him to begin.

"Based on what we were told before we began the dive, first thing to report is that the ship down there is definitely a World War Two designed corvette, and we're pretty sure it is the ship suggested by Captain Prendergast, *H.M.S. Norwich*. Despite the ravages of time and ocean currents, it's quite incredible that so much of the ship is still in once piece, though that may have something to do with the fact she's not entirely buried into the sea bed.

C.P.O Lomax and I are in agreement that, unbelievable as it may sound, the *Norwich* appears to have sunk and then landed on top of the submarine, which must have been lying silently on the bottom as part of her captain's evasion tactics. Sadly, he failed."

Cox now motioned to Lomax, who rose and turned on the screen of the monitor that stood at the end of the table. Instantly, those round the table found themselves watching a re-run of the *Watson's* progress as she made her dive on the wreck, with Cox now commentating.

"We can see quite clearly the damage to her starboard side," Cox went on.

"Would you say she was sunk by a torpedo?" George Baldacre, the Coast Guard asked.

"I'd say no," C.P.O. Lomax joined in the conversation. "A torpedo would have penetrated the hull and the explosive damage would have displayed a different pattern, with a smaller initial entry 'wound 'if you like, and more internal damage as the warhead exploded and the blast wave moved through the interior of the compartment where it struck. If you look at the bloody great hole in her side, and the way the plates have been blown inwards, I'd make an educated guess that she struck a mine."

"But surely the Germans weren't able to lay mines in the English Channel during the war?" Ross commented.

"No, Andy, they didn't," Charles Howell replied, "but we did."

"You mean she blundered into one of our own minefields?"

"No, Andy, that I very much doubt, but there were plenty of occasions where mines broke adrift from their moorings after being laid and were known as 'floaters', simply bobbing around in the open sea waiting to catch any ship unwary enough to run into them."

"Oh God," said Izzie Drake. "That brings a whole new meaning to the phrase 'friendly fire."

"I guess it does," Mike Sutherland said. "A whole ship's crew, by all accounts, lost to one of our own mines."

"A bad show, Mike," Howell agreed. "So, carry on gentlemen," he gestured to Cox and Lomax, who had waited patiently as the others talked, Lomax having used a remote control to pause the view on the monitor. He now set it going again and Cox took up the commentary once more.

Watson is of course too big for us to effect an entry into the wreck but we did send the ROV, that's a Remotely Operated Underwater Vehicle for our new friends," he explained, "in to have a quick look. You've probably seen similar things before if you've ever watched *Titanic.*"

Ross and the others nodded in the affirmative as the small, bright yellow ROV appeared as it left the deck of the submersible and filled the viewer for a few seconds until it slowly entered the cavernous hole in the side of the *Norwich.*

"C.P.O. Lomax is piloting *Moriarty* in this sequence."

"You gave the ROV a name too?" Carole St. Clair asked with a hint of surprise.

"Of course," said Cox. "Makes it more fun, and gives the vehicle a touch of personality."

Carole St. Clair privately thought these Royal Navy types were definitely a classic case of boys and their toys, but kept her opinion to herself.

"So, here we go," said Lomax as the *Moriarty* moved into the dark interior of the *Norwich*, its path highlighted by a series of very powerful headlights mounted on the ROV.

The others watched in awe as the little yellow vehicle made its way very slowly into the dark abyss of the *Norwich's* long dead compartments. It was evident to all that Chief Petty Officer Lomax was highly skilled in the operation of the ROV as it alternately glided and hovered as it probed deeper into the ship. It felt eerie to them as *Moriarty* showed empty corridors, twisted bulkheads and hundreds of tiny fishes, illuminated and twinkling like living stars by the ROV's powerful lights. A large crab scuttled across the sloping sand covered deck, startled by this alien invader into its current home. Ross and the others were relieved that no skeletal remains suddenly leaped out at them, disturbed by the movement of the ROV, but Lomax quickly put their minds at rest.

"Don't worry people, you won't see any bodies or human remains in there. They will have long ago disappeared. We didn't probe too far this time. We can go back again, but it was important to get an idea of the damage caused to the interior of the ship. We're moving into what would, I think, have been the wardroom now."

Having been so graciously entertained here in the *Wyvern's* wardroom, Ross and Drake especially felt the poignancy of seeing the smaller and long ago deserted wardroom of the *Norwich*. They could imagine the men who served on board this ship taking a few minutes in the midst of war to grab a quick bite to eat or a mug of tea, to rest between shifts or perhaps sit and write a letter to a loved one. Sitting beside Izzie Drake, Sergeant Carole St. Clair felt particularly affected by the sight, as she wondered if the *Norwich's* wardroom steward had had his own equally effica- cious cure for sea-sickness, similar to that provided by Leading Seaman Bowles here on the *Wyvern* and a lump formed in her throat as she wondered what the final moments must have been like for him and his crewmates as the ship blew up and the seawa- ter burst into her corridors and lower decks. Carole found herself hoping he hadn't suffered. A few rem- nants of dinner plates, a couple of spoons and what may have been a tin mug gleamed momentarily in *Moriarty's* lights and then were gone.

After another few minutes, and a brief examina- tion of what remained of the bridge, Lomax had ex- tricated the ROV from the interior of the wreck, sat- isfied there was nothing more he could do in the time he'd been allotted for this part of the mission.

Moriarty was slowly returned to its docking sta- tion on the submersible and then they watched, fasci- nated, as *Watson* glided imperiously over to the port side of the *Norwich* and closed in on the grim sight of whatever remained of the frogman's body, now fully illuminated by the powerful headlights of the *Wat- son.*

Lt. Cox took up the commentary again as the eerie sight came into closer focus.

"The poor bastard, excuse me ladies, is tethered to a surviving section of the port side dock rail. I'm not a pathologist or a specialist in forensics of course, but if you ask me, whoever did this chained him to the rail- ing first then cut through his air hose with a diver's

285

knife or similar instrument and he was left to thrash about, unable to get free as he drowned."

"The hallmark of a real sadist at work, I'd say," D.I. Jones spoke before anyone else could comment.

"I'd agree with that, Brian," Ross concurred.

The scene played on, on the monitor screen.

"Look closely," said Cox, "and I think you'll see that the diving suit is quite badly torn in places. The fact that water has entered the suit probably made you think it was a fully intact body when you saw those photographs you spoke of, but once we get our divers down there, I'm sure we'll find there's not much left of the poor bugger who was in that suit. But, the air tanks are still there and we should be able to trace them at least once we get the remains to the surface. Our second dive team is scheduled to go down in an hour now that we know the lay of the land, so to speak,"

"They're not using a submersible?" asked Izzie Drake.

"Yes, they are," Cox replied. "They're using *Holmes*, which differs from *Watson* in that it can be used for jobs like this. There's a hatch that allows one crew member to exit the craft to work outside while the other crewman keeps the vessel on station and can be called upon to use the mechanical arms as directed by the man outside."

Cox fell silent then, as the others watched the monitor closely, taking in the sad scene as the picture showed the dead frogman, or rather what was left of him, in much closer detail than they'd seen so far. As

Cox had intimated, they could now see the holes and gashes in the wetsuit, where the denizens of the deep had made inroads into the suit and doubtless feasted on the flesh and bones of the dead man, presuming of course, Ross thought, that it was a man. He didn't think this was the best time to suggest it could just as easily have been a woman.

"Okay, now we move on again," said Cox as the picture on the screen seemed to tip on its side for a few seconds, which indicated *Watson's* progress over the side of the ship and subsequent nose down position as they moved to inspect what lay beneath the keel of the *Norwich*.

"This is where things get really interesting," Lomax took over the tour. "I know you officers are interested in the body of course, but look here."

As he spoke the lights of the *Watson* illuminated the unmistakeable, sleek black shape of the U-Boat.

"It's hard for you to make it all out clearly if you're not familiar with such things, but take it from me, this was one hell of a disaster. From the positions of the two vessels and the fact that the keel of the corvette is so well buried into the deck of the sub it looks as if the ship sank quickly and in doing so, by a stroke of awful bad luck, landed directly on top of the U-Boat, trapping it on the sea bed. A lot of the stern end of the sub is buried well into the sea bed, but you can see the bow section clearly. Her bow planes are still in place, remarkably, in full horizontal position which tells us her captain had taken her down to the bottom and was holding position in the hope the corvette, which we assume was hunting him, passed over without sensing his presence."

They all watched enthralled as the sharp prow of the U-Boat came into clear view in the lights. They could make out the dark, threatening openings to the torpedo tubes and Andy Ross wondered how many times those tubes must have launched their cargoes of death in the months or years before the submarine met its own death here on the bottom of the English Channel. Lomax had fallen silent as he allowed the pictures on screen to speak for themselves. Everyone seemed to be watching in respectful silence as though all were aware that they were looking at the last resting place of maybe two hundred or more men in total.

Ross stood almost rigid as the lights of the submersible next picked out the U-Boat's deck gun, rusting and useless, but still looking lethal, pointing towards the surface of the sea as though waiting for the ghostly hands of her crew to spring to action stations to defend the sub from any and all comers. Ross shivered at the eerie thought. As though sensing his thoughts, in that strange way the two seemed to read each other's thoughts, Izzie Drake reached up to her full height and whispered in his ear.

"Still looks ready to fire, doesn't it, sir?"

"Hmm," Ross grunted, not able to say much as the emotion of the moment washed over him like a spectral hand.

The conning tower came next, its array of antennas and the periscope housing clearly still discernible though the small deck section had long since collapsed into the sub's interior. It was as the *Watson* slowly glided over the top of the conning tower and began to descend down the starboard side that Lomax spoke again.

"Now, this is where things get *really* interesting," he said, dragging out the word 'really' so it sounded like 'reeeeally'.

The others watched as the lights picked out a large hole in the side of the conning tower. One didn't need to be an expert to realise it had not been caused by the corvette landing on and crushing the sub into the sea bed.

"What the hell?" said Brian Jones.

"By jove," exclaimed Prendergast.

"Bloody hell," said Ross.

"Wow," Carole St. Clair frowned at the sight.

"Never seen anything like it," George Baldacre the coast guard added.

"Now, that's what I'd call unusual, not that I know much about it," Izzie Drake spoke quietly, putting things into some small degree of perspective.

In the few seconds they'd taken to make the array of comments, Ross had noticed that the hole in the side of the conning tower had quite obviously been made from the outside, as if a giant drill had somehow bored its way through the shell of the submarine and into the darkness that lay beyond.

"Looks like a giant lamprey's been feeding on it," Captain Howell now commented, having remained silent as they'd watched the images captured by his submersible crew.

"What's that?" Drake asked.

"A lamprey? It's a very archaic fish, Sergeant, I mean Izzie. It's an ugly little bugger with a big, round mouth at the end of its head. It latches on to its prey, for example a bigger fish, and literally bores its way into the other fish's body and eats it alive from the inside out."

"Blood hell," Drake exclaimed. "Sounds a real monster."

"In a way it is, said Howell, "but a very successful monster. The lamprey has been around for thousands of years and is still going strong, so it must be doing something right."

"Anyway, let's get back on course," said Prendergast. "What do you think you were looking at Lieutenant Cox?"

"Someone's been using some powerful underwater cutting equipment on her," said Cox. "They obviously knew what they were doing because it would have much harder for them to get through the double hull if they'd tried going through the sides of the sub, and the pressure hull, if still intact would have resisted even modern cutting equipment."

"So, it looks as if this is about the submarine and not the corvette," said Ross, thoughtfully.

"It must have been carrying something important," said Drake.

"Important and worth killing for," Brian Jones added.

"We need to find out what was on that submarine," Ross said.

"But to do that, we somehow have to identify the U-Boat," Prendergast added, "and that won't be easy, unless we can find something inside her to assist in the identification. Once upon a time, U-Boats carried their number on the conning tower, but the practice stopped during the war years." He seemed lost in thought for a few seconds and then something clicked in his memory. "Hang on though, there might be an easier way."

"We're listening, Captain." Ross said, expectantly.

"If my memory serves me right, and perhaps your friend Herr Haller can confirm this, the U-Boat builders were very proud of their craft and would usually inscribe the number of the boat they were working on into various parts of the boat, most commonly the periscope housing and the interiors of the torpedo tubes."

"Divers can check that out, sir, at least on the periscope housing," Lomax volunteered.

"That's right sir," Cox agreed. "I can brief Baines and Christie before they go down and tell them to check out the periscope housing. I doubt they'll be able to gain access to the torpedo rooms though."

"It's worth a try," said Captain Howell. "Brief them as soon as we've finished here, please Lieutenant."

"Aye, sir," Cox replied.

"And, Lieutenant?"

"Sir?"

"Tell them there's been a change in plan. Double the dive team. I want four men down there this time, two on the corvette and two on the U-Boat. Let's get this job done as fast as we can."

"Aye, sir," said Cox again.

"Gareth," Howell said to the marine lieutenant, still positioned at the doorway, "your men are all dive trained and qualified, right?"

"Yes, sir, they are."

"Okay, I want two of your marines to form the second dive team. Your men can take the sub while our lads take the corvette."

"Got it sir. I'll go and brief my lads."

"Good man," said Howell and the young marine saluted and went to ready his men.

"Any particular reason you're sending marines down to the sub, Charles?" Ross asked the captain.

"You're an astute man, Andy," the captain smiled at him. "I very much doubt we're in any danger out here. No one in their right mind is going to attack a Royal Navy frigate in broad daylight, but that's not to say there might not be something nasty waiting for us down there."

It was the retired submarine commander, Captain Prendergast who reacted first to Howell's words.

"You're thinking whoever plundered the U-Boat wreck might have booby-trapped her, aren't you, Charles?"

"It's a possibility," Howell confirmed. "If you'd been responsible for stealing God knows what from that wreckage, and if it was valuable enough to kill for, wouldn't you want to make sure nobody else found out what you'd been up to?"

"But wouldn't it have been easier to just blow up the remains of the submarine and the warship?" D.I. Jones asked.

"Not as easy as that," C.P.O. Lomax provided his answer. "Put together, the corvette and the sub constitute a sizable chunk of scrap metal, stuck on the bottom of the sea bed. It would take a bloody great explosive charge to blow the lot to smithereens, and the explosion would probably have been big enough that any shipping in the vicinity could have heard or felt the pressure waves from it and reported it to the authorities. This way, if the skipper's right, they lay sneaky little traps to catch the unwary and no one's the wiser."

"Thank you for that erudite explanation, Lomax," the captain grinned.

"You're welcome sir," said Lomax. "Couldn't think of a better word than sneaky, begging your pardon, sir."

"Probably right on the mark, actually," Howell replied.

"I'm sure Ridley's boys know what they're doing sir," Cox asserted.

As scheduled by the *Wyvern's* captain, one hour later, the much larger submersible, the affectionately named *Holmes*, took to the water. She held the *Wyvern's* second dive team, Lieutenant Dave Baines and Petty Officer Lee Christie. A fifth man, Chief Petty Officer Chris Dowling was at the controls, a last minute addition to the team that would enable both pairs of divers to work as couples, both for safety and because, as Howell pointed out, two divers could produce twice the results in half the time possible for one. *Holmes* could carry up to six people and so now held Dowling, Christie and Baines and the two marine divers, both petty officers, Al Sharp and Billy Kendall. Those two would both dive on the U-Boat, keeping a sharp eye out for each other amidst the possible danger of booby traps, as they'd been briefed. Dowling would remain on board the Holmes, keeping the submersible on station as the divers carried out their exploration, monitoring their air supplies, dive times, crucial to ensuring the divers well being, as well as being in a position to assist in case of unforeseen accidents. Gareth Ridley spent a good five minutes explaining to their guests the dangers associated with diving on such wrecks, particularly once the divers entered the dark and potentially wreckage-strewn compartments of both the corvette and the U-Boat.

As Ross and his comrades again held a watching brief on the bridge of the *Wyvern*, he and Drake both shared the feeling that they were about to find some, if not all of the answers to the mystery surrounding Aaron Decker's seemingly senseless murder."

Chapter 26

"It's just not cricket, you know"

Detective Chief Inspector Oscar Agostini placed the phone down on its cradle at the end of a most illuminating phone call. Andrew Montfort, one of the chief supporters of the university sports department, but especially the cricket club, had taken him by surprise with his call.

Agostini sat thinking for a minute and then picked up the phone again. When Paul Ferris answered his extension, Agostini asked him to find Sam Gable and Derek McLennan and send them to his office. Ten minutes later the two detectives found themselves in Agostini's office, wondering if they were about to receive some kind of reprimand for some unknown infraction they'd committed.

Seeing their body language and sensing their tension, the D.C.I. smiled and invited them to sit.

"Don't panic. You're not here for a bollocking. Far from it. You and the team have been working like Trojans in D.I. Ross and Sergeant Drake's absence, so just relax, okay?"

Both detective constables visibly relaxed their postures, and Sam Gable replied, "Thank you, sir. What can we do for you?"

Agostini looked at his desk, checking through the notes he'd made on an A4 pad as he'd listened to what Andrew Montfort had to say.

"Right, here goes. A few minutes ago I received a phone call from Andrew Montfort. Either of you heard of him?"

"I have, sir," Sam Gable said. "Isn't he some wealthy entrepreneur who supports various charities and good causes in the city?"

"That's right, he does," Agostini confirmed. "Well, apparently, he also gives his family name to an annual cricket match that takes place between Liverpool and Manchester Universities, the aptly named Montfort Trophy, no less. It seems Montfort is a great cricket fan and was there to watch this year's match, which Aaron Decker starred in apparently. He speaks very well, very posh, and rather olde worlde, if you know what I mean, all "I say, sir," and "Bad show" sort of thing. Seems he watched this year's trophy match, presented the trophy to the winners, Liverpool of course, and the man of the match prize to Decker and then jetted off the next day to Barbados where he has a private estate. He only returned to this country a few days ago and was shocked to hear of Aaron Decker's murder."

"And I take it he had something important to tell us, sir?" D.C. McLennan asked as Agostini paused for a second to draw breath.

"He did, McLennan, or rather, let's call it something of interest to us that may be of help in the investigation. According to Mr. Montfort, he was rather surprised when he first heard that Aaron Decker was sharing a house with Tim Knight."

Agostini paused again, for effect this time and it worked, as the looks on Gable and McLennan's faces confirmed.

"But we were led to believe they were good friends, sir, and the other lad in the house, Martin Lewis," said Gable.

"Yes, sir, all our inquiries so far have shown no evidence of any bad blood between them, apart from that one instance of Knight trying to pull Decker's girlfriend, but that was before Aaron and Sally got together so we couldn't see it being very significant and even Sally Metcalfe said it was all something and nothing," McLennan added.

"Hmm, well, all was not as clear cut as it appears according to Mr. Montfort." Agostini replied. "It would appear that Aaron Decker's closest friend on the team was the captain, Simon Dewar, and not, as he'd have you believe, Tim Knight. Montfort told me that when Decker was first spotted and included in the team there was some initial feeling against him among some of the players, this new arrival from America of all places, suddenly coming on the scene and showing our lads how the game should be played, but that soon passed as they realised what an asset young Decker was to the team. One man, however, apparently continued to hold something of a grudge against the new man."

"Tim Knight?"

"Correct," said Agostini in response to Gable's almost rhetorical question.

"Yes, and Montfort was quite adamant about it, told me that until Decker came along, Knight was the golden boy of the team, the one the girls wanted to be seen with and so on. That all changed when Decker joined the cricket team."

"So it's possible that Tim Knight did have a motive, however tenuous, for wishing Decker could be out of the way," said Gable, "though it's still a bit of a stretch to think he might have murdered Aaron Decker over being picked for a cricket team, surely, sir?"

"D.C. Gable, when you've been around as long as I have in this job, almost nothing will surprise you. I've seen murders committed for much less substantial reasons than being selected for the cricket team, I can assure you."

"Yes, of course sir, I just thought it unlikely."

"And under normal circumstances you'd probably be correct in your assumption, but remember this, both of you, murderers are not normal members of our society. Something sets them apart, something that allows them to step over the fine dividing line between what is and is not deemed acceptable behaviour by society. If everyone was like them, we'd be living under the laws of the jungle, kill or be killed, survival of the fittest and all that crap, if you understand my meaning."

"Yes, I see what you mean sir," Gable replied,

"That's an interesting way of putting it, sir," said Derek McLennan. "What you're really saying is you believe murderers may possess something like an aberrant gene, a fault in their genetic makeup that makes them somehow more prone to exhibiting the kill behaviour trait"

"Well done, McLennan, that's exactly what I'm saying, but of course, that's my own theory and there are others who would disagree with it I'm sure! Anyway, I want you two to go and see Mr. Montfort and get a signed statement from him. Once we have his words on paper, I think it'll be time for an official chat under caution with Mr. Tim Knight."

"You really think he's involved, sir?"

"As D.I. Ross said, Knight and Lewis are the obvious suspects, and sometimes, the obvious suspects are the best suspects, even though it might appear to be too simple a solution. But we'll wait until you've spoken with Montfort, so I suggest the two of you get a move on. Here's his address," Agostini said, handing a piece of paper across his desk, which McLennan took from him and took a quick look at the address.

"Nice," McLennan commented.

"Where are we going, Derek?" Sam Gable asked.

"Formby," McLennan responded. "Cheveley House, which I suppose will be some grand mansion overlooking the sea."

"I don't care if it's a hovel overlooking the Ribble in Clitheroe. Now go on, you two, we've a killer to catch."

McLennan and Gable were soon on their way, heading north towards Formby, after giving Paul Ferris a brief update on the news from the D.C.I. Paul Ferris took a break from his own computer search in order to key their information into his case file and then returned to his trawling of the internet for any inside information he might unearth relating to the Aegis organisation. So far, his efforts had proved frustratingly negative, but as always, optimism and his confidence that he would eventually find something, somewhere, kept him going as his fingers danced across the keyboard, his eyes intently scanning the screen on his desk.

* * *

"Do sit down, please," Andrew Montfort politely invited the two detectives after escorting them into a large sitting room in his Formby home. Not quite as large or as palatial as Derek McLennan expected, but it did overlook the sea, and did look rather grand from the outside, especially as visitors drove along a short but winding drive that was bordered on both sides by well established firs that formed an avenue, and then opened up to reveal full daylight as though exiting a tunnel, with the house sitting just beyond the gravel parking area, with a fountain situated in the centre, water gently cascading from the statue of a young woman holding a pail on her shoulder, from whence the water flowed.

The interior was even more imposing to Derek and indeed to Sam Gable, with what had to be genuine original oil paintings on the walls of the entrance hall, guarded it seemed by two gleaming suits of armour, each standing, holding vicious looking lances, either side of the large staircase that rose in a semi circle from the entrance hall towards the first floor. A mansion? Maybe not, but a beautiful country house for sure. Derek McLennan, brought up in a basic two-up, two-down semi-detached house in Crosby, was impressed!

Despite his obvious wealth and affiliation with the upper echelons of society, Andrew Montfort came across as easy to talk to and was warm and welcoming in his manner towards the two young detectives.

"I know your time is valuable so I took the liberty of ordering tea when I saw you pulling up outside. It will be here any time."

Right on cue, a young woman, dressed in traditional maid's uniform, black dress, white apron and a little white maid's cap, knocked and entered, carrying a silver tray, (McLennan guessed it had to be real silver), and walked across the room, placing the tray on the large coffee table that stood in between the sofa where McLennan and Gable sat and the large winged armchair in which Andrew Montfort had comfortably seated himself.

"Would you like me to pour, sir?" she asked, smiling at her employer as she spoke.

"No, thank you, Terri," Montfort replied, smiling back at the girl. "I'll see to it. I'll call if I need anything else."

"Okay, sir," said Terri, as she turned away and walked from the room, her heels clicking on the wooden border around the thick rug that took up the centre part of the room, finally closing the large, heavy looking door behind her

"Nice girl, Mr. Montfort," McLennan commented.

"Terri? Yes indeed, Mr. McLennan. I'm not one for all the old-fashioned master and servant stuff. Don't be fooled by the classic maid's uniform. Terri loves it, as if she's starring in an episode of *Upstairs, Downstairs.* She achieved a first class degree in English Literature last year and when she heard of my extensive collection of medieval English manuscripts she asked if I'd mind her visiting my library to carry out some post-doctoral research. I ended up hiring her to help me on a part-time basis over coffee and a discussion of Shakespeare's *The Merchant of Venice.* I did laugh when she asked if she could wear a 'proper' maid's uniform, but thought it did no harm to humour her request. If you weren't here, she'd be calling me Andrew and telling me about her latest boyfriend. But, you didn't come here to talk about my domestic arrangements. I presume you know what I told Detective Chief Inspector Agostini on the telephone?"

"Yes, sir," Sam Gable answered his question. "The D.C.I. would appreciate it if you'd go over what you told him once again with us and give us an official statement, for the record."

"Of course, Miss Gable," Montfort replied. "As I told Mr. Agostini on the phone when he asked if I'd see you right away, I'll do anything to help find poor Aaron's killer. I'm only sorry I was out of the country when it happened and only heard of his death on my return, or I'd have been in touch sooner."

"You mustn't feel bad about it," Gable said, reassuringly. Money or not, it was clear to her that Montfort had been shaken by the news of Decker's death and the old man was eager to help if he could. "There was nothing you could have done to prevent it, and you weren't to know what was about to happen when you left for Barbados."

"Quite," was Montfort's short response, which he followed up by shaking his head as he said in a quiet voice, "It just isn't cricket you know."

"Sir?" Gable was lost for a second.

"Sorry, Miss Gable, not cricket, you know? Bad form and all that, taking a young man's life when he had so much to live for."

"Yes, of course," she replied. "And you told D.C.I. Agostini you were surprised that Aaron Decker ended up sharing a dwelling with Tim Knight?"

"Very surprised, young lady, very surprised indeed."

Somehow, the fact that Montfort kept referring to them not by their ranks, but as Mr or Miss and in this case, young lady, seemed perfectly normal to Sam Gable, who wasn't in the least bit put out by what Agostini had described as his 'olde worlde' affectations and mannerisms.

"So, Tim Knight and Aaron Decker weren't the best of friends, as far as you knew?"

"Oh, don't get me wrong, they may have ended up as good friends, but back when young Decker first came on the scene, it wouldn't have taken a detective to work out that a certain amount of jealousy existed on young Tim's side of course. I only saw them on a few occasions back then, when I'd go along to watch the cricket team either in the nets at practice, or in Aaron's first few matches, when the jealousy seemed more apparent."

"So, are you saying the jealousy died away in time, sir?" Derek McLennan asked.

"On the surface, yes," Montfort said, "and of course, it's quite possible they did become closer as Aaron proved himself to be a quite magnificent cricketer, but it still came as a surprise when I learned they were sharing a house."

Thirty minutes later, armed with a signed statement taken down in her notebook by Sam Gable, the two detectives took their leave of Cheveley House, being waved off by the incongruous sight of Andrew Montfort and his erstwhile maid, Terri, standing side by side on the entrance steps of the house smiling together as the police car disappeared from view.

"I'll bet you any money the old boy's bonking that young maid of his," Derek McLennan said as he drove back in the direction of the city.

"Well if he is, that's their business, Derek, isn't it?" Sam replied. "She's not exactly under-age is she?"

"I know, but, I mean, he's old enough to be her father, maybe even her grandfather and, well, you know…"

"I do believe you're jealous of old Andrew Montfort, Derek," Sam grinned at him. "You can't believe an old chap like him might be getting in the pants of a young, gorgeous girl like Terri, where I have no doubt you'd very much like to find yourself, given half a chance."

"Sam!" Derek exclaimed.

"Oh, come on, McLennan," she laughed. "You're only human after all, and I must admit, she did have a great pair of legs, and the rest wasn't bad either."

Derek McLennan blushed bright red, his face an absolute picture as far as Sam Gable was concerned. No one on the team knew much about Derek's life out side of work, but Sam was now fairly certain that his out of work activities clearly didn't involve any young women at that time. *Was Derek a closet virgin?* she chuckled to herself.

"What?" Derek asked, hearing her quietly laughing to herself.

"Oh nothing, Derek," she replied. "Just wondering if Montfort keeps a harem of young women in reserve, waiting for him to summon them to his bedchamber, like some old lord of the manor. Then again, if Terri was the one who instigated the master and maid thing by asking if she could wear the uniform it could easily be her who's the one with the fetish for sex games and Montfort simply can't believe his luck."

"You've got a dirty mind, so you have, Samantha Gable,"

"Sometimes, yes Derek, I most definitely have," Gable smiled again and the two fell into a silence that lasted until they pulled in to the car park at Headquarters, and headed up to the fourth floor to report to D.C.I. Agostini, before hopefully heading out again to bring Tim Knight in for questioning.

Chapter 27

Prayers for the Dead

The second dive on the *Norwich* and the as yet unidentified *U3000/U966* had seemed to go on for ever to those waiting patiently on the bridge of *H.M.S. Wyvern*. Ross, Drake and the others had listened intently to the words being transmitted to the surface by the two dive teams, and Ross was at last beginning to understand just what the lure of the old German U-Boat had been for the crooked executives of the Aegis Institute, and why Aaron Decker had said that he thought he might be on to something that might make him a lot of money.

Team One had dived on the *Norwich* and despite no outwardly visible identification marks on the ship, Prendergast assured everyone it could only be the *Norwich*, based on its location and the type of corvette design she adhered to. Pictures coming up from the wreck reminded the watchers of those remarkable underwater shots of the *Titanic* as the divers with their hand held cameras moved silently through the eerie and long ago deserted corridors and companionways of *H.M.S. Norwich*. Meanwhile, everyone watched as the exploration of the wreck revealed one or two poignant reminders of the men who had served on board the corvette. As Baines and Christie swam slowly and carefully into the lower reaches of the corvette, their lights illuminated a familiar shape, trapped under a piece of collapsed and rusting metal, at one time part of a bulkhead. They all recognised it as a pipe, a personal item that belonged at one time to one of the men who bravely went to war on the *Norwich*. Most surprising and of even greater significance perhaps, was the discovery in the ship's engine room of the remains of an officer's cap, still hanging from one of the rusting handles of the ship's engine room telegraph, where possibly the chief engineer might have placed it while he wiped his sweat lined brow, perhaps seconds before *Norwich* struck the mine that destroyed her. Baines brought the telegraph into sharper focus and the watchers on board the *Wyvern* could see that the telegraph was set at 'full ahead' telling the Naval officers present that the *Norwich*, in all probability, had been at flank speed, searching for the submerged U-Boat at the moment she'd struck the mine.

Baines and Christie eventually arrived in the ship's forward section and there, about thirty feet from the bows, they came across the large, gaping hole in the ship's side, where she'd hit the mine, and seeing the twisted mass of metal, Captain Howell ordered them to take no chances by trying to explore further. He instructed the divers to exit the interior of the wreck, taking photos of any serial numbers they might be able to discern on any machinery that could help confirm the ship's identity and then to try to confirm that it had been a mine that had been the probable cause of the ship's demise. Charles Howell had seen enough and after a brief conversation with Anthony Prendergast, it was agreed that identification of the wreck as *H.M.S. Norwich* should be formally entered, provisionally into the *Wyvern's* log at that time.

Captain Anthony Prendergast, R.N. (Retired), knew his own work in connection with the *Norwich* would begin in earnest once he returned to shore, when the task of notifying any living relatives of the crew would begin with an extensive search to trace them, and procedures would be set in motion to have the wreck officially designated as a war grave.

No one felt like talking much at that point. Even Ross, Drake, Jones and St. Clair could sense the overwhelming sense of sadness that seemed to pervade all those present on the *Wyvern's* bridge.

Ross had by now come to understand that to the men of the Royal Navy, a ship was almost a living, breathing entity, an extension of the personalities of the men who crewed her, and in a case like this, the men who died with her. No sooner had those thoughts passed through his mind than he heard the sound of someone praying. Previously unnoticed by all except the Captain and First Officer, the ship's

Chaplain had arrived on the bridge and was now praying for the souls lost at the time of the *Norwich's* sinking.

Everyone's attention now turned to the second bridge monitor, where the two marine divers, Sharp and Kendall were making very slow progress in their dive into the interior of the German U-Boat.

* * *

At the same time as Ross and his people were watching the underwater scenes from the wreck site, and as McLennan and Gable were reporting to D.C.I. Agostini on their interview with Andrew Montfort, the man known as Finch sat at a desk in his apartment in the Bay Ridge area of Brooklyn, New York. Finch had been busy planning his next move after his conversation with Francis Kelly. Finch knew exactly what needed to be done and after due consideration he'd made a decision. Finch never rushed into things, which was one of the reasons he'd survived and prospered for so long in his line of work. Few people knew his real name, and those that did had no idea that he was anything other than a successful broker who'd made a small fortune playing the stock exchange for many years. In fact, Finch hadn't set foot on Wall Street for many years, any financial investments he made, and they were numerous, were handled on his behalf by a large brokerage house in the city.

Jerome Decker III would have been surprised and extremely disappointed to know that Finch was a former C.I.A. operative who had turned 'rogue' many years ago, and now ran his very own private 'security' service, selling his and his operatives' skills to the highest bidder, becoming a very rich man in the process.

Finch picked up the phone and dialled an international number, which was answered on the third ring. It was a simple ploy used by Finch and his people. Answer too soon or too late and it would indicate a problem, which could be anything from an operative having been compromised, or just an inopportune moment to take a call. Either way, it meant Finch would call back in thirty minutes and try again.

"Robin here," came the voice over the phone.

"Robin, it's Finch, you ready to go to work?"

"I am indeed," Robin replied, his accent immediately identifying him as English.

"Good. Listen up my friend. Here's what I need you to do."

Robin listened carefully for five minutes as Finch outlined the task that lay ahead of him, taking notes that he would burn as soon the call was over and he'd had chance to memorise them.

"You got all that?" Finch asked after briefing Robin on the job.

"Sure have, Finch. When do you want me to expedite the package?"

"It's of the utmost urgency, Robin. I'd like it very much of you could ensure delivery today. There'll be a large monthly bonus heading your way if you can deliver on time."

"Consider it a done deal," said Robin, a former soldier-turned mercenary who'd found a new and more lucrative career since joining Finch's enterprise. "Any paperwork involved?" he asked, a subtle way of asking for photographs or maps to assist in his assignment.

"Check your email in five minutes," Finch replied.

"That all?"

"That's it. Let me know when the job's done. Usual payment arrangements."

"Okay, Finch."

"Goodbye Robin," said Finch as he hung up and Robin found himself holding a phone connected to dead space.

Exactly five minutes later, Robin's computer gave a single beep, telling him an email had arrived. As promised by Finch the two attachments showed him his targets and exact directions to their location. Robin printed them out, cursing the fact he'd have to travel no more than twenty miles to carry out his mission. He enjoyed long distance travel, warm destinations, pretty women by a swimming pool, but no, Finch was sending him to bloody Liverpool!

Robin quickly packed an overnight bag, not intending to stay the night in Liverpool, but you never knew when plans might need to be changed at a moment's notice and anyway, he needed something to carry the tools of his trade in. His last thoughts as he looked round his flat one last time before locking up was how he hated Finch's stupid idea of giving his operatives the names of birds. *Robin, for God's sake,* he thought. *What am I, Batman's little buddy or something?*

Five minutes later he was on the road, heading along the East Lancs Road to 'Scouseland' as he disparagingly referred to the city of Liverpool. At the same time, Finch was boarding a Delta Airlines transatlantic flight from New York's JFK International Airport to London Heathrow. Finch was heading home to the UK, where he could maintain hands-on control of any clean-up operations that might become necessary if things went pear-shaped with the current situation.

* * *

The interior of *U966* had been kindly treated by time. There was little interior degradation of the main control room or engine room, which was sealed off from the rest of the sub by its watertight doors and the two divers, having entered through the hole that had been cut in the side of the conning tower, were feeling a little spooked by the appearance of the silent eeriness of the U-Boat, which had withstood the ravages of time so well. Those watching from the bridge of the *Wyvern* watched, enthralled, as Sharp and Kendall slowly moved through the deserted interior. As they reached the engine room, the two men joined forces to slowly open the watertight door, and even though the sea immediately began to flood into the compartment, they could clearly see what awaited them.

"Oh shit," Petty Officer Sharp suddenly exclaimed and dropped his powerful hand-held halogen lamp.

"What is it, Sharp?" Gareth Ridley asked his man over the comm. system.

Without a word, Sharp swam down to the deck and retrieved his lamp and then pointed it towards whatever it was that had startled him.

"Oh, dear God," Ross now exclaimed as he too saw the last remains of a body, still dressed in the rags of his uniform, that lay, resting beside one of the submarine's large diesel engines. The atmosphere inside the watertight compartment of the engine room had helped to preserve the body that appeared to be sitting on a stool, peaked cap jauntily propped on the head, sloping to the left side. Before they could do anything, the seawater rushed past them, sweeping the corpse to the floor of the engine room. *U966's* engineering officer Heinz Muller had remained at his post for nearly sixty years, still guarding his precious engines.

"Go no further," Howell ordered. "If there are other sealed compartments they might also contain human remains. We have to respect the dead, no matter what side they were on. Stick to the areas the interlopers have already opened up and let's see if we can find what they were looking for."

"Aye sir, understood. They seem to have concentrated on the for'ard section, so we'll head that way," Sharp acknowledged.

"That was awful," said Carole St. Clair as she exhaled, realising she had been holding her breath as they'd taken in the sight of the skeleton in the engine room.

"If there are more compartments that have remained sealed watertight since the sinking, there could be more remains in there," said Charles Howell. Unlike the *Norwich*, it looks like the sub remained free from the sea's encroachment until our unknown 'friends' came along.

"Oh God, that's so awful to think about," St. Clair said.

"There's one thing that's been bugging me about all this," Izzie Drake now spoke, trying to get back to the real reason for them being here.

"Go on, Izzie, what is it?" Ross asked, knowing that she'd obviously been thinking hard all the time they'd been watching the underwater drama unfold on the bridge monitors.

"Well sir, we're here because someone killed Aaron Decker and in the course of our investigation we found out he was interested initially in researching the company that had offered his girlfriend a job and in the course of so doing he became suspicious about what they were doing in the English Channel. He travelled down here to check them out and then, I'm assuming he followed them out to sea in a boat of some kind and discovered this very spot and came back to investigate by himself later. At some point he involved the historian Haller, who would have been his logical choice, given his expertise in maritime history, and we know that Haller then came down here also, did his best to find out what Aegis were doing, even hiring a boat himself and presumably doing what Decker did in following them out here. Am I right in all that so far?"

"I'd say you are, Izzie. Go ahead, I know you have a point to make here, and I've a feeling I know what it is, but let's wait and see if we agree."

"Okay," Drake continued. "Until we know more about the poor sod who was chained to the wreck down there, we can only speculate as to who he or she may be and what their involvement is, but we're still left with one big burning question as far as I can see."

"Which is?" Ross prompted.

"Well, sir, it's quite simple really. Decker heard about it through his connection to Sally Metcalfe, Haller heard about it from Aaron Decker, but, and this is the sixty thousand dollar question, how the hell did Aegis know about it, and even more important, what led them to believe there was anything valuable to be found on either of the two wrecks?"

"Bravo, Izzie. The same thoughts have been going through my mind too. It seems to me that someone in the Aegis set up had to have had some prior knowledge of the possibility of some kind of valuable cargo existing down there, in all likelihood on the U-Boat. So who told them? Who knows enough about the war at sea and in particular the German U-Boat war to have given them the information that sent them searching in the area in the first place?"

A light went on in Drake's mind at Ross's question and she instantly replied, "Haller? You really think he could be involved in this?"

"Why not? He's an acknowledged expert in the field and like anyone else, he could probably be bought for a large enough sum."

"But he seems too straight, sir, too legit to become involved in something like this."

"I know, Izzie, but if not Haller, then who else do we have? At present, nobody, so it's time we got someone to drive back up to Wrexham and put a little more pressure on Herr Klaus Haller."

"You want me to call Headquarters and get someone out there now, sir?"

"Yes, please Izzie, and send Dodds and Ferris. It'll do Paul good to get away from his computer for a couple of hours, and he's damn good at asking probing questions. Tell them to be respectful but let Haller know we have suspicions. They're to try and get him to open up if he is involved, but if he truly isn't he may know someone who could be helping the murdering bastards at Aegis."

Izzie turned and walked across the bridge, walking out onto one of the bridge wings, where she could talk to the team back home in relative privacy. After speaking to Paul Ferris, she returned to watch the progress of the divers with the others.

* * *

Sharp and Kendall swam slowly through the flooded forward compartments of *U966*. Whoever had found the submarine and broken through into its interior quite clearly hadn't given a damn about preserving any human remains that might have been present. Any such remains would by now have floated clear of the U-Boat's hull and been lost to the sea forever. Prendergast had vowed to himself that at some point in the future, he would contact the German Navy and arrange a joint recovery operation to access the sealed rear compartments of the submarine in the hope of recovering any preserved remains. For the time being though, he watched with the others as the two divers explored further into the eerie wreck.

Kendall was the first to break the silence that had accompanied their progress since the ill-fated foray into the engine room.

"I think we've found what they were looking for," he reported.

"What do you see, Kendall?" Captain Howell asked.

"Hang on a minute, sir," the diver replied.

Ross and the others watched as Sharp swam in front of the camera, which Kendall held steady as the other man reached down and indicated a large packing case, still attached to one of the forward torpedo room storage racks by thick canvas webbing straps that had stood the test of time remarkable well.

"There are two more of these boxes down here," said Kendall, "but by the looks of things there must have been others. There are more of these webbing straps here that look as if they've been recently cut. I'd say whoever has been working in here has only half-finished the job."

"But Decker was here a year ago, sir," Drake commented. "Why has it taken them so long to remove whatever they were after?"

"That's an easy question to answer, Sergeant Drake," Howell said. "Yes indeed," agreed George Baldacre, the coast guard, who hadn't spoken much at all since they'd begun to watch the dive operation. "I think what the captain was going to say, and excuse me for butting in Charles, is that you can't just turn up in the English Channel with a bloody great salvage tug and begin exploring the sea bed without anyone knowing about it. This is, remember, one of the busiest sea lanes in the world and they'd have been noticed and questions asked. I would guess they spent a long time in small boats or even in a submersible of their own, simply checking out the wreck site, and then eventually sending divers down much as we have, but only for short periods at a time so as not to arouse suspicion. The weather would have played an important role too. They set up their cover story to fool us and the other maritime authorities but I still don't understand how the hell they managed to force their way into the submarine's conning tower. What the hell did they use?"

Ross was impressed with Baldacre's theory which seemed to fit all the facts and he now came up with a theory of his own.

"You said they might have used a submersible, George. Charles, tell me, could a civilian organisation like Aegis have anything like the *Holmes* or *Watson*, you know, a submersible with all the mechanical grabs and arms and so on, at their disposal?"

"Of course," the captain replied. "Such things are not restricted to the Royal Navy, Andy. Most ocean exploration companies have them nowadays."

"And is there such a thing as an underwater drill?" Ross ventured.

"Bloody hell, he's right sir" Ridley exclaimed. "That's how they did it. They must have used something like 'the worm.'"

"Er, what's the worm?" Izzie asked.

"It's a special tool we have at our disposal," Howell replied. "It is, in effect a large drill bit, an augur that can slowly cut through the hull of a ship. We only use it for salvage purposes but if they have something similar, they could easily have used it as a break-in tool to gain access to the U-Boat's interior."

"Bloody hell, sir, look here," the startled voice of Petty Officer Kendall pulled all eyes back to the monitor.

"Jesus Christ," Sharp added as the beam from his lamp shone on one corner of the packing case which had become rotten and fallen away, probably since the sea had been allowed to encroach into the compartment thanks to the thieves as everyone now thought of them.

"Is that what we think it is, Kendall?" Captain Howell asked his diver.

"I believe so, sir. I think this is part of a horde of bloody Nazi gold. The bastards who did this are nothing but a bunch of murdering grave robbers."

"Gold!" D.I. Brian Jones exclaimed as his eyes took in the sight.

"And it's been down there all those years," his sergeant, Carole St. Clair added. "But like Izzie said earlier, how did the Aegis people know it was here?"

"Someone had to know it was on the submarine," Jones said. "Andy is probably right that this Haller chap must know something."

"But that doesn't add up either," Ross suddenly said.

"Why not, Andy?" Jones asked.

"Because he wouldn't have given us the exact location of the wreck site if he was part of the conspiracy. That would have been stupid beyond belief. No, there has to be someone, somewhere who knew about the cargo this sub was carrying and who got the Aegis people involved, probably for a share of the loot. Before we even begin to find out who it is, we need to identify the U-Boat, Captain Howell," Ross said to Charles Howell, in a seriously official tone of voice.

"Indeed we do," the captain replied and then he spoke to the divers.

"Sharp, Kendall, did either of you look for the maker's plate in the control room? It should have been bolted somewhere on the superstructure. They always did that, I think."

"That's right," said Prendergast, "like a birth certificate. It would have the boat's number, date of

321

launch, where it was made and other specific information."

"We didn't see it, sir," Sharp replied, "But I don't think we need to look for it."

"And why's that, Sharp?" said Howell.

Sharp pointed towards the crate again and Kendall focused the camera to a close up view. The watchers could now see a series of stencilled numbers and letters on the packing case and what appeared to be some lettering below.

"Looks like one of the crew got bored and indulged in a spot of graffiti," said Sharp. "Anyone up there speak German?"

"I do," said Gareth Ridley. He moved to the front of the watchers and looked at the screen as the words came into focus.

One of the crew had indeed been busy during a few idle moments on the last voyage of *U966*. Underneath the official lettering, someone had etched *U966, Adolph postboten* into the side of the crate and filled the lettering in with what had probably been oil or diesel fuel oil, turning it black and still readable after almost 60 years.

"*U966* is obvious," said Ridley and the words translate as *Adolph's postman.*"

"Well done you two, and thank you, Lieutenant," Howell said, without revealing that he too spoke perfect German. Better to let young Ridley feel he'd contributed substantially to the mission.

"*U966*," said Ross. "Well, at least now we know the sub's number we might be able to discover more

322

about her. Izzie, get back on the phone to Ferris. Tell him what we've found and make sure he knows Haller is no longer a viable suspect. Treat him as a valuable witness and find out if he knows anything of the history of *U966*. He's the expert historian after all."

"Right you are, sir," Drake replied as she stepped out on the port wing of the bridge again to call Paul Ferris.

Captain Howell meanwhile, had been in a huddle with his first officer, Mike Sutherland. Turning to Ross, he spoke in a hushed tone.

"Andy, I know this all began with your request for help in a murder investigation but now we know what we're dealing with, I'm sure you can see that as far as the Royal Navy is concerned, this matter goes much further than that. I will of course be reporting everything we've found to the Ministry of Defence and I'm sure they will launch a full scale inquiry into both wrecks down there, particularly as we seem to have unearthed an amount of Nazi treasure which it's clear to see was being transferred out of Germany to some secret location, possibly South America, knowing the Nazis had connections over there during the war. We'll continue to assist you of course but I think it's safe to say we'll be joined by a much larger salvage team and possibly a specialist salvage vessel sooner rather than later. Will you be expecting to stay and see what else we discover?"

Ross thought for a few seconds before replying.

"I don't think so, Charles. Once we get your doctor's report on the remains of the frogman and the remains sent to the local medical examiner, I think our usefulness here will be at an end. I'm sure D.I. Jones and Sergeant St. Clair will be happy to be our eyes and ears on the case down here while we go back to Liverpool to continue the investigation."

"We'll be more than happy to work the case from our end," Brian Jones replied. "We're only a phone call away at any time and you only have to let us know if we need to be doing anything to help push the investigation along and we'll be on it right away, won't we, Carole?"

"Without a doubt, sir," Carole St. Clair agreed.

"Thanks," said Ross as they all turned to watch the final minutes of the dive. Lieutenant Commander Douglas Sykes, the *Wyvern's* senior medical officer was still busy at work on the remains of the frogman and Ross was keen to find out what he'd discovered.

Leaving the others to watch the submersible begin its ascent from the deep, Ross and the other police officers now made their way to the *Wyvern's* sick bay, escorted by a young naval rating. Once there, Ross politely knocked on the bulkhead at the door to the sick bay and was ushered in by one of Sykes's sick berth attendants. The grim task of opening the wetsuit to examine the remains had already been undertaken by Sykes and two of his sick-berth attendants, and the rest of the procedure was now watched closely by Ross, Drake and the two Cornish police officers.

As expected, the denizens of the deep had made many a meal of the dead man, or woman, and Sykes and his men had been able to recover nothing more than a few well-picked bones from the interior of the wetsuit. Any hopes Ross might have had of identifying the body from its remains were dashed almost as soon as the examination had begun, but then, just as he was beginning to think they'd run into another brick wall in the investigation, Doctor Sykes suddenly perked up as his hands emerged from the wetsuit holding something silver in colour, attached to a thin chain of a similar metal.

"Aha," said Sykes, almost triumphantly, "what do we have here, I wonder?"

"What is it Doc?" Ross asked quickly, taking two steps towards the examination table in the centre of the *Wyvern's* sick bay treatment room.

"A silver St. Christopher medallion, Inspector, still with its chain attached." Sykes turned it over and smiled as he passed it to Ross.

"Take a look Inspector. It's engraved on the back."

Ross looked closely at the medallion, which was no more than an inch and a half in diameter, but big enough for him to clearly make out the engraving on the back.

"T.J.K. LOVE FROM J.D. 6.6.2000," he read aloud for all to hear. "If this doesn't help us to identify the body, nothing will."

"Oh Christ," Brian Jones exclaimed as Ross passed the St. Christopher around for the others to examine.

"Brian?" Ross questioned the Falmouth detective's reaction, without failing to notice Jones's face had turned pale as a sheet.

Replying to his own sergeant rather than directly replying to Ross, Jones spoke quietly as his shoulders appeared to sag.

"You know who this is, don't you. Carole?"

"Surely it can't be," St. Clair replied. "Everything pointed to him doing a runner, sir. We had evidence…"

"Faked evidence, obviously," Jones said, his voice cracking with emotion.

Ross had listened to the exchange between the Falmouth detectives and now tried again to reach past Jones's obvious shock.

"Brian, I'm sorry, but please talk to me. It sounds to me as if you both have a bloody good idea who our victim is. Take a deep breath, and tell me, for God's sake."

"Carole, would you…?" Jones said, turning away from the sight of the remains on the examination table and reaching out to the nearby bulkhead to support himself.

Carole St. Clair cleared her throat, nodded at her boss and turned to Ross.

"Sir, you'll recall we told you that only a few locals were ever employed by Aegis at their Falmouth facility, and even then, only in pretty menial jobs, nothing that would have given them access to anything important that Aegis might be working on?"

"I remember, Carole, please go on."

"Well sir, one of those locals was Thomas Joseph Knowles, known as T.J. to his friends. T.J. was employed as a security guard by Aegis. His job was restricted to patrolling the grounds of the facility at night, ensuring nobody broke into the place. None of the security guards have access to the main buildings there apparently. This was just routine exterior patrol work. T.J. was out of work for a while, so grabbed the chance to earn a few pounds when this job was advertised.

He'd been going out with a local girl, Julie Dakin for about two years when Julie announced she was pregnant. Next thing anyone knew, T.J. disappeared one day about a year ago. Julie received a text message from him saying he wasn't ready to be a father and he'd gone away to think things over, to decide what to do next. A week later, she received a postcard from London, saying he was staying in a B & B in Whitechapel, that he was well and didn't know if or when he'd be coming home. She kept trying to reach him by phone and text message, and received another text a fortnight after the postcard. He said he was sorry, but he couldn't be a dad. He said he loved her, told her to take care of herself and that was the last thing anyone heard from him."

St Clair paused for breath. Somehow, Ross had a feeling he knew how this story might end, but he waited and allowed her to carry on.

"When nothing was heard from T.J. after another two weeks passed, Julie, who was already beside herself with grief, asked her uncle to look into his apparent disappearance. Julie Dakin is D.I. Jones's niece, Inspector Ross."

"I guessed as much," said Ross. "Brian, I'm sorry, this has been a real shock for you, but we need to know what happened next."

Jones acknowledged Ross with a nod and gestured for St. Clair to continue.

"Everyone knew this to be out of character for T.J. He absolutely adored Julie. They were childhood friends, and their friendship turned to something more as they grew older. No way would he have run off and left her in the lurch, or so we all thought. Julie gave birth to a little girl a few months ago, called her Kerry."

Having finally composed himself, Brian Jones pushed himself away from the bulkhead and walked closer, looking down with sadness at Thomas Knowles's remains.

"We did all we could to find him, Andy. I even went up to London and trawled the B & B's in Whitechapel. Those bastards were clever, I'll give 'em that. I actually found a place where a young man matching T.J's description had apparently stayed for a week, before moving on, according to the land-lady, who also said she hardly saw him, so her confirmation of his identity was a little suspect, but I couldn't argue about the fact that the handwriting on the postcard looked a perfect match for his. The bastards must have taken him and made him write it before killing him. They were too clever for me, I have to admit."

"But what would he have had to do with all this?" Izzie Drake asked.

"T.J. was an expert diver, Izzie. He was also round about the same age as Aaron Decker and it's possible that Aaron met him while he was down here, maybe in one of the pubs in town, found out he was employed by Aegis and somehow convinced T.J. to help him look into what they were up to. T.J had a great sense of adventure, and also knew right from wrong, so I could easily imagine him being talked into helping Aaron in his quest, particularly if Aaron offered him some kind of financial reward. Like I said, he'd been out of work for a time, so he'd have jumped at the chance to earn a few quid."

Ross had been thinking as Jones spoke and now voiced his agreement with the Falmouth detective's hypothesis.

"You know, Brian, I think that's probably exactly what happened. I can't see anyone other than Aaron, or at a push, Klaus Haller asking him to dive on the wreck site. In fact, it could have been Haller rather than Decker who recruited him. Decker could dive himself, Haller is too old, and might have wanted confirmation of what Decker had told him. But if he did get T.J. to help him, why didn't he mention it when my people spoke to him before?"

"Seems every mystery in your case leads to yet another one," Jones observed and Ross couldn't really argue with his point.

"Is there anything else you can tell us about the remains of... er, T.J., Doctor Sykes?" Ross asked, trying to return to a less personal perspective.

"Not really," said the *Wyvern's* medical officer. "There just isn't enough here to carry out a post mortem on, I'm afraid. Obviously, we'll forward the remains of Mr. Knowles to the medical examiner's office in Falmouth as soon as we dock, but I doubt you'll get much more from him, Inspector Ross."

Ross thanked the doctor and quietly signalled for Drake and St. Clair to follow him out of the medical centre. Seeing them and realising Ross's intent, Doctor Sykes also beckoned to the two sick berth attendants who likewise followed him through the door, leaving Detective Inspector Brian Jones alone with what remained of the man who was the father of his niece's baby girl.

Chapter 28

A history lesson

Nick Dodds and Paul Ferris sat opposite Klaus Haller in his comfortable cottage in the Welsh town of Wrexham. Haller had welcomed them into his home and made them wait to talk to him while he'd made fresh coffee for the three of them.

He'd then listened intently as they'd conveyed the information they'd received from Izzie Drake.

"*U966*?" he mused. "I know the history of most of the better known U-Boats of the war, detectives, but you must forgive me if this one doesn't immediately spring to mind."

"But can you help us to trace its history, Herr Haller?" Dodds asked him.

"But of course. I did not mean that because I have no personal recollection of it that I cannot find out what you want. Please wait while I conduct a quick search."

Haller rose from his armchair and walked across the room, re-seating himself at his small desk that held his small personal computer, switching it on and then waiting as it whirred and finally beeped to signal it had fully booted up. The historian opened his personal files and within a minute, had located the one he was looking for.

"Ah, here we are, gentlemen," Haller said quietly, continuing to read as he spoke. "Now, this is a little odd."

"In what way, sir?" Ferris asked.

"Well, *U966* was one of the type VIIC boats, launched in 1943 and scuttled later that same year after being badly damaged by an aerial depth charge attack in the Bay of Biscay. Yet the shape of the vessel in the photos Aaron took resemble more the much later type IXD U-Boats, which were all built slightly later in the war. They were more than five hundred tons heavier and almost ten metres longer than their predecessors, but records indicate they had their torpedo tubes removed and were converted for transport purposes, essentially making them nothing more than freight carriers, but this boat looks to be a fully functional craft and there is something else about it that I cannot quite put my finger on at this moment. It may come to me in time. One thing I can tell you for certain though is that this U-Boat, whatever its maker's plate or any other identification marks may say, is most certainly not the original *U966*. For some reason, she was redesignated as *U966*, as a subterfuge, so there must be something secret about the U-Boat itself, or about someone or something on board when she sailed. You say she was being used to carry cargo of some kind?"

"That's correct, Herr Haller," Ferris confirmed. "Detective Inspector Ross has authorised us to give you certain information which he hopes you will keep in confidence."

"I wish nothing more than to help in this matter, so yes, you can be assured of my discretion in this matter, and you have really piqued my interest with the mention of this boat. Please wait while I see what else I can discover."

Dodds and Ferris looked on as Haller opened up page after page of information on his computer. Ferris, the murder investigation team's collator and resident computer expert was impressed by Haller's dexterity and speed in operating his machine. The historian soon had something to tell them, though his face betrayed a look of puzzlement, which Ferris noticed right away as Haller looked at them.

"What is it, Herr Haller? You look as if something is wrong."

"Now wrong, exactly, Constable Ferris, but, shall we say, a little odd?"

"Please explain, sir."

"Well, it would appear that *U966*, that is to say, the ersatz, you would say, false *U966* was placed in reserve at the beginning of 1945. In essence, she was being kept in port, in Kiel, and held in a constant state of readiness for what were deemed 'special operations.' That term could have meant almost anything in those days, but what interests me is that she'd been operating at sea for some time and her captain was a highly decorated officer who had previously commanded a most successful U-Boat during the Battle of the Atlantic. His previous boat had been badly damaged and needed extensive repairs after his part in a Wolf Pack operation against allied convoys, and he was then transferred, along with a sizable number of his crew to the *U3000*. But we know that *U966* was sunk two years earlier so someone went to great trouble to create a false record for this 'new' *U966*, long before she sailed from Kiel, possibly before her captain was even aware of it."

"That sounds suspiciously like a clever cover story," said Nick Dodds.

"Ja, very much so, Constable, especially as the records then go on to state the boat was lost with all hands, in May of 1945, having sailed from Kiel in March but gives no approximate position or even what heading she was last reported to be following. That is not like the usual German efficiency. It sounds as if *U966*, it is easier for you if we stick to that number I think, was dispatched on a secret mission around a month before Hitler's suicide. If, as you say, she was carrying gold bullion it is likely to be either a cargo of part of the immense of amounts of gold the Nazis stole from occupied countries, or part of Germany's own gold reserves. Hitler remained convinced almost to the end that he could revive Germany's war effort and rumour has it that he was ferrying looted art treasures and gold bullion to sympathetic nations in South America for some time in the final months of the war. Let me see next, what we can discover about her captain. Ah, here we are, *Korvettankapitän* Max Ritter, holder of the Knight's Cross with Oak Leaves, a much respected U-Boat commander, gentlemen. Now, his name I do recognise, though how he ended up on this *U966*, ferrying gold across the sea, I do not know. Someone in high authority must have been involved to have had such a man's records changed to include this false 'cover story' as you call it. I can think of only one man who would be responsible for this."

"And who would that be?" Ferris asked.

"Admiral Wilhelm Canaris, Constable, head of the *Abwehr*, the Nazi's military intelligence service, probably in collusion with Admiral Doenitz, who headed the U-Boat arm of the Kriegsmarine. They obviously went to great lengths to disguise this boat, its crew and its mission."

"Even I've watched enough on the history channel to know that the decorations you quote mean Ritter was highly decorated, Herr Haller," said Ferris. "But if he was so well thought of, is it not possible he was selected for the mission precisely because of his bravery and loyalty to the Reich, that he was well aware of his mission all along? A good officer would go along with such a subterfuge if it was for the benefit of the war effort, surely."

"Yes, of course," Haller replied thoughtfully, "and there may be something in that after all when you consider who he worked under."

"Such as?" Dodds asked.

"Well it says here that his immediate superior was *Kapitän zur See*, Heinz Schmidt, who was himself the close aide to Admiral Werner Stein. Stein was well known to be close to Hitler and Schmidt was an ardent Nazi, so I can easily believe them selecting Ritter for such a task, but it is strange..." his voice tailed off thoughtfully.

"What's bothering you, Herr Haller?" Ferris asked, seeing the historian appearing to debate something in his own mind.

"Her course, Constable Ferris, her course is all wrong, but wait, no, perhaps not so crazy after all."

"Do you mind explaining, sir?" Ferris pressed Haller to elaborate on his thoughts.

"How is your German geography, gentlemen? Oh never mind, just look here." Haller beckoned the two detectives to come and look at a map he'd just opened up on his desk. Using a pencil as a pointer, he began to explain. "Here's Kiel," he indicated and then using the pencil, he traced what would have been a U-Boat's usual route around the coast of Denmark, across the North Sea and into the Atlantic via the northern route, past the northern British Isles and on towards Greenland. He then traced a totally different route, one which placed *U966* in the English Channel before breaking out into the Western Atlantic.

"I would wager that Schmidt planned a route that sent *U966* on a circuitous route, away from the usual U-Boat areas of activity, thinking there was less chance of accidental interception of the submarine by patrolling warships."

"He got that bit badly wrong then, didn't he?" Dodds commented.

"You appear to be correct," Haller agreed. "I think also, that if the ultimate destination of *U966* was South America or perhaps one of the island chains, The Bahamas for example, it would in fact save time and fuel by taking this route, especially if Ritter was under orders to remain submerged as long as possible."

Dodds and Ferris looked at the plot that Haller had drawn on the map and it did appear to both men that the overall length of the voyage would have been shorter using the route he'd mapped out.

Ferris now asked the same question that had been niggling at Izzie Drake down in Falmouth.

"Herr Haller, even accepting the truth of all you've told us, how did the people at Aegis learn of the position of the submarine, or even learn of its existence?"

"I have been thinking of that question as we have been talking," Haller said, "and it seems to me there are only two people who might know the answer to that."

"You know who they are, Herr Haller?" Dodds asked, feeling stupid as he did so, *Obviously Haller knows or he wouldn't have said there were two people would he?* Nick Dodds thought.

"While we have been talking I have checked on the histories of both Schmidt and Stein, gentlemen. Stein died in 1965, but was survived by a son, Ralph, who was born in 1946 which would make him fifty-seven years old now. Schmidt was thirty when the war ended and is, as far as I know, still alive, obviously in his eighties now, and my records show he was last known to be living in a retirement home near Rothenburg in Bavaria. It is possible that Schmidt knew the course that *U966* was to follow and may now be trying to locate the gold or, perhaps, Stein left the same details for his son to find and he is now working in league with the people at Aegis to take the gold and share it with them in return for them doing the work of recovering it."

"Do your records show where Ralph Stein lives, Herr Haller?"

At that point, Haller paused as if for dramatic effect before replying.

"My records show only information relating to persons who have served in the Kriegsmarine, or since its inception the modern-day German Navy which replaced the Kriegsmarine after it was disbanded after the war, gentlemen, but luck is with us. Ralph Stein served for eight years in the navy and his last known address places him in Rostock, close to the Baltic Sea."

"Which by itself means little of course," said Ferris, unless..." he hesitated. "Can you do a search please, Herr Haller and see if Aegis has any business interests in that area of Germany, please?"

"Of course, let me see now... ah, here it is. Constable Ferris, you are indeed a clever man. When Communism fell and Rostock became part of the new reunified Germany, they invited many foreign companies to the town to assist with rebuilding and modernisation and the Aegis Corporation is listed as one of those companies and indeed they still maintain an office in the city and a small facility on the coast near the city's Baltic port at Warnemünde a few miles away. I explain, of course. Rostock is a few miles inland from the coast and its port facility is actually on the Baltic at the head of the river Warnow, on which Rostock stands."

"Herr Haller, you have been a great help," Ferris said. "Please, can you print this information for us? We may need to talk again and in the meantime, as we asked earlier..."

"I will say nothing of your visit, Constable, I promise. I only hope I am helpful in finding out who killed that poor young man. It is for me a great pity that the life of any person is considered less than the value of a few gold bars. In the meantime I will continue to investigate the anomaly of the change in the U-Boat's number and if I find anything I will of course telephone you or your superiors in Liverpool."

Ferris and Dodds thanked Klaus Haller, and were soon motoring back to Liverpool, eager to speak to Andy Ross as soon as they could. Hopefully his mobile phone would be in range by the time they got there.

Chapter 29

Agostini's 'Lightbulb'

Detective Chief Inspector Oscar Agostini had until recently shared the same rank as Andy Ross. When his predecessor as head of the murder investigation team, Harry Porteous, announced his retirement, his job and a promotion was offered to Ross, who turned it down, preferring to remain 'in the field' on active investigations. Ross was delighted when his old friend and one-time partner, Detective Inspector Oscar Agostini was promoted and handed the job.

The two men had worked together many years earlier and had remained firm friends ever since, and Ross had no problem in working for Agostini, the pair retaining a respectful but friendly working relationship during office hours whilst being able to remain as before in their own time.

As Agostini waited for Ross and Drake to return from Falmouth, and as the rest of the team continued to gather other pieces of the jigsaw this case had become, he sat at his desk, pondering. Though not out on the streets any longer, Agostini was still a detective and a damn good one at that and this case had so far proved something of a nightmare.

The D.C.I. now decided to use one of his old techniques, one that had proved valuable in the past. He began to mentally sift the facts and the fictions of the case so far. By the fictions, he meant the idle suppositions and wild theories that often enter into difficult inquiries.

As he saw it, the case began not with the murder of Aaron Decker, but long before that when someone gave information to another person at the Aegis Institute about the possibility of there being a cache of Nazi gold on a shipwreck in the English Channel. He now believed, with the information gleaned from Klaus Haller, that that person had to be either Ralph Stein or Heinz Schmidt.

There had to be a crooked executive or group of executives within the Aegis organisation. The company was respected around the world and it was inconceivable that the entire set-up was involved in illegal activity. No, Agostini concluded, there had to be a rogue element present and he and his team, possibly with help from Interpol and perhaps the resources of Jerome Decker's C.I.A. affiliates had to find whoever was leading that group. His personal favourite at present was Francis Kelly. He was sure that at the time of Aaron Decker becoming involved in the case, the perpetrators quite possibly knew nothing about his father and his position in the C.I.A. their first big mistake, Agostini concluded.

At some point in the case, Aegis Oceanogaphics made a job offer out of the blue to Sally Metcalfe, Aaron's girlfriend. Sally's father owns a haulage company that had done some work for Aegis in the past and apparently Sally was offered the job based on this connection.

Aaron had decided to check out her prospective future employers and something aroused his suspicions about Aegis's activities. He consults a respected historian, Klaus Haller who in trying to help Aaron gets cold-shouldered by Aegis, but cleverly follows their ship out to the wreck site from a distance and notes the location. He passes this to Aaron who goes to Cornwall, dives on the wreck, and later manages to hire this local lad, T.J. to help him. T.J. Agostini supposes, gets found out and eliminated by the Aegis people, so when he doesn't hear from him, Aaron returns to Cornwall, dives on the wreck himself and takes the photos we now have.

Agostini paused in his reflections. Why had so much time passed between Aaron finding the body chained to the wreck and his murder? Only one answer. Agostini recalls Aaron having told someone, was it the girlfriend, that he'd found something that could make him a lot of money? Perhaps he didn't mean the gold on the submarine, as he probably wasn't really aware of the cargo on the submarine, but he could have been blackmailing someone at Aegis, by threatening to reveal the presence of the body and where the wreck site was. That was surely a motive for murder. At this time, Agostini couldn't know that Aegis had tried and failed to buy Aaron Decker's silence.

Aaron was killed while his two housemates, Tim Knight and Martin Lewis were in the house, asleep by their own testimony. Sally was also drugged but not sufficiently to harm her permanently. Why?

By the Occam's razor principal, Knight and Lewis were the only possible killers but there was no evidence to link them to the murder, and no apparent motive for either of them to want to harm Aaron.

"Bloody hell," Oscar Agostini shouted out to the walls of his office. He'd had a personal 'light bulb' moment thanks to his old tried and tested method of singularly brainstorming the case in his head.

He suddenly felt he knew what they'd been missing. The key to cracking the case lay not below the English Channel or on the university cricket pitch, or in a care home in Bavaria, or on the Baltic coast though he was sure that was probably where it all began but somewhere and with someone they hadn't even considered up to this point. Sitting quietly at the periphery of the case was someone they hadn't even spoken to so far. Again, Agostini asked himself that one final question just to make sure of his thoughts. Why hadn't Sally Metcalfe been murdered along with Aaron Decker? It would surely have been easy enough to kill her at the same time, and would leave less chance of her being a witness to anything. The answer was still the same one he'd just

343

arrived at. Was Sally Metcalfe a killer? Did she collude with Knight and Lewis to murder her boyfriend? No, of course she didn't, but the man who was probably responsible for carrying the pilfered gold from Cornwall to its final destination, somewhere in Europe to one of Aegis's facilities on the continent, and who must have known what was planned for Decker could only be her bloody father!

Oscar Agostini picked up the phone. He had some calls to make.

Chapter 30

Robin

Robin parked the stolen Land Rover a little way down the road from the house shared by Tim Knight and Martin Lewis. Thankfully, most of the residents were still at work, college or whatever, he didn't really care. The email he'd received from Finch had been wonderfully comprehensive and Robin was fully conversant with their day to day routine.

Knight was at cricket practice, so could wait a little. Lewis was at home, but his file indicated he'd be leaving home any time now to spend an hour at the gym three streets away, which he visited twice a week. Luckily for Robin, this was one of those days.

Sure enough, five minutes later a man matching the photograph Robin held in his left hand emerged from the house with a back pack over his shoulder, headphones in place as he listened to some kind of music and began a slow jog along the pavement in the opposite direction from where Robin was parked. Perfect!

Lewis reached the end of the street and pressed the button on the pedestrian crossing, and waited for the lights to turn green in his favour, red for the traffic. Robin calmly pulled out of his parking space, and with military precision, judged his moment perfectly, flooring the accelerator pedal just as the lights switched and Lewis started to cross the road. At the very last second, Lewis heard, maybe sensed the sound and approach of the onrushing vehicle as it came towards him and too late, tried to avoid it. The Land Rover literally propelled Martin Lewis like a rag doll into the air, his body bouncing up off the bonnet of the vehicle before sailing over the roof to land in the road, broken, bloody, and very, very dead. It all happened so quickly, Robin was clean away before a young woman, pushing a toddler in a pushchair, realised what had happened before her eyes and began to scream. A full twenty seconds passed before another car turned into the quiet street, the woman frantically flagging it down and the driver running to the nearest phone box to dial 999 to summon the emergency services.

Robin drove carefully, keeping to the speed limit, and returned the Land Rover to the multi-storey car park he'd taken it from, deliberately leaving it on a level higher than he'd stolen it from. Confuse the enemy; that was his strategy. He walked to where he'd left his own car and casually drove out of the car park towards his next 'appointment' with death.

As the virtually new, 2003 model Lexus carrying Robin sedately proceeded towards his next target, another car, this one carrying Ferris and Dodds happened to pass him travelling in the opposite direction. The two detectives, having reported to D.C.I. Agostini were on their way to pick up Knight and Lewis for further questioning, hoping to find the two men at home at that late hour in the afternoon. The Lexus was Robin's own car, hadn't been reported as stolen, was adhering to the speed limit, so there was nothing overtly suspicious about it, just another car on the road, eliciting barely a glance from either man as they passed side by side for a brief second with the killer of Martin Lewis. Robin was using his own vehicle so he could carry out part two of his mission and then simply drive away, home in time for supper.

A few minutes later, Ferris pulled up as they took in the scene ahead. Two police patrol cars, an ambulance and a scene of general pandemonium greeted them as they attempted to approach the house on Manor Court.

Despite the terrible injuries caused by the impact of the Land Rover on the body of Martin Lewis, his face, though bloodied, was instantly recognisable to Ferris and Dodds.

"Shit, shit, shit," Ferris shouted. Holding up his warrant card, he barked at the nearest constable, "What the fuck happened here?"

"Looks like a hit-and-run," said the young officer. "The young woman over there with the kid in the pushchair seems to be the only witness, but she said it all happened so fast, it hardly registered with her mind at first. By the time she realised what had happened and started screaming her lungs out, the car that hit him was long gone."

Ferris shared Ross's belief that coincidences were often just too convenient in explaining away sudden events like this. It had to have been deliberate.

"Nick, for fuck's sake get to the house. Check and see if Knight's there. I think this was a cold-blooded murder. Someone wants to make sure we don't talk to this pair of scallys."

Nick Dodds set off at a run towards the house as Ferris got on the radio to headquarters, quickly being patched through to D.C.I. Agostini.

The horrified chief inspector cursed and immediately asked if Knight was safe in the house.

"Dodds is checking, sir. Hang on, he's coming back."

Still running, Dodds breathlessly shouted to Ferris from ten yards away, "Not there Paul."

"I heard that," Agostini said. "Where the hell is he?"

"I don't know, sir. Any suggestions?"

"Let me think, Ferris. It sounds as if the bastards know we're getting close, and are trying to eliminate anyone who can connect them to the case. Looks like we were right to eventually latch on to Knight and Martin."

"But why would they kill their friend, sir?"

"Probably for the oldest motive in the world, Ferris, money. When this is over, I'll bet we find those two were paid a handsome sum to eliminate poor Aaron Decker."

"Bastards," Ferris said loudly, and then, "Sorry, sir."

"Don't apologise, Ferris. Those are my thoughts too. Look, you and Dodds knock on a few doors, and get those uniformed lads on the scene to help you. See if any neighbours are at home and if any of them know anything about Knight's routine. We might get lucky if one of them knows where he might be."

"Okay, sir. I'll get back to you ASAP if we find anything out."

"Good lad, Ferris. Now go, don't waste time. Tim Knight is in danger. I'm certain of it."

As the ambulance carrying Martin Lewis's body pulled away slowly with no need for sirens or flashing lights, Ferris and Dodds, in company with the four uniformed constables from the patrol cars, began knocking on doors.

Nick Dodds appeared to have struck lucky when one elderly man who lived opposite Knight and Lewis and who had come out to see what the commotion in the street was all about informed the detective that he often talked to Knight about cricket, being a fan himself, and he knew Knight often went to net practice after completing his studies. He knew this to be one of those days as he'd seen Tim Knight leaving his home that morning carrying his cricket bag, containing his bat and pads.

"Thanks, Mr. Collins. You wouldn't happen to know where Tim goes for net practice would you?"

Dodds asked hopefully, though his luck ran out at that point.

"Sorry, young man," said Collins. "I've no idea, but you could try the university. That's who he plays for isn't it?"

"Yes, of course," Dodds replied. He knew full well that the university was a large and sprawling microcosm of a community, with more than one playing field in more than one location. If Tim Knight was in imminent danger, he realised they needed to move fast in locating him.

"Damn," said Ferris when Dodds reported Mr. Collins's information to him. "They wouldn't hold net practice on the main playing surface would they? I know sod all about cricket, Nick. I'm a soccer fan, like you."

"So who might know?" Dodds mused aloud and then brightened up as he said, "Sally Metcalfe."

"His girlfriend?"

"Sure. She must have gone along now and then to watch him practice and then maybe gone on to the pub for a drink or back to the house for a sweaty shag?"

"Nick, you've got a dirty mind mate," Ferris grinned.

"Yeah, I know," Dodds laughed, "but she's a bit fit that girl of his, you must admit, with that long blonde hair, great legs and a nice pair up top. I wouldn't mind a quickie with her, that's for sure."

"Nick, we don't have time for this, and I'm a married man, remember? We need her number, now, you bloody pervert."

"Hey, just fantasising, you know? I don't know her number, do you?"

"No, but wait," said Ferris quickly putting in a call to Sam Gable at headquarters.

"Sam's got it," he said triumphantly, "and she just phoned Sally while I held on. The nets are at the Mile End playing field, let's go."

Leaving the uniformed officers to continue their house to house inquiries for witnesses to the death of Martin Lewis, the two detectives dived into their car and sped off with a squeal of tyres in hopes of reaching Tim Knight before the as yet unidentified assailant. Meanwhile, Control were sending the nearest uniform branch patrol car to the Mile End Sports Ground as back up. If possible they would detain Knight until the detectives arrived.

Tim Knight, knowing nothing of the events of the last hour or so had showered and changed at the end of practice, and was walking out of the practice ground with Simon Dewar. At the car park, Dewar offered Knight a lift in his car, but fatefully, Tim Knight said he would walk to the nearby pub, The Journeyman, have a drink or two and then get a taxi home. Tim waved at Dewar as he pulled out of the car park and began to walk towards the pub. He had only gone a few yards when a voice from behind made him stop.

"Mr. Knight?" said a tall uniformed policeman.

"Yes?" Knight replied. "Can I help you?"

"Actually you can, sir," said the officer who came closer to Tim and smiled.

"Is this to do with Aaron?" Knight asked.

"Oh, yes, you could say that," the policeman replied, quickly checking there was no one else around and then removing his right hand from the pocket into which he'd slipped it when he first saw Knight.

Before Tim Knight could react, the man raised his hand and quickly stabbed a tiny, dart shaped needle into the young man's neck.

"What the hell? What do you think you're…"

Tim Knight never got to finish his sentence as the fast acting poison hit his nervous system. His body appeared to go into an instant seizure, breathing arrested and cardiac arrest followed in seconds, and the young man was dead before his body hit the ground.

Robin walked away without hesitating, job done. As he climbed into his car, parked around the corner from the street where Knight lay dead, a police patrol car sped past on its way to the sports ground. The two constables, seeing what appeared to be another of their own, waved and Robin waved back. That was the moment when they first saw the body of Tim Knight lying on the ground and the senior man in the car made a leap of faith in his decision making and told his partner to swing the car round and go after the officer they'd seen a few moments ago. Constable Les Dunn had quickly realised a uniformed officer wouldn't be driving an unmarked car and was convinced the man was bogus, and probably the killer of the man on the ground.

"Radio it in, now," he shouted at Constable Danny Jewel as he switched on the siren and lights and set off in pursuit of the blue Lexus driven by Robin.

Less than twenty seconds later, Ferris and Dodds arrived on the scene and almost simultaneously heard Jewel's message to control and saw the body of Tim Knight on the ground.

Making a fast decision, Ferris dropped Dodds off at the scene to call headquarters and await the arrival of the forensic and medical teams. He then sped off to join in the pursuit of the Lexus.

Robin couldn't believe his bad luck. He'd almost been clean away when those stupid plods had arrived in the patrol car, and put two and two together. Now, he threw the car round turn after turn as the police Peugeot screamed along within a hundred yards of his rear. It had been six years since his last foray into Merseyside in general and Liverpool in particular and that had been solely for the purpose of visiting Goodison Park on a rare meet-up with his younger brother, Malcolm, to watch an Everton versus Manchester United football match. Mal, married with two kids and a pretty wife, and neat semi-detached suburban house was nothing like his brother, lived in a smart suburb of Chester and the pair found it easier to maintain a passing relationship rather than a close one, exchanging cards on birthdays or at Christmas, only meeting once or twice a year when Mal would bore him to death with happy family news and the latest on their mother's failing state of health. Robin always wondered how the old girl had lasted so long, her lungs buggered up from a lifetime of smoking twenty a day and her joints riddled with arthritis.

His unfamiliarity with his surroundings now meant that Robin was lost in a maze of unknown streets and roads that could lead anywhere. The damned patrol car seemed to be getting closer. Another slice of ill fortune for Robin had placed Les Dunn behind the wheel of the chasing car. Dunn was qualified as a high-speed chase driver and his skills behind the wheel were honed to a fine art. Whatever Robin could do, Dunn could react to instantly.

Back at headquarters, Oscar Agostini wasn't sitting idle either. Galvanised by the opportunity to apprehend the killer and perhaps grasp an opportunity to crack the case wide open, the D.C.I. soon had an all points bulletin out on the airwaves, and consequently, every patrol car and beat officer in the city was quickly appraised of the ongoing chase and was on the lookout for the blue Lexus, its registration plate number having been provided by P.C. Jewel in the chasing car.

Robin, determined not to be taken lightly, reached under his fake policeman's jacket and withdrew his trusty Glock from its shoulder holster. He only took a couple of seconds to extract it and place it on the passenger seat but that momentary lapse in concentration would cost him dear.

Seemingly appearing from nowhere a second police patrol car suddenly pulled out from a side road to join in the pursuit of the Lexus. Seeing the new chaser in his rear view mirror, Robin instantly pushed his foot down hard on the accelerator, and as he did so, an elderly lady in an old black Fiat Panda pulled out of a side road directly in front of Robin, who tried, too late, to swerve around her. The Lexus swiped the rear quarter of the Panda, hit a parked Ford Focus and bounced into the air, turning an almost graceful cartwheel as it flew over the Ford, almost in slow motion in the eyes of those watching and struck a lamp post head-on with a sickening sound of crunching, tearing metal as the pre-stressed concrete structure buried its steel reinforced body into the speeding car's engine compartment. As the car's air-bags deployed, Robin was aware of a sharp pain in both legs as the car's momentum continued its forward motion and his legs were crushed as the lamppost broke into the passenger compartment of the Lexus, and then, everything went black.

Ferris appeared on the scene within minutes, and ran swiftly from the car to take stock of the situation. The old woman in the Panda appeared to be fine and Ferris gave her into the care of one of the constables to await the arrival of the medics.

"Is he alive?" Ferris asked P.C. Dunn immediately as he stepped closer to the crashed car.

"I think so," Dunn replied. "It's my guess the airbag saved him from fatal head damage, but he's out cold, that's for sure."

"That was some nifty driving by the way," Ferris complimented him, and Dunn basked for a moment in the congratulations.

"Thanks. I'm assuming we arrived after he'd killed that poor guy in the street back at the sports ground?"

"That's right," Ferris confirmed. "And another one at Manor Court before that."

"Bloody hell," said Dunn. "A real busy chap eh?"

"Looks that way," Ferris said. "Look, we need to seal the road off until the medics arrive. Can I leave you and your lads to see to it? I need to follow this one up."

"Sure," Dunn replied and he led Jewel and the two officers from the second patrol car to take care of making the area secure, just as the ambulance arrived, blues and twos announcing their arrival well in advance.

"How is he?" Ferris asked the paramedic who had just finished examining the man in the Lexus.

"Both legs broken and probably a severe concussion, maybe other internal injuries. We'll know when we get him back to the Royal," referring to the Royal Liverpool University Hospital, which Ferris found rather ironic considering the circumstances.

"What about getting him out of the car?"

"The fire brigade will be here in a minute. We'll need their help to get him out without damaging his legs further."

A quick examination of the old lady in the Fiat confirmed she was shaken up but not badly hurt, leaving Ferris to concentrate on his number one priority.

Right on cue, the fire brigade arrived on the scene, the crew quickly assessing the situation and Ferris stood well back and watched as the fire-fighters used cutting equipment to extricate the man from the concertinaed front end of the Lexus.

As soon as they'd managed to extract him from the shattered front compartment of the car, the paramedics took over, immediately hooking Robin up to a drip and immobilising both legs and his neck.

Ferris radioed to Control, asking them to instruct Nick Dodds to meet him at the Royal and then followed the ambulance as it sped through the busy city streets to the hospital, where Robin was rushed through the Accident and Emergency Department and into surgery, where the doctors began their work.

Ferris was soon in touch with D.C.I. Agostini, who instructed him and Dodds to remain at the hospital until he arranged for uniformed firearms trained officers to be sent to mount a round the clock armed guard on the killer. Agostini would also ensure a detective presence to be in close proximity to the killer at all times, and would send someone to relieve Ferris and Dodds as soon as possible. He wanted a full and detailed report on the events of the afternoon.

Ross and Drake were arriving back at headquarters just as D.C.I. Agostini was being informed by

Sam Gable of the results of the search to identify the
owner of the blue Lexus.

Chapter 31

Hail, hail, the gang's all here

Ross and Drake walked in to the squad room within minutes of Ferris and Dodds having returned from the hospital. Oscar Agostini welcomed them home, at the same time berating them for coming into headquarters instead of going home after their long journey from Cornwall.

"We both needed to check in here first, sir," said Ross, "just to make sure the place was still in one piece," he grinned.

"We can manage to blunder along quite well in your absence, Andy," Agostini countered and then proceeded to give the pair a brief update of their progress while Ross and Drake had been on the South Coast.

Ross was delighted with the news that they had the killer of Knight and Martin under wraps in the hospital, even more so when Derek McLennan, looking up from his desk, added a piece of new information.

"I've got a name for the driver of the Lexus, sir. Well, at least I'm assuming it's him. A check with D.V.L.C. indicates the registered keeper of the Lexus as a Graham Young, with an address in Manchester. Wonder why he was stupid enough to use his own car?"

Everyone knew that the Driver and Vehicle Licensing Centre in Swansea was the fount of all knowledge when it came to information relating to cars on Britain's roads, but that the 'registered keeper' of a vehicle was not always the actual owner, though in most cases it was. They hoped this would be the case with the Lexus.

"Probably expected a quick in and out job and less chance of being pulled than in a stolen car. Do we have anything on this Graham Young?" Ross asked.

"Haven't had time to check him out yet," McLennan apologised. "I'm getting on it now, sir."

"Good lad Derek." Ross said, giving Derek an encouraging pat on the shoulder.

"It's good to have you both back," Sam Gable added as she handed mugs of coffee to each of them.

"Thanks, Sam. We needed this," Izzie Drake said in thanks.

"Where's D.C. Curtis?" Ross asked, noticing the missing face from his team.

"At the hospital, keeping an eye on the Lexus driver," Agostini provided the answer. "He volunteered to take the first shift. I was willing to bring in some help from Division but the team wanted to keep it within the squad as we've come so far."

"I'm taking over from Tony later, sir," said McLennan.

"And I'll be relieving Derek in the morning," Sam Gable added.

"Nick and I will cover the rest of the day tomorrow," Ferris said, as Ross felt a sense of real pride in his team.

"Right, you two," Agostini now said, putting on his most forceful tone of voice, "I'm ordering you both to go home to your spouses, have a hot bath or shower, enjoy your evening, and come in bright and fresh in the morning. We all want to hear your news from Falmouth, but it's getting late in the day and we're not going to get much more done today. Andy, just give me ten minutes in my office first before you go."

"Right, sir. You're the boss," said Ross, who sent Izzie Drake off home while he accompanied the boss into his inner sanctum. Agostini spent five minutes appraising Ross of his theory regarding Sally Metcalfe's father. Ross, who'd seen Agostini perform this particular 'trick' before with his single minded brainstorming sessions agreed it made sense.

"Why the hell didn't I make that connection myself?" he asked.

"Not your fault, Andy," Agostini replied. "You, like the rest of us, had to take in so many facts and theories at once, the glaringly obvious got lost in the middle of everything that was happening around us."

"Hmm, kind of like not seeing the wood for the trees," Ross agreed. "Like bloody Knight and Martin. We should have pressured them more to begin with, but we had no evidence at all to link them with the murder of Aaron Decker."

"Again, not your fault, Andy. We're up against some very clever people here, mark my words. They've been very good at covering their tracks so far but they've suddenly slipped up today."

"Yes, they have. I wonder why?" Ross mused, thinking aloud.

"I have a theory they thought we were closer than we really were, Andy. You and Drake going down to Falmouth and the Royal Navy sending the frigate to help in the investigation must have really put the frighteners on them. They obviously want to silence anyone who can connect Aegis to the killings and the wreck site."

"I agree, Oscar," said Ross, using his friend's first name as they were used to doing in private. "But that means anyone who knew about the wreck who wasn't involved in their operation could be in danger too."

"Don't worry, I thought the same thing. A couple of detectives from the North Wales Constabulary picked Klaus Haller up a couple of hours ago and he's in protective custody. They're going to transfer him into our care tomorrow. We'll put him under guard in a safe house until we catch these bastards."

"Let's hope we catch them soon, then," Ross said. "They're a bunch of cold, heartless bastards, for sure.

Young Decker, the lad T.J, in Cornwall, Knight and Martin, though I can't feel too sorry for them, and God knows how many more, all dead in order to satisfy someone's lust for bloody gold."

"I know, Andy, I know. I've been in touch with D.I. Jones and his boss in Falmouth while you and Sergeant Drake were on the road, and they're aware of what's happened here today. Jones's boss, D.C.I. Small, has agreed to institute round the clock surveillance on the Aegis facility in Falmouth. As soon as we get one slightest scrap of evidence that links them to the wreck or even one of the murders, his people will swarm over the place like a pack of angry wasps."

"We're getting closer, and catching this fellow this afternoon could just be the break we need to open up the whole can of worms."

"I hope so, Andy, now do me a bloody favour and go home to Maria. You look bloody knackered!"

"Okay, I get the point," Ross laughed. "See you in the morning."

"Sleep well, Andy," Oscar Agostini said as Andy Ross walked from the office.

"You too, boss," Ross said as he quietly closed the door behind him, looking forward to an evening at home with his wife. He knew tomorrow would likely prove to be a very busy day.

* * *

Sam Gable was the only member of the team missing from the following morning's briefing. She was at the hospital, keeping watch on the man they now knew to be Graham Young. Curtis and McLennan, despite having both spent most of their night in a similar role, had both arrived for the briefing, anxious to hear what Ross and Drake had discovered in Falmouth and to be involved in the continuing investigation. Both men had decided that sleep could come later,

Ross looked his usual self again, the tiredness of the previous day wiped out by a romantic evening spent with Maria, who'd ensured her husband received a fitting welcome home, a great meal, one of his favourite DVDs to relax with, followed by a couple of hours of conjugal bliss before they'd fallen asleep in each others' arms.

Izzie Drake had enjoyed a similar return to her new husband. Peter had swept her off her feet as soon as she'd walked through the door and in a reverse of Ross's evening timetable, had immediately whisked her off to bed, from where they emerged much later, before showering, ordering a meal from their favourite Chinese takeaway, and then skipping the movie part of the evening as they fell into bed once more. Eventually, they ended up much the same as Andy Ross and Maria, fast asleep, holding each other in a loving embrace.

Both inspector and sergeant felt ready to push the case towards a conclusion, but unusually for him, Ross announced he was initially handing the briefing over to D.C.I. Agostini. His reason for doing so soon became clear as the chief inspector quickly outlined his theory relating to the potential involvement of Sally Metcalfe's father.

As he came to the conclusion of his idea, Agostini summed things up.

"Like a lot of police officers, we may have blundered a little in the beginning, not by anyone being at fault, but because the simple solution actually looked the most unlikely one, and didn't appear to fit any of the known facts. As the case grew more and more complicated we lost sight of the little things, the obvious things, as our very clever adversaries probably expected us to.

I decided to strip the case bare of all its complications, start from scratch, and see if a dog is just a dog is just a dog after all."

"Eh?" Curtis said quietly, only to receive a dig in the ribs from Derek McLennan. Agostini had heard him though.

"D.C. Curtis, all I mean is that just because you start out thinking a dog stole your sausages, but then someone tells you they saw a boy running behind a dog with a string of sausages in his mouth, and then a man appeared on the street offering cheap sausages for sale, it doesn't mean the man and boy were responsible for the dog stealing the sausages. The boy could have been trying to catch the dog to get the sausages back, and the man was probably a legitimate door to door butcher, got it?"

"Er, not really sir, sorry."

"Oh well, never mind," said the chief. "D.C. Ferris, I want you to use your extensive skills on the computer to check out Metcalfe Logistics. I ran a quick search on my own computer before coming to the meeting. Sally's father is Jeffrey Metcalfe, aged fifty five, and the company has depots here and in Spain as she told us in her statement. But, it would appear they own a subsidiary company, Advance Transportation, which operates an international freight service, which could be very useful for anyone wanting to ferry illicit goods from country to country. Use every tool at your disposal, Ferris and see what you can find."

"Right sir," said Ferris.

"Now, I'm sure D.I. Ross has a lot to tell us about his trip to Falmouth, so please, let's hear it, Andy."

"Thank you, sir," said Ross and between them, he and Izzie Drake spent the next twenty minutes giving the team the full run down on the events of the last few days on the south coast, the identification of the wreck of the *Norwich*, the revelation of the gold bullion on board the old U-Boat, and the final, tragic identification of the frogman who they'd all seen in the photos taken originally by Aaron Decker."

"So, D.I. Jones is continuing the investigation from Falmouth too, sir? Dodds asked.

"Yes, he and Sergeant St. Clair will be in daily contact with us, so be ready to speak to them if you happen to answer the phone when they call, introduce yourselves and work with them. We're all on the same case, remember that."

"Okay, sir, no problem," said Dodds.

"Do we know how this T.J. character came to be involved with the case, sir?" Derek McLennan asked.

"We don't know for sure," Ross replied, "but we think it's a safe assumption that Aaron Decker found out he worked at the Aegis facility and made contact with him and somehow convinced him to help dig up the dirt on his employers."

"So, what now, boss?" Curtis asked.

"Now, Tony, we first hope we can get something from Graham Young. Sergeant Drake and I are going over to the Royal in a while to see if he's ready and able to talk yet. With a case like this, I want him out of the hospital and safely under lock and key as soon as possible. If his employers know we have him and are afraid he'll talk, they might try to have him eliminated before he can spill the beans and blow their operation out of the water."

"Nice analogy, sir," Drake smiled.

"What? Oh, yeah, out of the water. Completely unintentional I assure you," he grinned back at her.

"Meanwhile, Klaus Haller is being brought to Liverpool today. He'll go straight to the designated safe house where we can keep him protected at all times. Thanks to D.C.I. Agostini, Interpol are looking into the activities of Ralph Stein and Heinz Schmidt. If either of them is involved, as I suspect will be the case, we'll soon know about it. Derek, you seem to get on well with Herr Haller. Once he's in the safe house, go and see him. Try and find out if there's any way he can help us trace any other living relatives of the men who sailed on *U966*, or *U3000*, or whatever the

Germans called her. Bloody confusing, changing the number the way they did."

"But they must have had a reason sir," Drake said, after having been silent for some minutes. "What if the U-Boat itself formed part of the secret?"

"Go on, Izzie, what are you thinking?"

"Well sir, changing the number of the submarine only makes sense if the Germans didn't want it identified it were sunk or captured by the allies. What if it held some secrets that they wanted to cover up at any cost?"

"Such as?"

"I've no idea, sir. It was just an idea."

In fact, Ross thought it a very good idea that could help their case if they could discover exactly what the extent of the Nazis subterfuge really added up to.

"Derek," he looked at McLennan.

"I know sir, ask Haller."

"Good lad, Derek," Ross said, at the same time thinking what an excellent and intuitive detective Derek McLennan had become in the four years he'd worked under Ross. From a young, idealistic, and naïve young man, McLennan had grown to be a first class investigator with a quick brain and a burning desire to see justice prevail in every case he worked.

* * *

Despite his wife being a doctor, Andy Ross hated hospitals. Something about the smell, the almost institutional colour scheme so typical of such places, the stagnant over-heated air-conditioned air, an all-pervading smell of overcooked cabbage and the constant hubbub of sounds that assaulted his ears on every corridor, made him want to turn and run back out into the fresh air as soon as humanly possible.

After pausing to say hello to Sam Gable and then sending her to the cafeteria to grab a coffee and a bite to eat, Ross and Drake nodded their hellos to the uniformed guards on duty outside the door to the room where Graham Young lay, both legs elevated and securely wrapped in plaster casts. His head was also bandaged, Gable having informed them the doctor had recently informed her that Young was also suffering from intra-cranial bleeding and might need additional surgery to relieve the pressure on his brain.

While travelling to the Royal in their car, Ross and Drake learned more about Young, when Agostini himself contacted them to let them know that Young's fingerprints had led to a positive identification. They now knew that Young was a former sergeant in the Parachute Regiment, who had been dishonourably discharged following an assault on a superior officer. Young had served twelve months in the military prison at Colchester after first striking and then breaking the arm of a Lieutenant who had reprimanded him for smelling of drink while on duty. Since his discharge, Young had apparently been working as a mercenary for some years, but had recently fallen off the grid and his whereabouts and employment details for the last three years were a blank to the authorities.

"Well, well," Ross said, looking down at the figure lying in the bed before him, "looks like you have quite a chequered past, you murdering bastard."

"Do you think he can hear us, sir?" Drake quietly whispered in Ross's ear.

"I doubt it, Izzie, not yet anyway. When he comes round, I want one of our people with him with a recorder so anything he says won't be missed. If we're lucky, he'll be a bit disorientated when he starts to wake up and you never know what he might inadvertently blurt out without him realising he's said it."

"You're a sneaky bastard sometimes, Detective Inspector, you know that don't you?" she smiled.

"But of course, Sergeant Drake," he smiled back at her. "When we get back to headquarters, draw up a rota, Izzie, so we've got someone with Young every minute, day and night, until he wakes up."

"Right sir. Why don't we go see if the doctors can tell us when that's likely to be?"

"You go, Izzie. I want to stay here and get a good long look at this piece of dung. There's a lot he can tell us if we can break him down, but given his background, that's not likely to be an easy task."

"Okay, won't be long," Drake said and she was gone in a second, leaving Ross alone with the killer of Tim Knight and Martin Lewis, themselves a pair of cold-blooded killers for money as far as Ross was concerned.

As Ross waited for Izzie's return, Young stirred, and much to Ross's surprise, his eyes suddenly snapped open. Seeing Ross towering over his bed,

Young seemed to sense just who and what Ross was. In a rasping, dry voice he croaked, "Fuck off, copper," and then closed his eyes again.

Ross quickly went to the door, and ordered one of the constables on guard duty to go and summon a doctor. The nurses station was mere yards away and the P.C. reported that the patient was conscious. A doctor appeared as if by magic within a minute and joined Ross in the room at Young's bedside.

"Good morning, Inspector. I'm Doctor Starling," the doctor introduced himself.

"He woke up, swore at me, then closed his eyes again, Doc," Ross informed the doctor, who proceeded to examine the patient. When he lifted Young's eyelid, Young sprang to life again, protesting at Starling's intrusion.

"Ah, good to see some response from you, Mister Young," Starling said, completely unfazed by Young's reaction. "Try to lie still. You're in the Royal University Hospital. You have two broken legs and scans show you have an intra-cranial bleed."

"Meaning?" Young croaked.

"Meaning you have a potentially serious injury. We may have to operate to prevent pressure building in your head and in turn putting pressure on your brain."

"Can I talk to him, Doctor Starling?" Ross interrupted.

"In a minute, please, Inspector," Starling rebuffed him, as Izzie walked back into the room, surprised to see the doctor with Ross.

"Oh, I just got back from talking to Doctor Clemence," she said, "he got the call from the nurse to say Young was awake and..." and in less than a second, Ross leaped at Starling, knocking him down and pinning him to the floor.

"Cuffs, Izzie, *now*," he shouted and Drake responded instantly, handcuffing the man on the floor as Ross kept him pinned down. Once the prisoner was secure, Ross pulled him to his feet. Starling scowled at Ross and Drake, but could do nothing to prevent Ross from delving into the pockets of his white coat, his right hand emerging with a syringe loaded with a clear liquid.

"Well now, what have we here?" Ross said as he held the hypodermic up for Young to see. "It would appear someone didn't want to take a risk on you talking to us, Mister Young."

"Bastards," was the monosyllabic reply from the man in the bed.

"I take it my return was a timely one," Drake observed.

"Definitely," Ross confirmed as the door opened to admit Doctor Clemence.

"Oh, hope I'm not intruding," Clemence said, as though seeing a man dressed a doctor being held in handcuffs by two police officers in a patient's room was a normal, everyday occurrence in his life.

"Not all, Doctor," Ross replied. "Just a minute and we'll get this impostor out of your way."

Ross called the armed constables into the room and handed Starling over to them.

372

"Get this piece of scum down to headquarters," he ordered. "I'll let them know you're on your way in. Sergeant Drake and I will stay with the patient, along with D.C. Gable when she gets back, until you return."

"Yes sir," the two men echoed each other as Ross took out his mobile phone and called D.C.I. Agostini, who would personally begin interrogating Starling as soon as he was delivered to headquarters.

"Perhaps you'd like to check him over, Doctor?" Ross said to Clemence, who nodded at the detective and then carried out his examination of the patient.

Young remained silent throughout, and Clemence finally stood back from the bed, and turned to Ross.

"He's going to make a full recovery, Inspector, though it will be a while before he's walking again."

"Good," said Ross.

"Yes, well, whatever he's done, he's still my patient and it's my job to patch him up the best I can."

"I know, Doc, but it just seems a waste of taxpayers money to pay for all that treatment for a piece of murdering shite like him."

"Not for me to debate," said Clemence.

"Sure, I won't make it difficult for you," said Ross. "I just want to talk to him."

"Well, I have no objection to that. If you need me, I'll be outside for a few minutes at the nurse's station."

"Thanks, Doc," said Ross and Clemence made his way out of the room, leaving Ross and Drake with Graham Young.

"Well now, that was a turn up for the books wasn't it? Your friends certainly didn't waste any time in trying to silence you, did they?" Ross said to Young who glared back at him.

"Don't tell me you're going to keep silent to protect them after that?" Drake asked. "You ought to be bloody grateful to Detective Inspector Ross here for saving your worthless life."

"Worthless to you maybe, darlin' but not to me," Young replied in his hoarse, croaking voice.

"Well if you don't want your pals coming back to try again, I suggest you tell us what we need to know," Ross said as he stood staring hard at the man in the bed.

Young stared back, still perhaps feeling the effects of the anaesthetic, his eyes seeming to lose focus for a few seconds. In fact, he was quickly mentally weighing up his options. As soon as the bogus doctor had introduced himself to Ross as 'Doctor Starling' Young had instantly realised that the man was another of Finch's operatives and could only be in his room for one purpose. He'd been unable to react quickly or shout a warning to the policeman, but thankfully the real doctor coming in to the room together with Izzie Drake's words had alerted Ross, who'd reacted with surprising speed in taking the man down. Young could only guess at the contents of the syringe Ross had taken from Starling's pocket, but guessed it would probably prove to be the same cyanide compound he'd used on Tim Knight. Fast acting and bloody awful way to die, but over in seconds.

Finch obviously didn't trust him to keep his mouth shut, or maybe that was the American's way of dealing with any of his operatives he felt had failed him. Either way, Graham Young knew he had to make a decision, and as self-preservation was always his priority, the appeal of living to fight another day overrode any thoughts of 'honour among thieves' or any of that old-fashioned malarkey.

Young appeared to Ross to slump back against his pillows and exhaled a deep and almost reluctant breath as he looked up at the Detective who'd just saved his life, and pointed to the water jug on the cabinet beside his bed. Ross nodded to Izzie Drake who filled a small plastic drinking cup with a straw from the jug and held it out to Young. He managed to take and hold the cup while he took a few sips of the already slightly warm water, enough to lubricate his dry throat.

He passed the cup back to Drake without a word, and Izzie placed it back on the cabinet as Ross began to lose patience.

"Well, come on, Young, what's it to be? We know you murdered Tim Knight and Martin Lewis, so you're caught bang to rights on those killings. If you don't want us to start digging further, maybe get Interpol to look into a few unsolved murders across the continent, I suggest you talk to us." Ross turned to Drake, winking at her as he spoke.

"You never know, Izzie, this bastard might have killed more people over the years, maybe in Germany, Greece, Albania, Turkey, oh yes, Turkey or Al-

375

bania would be good ones. I don't think Mr. Young here would receive a very warm welcome in either a Turkish or Albanian prison would he? Of course, if he confesses all, we might be able to keep him here and make sure he serves a nice, long, warm and comfortable sentence in a good old, civilised British prison, but just think of the things we've heard about what happens to good looking chaps like Mr. Young at the hands of the guards, never mind the inmates in Turkish jails especially. Brings tears to your eyes just thinking about it."

"God yes, it does sir. Must say I've never understood what makes men want to do that to other men, but hey, whatever floats your boat, and all that."

Young had heard enough. Ross may have been bluffing about Interpol, but then again, maybe not, and he certainly didn't want them to know about the jobs he'd carried out over the years, including a couple in Turkey. No way was Graham Young going to allow himself to become a faggot for some fat, dirty, unwashed Turkish bastard of a prison guard. He actually subconsciously cinched the cheeks of his backside together as he sighed again and looked up at Ross, who knew instinctively he'd got his man.

"Well, Young? Anything to say?" he asked once again.

Graham Young almost choked on the words as he finally spoke, hatred for his adversary still clear in his eyes, but the words he spoke were just what Andy Ross wanted to hear.

"Alright," he said. "What do you want to know?"

Chapter 32

Finch Unmasked

The excitement among the team at headquarters was palpable as everyone began to believe they were finally closing in on the solution to the case. No sooner had Ross and Drake arrived in the squad room, after arranging for Graham Young to be transferred to another hospital room, under a false name, with armed guards present inside the room rather than outside the door, than the squad received an unexpected visitor.

Jerome Decker III appeared to have aged ten years since the case began with the murder of his son. He at first expressed total surprise at the revelation that his son had been murdered by his two housemates, two men Decker had met and thought to be Aaron's friends. Ross had made him sit down and compose himself as memories began to flood the C.I.A. man's mind.

After a couple of minutes, Decker stood and walked across to where Ross was in a huddle with Agostini and Drake.

"I actually came to bring you some information," Decker said, as he walked up behind them, making them jump in unison.

"Oh, sorry," he apologised.

"No, please, go on Mr. Decker," Agostini said. "I'm presuming those inquiries you were going to get your people to make have borne fruit?"

"In a way, yes," Decker replied. "It seems that the Aegis Institute is to all intents and purposes innocent of any collective or corporate wrongdoing, Chief Inspector, but, my operatives in various locations, have, shall we say, unearthed something interesting?"

"Go on, please," said Ross.

"Okay, with the reports I was receiving, a pattern gradually emerged. You guys already know that for some reason, Aegis has been employing salvage experts to head up some of their facilities and where we identified such people we concentrated our inquiries. We found the men employed to run those facilities all appear to live a little too well, you know what I mean, cars or houses a bit too extravagant for their status in the company and so on. Taken individually it wouldn't add up to a hill of beans and they wouldn't ever have expected a major investigation into their little scam, well a big scam in fact. Everywhere that Aegis has carried out supposed environmental studies or oceanographic research into coastal erosion by wave action or whatever, some kind of historical site has been found nearby, or an ancient wreck or the ruins of an underwater city, and so on. Pretty innocent so far, yes?"

Everyone in the room was listening now and they collectively nodded, like puppets being manipulated by invisible strings, Paul Ferris thought to himself. Decker continued.

"Okay, but, in these cases, it seems that Aegis only arrived on the scene after they made representations to the governments or at least the local regional governments responsible for these locations."

"They weren't invited, then?" Ross asked.

"Not in one single case," Decker confirmed, "and in all those cases the man who made first contact was none other than Francis Kelly, whose official title by the way is Executive Vice President in charge of Overseas Development. My friends at the F.B.I have informed me that Kelly lives in a house comparable with that of Aegis's CEO, but that he also owns a large beach front property in Malibu, a condo in Florida and holiday villas in four European countries, all countries that have an Aegis facility present on their shores."

"But okay," said Ross, "I can accept that Kelly is running a crooked operation, ripping off governments around the world, stealing national treasures or items of historical significance, but my question is, how the hell are they locating these sites in the first place?"

Instead of a reply, Decker picked up a large manila envelope he'd earlier placed on a nearby desk and extricated a large ten by eight inch photograph that he first passed to Ross, who in turn passed it on to Agostini and the others.

"Are you serious?" Ross asked.

"Deadly," said Decker.

"But that's a...a"

"Submarine, Sergeant Drake, exactly," said Decker as Izzie hesitated with the shock of the revelation.

"You're telling us that Aegis has the use of a submarine?" She gasped.

"No, Sergeant, not *a* submarine, *four* of the damned things."

"Where the hell did they get them from?" Ross asked incredulously.

"In 1991, the Soviet Navy effectively ceased to exist with the fall of Communism," said Decker. "You've maybe heard stories of the old Soviet Fleet lying rusting away in various dockyards around the old Soviet Union. Well, that's true but some enterprising Russian entrepreneurs, usually high up in the new democratic but equally corrupt government have made millions of dollars over the years by secretly selling off various parts of the fleet, at least parts that were still operational. The sub in that photo is a Kilo class boat, non-nuclear diesel electric powered. We think they have two of those, plus a couple of Juliett class guided missile subs."

"That's almost unbelievable," a shocked Oscar Agostini managed to gasp.

"Unbelievable but true," said Decker.

"And is that what I think it is behind the conning tower?" Ross asked, looking closely at the photo.

"They call it the 'sail' nowadays, Inspector, not the conning tower," Decker pointed out.

"Oh, right, I stand corrected, but the question remains, is that a bloody great submersible on the deck behind the... sail?"

"It is," Decker confirmed, "and that's how they are finding these sites. They have modern submarine technology with the ability to scan the terrain of the sea bed, and carrying their own submersibles means they can carry our covert examinations of the target areas to see if they're worth 'grave robbing' for want of a better term."

"So they find themselves a possible target, check it out, and if it's a possible source of wealth, they move in with some sort of legitimate offer to the relevant authorities and then proceed to strip the assets from the poor sods who think Aegis is doing them a service."

"That's exactly the way my people read it, Inspector," Decker confirmed.

"But how is this Kelly guy keeping all this secret from his bosses?" Drake asked.

"Easy," said Decker. "As far as the executives of Aegis know, Kelly's people are carrying out legitimate research or whatever, and Kelly and his cronies carry on doing what they do under a cloak of legitimacy."

"But what about the submarines? Why don't they tell the countries they are working for about them?" asked Derek McLennan.

"Politics, Detective," said Decker. "No way do the Aegis board want anyone to know they are sailing around the oceans in a small fleet of former Soviet attack submarines, for obvious reasons."

"Sure, I see," said McLennan.

"It seems clear to me," said Decker. "Kelly and his highly specialised team of crooked operatives have gained control of one or more of the submarines, and using some form of intelligence gathering system that I'd love to infiltrate, they are managing to target specific areas that might yield massive personal profits if they can first of all negotiate a legitimate contract with the relevant government, and then they send one of their subs in to confirm the possibility for profit. If there is nothing in it for them, they allow a normal Aegis research team or exploration vessel to carry out the contract and everything is perfectly legit, a perfect cover in fact for the shady operations that develop when they identify potential, illegal profit making enterprises. It also serves a purpose by keeping the main board of the Aegis out of the loop because all they see are normal, oceanographic studies or environmental investigations being carried out by their people and equipment."

"But, how do they cover up the crooked operations?" Ross asked the C.I.A. man.

"That should be no problem for Kelly either," Decker replied. "Look at the Falmouth job, as I'll call it. Aegis Oceanographic in the States are aware only of the legitimate side of the operation taking place in the English Channel, as Herr Heller discovered when he contacted them. So, they have instant plausible deniability which is genuine because Kelly's people are running the salvage and plundering of the wreck site as what we'd call a 'Black Op' with only a small number of people aware of the true nature of what they're up to. I'll bet if we could access their records, we'd find a team of scientists and underwater specialists are in fact gathering data on the environmental issues surrounding not just this site, but others in the English Channel, with only Kelly's gangsters actually working this particular site."

"That's absolutely diabolically brilliant," Oscar Agostini grudgingly admitted.

"Yes it is," said Decker, "and Kelly obviously has enough personal finance behind him to run these special operations without disturbing the company's finances and raising suspicion."

Ross had remained virtually silent throughout Decker's report, realising also just how far reaching the intelligence gathering skills of the C.I.A, could reach into the lives and the operations of people and organisations around the world. Having heard what Decker had to say, he felt it an opportune moment to fill in the assembled group of detectives and Decker on what he and Drake had learned in their time at the bedside of Graham Young.

"All you've said makes sense, Mr. Decker and tends to fit what we've learned from Kelly's hired killer,

Graham Young. As soon as he realised that Kelly had sent a man to eliminate him after he'd fallen into our hands, he became a little less reluctant to cover up for his employer who must be one hell of a ruthless man,"

"He did what?" Decker asked and Ross, realising that Decker wasn't aware of recent events at the hospital, quickly brought him up to date with what had occurred in Young's room.

"Holy cow," Decker retorted. "Ruthless indeed. Please go on, Inspector Ross. Sorry for the interruption."

"Well," Ross began again, "according to Young, the boss as he put it, employs a team of specialist 'damage limitation experts' as they call themselves to make sure the illegal operations remain secure from outside interference. The man who heads up this team, mostly former mercenaries and Special Forces personnel, is known only as Mr. Finch. All the members of the team are known by code names, in Young's case, his is 'Robin'. That's what gave the bogus doctor away to Young at the hospital although he couldn't cry out to warn us at the time. When he introduced himself to me as Doctor Starling, another bird's name, Young knew right away he was as good as dead. If the real doctor hadn't come in to the room at that moment, with our own 'bird,' Sergeant Drake of course, it's likely Starling would have asked us to leave while he carried out some bogus examination of the patient and would have injected Young with the assumed poisonous contents of the syringe we took from him."

"Sorry to interrupt again," said Decker, "but where is this Starling guy right now?"

"In custody," said Ross, "cooling his heels under guard in an interview room waiting for me and Sergeant Drake to question him." "That's great," Decker enthused. "So, you have two of the bastards under lock and key."

"Yes," Ross agreed, "but from what Young told us, each of these men is a highly trained killer, ready to kill at a minutes notice without conscience. None of them are privy to the running of the organisation and all work for the man known as Finch who in Young's case at least, contacted him initially by email. After a few messages between them, a meeting was set up and Young was hired as a 'security consultant' and given the name 'Robin'. I doubt any of them has access to Kelly. Young says he's never heard of him, and I tend to believe him. Having someone try to kill you in your hospital bed tends to focus the mind and destroy any old allegiances in my experience."

"So, how we can use them in trying to crack the case, sir?" asked Derek McLennan.

"Well, Sergeant Drake and I have concocted a plan," Ross replied and nodded to Drake, who continued.

"We hope to use Young as bait," she said. "Young doesn't want to spend the rest of his life looking over his shoulder, so he's agreed to help us. In return, we'll recommend he be tried over here and not handed over for extradition if anyone else comes seeking him for previous crimes. He knows we can't make

385

promises but he's trusting us to do our best. We'll let word slip out that Young is talking and is being held in a safe house, which he will be, but not at the address we'll leak.

Young thinks it likely that Finch might just try to finish him off himself once word leaks that Starling failed. He says Finch is an arrogant so and so and it would be just the way he'd work things to make sure Young is out of the way for good. If he can't trust Starling then he'll try to finish the job himself."

"But why eliminate Young if he can't tie them to Kelly?" McLennan asked.

"Because Young ties in to Finch, and Finch is obviously connected to Kelly and if we establish that link we might just be able to bring the whole house of cards down. Finch must be worried and therefore Kelly is too."

"So really the man we want is Finch?"

"That's right, Derek," Ross replied this time. "Even Young thinks Finch knows enough to identify Kelly as the brains behind the operation. He's bragged to 'Robin' that he knows enough to cause trouble for the paymasters if they try to dupe or double cross him."

"But I thought Finch was in America," McLennan probed further.

"Young doesn't think so," said Ross. "Kelly is, but not Finch. Young believes Finch is the head of security for the UK, maybe Europe too, but even though Finch talks with a U.S accent and tries to make Young believe he's in the States when he speaks on the phone, Young says sometimes there are none of the distinctive sounds present on the line like you get from an international call when he speaks to Finch. He's convinced Finch spends time in both countries and if this is where the action is this is where he'll be."

"This Finch guy sounds a slippery customer," Jerome Decker interjected.

"Yes he does, Mr. Decker, and listen to this. Young told us he believes Finch is ex-C.I.A."

"What?" Decker exploded. "I need to find out who that rat is. I'll personally drown his ass in your River Mersey if I can get my hands on his sorry throat. Did Young or Robin, whatever his name is give you a description?"

"Yes he did," Izzie Drake replied to his question, taking out her notebook from her shoulder bag. "Young says he only met Finch once, when the other man interviewed him for the job."

The others coughed and almost laughed at the description of hiring a hitman at an interview.

"I know, I know," said Drake, knowing what they were chuckling at, "but that's what Young called it. Anyway, he says Finch was around forty to forty-five years old, just short of six feet tall he thought, though the man was seated most of the time. Young has travelled extensively and he was certain Finch's accent put him as being from New York, though he'd tried to refine it a little. He had brown hair, thinning on top with a hint of grey at the sides, brown eyes, and had an Italian look about him."

Ross couldn't help but notice a look of intense concentration on Decker's face, one eye was almost closed, and his head was slightly tilted to one side, as though he was accessing some long buried memory bank in his brain. Meanwhile, Izzie Drake continued.

"Young said the one feature that made Finch stand out was something he only noticed when he shook hands with Finch as they were parting company. He said he couldn't help noticing that Finch had no little finger on his right hand and something made him look at the other hand and Finch was missing the little finger on that hand too."

Jerome Decker virtually exploded as recognition swept through him.

"Lambert," he shouted so loud everyone in the room was totally shocked by his outburst. "Fucking Randolph Lambert," his voice grew even louder.

Ross placed a hand on Decker's right shoulder in an attempt to calm him down.

"Mr. Decker, please, calm down. I take it you know who this man is?"

"I do, Inspector Ross," said Decker, lowering his voice to a reasonable decibel level. "Randolph Lambert was a first class operative until he was captured on a covert mission into Iraq during the first Gulf War. Saddam's Secret Police had him for nearly three months, tried everything to get him to betray his two fellow agents who were with him in Tikrit. They cut one of his fingers off and he didn't talk. They cut off his other little finger and he still didn't talk. When they cut off the things you didn't see, two toes from each foot, and then began beating his bleeding feet, Lambert cracked. Who could blame him? Thing is, before the Secret Police could act on his informa-tion, the building they were in was assaulted by an extraction team ordered in by his co-agents in the town. They took one look at what those bastards had done to Lambert and shot them where they stood. Lambert was treated and repatriated to the States but due to his injuries he wasn't considered suitable for field work any longer. He was given a desk job but it soon became evident his mind had gone. He blamed the Agency for what had happened to him, said we should have got him out sooner, which we would have done if we'd known where they were holding him. He was subjected to a psyche evalua-tion which deemed him unfit for service so he was pensioned off, invalided out of the service. He made a lot of noise at the time, saying he'd been betrayed by those he'd fought to protect and was eventually placed in a psychiatric hospital. He was resourceful though and escaped and has been living off the grid until now. He's obviously using his former skills to run his own squad of highly paid mercenaries in a pseudo-security operation on sale to the highest bid-der"

"You sound as if you knew him well, Mr. Decker," said Ross, speculating that there was a punch line to all this.

"I did, Inspector Ross," Decker confirmed. "I was the person he blamed the most for his capture. You see, I was his handler, his superior officer. I sent Randy to Iraq in the first place. His mind somehow twisted into holding me responsible for his capture, incarceration and torture. The fact that I organised the team that eventually broke him out of there and took him home got lost somewhere along the trail. Now he's responsible for the death of my son."

Decker's head slumped into his shoulders as his words dried up.

The room fell silent. For a while, nobody could think of a word to say. Ross, Drake, Agostini and the rest of the team quickly realised that finding those responsible for Aaron's murder had now taken on an even greater significance for Jerome Decker III.

"You can't think Lambert knew right from the start that Aaron would become involved, surely?" Drake asked the American.

"No, Sergeant Drake, I don't. But once he knew someone was poking around in his UK operation and then discovered it was Aaron, he would have had a perverse sense of revenge in ordering his murder. Gentlemen, ladies, rest assured, I will do everything in my power, personally and professionally to bring him down, and all those connected with him. Aaron's killers may be dead, but the ones who ordered his death and maybe others are still free. I hope this doesn't close the case for you, Inspector Ross?"

"Far from it," Ross replied. "There's still the matter of the death of T.J. Knowles in Cornwall and the involvement of Sally Metcalfe's father in transporting stolen artefacts and bullion to be taken into consideration, plus his possible connection to Aaron's death."

Decker appeared stunned.

"You really think Metcalfe could have been involved in Aaron's death? He was his daughter's boyfriend for Christ sakes."

"Someone helped to set up the whole scenario here in Liverpool. Someone told them where Aaron and Sally would be that night. Who better than her own father?" Ross added.

"Jesus H. Christ," Decker exclaimed. "This gets worse by the minute."

"Yes it does, Mr. Decker, and now I need to ask you to let us get on with our jobs and try to close the net on these bastards. Any help you and your people can give, as long as it remains focussed outside the United Kingdom, will of course be appreciated."

Decker nodded his agreement.

"Anything, Inspector, anything at all."

"Thank you," said Ross as his face seemed to set into a hard and determined look as he spoke to his team.

"For now, everyone, we have a sting to set up, a trap to bait."

Chapter 33

A singing canary and a history lesson for Tony Curtis

In order to put their plan to lure the man known as Finch into their trap into operation, Ross and Drake spent an hour in the company of Graham Young, the killer now so concerned with his own self-preservation that he was to use Ross's awful pun, 'singing like a canary' in his efforts to deflect blame onto those responsible for the plot that had led to the deaths of Aaron Decker, T.J. Knowles, and the two housemates, Tim Knight and Martin Lewis.

Everything he knew, he told the detectives, until eventually they managed to build up the best picture they possibly could of the man known as Finch, a.k.a. Randolph (Randy) Lambert.

Ross's next move was to contact D.I. Brian Jones in Falmouth. He needed to give the Cornish detective the news of Young's capture.

"Brian," Ross said as Jones answered his extension at the police station in Falmouth, "glad to catch you in the office."

"Hello, Andy. Something tells me, by the sound of your voice, that you have news to impart."

"Very astute my friend, and yes, I do. We have the killer of T.J. Knowles in custody, though not before he'd managed to kill the two men who carried out the murder of Aaron Decker."

"Bloody hell," Jones said loudly down the phone. "Sounds like you've been busy up there."

"We have, Brian, but I'm only sad we were one step behind them most of the way and just too late to save Knight and Lewis, Aaron Decker's housemates."

"Why the hell did they kill their own friend?" Jones asked an obvious question.

"Money, mostly, Brian. According to Young, Knight had the bigger incentive, because believe it or not he was jealous of Aaron's prowess at cricket and he also coveted Sally Metcalfe, Aaron's girlfriend. Lewis was the follower, the weaker of the two, but he'd run up some nasty gambling debts and saw this as a way out of hock, and a new start."

"Bloody hell," Jones's Cornish accent seemed to grow stronger as he became more animated. "I can scarce believe it. Andy, did this Young character tell you what happened to T.J?"

"He did, Brian. Seems young Aaron met him in a pub in Falmouth as we thought, got talking to him and found he worked for Aegis. T.J. must have shot his mouth off a little about being fed up with the poor

wages Aegis was paying to their U.K staff and Aaron
targeted him as a potential helper. When he told T.J
what he thought Aegis was up to, T.J was happy to
join forces in the hopes that there'd be something
in it for him. Aaron must have told him there was
the potential to make some money. I think Aaron's
real plan was to find out what Aegis was up to and
simply blackmail them. Gold bullion was outside the
realms of what Aaron could possibly carry or sell on
so blackmail makes sense. All he had to do was come
up with enough proof of exactly what they were up
to. I think he was killed because he'd made contact
with Aegis and tried to put his blackmail plan into
operation. He used Haller to establish the credentials
of the wrecks once he knew Aegis was diving on the
site. God knows how many dives he and T.J. made
over the months but they eventually figured it out.
Of course, we all know how it all turned out, Brian."

After a moment's silence, Jones asked Ross the inevitable question.

"So, what happens now, Andy?"

Ross outlined his plan, as agreed with Agostini,
which met with immediate approval from Brian
Jones.

"Anything we can do to help, let me know," the
Falmouth detective offered.

"I'm sure we'll need you and your people at some
point, Brian. Probably be an idea to let your guvnor
know the score, and be ready for a call. We're obviously going to have to hit the Aegis facility down
there before long, but first we need to get our hands

on this Finch character and hopefully cause some panic in the minds of the top man in the organisation."

"And you think it's this Kelly character, right?"

"Maybe, but there's a possibility he may be the front man for someone higher up in the Aegis hierarchy."

"Bloody hell, Andy. Just how far does this thing reach?"

"Hopefully, we're not far from finding out, my friend. By the way, how are our Navy friends getting on down there?"

"I thought you'd never ask," Jones replied. "The *Wyvern* was joined on station as they call it by a Royal Fleet Auxiliary salvage tug, the *Whitehaven Castle.* Don't be fooled by the word 'tug' Andy. I had a mental picture of something like you see pushing ocean liners around in the movies, but God, this thing anchored off Falmouth the day before yesterday and it's bloody massive, even bigger then the *Wyvern.* She's not a very pretty ship, nothing like a sleek warship like the *Wyvern* but Cap'n Howell says the *Whitehaven Castle* has instantly speeded things up and they anticipate completing their investigation of the wreck of the *Norwich* in a few days time, after which she will be designated as an official war grave. The Navy is holding a memorial service at sea for the crews of the sub and the *Norwich* too and I'd really like you and Izzie to come down and see that short ceremony of dedication, if you're able to, Andy."

"Of course we'll be there, Brian. I'll get it cleared with D.C.I. Agostini today and you can then book us in to the Hope and Anchor again if you don't mind."

"No problem, Andy."

"Any news on the U-Boat, Brian?"

"They're working on the submarine today. I'll call you as soon as I know anything with an update."

"I'd appreciate that, thanks Brian."

"So what's next for you guys up there?" Jones inquired.

"My D.C.I. is talking with his boss, Detective Chief Superintendent Hollingsworth about involving our friends across the pond. We are going to need the Americans' help if we're to bring Kelly to justice. We can't touch him as long as he's in the States, but the F.B.I. can. And then of course, we've got Aaron's father, the C.I.A. man and his contacts working the Continental Europe angle. Hollingsworth will also liaise with the other European police forces in countries affected by Aegis's crooked operations. Hopefully we can bring the whole lot down in one fell swoop in a single well co-ordinated operation."

"Blimey," said Jones. "You make the whole thing sound like a bloody military operation, Andy."

"It seems like it, doesn't it? Anyway, this whole thing harks back to World War Two with the sinking of the *Norwich* and the *U966*, or *U3000*, or whichever you want to call it, Brian, so it's rather appropriate we should use military style planning to bring these murdering bastards down, don't you think?"

"There's no arguing with that," Jones agreed. "So this Chief Super of yours, do you think he can swing it with the Yanks and all the Euro-forces."

"He's a she, actually," Ross corrected his Cornish counterpart. "D.C.S. Sarah Hollingsworth is one damned tough cookie, Brian. Good looking, brains, and a clinical and analytical mind. She's been in the job three years now and I can tell you, if anyone can pull it all together in a short space of time, she can."

"Wow, she sounds like a real firebreather," Jones quipped.

"Well, I've heard she can be a bit of a dragon in meetings," Ross joked and the two men shared a brief few seconds of laughter.

* * *

Klaus Haller was in his element. Safely ensconced in a safe house organised by Merseyside Police, located a few miles east of the city in St. Helens, with two armed police officers inside and two more outside for his protection, plus the company of Detective Constable Tony Curtis, who'd been sent to check on his progress, Haller was a busy man. Curtis had taken the place of Derek McLennan in visiting the historian when Ross informed them that McLennan was needed for a special assignment, related to the current case. Very mysterious, Curtis thought, but Ross said no more.

The German historian was proving a real asset to the investigation. Even as Ross and his team were thinking along the same lines, Haller had decided that someone with a connection to the strange circumstances surrounding the false *U966*'s last mission had to be connected to the current case. Of course, there was old Hans Schmidt and Ralph Stein, but Haller's own inquiries showed that Schmidt, now old and infirm, was suffering from Alzheimer's disease and could be easily eliminated as a suspect. Stein was a possibility but though he lived close to an Aegis facility, his life since leaving the Kriegsmarine had been an exemplary one and his chances of being involved, at least to Haller, seemed tenuous to say the least.

Being the historian that he was, an established academic and expert in his field, Haller had devised a new theory, one he now sat explaining to D.C. Curtis.

"We must remember," Haller began, "that the boat we are now referring to as *U966* was in fact *U3000*, sailing under a false designation. We know there were no survivors from the sinking of the U-Boat, but we Germans, and the Nazis in particular have always been known for keeping scrupulous records, D.C. Curtis. So, the crew records for *U3000* must have been altered to show the men of *U3000* to be serving on the false *U966*. There is no way the boat would have sailed without a full crew and cargo manifest being compiled, which leads me to believe we may have missed another person, two perhaps, who may have been aware of the nature of this *U966*'s mission."

Tony Curtis was a bright and quick-thinking young detective and without further prompting, he quickly latched on to Haller's train of thought.

"Clerks, administrative staff, that's what you're getting at, isn't it, Herr Haller?"

"*Sehr gut,* forgive me, I mean to say, very good. Yes, that is what I am getting at. Now, my research while I have been in this nice house you have accommodated me in has thrown up two names. The first was the senior dockyard superintendent's secretary at the Kiel Submarine base, Brigitte Kraus, who was responsible for maintaining all such manifests as I previously mentioned. The second is Helene Schneider."

Haller paused and waited for Curtis to accept the bait in his hesitancy.

"And she is, or rather, was?"

"Helene Schneider, Detective Curtis, was at the time of the redesignated *U966's* voyage, the personal secretary to Admiral Stein. She was only twenty at the time, and is now seventy-eight years old, but in full health, as I have discovered."

"You think this Helene Schneider is the one, don't you, Herr Haller?" Curtis astutely observed.

"Oh yes, I do, I most certainly do, Mr. Curtis," said Haller as the excitement in his voice grew by the second, "though not directly. Fraulein Schneider married in 1950, and records show she gave birth to three children in the next ten years. Helene married a former naval officer, Jürgen Reinhardt, who was unconnected to the U-Boat arm of the service. Now for the interesting part, D.C. Curtis. She had two daughters, Lotte and Inge, and a son, Anton. Life in post-war Germany was hard, though the Reinhardt family were fortunate to live in that part of Germany you called West Germany, and not in the so-called German Democratic Republic, East Germany to you, and controlled by the Soviet Union. The best way to make a good life in those times was through a good education and Helene and Jürgen encouraged their children to make a good future for themselves.

To cut this short, Anton went to university in Heidelberg and is now a respected research chemist working for a large pharmaceutical company, involved in developing new drugs to combat various cancers. Lotte never married and is a journalist for a feminist magazine based in Munich, where she lives with her lesbian lover, Hilda Neumann. This leaves us with Helene's youngest daughter, Inge. Whether by coincidence or design I cannot say, but Inge Reinhardt, while studying history, much like Aaron Decker met and fell in love with a much older man, named Robert Ackermann."

Haller paused for breath and took a sip from the glass of water on the table in front of him. Curtis did the same. He found it strangely enthralling listening to the passionate way the German historian related this story to him. History had never been a favourite subject of his at school, but somehow, Klaus Haller had the knack of making the events and the people he talked about come to life in the listener's mind. After audibly clearing his throat, Haller continued with his story.

"Now, where was I? Ah, yes, Robert Ackermann. You will not have heard of this man, D.C. Curtis..."

"Oh for God's sake, Herr Haller, call me Tony, please. No more of the D.C. Curtis or 'detective' and all that crap. It'll save a lot of time."

"Very well, and thank you," Haller smiled at Curtis, feeling he had made a friend of sorts in this young and very attentive detective.

"So, as to Robert Ackermann. During the war, Tony, Ackermann was on the staff of Grand Admiral Karl Dönitz, head of the U-Boat arm, close confidant to Adolf Hitler and later President of Germany for a short time following Hitler's death. Inge was not concerned with Ackermann's war service, quite clearly and she and Robert later had a son, born in 1960, who they named Erich. Now, in 2003, Erich Ackermann is of course a grown man of forty-three years of age, and this is where I believe you should make a phone call to Detective Inspector Ross, Tony."

Haller sighed, fell silent and leaned back in his chair, a knowing smile on his face.

Curtis in turn smiled back, and waited.

"Okay, Herr Haller, let's hear it," he said after a few moments' silence. "I can feel a punchline coming on."

"Haha," Haller giggled quietly. "I am aware of this phrase, punchline, and yes maybe you will take it as such when I tell you that Erich Ackermann is a financial genius, who has made a small fortune, as I believe it is called, by playing the world's stock markets, and by speculating on some very risky financial ventures over the years, but he is also the European Head of

Finance for the Aegis Institute, a position he acquired as a result of being listed as a major shareholder in the company. Not only do I suspect Ackermann of having inherited his father's papers, including details of the voyage of *U966*, but I think you will find he has been the driving force behind the Aegis plan to steal the gold from the wreck of the submarine."

Tony Curtis fell silent; his mouth moved a couple of times though no sound came forth as he assimilated Haller's information.

"Herr Haller, you're a genius. How the heck did you find all this information? We're supposed to be the police, not you, and yet you've uncovered all this in no time at all."

"I thank you for the compliment, Tony, but it took no genius to fathom this conundrum out. You must remember that I am German, my friend, and so when it comes to researching anything to do with the Kriegsmarine and the modern German Navy, first of all I am a world-renowned expert on the subject, and have access to many databases your people would not know exist, many written in German of course and by the same token I can also access information about their families and descendants in a similar way, though that takes a little more expertise and the opening of a few, how do you say, back doors?"

"You mean you've hacked into their systems?" an incredulous Curtis ventured, surprised that a man like Klaus Haller would not only have the skills to be a computer hacker, but was prepared to use them.

Haller chuckled. "Sometimes, in order to get at the truth it is necessary to take a crooked path, do you not think, my young friend."

"Well, yes, I suppose so," Curtis agreed, not sure if by doing so he was condoning an illegal act, *but what the hell*, he thought, *if it helps catch a killer...*

Allowing his mind to end its personal internal ethical debate, Detective Constable Tony Curtis pulled his mobile phone from his pocket and dialled D.I. Ross's number.

Chapter 34

The Traitor

Andy Ross was pleased with the way his plan was coming together. He'd been delighted beyond belief with Klaus Haller's information, and thanks to Oscar Agostini's intervention with Detective Chief Superintendent Sarah Hollingsworth, not only had the New York office of the F.B.I been brought into the case, actively investigating the internal finances of the Aegis Institute and also having placed a watch on the activities of Francis Kelly but D.C.S. Hollingsworth had acted immediately on the information supplied by Haller, and now the German police in the form of the *Bundeskriminalamt*, Germany's Federal Police Force was involved and were now investigating Erick Ackermann and the activities of Aegis in Germany. The Germans were also liaising with their counterparts in Greece, Italy and Turkey, all countries where the arms of the Aegis octopus of criminal activity was thought to have spread its tentacles.

In order to bring the case to a logical conclusion in the UK, however, it remained for Ross and his team, together with Brian Jones of the Devon and Cornwall Constabulary, to link the deaths of Aaron Decker, T.J. Knowles, Tim Knight and Martin Lewis to Francis Kelly in New York and secondly, to bring Sally Metcalfe's father to justice for his part in the operation in transporting the stolen bullion around Europe and possibly setting Aaron Decker up to be murdered. Ross and Drake had concluded that Metcalfe must have had modifications carried out to Advance Transportation's vehicles in order to conceal the whereabouts of the gold when they crossed various borders on the continent, a theory Agostini wholeheartedly agreed with.

Now that the various European police forces were actively investigating the activities of Aegis Oceanographics, Ross could concentrate on the next phase of his plan, that of luring the man known as Finch, a.k.a Randolph Lambert into the open and then using him to implicate Kelly.

When Oscar Agostini asked Ross how he planned to execute such a plan he replied,

"Easy, Oscar, one of our detectives is corrupt, a leak and is ready to reveal the details of our investigation to Kelly."

Agostini smiled, knowing Ross had a plan up his sleeve.

"Okay, Andy, and just who is this bad cop?"

"Derek McLennan, sir. Of course, he doesn't know it yet, but I'm sure he'll want to volunteer once I explain the plan to him."

"Is your D.I. serious?" Agostini asked Izzie Drake, who was standing behind Ross, her bottom resting on the edge of his desk as the three of them discussed Ross's plan in his small office.

"Deadly serious, sir," she replied. "Derek'll be made up to have the chance to play James Bond."

"You've considered the potential danger to McLennan I presume?" Agostini said.

"We'll have men watching him all the time, sir. Derek McLennan is a top class detective. He can do this. We have a good cover story for him. He sat his sergeant's exams recently. We don't know the actual results yet but we can put the word out that he's failed and he's really bitter at not getting the opportunity to move up in rank."

"You really think you can pull it off, Andy?"

"Yes, I do, sir. Finch is bound to be panicking, knowing we have both Starling and Robin in custody. If Derek can convince him they are both spilling their guts to us, he's going to want to silence them. The fact we haven't got them in a regular prison, or prison hospital in Robin's case, adds to the fact that he will see we're trying to keep them well out of reach of him or any hired killers he might be able to use behind bars. So he'll be desperate to eliminate the pair of them before they can do irreparable damage to his organisation. Derek will contact Finch on Robin's mobile phone, which he'll have supposedly 'borrowed' from the evidence locker, and offer to sell him the locations of both men, but only on a cash basis and at a one to one meeting."

Agostini thought it through for a minute before making his decision.

"Okay, Andy. If McLennan is willing to try, let's do it."

Relieved, Ross could only thank the D.C.I. and he and Drake left to brief Derek McLennan on Ross's proposal. The detective constable was immediately enthusiastic about the idea, and was grateful to Ross for the faith the D.I. was willing to place in him and his abilities. Derek had indeed come a long way since those early days as a young, rather gauche and naïve D.C. Now, he realised, Andy Ross trusted him totally and he intended to repay that trust by carrying off the undercover sting to the best of his ability.

It was agreed that before they went ahead, the Press Liaison Officer, George Thompson would be brought on board. Thompson would 'plant' a story in the Liverpool Echo's evening edition through his contact there, Terry Wallace, a reporter Ross knew could be trusted, having dealt with him during the Brendan Kane and Marie Doyle case four years previously in 1999. The story would report that two men, believed to be connected to the death of local student and sporting hero Aaron Decker, had been apprehended in two separate incidents in the city, and were now under guard in separate locations where they were providing the investigating officers with a plethora of useful information which the police hoped would lead to an early arrest of those behind the murder of the popular young sportsman.

* * *

Paul Ferris, meanwhile, had been far from idle. His investigation into the activities of Jeffrey Metcalfe and his two businesses, Metcalfe Logistics and Advance Transportation was proving interesting. Although Metcalfe Logistics appeared to be perfectly up front and legal in every respect, Ferris had discovered that the subsidiary business, Advance Logistics, had originally been set up and incorporated on the island of Jersey in the Channel Islands, well known for its status as a virtual tax haven for many companies.

It had become evident to Ferris that any business carried out on behalf of the Aegis group over the last three years had been directed through Advance Transportation and not Metcalfe Logistics. Even more interesting to the team's computer whizz-kid was the fact that although Metcalfe Logistics was listed as a Public Liability Company with shares readily available through any legitimate broker, Advance Transportation was a simple private company, sole proprietor, Jeffrey Metcalfe. In other words, the activities of Advance were under the sole control of its owner.

Having found that much, Ferris had moved on to trying to trace the movements of Advance Transportation's small fleet of lorries. To do so, he needed to call on a certain outside resource, a computer geek, a friend, and one of the finest hackers he knew that wasn't actually in jail.

Frankie Trout's saving grace was that he never actually obtained any financial reward as a result of his 'prying' into other people's business. Ferris had met him when he'd caught him trying to hack into the Merseyside Police Personnel Records. Frankie, horrified at being discovered 'with his hands in Aunty's panties,' as he himself described it, thought he'd been apprehended by a 'super hacker' and only later found that Ferris had stumbled on him quite by accident.

Frankie had been able to assure Ferris he only did it to prove to himself he could, which was true of most of his more outlandish 'adventures' in the world of cyberspace. As a result, Ferris was able to use Frankie's expertise in cases where an 'invisible' presence was required, and here and now was one of those occasions.

Five feet five in height, with hair that resembled a young John Lennon during his Maharishi days, and pale green eyes sunken into his head through an apparent lack of a good night's sleep in the last ten years, Frankie answered the phone on the first ring, automatically recalling and recognising Ferris's mobile phone number as it showed on his screen.

"Paul Ferris, my friend," he replied, knowing full well this was no social call. "Tell me what you need."

"You don't mess about, Frankie, do you? Let's get straight to the point huh?"

"Why beat about the bush? We both know you only call me when you want me to do something ille-

409

gal for you, *Detective Ferris.*" He emphasised Ferris's name and rank as he smiled into the phone.

"Watch your mouth, there Frankie. If not for me, you'd be doing ten years in Walton jail, mate, so be grateful I let you do me these little favours now and then."

"Yeah, yeah, right. I'm real grateful, Mr. Ferris, sir. You do realise if any of my geeky mates find out about me helping you I'll probably get chucked out of the Liverpool Geeks and Weirdos Society."

Not sure at first if Frankie was serious, Ferris merely laughed, then realised his tame hacker was simply being facetious.

Frankie laughed along for a few seconds and then asked Ferris what he needed. The detective explained, assuming of course that Metcalfe, like most modern businessmen kept his company records on computer. He warned Frankie that the man might keep anything illegal or secret on a separate, personal computer.

"No problem, Mr. Ferris," Frankie said when Ferris fell silent. "Just tell me where the mark lives. I'll be able to trace any IP addresses located at his home or work. Just leave it to me. Shouldn't take long."

"Really?" Ferris queried.

"Simple task really," Frankie replied. "Ah well, maybe one day you'll bring me a real challenge."

"What, like hacking into the accounts of the Bank of England?" Ferris laughed.

"Oh no, been there, done that. I mean something really difficult."

Ferris stopped laughing.

"Frankie, you haven't? Wait, don't answer that. Just get on with what I want, okay?"

"Sure, Mr. Ferris," Frankie replied. "I'll get back to you soon."

The phone went dead as Frankie hung up and Ferris sat looking at the silent device he held in his hand, wondering, *The Bank of England?* No, surely not. Then again...

Chapter 35

No Headstone on a Sailor's Grave

With plans in place for the operation to lure Randolph Lambert, a.k.a. Finch to Liverpool, Ross and Drake once again made the long journey to Falmouth, where the evening found them in familiar surroundings, enjoying a meal at the Hope and Anchor, prepared expertly by Hope Severn. Her husband Thomas had welcomed the two detectives back to his establishment and insisted they call him Tommy. Now they were returning guests, they were regulars as far as he was concerned and thus classed as friends.

This time, there was no old Mrs. Twining or her equivalent in the dining room as they enjoyed their meal. They were however, joined for dinner by Brian Jones and his sergeant Carole St. Clair. The two Cornish detectives were there to bring Ross and Drake up to date on the salvage operations in the Channel.

There had proved nothing unusual or remarkable about the wreck of the *Norwich* apparently, but the team from the Fleet Auxiliary vessel *Whitehaven Castle* had made a remarkable discovery. The wreck of the *U966*, finally revealed in the brilliant high powered underwater lights of the *Whitehaven Castle's* submersibles and dive teams, had given up a secret nobody had expected.

Brian Jones explained as the four enjoyed the redoubtable Hope Severn's superb cooking.

"Charles Howell on the *Wyvern* and his chief engineer tried their best to explain it to us. We saw what looked like an extra torpedo tube on each side of the U-Boat but the tube looked wrong and seemed to run all the way along the lower part of the submarine's hull with corresponding tube exits at the stern. Once the divers identified the exterior anomaly they explored further within the sub's interior until they found what they were looking for.

It seems *U966* was an experimental craft, Andy. She not only carried the gold that Hitler wanted to reach his ex-pat Nazis in South America but she was fitted with what the Navy guys are calling a Hydrodynamic propulsion system."

"I see," said Ross, "and what is a Hydrodynamic propulsion system?"

"Explained in simple terms, Andy, it's a system that sucks in seawater from the front, passes it through something like a ramjet inside the sub and then expels it at great pressure from the rear to propel it at great speed, virtually silently. Imagine if that bloody technology had been put to use by the Nazis. They would have had a 'stealth submarine' as early as 1945, and the ability to strike at our naval and civilian vessels and attack our ports and coastal towns from a fleet of undetectable submarines."

"In other words, that one U-Boat might have changed the course of the war," said Izzie Drake.

"Well, yes and no," Jones responded.

"How come?" Ross asked.

Jones coughed as a piece of food caught in his throat. As he sipped from a glass of water, Carole St. Clair continued.

"It was probably too late in the war for it to have had any real effect on the outcome of the conflict according to Captains Howell, and Prendergast. Anthony Prendergast knows the history of the war at sea better than anyone else in the UK according to Charles Howell. Anthony says that Germany was already on the verge of collapse by the time *U966* or *3000* left Kiel. God it's bloody confusing, these two different numbers, don't you think?"

"Let's stick with *U966*," Ross decided, as that's the number she sailed under, okay?"

"Suits me," Jones agreed, and Carole St. Clair added, "It'll save space in my notebook too."

"Good enough," said Jones. "So anyway, Anthony Prendergast says that Hitler was so out of touch with reality by then he probably did think he could still win the war and in all seriousness, he ordered the experimental U-Boat to set sail for a secret destination, carrying enough stolen gold to finance the building of a fleet of his new super U-Boats. Prendergast thinks the sub was probably headed for a rendezvous with Nazi sympathisers in Argentina. I am left wondering why they didn't use the new propulsion system on that last voyage."

"Why Argentina?" Izzie asked, as she added, "Maybe it wasn't working properly."

"That would make sense," Jones tried to give a rational explanation. "I've been reading up on the history of the Second World War since we got involved in this case, and after the divers found evidence of this Hydrodynamic thingy system, I went a bit further and looked up as much as I could on the Nazis and their search for new technology."

"And what did you find, Brian? Anything interesting?" Ross asked his Cornish counterpart, impressed with the fact he'd delved into the mists of time to try to pour light on the present."

"I was amazed," Jones replied. "The Nazis were obsessed with developing so-called Super Weapons. They used their best scientific brains, plus God knows how many captive scientists and engineers in Hitler's almost manic quest to come up with what we'd call 'weapons of mass destruction' today. Most of us have heard of the V1 and V2 rockets of course but it seems they were working on much more, including the equivalent of today's intercontinental ballistic missiles which could have drastically changed the course of the war. Historians have actually found the ruins of several test sites and underground research facilities where these projects were worked on. They used slave labour to excavate these sites and again to do the manual labour of maintaining them, simply killing the poor bastards when they couldn't work any more."

"That's inhuman," said Izzie.

"True," said Carole St. Clair, who'd obviously been aiding her D.I. in his research, "but they did far worse, Izzie. At one site, the historians found the remains of hundreds of bodies, hastily buried in pits dug only a few feet into the ground. Forensic anthropologists who examined the bones found many of them contained traces of radiation."

"Radiation?"

"Exactly," Jones re-entered the conversation. "They concluded, together with the historians and archaeologists, that the Nazis probably tested the contents of the experimental warheads on those poor sods, who the anthropologists identified as being mostly of Slavic or Jewish origins, so probably they were Russian P.O.W.s and concentration camp inmates, shipped to the site to be used as human guinea pigs."

"Fucking hell, Brian," was all Ross could manage to say.

"My thoughts exactly, Andy," said Jones. "Anyway, the Nazis had lots of similar facilities all over occupied Europe, working on new aircraft designs, ships, submarines, poison gas filled torpedoes, all sorts of diabolical stuff. Thankfully they never got to develop most of them. Seems the RAF, thanks to some bloody great intelligence work by the resistance in some countries and by their own aerial reconnaissance, identified a lot of these sites and bombed the bastard things out of existence."

"Thank God they did," Izzie Drake replied as Jones fell silent.

"So you think they developed this new propulsion system at one of these sites and then tried to smuggle the technology out of Germany when it looked like they might be losing the war in Europe?"

Jones now returned to Izzie's earlier question regarding Argentina being a possible destination for the disguised submarine.

"There's evidence, according to Prendergast, that a large group of Nazi military personnel and scientists were gradually ferried across the Atlantic towards the end of the war, first of all to escape the constant bombardment of Germany's cities by the RAF and the U.S. Army Air Force, and secondly to continue their work on various Nazi super-weapons, designed to give Hitler a final decisive victory in the war. In case you're wondering the U.S. Air Force as we know it today didn't become a separate force until late in 1947, according to the great sage, Prendergast." Jones smiled and the others smiled with him.

"So, come on, Brian, what does Prendergast think the Germans intended to do if the U-Boat had made it to Argentina?"

"He thinks the Nazis had set up a secret base, run by senior naval officers and crack scientists, where the production of these super-subs could be carried out. It was probably Grand Admiral Doenitz's plan to continue the war after the fall of Berlin, but even he couldn't have anticipated Hitler's suicide and the rapid decline and fall of the Third Reich after his death as the Allies overran the Fatherland and its occupied territories. It was interesting to note the actual spelling of his name was Dönitz. Doenitz is the Anglicised spelling apparently. The old bastard lived until 1980 and died peacefully at the age of 89. Anyway, the point is, bringing things bang up to date, that the technology employed by these new U-Boats was so advanced that even today, it could be worth a fortune, not specifically for submarines, which have changed dramatically since the advent of nuclear propulsion but simply as a highly efficient system of propulsion for surface vessels, reducing the dependence on oil for any nation possessing it."

"Sounds to me as if the technology for this hydrodynamic propulsion system could actually be worth more in the long run than the gold the *U966* was carrying," said Ross.

"Exactly," Jones agreed, "and that, Andy, definitely gives anyone who wants to possess the technology a bloody big motive for murder to obtain it, develop it commercially and to prevent others getting their hands on it."

"Brian, my friend, I think between us all, and with thanks to you and Anthony Prendergast, we may have arrived at the true reason behind everything that's happened."

"There is another option we haven't considered too, sir," said Drake, who'd been following the conversation closely.

"Go on, Izzie, what have we missed?"

"Well sir, I was just thinking; we're all presuming that the whole idea of this exercise was for Aegis to steal and develop the new technology themselves, right?"

"Yes, that's how it seems."

"But with the world's dependence on oil, what if Aegis was being paid by a separate interested party to get hold of the Nazi technology and sell it on to them?"

"And who are you thinking of, Izzie?"

"The people who would stand to lose most if such technology came into being of course, sir."

"Of course," Ross realised what Drake was thinking. "You mean the Arabs."

"Exactly sir. It might be unlikely, but it does bear thinking about. Some of the Arab nations would stand to lose billions of dollars if this new propulsion system came into being."

"But surely," Jones interjected, "it would make more sense for Aegis to just go ahead and develop the system themselves, and make a fortune from building ships and so on that used these engines and selling them to shipping companies all over the world."

"If this Kelly chap is as greedy as we think, I'd say that would depend on how many billions the Arabs would pay to possess and bury that technology," Drake replied.

"A good point, Izzie," Ross said, "and certainly an option we shouldn't discount out of hand until we know more. Thanks for your input. Good to see your brain hasn't been totally befuddled by the joys of marital bliss."

Laughter ensued as everyone took a few seconds to escape from the gravity of the discussion, but then Ross motioned for them to return to the matter in hand.

He went on to explain in detail the information provided by Klaus Haller. It now appeared that the path to the solution to this complicated and convoluted case both began and ended with Erich Ackermann. Now they knew that, and once Ross explained the basis of his plan to bring Finch out into the open as a means of getting to Kelly, he felt it was only a matter of time before they brought those responsible for so many deaths to justice.

Dinner over, the four detectives retired to the bar where they sat and enjoyed a single drink together, a nightcap to bring the evening to a close. Jones and St. Clair bade the Liverpool duo goodnight when their shared taxi arrived, the two living quite near to each other, or, as St. Clair put it, "Tight bugger won't stump up for a second taxi for me when he can get away with only paying for one."

"Now come on Carole, you know very well I've got a wife, a mortgage and three credit cards to support."

The group enjoyed a quiet laugh on the steps of the Hope and Anchor, and as the taxi's rear lights disappeared from view, Ross and Drake made their way to their rooms, both phoning their respective spouses before going to bed, ready for a good night's sleep and a busy day in the morning.

"You were right, Brian," Ross observed as the helicopter that had picked them up from Falmouth neared the Royal Fleet Auxiliary Vessel, *Whitehaven Castle*. "She's certainly an ugly duckling, that's for sure."

"Ugly maybe, but from what we've seen she's a hell of a ship," Brian Jones said with clear admiration in his voice. The Westland Lynx Mk8 banked slightly to port, giving the passengers a better view of the R.F.A. ship as they turned to make their landing approach.

The dull grey ship had an ungainly appearance, its upper decks seemingly a mass of derricks, cranes and gantries, the few crewmen visible from the Lynx resembling ants scurrying around as they made their way towards the ship's helicopter landing pad, clearly identifiable by the large white 'H' painted on a section of the upper rear deck. A little way to the south of the salvage tug, the sleek lines of *H.M.S. Wyvern* could be seen by the Lynx's passengers, the raked bow and narrow beam of the warship contrasting sharply with the ungainly behemoth of a ship that waited to greet them. Quite clearly, the *Whitehaven Castle* was the type of ship that, had it been a child, only a mother could love. The closer the Lynx got to the ship, the smaller that 'H' and its surrounding circle of clear deck appeared to Ross and his companions.

Closer and closer, the deck appeared to be rising from the ocean to meet their rapid, (in Ross's mind), descent. Ross, never a great flyer, was about to start saying a prayer when the pilot pulled back on the collective, and the helicopter flared out and made its final approach to the deck, seeming to Ross to literally thump on to the *Whitehaven Castle*, despite the obvious suspension springs in the undercarriage easing the shock of final touchdown. Realising he'd been holding his breath, Ross let out a massive sigh. Izzie Drake, who'd noticed her boss's nervousness on the final approach, touched his arm and gave him a reassuring smile.

"Nice soft landing that," she said facetiously.

"Yes, hardly knew we'd touched down," Carole St. Clair added, obviously much happier flying than sailing.

"You alright, Andy?" Jones asked. "Your knuckles have turned a bit white."

Seeing them all grinning sheepishly at him, Ross knew they were having a laugh at his expense.

"Alright you horrible lot," he said, regaining his composure. "Let's get out of here. There's a reception committee waiting for us by the look of it."

Despite his best efforts, Andy Ross still managed to stagger a little as his legs touched the deck, and it took him a couple of seconds to regain full equilibrium. As he did, Captain Charles Howell of the *Wyvern,* Anthony Prendergast of the Royal Navy's Archives Section, and another man strode towards them.

Charles Howell made the introductions, as the new man, a reasonable replica of Captain Birdseye with his long white beard, rotund figure and an unlit pipe dangling from his mouth smiled at the newcomers. The man was a veritable giant, too. Ross estimated his height at around six feet four or five.

"Ladies and gentlemen, say hello to the master of the *Whitehaven Castle*, Captain James Ramsey. James, this is Detective Inspector Andy Ross from Liverpool, D.I Brian Jones from Falmouth and Sergeants Izzie Drake and Carole St. Clair."

"Welcome aboard to you all," Ramsey spoke as he reached out to shake hands with each of his visitors. Ross thought the captain had a handshake that could crush granite, firm and assured, and the man exuded confidence. He'd already been informed by Jones that the Royal Fleet Auxiliary was manned by civilians, not Royal Naval personnel and he could instantly see the difference as he took in the appearance of Ramsey's uniform. Similar in some respects to the military uniform it was however different enough to the naked eye to make the distinction between civilian and military.

"Please follow me," Ramsey said as he turned and beckoned the newcomers to follow him as he led them from the exposed helipad to the warmth that awaited them as they passed through a large steel door and entered one of the ship's many large 'warehouse' facilities where repairs and other vital work could be carried out. For now though, this particular area had been set up as the control room or 'hub' for the continuing exploration of the wreck site. Numerous monitors stood against one bulkhead, each one manned by a seaman who appeared to be analysing everything that had been previously recorded by the dive teams, frame by frame, missing nothing as they searched for anything that would add to the historical records of what had taken place between these two old adversaries during the cold dark days of World War Two.

Captain Ramsey excused himself for a minute, allowing them to take in their surroundings. Ross and the others were amazed at the array of information presented on the various screens. They were able to see the record of everything that the crew of the *Whitehaven Castle* had achieved since arriving on the scene of the dual wreck site. Some of the screens were replaying the same footage over and again as analysts busily examined the pictures in detail, recording their findings and opinions onto voice recorders as they picked up on every tiny detail from earlier dives, and other screens showed static images, those which the experts wanted to examine in closer detail, or that presented them with evidence to help in the examination of the wreckage of both the corvette and the U-Boat.

Ross sensed a presence behind him and turned to see Captain Ramsey approaching with three newcomers in close attendance. Ramsey wasted no time in introducing Ross and his companions to the smiling trio who accompanied him.

"Ladies, gentlemen, please say hello to these gentlemen who will be carrying out our simple act of remembrance for the crews of the *Norwich* and the

U966, or, as we have been informed of its correct designation, the *U3000*."

Ramsey then introduced Father Roland Green representing the Roman Catholic Faith, Giles Parker from the Church of England and finally, Pastor Konrad Völler from the German Evangelical Church, representing the German Navy.

Father Green spoke for the others after a round of handshakes was completed.

"Detective Inspector Ross, and all of you who have helped in this finding of the two vessels that lie below us on the seabed, on behalf of myself and my colleagues in Christ, I thank you for your dogged determination and your efforts to ensure that the men who were lost on that fateful night in 1945 will no longer be merely part of a forgotten page in history."

Ross went to speak but Green held a hand up, stopping him as his words began.

"No, please, do not be modest, as I'm sure you were about to be. We are here to ensure those men are commemorated today, not as men of war, as they surely were at the time, but as human beings, as husbands, fathers, sons, brothers. You and your people, police officers and naval personnel have all contributed to this moment, and we thank you."

Andy Ross felt a lump in his throat, touched by the simple gratitude expressed by the priest and echoed by his two fellow ministers.

"Thank you," he said, struggling to find words appropriate to the moment. "We were just doing our jobs, all of us, but I'm sure I speak for everyone involved in locating these two ships, and that includes my team back in Liverpool, even young Aaron Decker and T.J Knowles, whose deaths, in retrospect, led to us being here today. Anyway, thank you."

As Ross fell silent, feeling slightly awkward and a little embarrassed, the sound of a helicopter could clearly be heard as it landed on the deck outside the hangar-like room they occupied.

Charles Howell spoke up at that point.

"Aha, sounds like our other guests are arriving. Do excuse me for a few minutes," and he turned on his heel and marched out through the nearest bulkhead door.

"It's beginning to look like we're having a real gathering here today, Andy," Brian Jones commented. "I wonder who's arriving now."

The answer arrived soon afterwards as Captain Howell led another officer, resplendent in the full dress uniform of the German Navy into the operations centre, as they'd by now been given its title.

"Let me introduce you to Kapitän Franz Steiger," Howell said as the German officer snapped to attention and saluted the small group. "He's the official representative of the German Navy. He has a small contingent of naval ratings on deck who will join with men from the *Wyvern* in firing a salute to the dead after the short service of remembrance.

Steiger greeted Ross warmly and the next hour passed quickly for everyone as final arrangements were made for the service to commemorate those who'd died all those years ago.

When the time came, Ross was particularly moved by the words of Pastor Völler, which included:

"These men, who never met face-to-face, but who were forever joined in death, served and died for their countries. In the case of the crew of the *U3000*, sailing under false identity as *U966* they were all young men who served an evil regime, but these were not evil men. The Germany they lived in was not like the Germany of today. It was not possible to be a conscientious objector to the war in my country during those dark days, as many priests, much like me, discovered to their cost. It was a case of serve or die, perhaps quickly at the end of a rope or slowly in a concentration camp, so they served, whether they believed in the cause or not. Yes, it is true that some followed the ravings of the madman who rose to power in our nation at that time, but the vast majority did not. They were ordinary men, sailors of the Kriegsmarine, and their foremost pride was in their *Kapitän* and their boat. They did their jobs, as did the brave men of *H.M.S. Norwich*, without thought for themselves, only for their fellow crewmen and their ship. How these men died that night long ago is less important than the fact that they died in the service of their countries, in the cold, dark, moonlit waters of the sea, far from home and family, one minute vibrant, alive, maybe sharing a joke with their fellows, and then pitched into the darkness of death, either in the water, in an explosion, or in the case of the men in the submarine, from a slow, lingering death as their air ran out. We remember them not as foes, but as human beings, as brave men and we salute them all and commend their souls to God."

The other two ministers spoke similar words, and Izzie Drake wiped a tear from her face as Kapitän Steiger now stepped forward, side by side with Captain Howell, each man carrying a large wreath, Howell's in a mix of red and white flowers, the colours of the Royal Navy's white ensign, and Steiger's in the red and yellow of the German Navy ensign with black ribbons to complete the colours of their flag.

Steiger spoke briefly.

"It is my wish to recite for you a poem," he said. "It was written by your English poet, Brian Porter, and is called *No Headstone on a Sailor's Grave*. It was, I understand written to commemorate the men of your Merchant Navy, many of whom lost their lives during the Second World War, but I believe the sentiments of the poem are appropriate to the events of today."

Taking a piece of paper from his pocket, Steiger cleared his throat, and began by reading the title, followed by the words of the poem.

"*NO HEADSTONE ON A SAILOR'S GRAVE*[1]

Third day now, and still no sign of any rescue boat,
Please God, how much longer on this ocean must we
float.
Poor Lofty's fell asleep again, I'm afraid he's getting
weaker.
Truth be told, I think that our chances are getting
bleaker.

She went down so very quickly, it happened all so fast.
Torpedo in the hold I think, judging by the blast.
So cold, wet and hungry, no fresh water to drink.
Must keep baling though, don't want this thing to sink.

Lofty seems delirious, he thinks he's home in bed,
Strange how things like this put all these daft things
in your head.
Maybe my mind will start to go, if we're not found quite
soon.
Maybe tonight I'll be looking up, and howling at the
moon!

---

1. *No Headstone on a Sailor's Grave* is from *Lest We Forget, An Anthology of Remembrance,* by Brian L Porter, published by Next Chapter.

429

I wish someone would find us, I'd kill for a cup of tea.
But all I can see for miles around is nothing but open
sea.
Perhaps they'll never find us, don't even know we're
here.
Wasn't much time for a mayday call, will anyone shed
a tear?

I'm sleepy now, I must admit, can't go on for very long,
I think I'll soon be listening to the sound of Neptune's
song.
If anyone should find these words, say a prayer for
Lofty and me.
And please, throw a few rose petals on our grave be-
neath the sea."

Steiger bowed his head as he came to the end of
the poem, and then walked slowly to the deck rail of
the *Whitehaven Castle*, where he stood silently and
saluted over the rolling waves of the Channel, as he
cast the page containing the poem into the breeze.
The assembled group watched as the light breeze
caught the flimsy sheet of A4 paper, and for a few
seconds the poem and its poignant words seemed to
fly of its own volition, swirling up and down, back
and forth as though on wings of faith, until the breeze
relented for a few seconds and the page floated gently to land, printed side up, on the undulating swell
of the ocean, where it remained for at least a minute
until, saturated by the waters of the English Channel,
No Headstone for a Sailor's grave, silently and with

an uncanny sense of reverence, slowly disappeared beneath the waves, gently floating down in a silent pirouette towards the shattered remains of the two former warships, where, perhaps, the ghosts of those who'd sailed in them waited to receive it. Charles Howell next walked forward to join him at the ship's rail and together the two men threw their respective wreaths onto the waters below in their final, joint act of remembrance, each man saluting in farewell and respect to those who'd met their deaths in a watery grave, almost sixty years earlier.

Not a word had been spoken by anyone on deck as Steiger had read the poem, or as the wreaths were thrown down to the sea and everyone present had been moved not just by the poet's words, but by the German officer's emotional delivery of them.

Now, as though by prearranged signal, the single deck gun of the *Wyvern* burst into life, a single round fired in salute to those who'd perished on the two vessels on the seabed. Next, a loud command of 'fire' from none other than Marine Lieutenant Gareth Ridley who had appeared as if by magic as far as Ross's party could see, was followed by a fusillade of rifle fire from the joint contingent of Royal Naval and German Naval ratings in a second and reverberating salute.

Ross and Drake, and the others couldn't fail to be moved by the ceremony, which was then brought to a close by the Reverend Giles Parker, who led those present in the Lord's prayer, after which, another surprise for the visitors as a small company of youngsters were led onto the deck by the choirmaster of Exeter Cathedral and as they began their rendition of *'For those in peril on the sea'* with the officers and men on deck joining in lustily, Ross saw tears streaking the face of Izzie Drake. Never had he seen his sergeant so moved and emotional. At the same time, he noticed Brian Jones and Carole St. Clair also appeared highly emotional, remembering of course the family connection for Brian Jones to T.J. Knowles.

Lunch was served soon afterwards, with Captain James Ramsey proving to be a genial host, and the food served by the *Whitehaven Castle's* chef, quite superb. Ramsey explained that their chef was a former Cunard employee, who had served aboard the *Q.E.2* for some years. When asked by Carole St. Clair how he came to be serving on a Royal Fleet Auxiliary salvage tug, Ramsey simply tapped the side of his nose with one finger and with a knowing wink, replied "Don't ask."

The Naval personnel, plus the visiting clerics were all keen for Ross to tell them the story of how they all came to be meeting on this day and the D.I. did his best to inform them without giving away too many salient details of the case, which as he explained, was still an ongoing criminal investigation. He explained that he would love to say more, but knew they'd understand his reticence, which they all of course reluctantly accepted.

Their hosts however were not so reluctant in divulging their knowledge of the underwater examinations of the two wrecks.

First of all, Charles Howell went into more detail about the submarine's revolutionary technology, the hydrodynamic propulsion system. As a former submariner himself, Anthony Prendergast was especially interested in knowing as much as they could tell him about the discovery. The system, as far as Howell was able to describe it worked like a sort of snake, propelling the submarine along using the same principles as jet engine propulsion, but using water instead of air as the medium by which to create the necessary energy.

Ramsey explained that they had finally broken through to the still watertight areas of the U-Boat and by using state of the art compressed air technology had succeeded in preventing them becoming totally flooded. In so doing, they had found the decomposed remains of another twenty five of the *U3000/U966's* crew. Most of them had been identified from their identity tags. A couple, obviously in breech of regulations hadn't been wearing theirs and would remain unidentified.

He went on to say that they were welcome to view the films taken by the divers who had located the remains if they wished to, though Ross and his people couldn't decide if they wanted to take that step, as Ross himself felt it to be perhaps an intrusion too far into what was in effect the grave of those who'd died in her.

Charles Howell agreed with Ross to a point but he explained that by identifying those men, the German Navy had been able to locate a number of surviving family members, descendants of the dead men and it was hoped to invite them, as well as any other legitimate family members of the known crew, plus the living relatives of the crew of the *Norwich*, to attend a joint service of remembrance in the near future, probably in Exeter Cathedral. Everyone thought that to be a good idea and by the time came for Ross and his party to board their helicopter for the journey back to Falmouth, friendships had been formed and promises made to keep in touch, which everyone intended to keep. Ross was especially touched when Anthony Prendergast, on behalf of the Ministry of Defence, passed on an invitation for Ross's entire team from Liverpool to attend that service when it took place, as a way of thanking them all for finally helping the dead to be properly acknowledged and their last resting place confirmed. Ross felt proud of his team, and said he'd do his best but it would depend on their case load at the time of the service. Brian Jones and Carole St. Clair were also invited, and they gratefully accepted right away.

The return flight in the Lynx was smoother than the outgoing leg of their day's journey, but Andy Ross was glad to finally find his feet on *terra firma* later that day and after he and Drake said their farewells to Jones and St. Clair and picking up their bags from the Hope and Anchor, they began the long and arduous journey back along the motorway system towards Liverpool where the next day, Ross hoped, just might prove decisive in bringing the case to its finale.

Chapter 36

A Set-up

Randolph (Finch) Lambert lay on the bed in his hotel room, situated in a quiet street in Bloomsbury, London. The television was playing quietly in one corner of the room, the sound turned down so low that its effect was little more than white noise on Lambert's senses. The flickering picture depicted some inane comedy movie he'd never seen before and certainly had no wish to see again in the future.

Lambert was planning, working out how to first of all find out where Robin and Starling were being held, and secondly how he would then find a way past the inevitable police defences around each man. Lambert was certain the police would have put armed guards in place. He was confident enough to assume Starling's silence but Robin was another matter. He wasn't stupid and must have realised that Finch had sent Starling to eliminate him. He was, as far as Lambert knew, still unconscious in hospital. The police had only released the information that the man responsible for two murders in the city was being treated for multiple injuries and may have suffered brain damage. Brain damaged or not, he needed to make sure that Robin never recovered sufficiently to tell the police what he knew about Finch's organisation. As one of his most trusted operatives, Robin knew more than most, perhaps too much, Lambert thought in retrospect.

Having flown to Heathrow as Ralph Kerr, one of his many aliases, he was confident that he had arrived unnoticed into the United Kingdom. Sadly for Lambert, that was his first mistake. Unbeknown to him, Graham Young, (Robin), was recovering well from his injuries and was proving to be a veritable goldmine of information in his attempts to avoid being potentially handed over to one of the foreign powers with a less than civilised policy towards imprisoned killers. He knew of more than one member of his profession for example who had been sentenced to lengthy spells in Turkish prisons, only to suffer appalling and inhuman cruelty at the hands of sadistic warders, including gang rape, severed fingers and toes, starvation and brutal whippings and beatings. By contrast, a prison sentence in Britain would be the equivalent to a stay in a holiday camp.

His thoughts were interrupted by the ring tone of his mobile phone. Lambert reached out, picking the phone up from its place on his bedside cabinet. Looking at the screen, a puzzled look appeared on his face as he recognised the caller's number. With one eyebrow rising, Spock-like he saw Robin's number displayed. *How the hell could he be calling me?* he thought, knowing only too well that the man was in police custody, supposedly unconscious and unable to communicate.

More curious than suspicious, Lambert pressed the green answer button on the phone, held it to his ear and listened without saying a word.

"Hello?" an unknown voice with a distinct though not overly heavy Liverpool accent spoke to him. Lambert remained silent, waiting.

"Hello? Mr. Finch?"

Lambert continued to wait, saying nothing, trying to draw the unknown caller out.

"I know you can hear me," the voice said. "If you're wondering who I am and why I have Robin's phone, let's just say for now, that I'm someone who can help you."

"And just how can you help me? Just what do you have that I want, and who the fuck are you, some copper trying to get me to talk?"

"As it happens, Mr. Finch, I am a police officer, but one who may be prepared to provide you with information that could prove to be beneficial to both of us."

Lambert fell silent for a few seconds, his mind quickly evaluating the information from the unknown caller. This could be a godsend or it could be a trap. He needed to know more. A bent copper on the investigating team could prove to be manna from heaven if this guy knew how he could get to

Robin and Starling, and could help him in his quest to eliminate them.

"Do you think I'm some sort of moron?" he asked the mystery caller. "You call me on Robin's phone, but you could be anyone, a passer-by who picked it up at the scene of the accident, a thieving hospital orderly, almost anybody in fact. Why should I believe you're a copper or that you want to help me?"

At the other end of the line, Derek McLennan smiled to himself. Detective Chief Inspector Oscar Agostini, listening to every word through an earpiece connected to Derek's phone nodded to McLennan to move onto the next part of the attempt to 'hook' Finch.

"Okay, I know you're suspicious," said McLennan. "I would be too, so just listen, okay? I'm not going to give you my name yet, that could prove to be bad for my health in the long term, but I am part of the team investigating the murders of Tim Knight and Martin Lewis. I've sort of 'borrowed' his phone from the evidence locker. They know a lot about what's going on, Mr. Finch. They also know it was probably you who sent Starling to kill Robin, and that means you have unfinished business to take care of."

"Even if that's true, and I'm admitting nothing," Finch replied,

"why should I trust you?"

"Because I'm your only hope of getting to both men without being gunned down by armed police officers before you can reach them; that's why. Okay, you want to know why I'm prepared to help you, right?"

"It would help," said Lambert.

"I've been a police officer for nearly ten years, Mr. Finch. I was ambitious, and a good copper too. Thing is, I've taken my sergeant's exams three times, and just because I'm no bloody good at taking exams, I've failed every time. My chances of ever making sergeant or going any higher are just about zero. I don't intend to be a lowly detective constable for the rest of my life, ending up in some out of the way station out in the sticks because I never had what it took to climb the promotion ladder. I've seen enough old stagers like that already in my time, just plodding along towards early retirement, sitting behind a desk doing the Daily Mail crossword until another piece of paper comes along to be filed. I want money, Mr. Finch and I'd rather have it while I'm young enough to enjoy it."

Randolph Lambert said nothing for a few seconds, wondering if he could take a chance on this unknown man being straight with him. There was still the possibility he was a plant, a Trojan Horse, and a part of a ploy to entrap him. Finally, he made a decision.

"Okay, I still don't know if I can trust you, but let's say you're telling the truth. Tell me something that the police know that isn't general knowledge. Convince me you're close enough to the investigation that I can trust you to be able to get me what I want."

"Okay," said McLennan. "We've found out that Robin and Starling work for you in a 'mercenary for hire' security organisation, hiring yourselves out to the highest bidder, At present you're working for the Aegis Institute, and you need to eliminate anyone, including your own people, who might be able to tie you into your boss in the States, thus compromising both him and you. The only evidence we have is circumstantial at present but if Robin and Starling agree to talk, then we can probably get enough evidence to come after you and your boss, Mr. Finch. It would appear your only hope of preventing them from talking, which I'm sure Robin will be happy to do when he learns you tried to have him killed, is to make sure neither man is ever in a position to implicate you directly."

"I think you and I should meet," Lambert said after a brief pause for thought. "If I think I can trust you, maybe we can come to a deal. If not, then I promise you that your future will be a very short one. Do I make myself clear?"

"Clear as crystal," Derek replied, his voice confident and unwavering.

"Give me a name I can call you," Lambert said.

"I tell you what, you can call me Raven," said McLennan. "That should sit nicely with your obsession with our feathered friends."

"Right, Raven it is." Lambert checked his watch, estimating how quickly he could get to Liverpool. If this copper was actively working on the investigation there was no way he could leave the city to meet him halfway.

"When do you go off duty, today, Mister Raven?"

"Six p.m." McLennan replied, "assuming nothing crops up needing overtime."

Lambert had visited the city of Liverpool twice in the past and his knowledge of the place was limited so he decided on a nice, public place where both he and his would-be informant could meet without being overheard, and where he would be able to spot any surveillance team in an instant. After all, that was part of his business. They couldn't fool him.

"Is there still a McDonald's on the concourse at Lime Street Station?" he asked.

"There is," said Derek.

"Seven thirty this evening; be there. I'll be wearing jeans and a black leather jacket and a New York Yankees baseball cap. I want this done quickly, so whatever you think you can do for me, it has to be done tonight. I don't want to be in your damn city when the sun rises tomorrow, got that? And you'd better not be trying to trap me, copper," he said, his voice suddenly full of latent menace.

"Trust me, Mr. Finch. Ordinarily I would never even dream of doing something like this, but Starling and Robin are just a pair of murdering bastards who probably deserve nothing better than a bullet in the head. What I have planned to get you to them can be done tonight, tomorrow, any time at all, so there's no problem there, and, like you say, the sooner the better really. What you do to them won't make me lose a minute's sleep, but there's a condition to me helping you."

"Oh yeah, and what's that?"

"Nobody else gets hurt, okay? I don't want any fellow officers ending up as collateral damage. If you can't agree to that, then the deal's off."

"Okay," Lambert agreed readily, obviously lying, as McLennan knew. "We'll do it your way. Now, how will I know you, Mister Raven?"

"You won't," said Derek. "But I'll know you from the description you just gave me. Sit anywhere you like and I'll come to you."

"Okay," said Lambert, "but you haven't told me how much you want for this information."

"Oh, don't worry; it'll be something you can afford. We'll discuss it when we meet," McLennan said, growing more in confidence with every second.

"Okay, Raven, don't be late," Lambert said and before Derek could say another word, the line went dead.

Derek McLennan hadn't noticed until the phone went dead in his hand, that he was shaking from the raw emotion of talking to the cold-blooded killer on the other end of that call. Agostini however, congratulated the young D.C. having been impressed by his handling of the conversation.

"Thanks a lot sir," Derek said in response to the D.C.I's flattery. "I hope I sounded more confident than I felt."

"You were great, McLennan, really. I wasn't sure you could pull it off but you did. I think you've actually got him hooked."

Ross had been listening from the next room, knowing his presence might serve to make Derek more nervous than needs be, and now came smiling into the room, accompanied by Izzie Drake, adding his congratulations to those of their boss.

"You were damn good there, Derek. Well done."

"Thanks, sir," McLennan replied.

"Of course, tonight will be the tricky part," Ross went on. "You're going to have to be totally convincing, Derek. This is no amateur we're dealing with. One slip and you could be in real danger, you do know that don't you?"

"Yes, I do sir. I wouldn't have volunteered if I didn't think I could pull it off."

"Good lad," Ross smiled again and patted McLennan on the shoulder. "Don't forget, we'll have you under surveillance all the time you're with him. Don't worry; he won't be able to make our people. Sam Gable will be there as a Mum with a baby in a pram, not a real one of course, and Izzie and Tony will be a courting couple, canoodling in McDonalds. I'll be a ticket inspector, already agreed with the station authorities, who think we're looking for a drug dealer. And just to be on the safe side, we'll have a police marksman up in the roof, with a rifle trained on Finch the second he's in view on the concourse and another couple of armed officers will be positioned in a diesel locomotive that will be conveniently stood at the buffers closest to the concourse."

"Tell me again why we can't just pick this bastard up the minute he sets foot in Liverpool?" Izzie suddenly asked; her concern for Derek uppermost in her tone of voice.

"Because, Sergeant Drake," Agostini provided the reply, "as much as we may know just who and what this man is, we have no hard evidence that proves he's committed an offence on British soil. He's clever, and covers his tracks very well indeed. We have to have something concrete to pin on him. We need him to attempt to kill one or both of his men and then, by God, we'll have the bastard."

"What about attempting to bribe an officer? Didn't he just do that with Derek?"

"No, he didn't. McLennan called him, remember, and offered to sell us out to him. His phone will no doubt have a record of the call he received so all he'd need to do is prove we called him and then claim entrapment. We have to do it this way. I know you're concerned for McLennan, but he's a big boy, and he can handle the situation."

"I'll be fine, Sarge," McLennan reassured her. "All I have to do is convince him I can lead him to Graham Young and we'll have him."

"I hope you're right, Derek," Drake said, not entirely convinced.

* * *

The evening traffic had eased off by the time Derek McLennan made his way into Lime Street Station. He couldn't help but be impressed every time he entered the place. The architecture of the railway station, with its arches and façade that was once the North Western Hotel, reminiscent of a French Chateaux

444

was without doubt one of the most impressive mainline stations in Britain but for now, Derek pulled his mind away from such thoughts and made his way towards the arranged meeting place.

Finch wasn't there yet, so he bought a coffee and seated himself at a table that afforded him a good view through the large plate glass window, enabling him to see anyone coming or going from the restaurant. He knew that Ross was already in place, having seen him at the ticket barrier as he walked along the concourse. Somewhere above him, he knew a police marksman was hidden, rifle in hand, ready to act if Derek needed immediate help. He'd noticed a diesel locomotive standing just where Ross had said it would be, and knew two more armed officers, dressed in railway uniform would be scanning the concourse continuously.

Sipping his coffee, Derek checked his watch. He was too early, Lambert, or Finch wasn't due for ten minutes unless he too put in an early appearance. The double glass doors swung inwards as a couple entered, laughing and talking, eyes only for one another. A swift double-take told McLennan his close back-up had arrived. Izzie Drake was virtually unrecognisable from her day to day on-duty appearance. Her hair had changed from its usual shoulder-length brunette to long, blond tresses, with a sexy fringe, (Derek thought). For a second he couldn't take his eyes from Izzie's legs. In her short, black mini skirt and two inch heels, she looked incredible, Derek decided. The silky white blouse accentuated her breasts and Derek McLennan almost fell off his seat as he finally realised it *was* Sergeant Izzie Drake he was ogling. Pulling himself back to reality he now realised the man she was with was his friend and colleague, D.C. Tony Curtis. With long but neatly styled hair, which Derek had to assume was a wig, expensive shoes and a sharp three piece suit in a pale blue pinstripe, Curtis reminded Derek of a well-heeled pimp or drug dealer. Maybe that was his cover, Derek smiled to himself.

"See something funny, or maybe something you like, Mr. Raven?"

McLennan looked up to see the man he was due to meet standing at his shoulder, dressed as Finch had said he'd be, down to the New York Yankees cap. He'd been so engrossed in watching Izzie Drake's totally transformed look that he'd taken his eye off the door for a few vital seconds, allowing Finch to take him by surprise, a mistake he rapidly decided he mustn't repeat if he was to succeed in his undercover role.

Looking up at the new arrival, Derek could only say, "Finch?"

"That's Mister Finch to you, Raven. Not much of a copper are you? You were so busy ogling the Tom over there; I could have walked right up to you and blown your fucking head off."

Derek decided to play dumb, to play along with Finch's initial impression of him.

"You think she's a prossie?"

"Are you thick? Of course she is. Skirt that short, almost showing everything she's got? Nice shapely

446

ass and great legs though, I'll grant you, but I'll bet you she opens 'em more times in one night than you get laid in a year. Her pimp's probably brought her here to deliver her to a client for the evening. Less chance of being picked up by your lot if he hands her over in a place like this."

"Right, yeah, I see what you mean," said Derek. "So, anyway, why don't you sit down? Can I get you a coffee or tea or something?"

"This isn't a social call," Finch replied. "Let's talk," and the man sat down opposite McLennan, who couldn't help noticing his eyes. Finch's eyes were dark pools, almost lifeless in their appearance as though he saw the world through a soulless veneer with not a hint of emotion visible in his countenance. As Finch/Lambert took his seat, Sam Gable entered the cafeteria, pushing the door open with her bottom as she reversed into the place with her 'baby' in the pram that she towed in with her. Unlike Izzie Drake, Sam was 'dressed down' in a quilted jacket that had seen better days, well worn jeans and a harassed look on her face as she looked around for a place to sit and park the pram without causing an obstruction. She didn't give the two men at the table a second glance, just hurried past, another stressed out, care-worn young mother, eager for a cup of tea and a sit down.

Finch wanted to get his business concluded as fast as he could.

"Assuming you've got information that I want to buy, just how much do you expect me to pay you for it, Raven?"

"Short and to the point, I like that," McLennan replied, now recovered from his earlier lapse and getting back into the role of bent copper. "I want twenty thousand for each location."

"Twenty thousand pounds? You can't be serious, Raven. You must think I'm stupid."

"Far from it," McLennan replied. "If either of those men talks, it could completely compromise you and give my bosses a good reason to pick you up and charge you with conspiracy to commit murder. I'd say forty grand for the two of them is a bargain if it helps to keep you out of jail. Oh yes, and another thing; I'm not sure how your bosses would react if you did get arrested, Mr. Finch. Maybe you'd be the next one with a contract taken out on your life. I'll bet you know enough to bring your bosses down, Think about it."

Derek McLennan was growing into his role by the second, any earlier hesitancy completely gone. He felt he almost had Finch hooked. Now, the only question was whether Finch would accept his terms or try to negotiate. Finch had to be desperate; he had no other way of locating the two men, or of finding a way to actually get close to them. Derek represented that chance and both men knew it. A few seconds passed in an awkward silence before Finch suddenly reached a hand across the table and said "Done, you thieving bastard."

Derek reached across and the two shook hands on the deal.

"You won't regret it, Mr. Finch," he said as he sat back in his uncomfortable plastic chair again.

"I'd better not," Finch grinned at him as he went on, "I'd have paid twice that amount if you'd pushed me, so I guess I got a good deal. It's easy to see this is the first time you've done anything like this."

"Yeah, well, I just want enough to maybe resign from the force, start a little business of my own maybe, somewhere new, you know; a fresh start."

"Right, well, I don't give a shit what you do with the money. Just tell me what I need to know."

"Not so fast," said McLennan. "I want fifty percent up front, the rest when you're satisfied the job's done."

Finch smiled as he reached into his inside pocket, so intent on his dealings with McLennan that he failed to notice the 'hooker' sitting at the far side of the cafeteria as she fiddled with something in her handbag. In fact Izzie Drake was pressing the shutter button on the camera cleverly hidden in the clasp of her handbag, a handy gadget Ross had borrowed at short notice from a friend in the drug squad. They now had, if nothing else, Randolph Lambert passing money to Derek, as payment for information that would lead to attempted murder.

"There's ten grand in there," Finch said to Derek. "Take it or leave it as a down-payment. You don't think I'd carry all that cash around for a first meeting do you? You get the rest after the first hit. I'll know you can be trusted then and I sure don't intend to hang around after the second one to have a nice chat with you to hand over the rest. You won't see me again after that, you have to appear clean, so we have to make it look good. I don't want your friends realising you've sold them out and closing the door on my escape."

"So what do you suggest?"

"You get me in to Robin's room. I take care of business. We meet at a place of your choice, in the car park, wherever you want. I hand over the cash and head off to take care of Starling."

"Wait a minute. I've already thought of an easy, painless way in."

"Go on, I'm listening."

"I can come and go as part of the team, so I propose I go in with a nice flask of coffee, suitably drugged and as soon as they fall asleep, I get out of there, and drive to the next location, ready to meet you there. I then call you in, give you the directions to Starling's location and you do what you have to do. You get what you want and no one gets hurt."

"Apart from Robin of course," Finch grinned. "I like it. You're sure you can pull the drugged coffee thing off?"

"Of course, I can later say I left my flask unattended for a few minutes at the nurses' station and you must have crept up and dropped something in it while the nurse was taking me to see the duty doctor. Don't worry, I'll make sure she and I are away long enough for it to have happened in theory."

Finch was obviously so keen to see the end of Robin that he accepted the plan without too much thought, as Ross had imagined he would.

"What time do we go in?" Finch asked.

"Three in the morning, that'll be the best time right in the middle of the night shift. There's only one nurse on duty at that time, and I can deal with her and the guys on guard, no problem. All you'll have to do is walk in and do the job and walk out again. Nobody will even see you. Here, take this."

McLennan passed a cheap basic pay-as-you-go mobile phone to Finch. I have one like it. Yours has my number programmed into it. This is how we stay in touch. Once the job's over, you can dispose of it."

"You've worked it all out, haven't you?"

"Yes, Mr. Finch, I have. I'm not as stupid as you may have thought."

"Okay, Mr. Raven, so you want me, where, just before 3 a.m?"

"Be in the main car park of the Royal Hospital. I'll tell you where to find Robin when I meet up with you."

"Okay. But listen to me, Raven. This had better work or you will live to regret it."

"Trust me, it'll work," said Derek.

Without another word, Finch rose and walked out of the cafeteria. None of the undercover officers approached Derek or made any contact with him, just in case Finch was lurking somewhere nearby, watching Derek in case of a double-cross.

Derek waited two minutes before he also got up from his seat and walked out to the car park. He drove all the way home before picking up the phone and calling Andy Ross who was delighted things had gone so well. Everything was set up, now all they had to do was wait for dead of night to fall on the hospital.

Chapter 37

German efficiency

Following the telephone update from McLennan, and with Derek safely at home with instructions to get something to eat and then put his feet up for a couple of hours, Ross and Drake joined D.C.I. Agostini and the rest of the team in the squad room where they held a quick debriefing session on Derek's meeting with Randolph (Finch) Lambert.

"He did a good job, that's for sure," Ross said.

"I'm pleased to hear it," Oscar Agostini replied. "It could have all gone badly if Lambert had caught on to our little plot."

"Derek was rather amazing, sir," Sam Gable observed with real admiration in her voice for her colleague.

"He was," Curtis agreed, "but I thought his eyes were going to pop out when saw you in that miniskirt, Sarge," he said to Drake.

"I'm just glad Peter couldn't see me dressed like that," Drake said. "His eyes would have popped out of his head at the sight of me in that skirt," she grinned.

"Hey, Sarge, you never know, he might fancy you looking like that, want to go in for some dressing up games at bedtime; you know what I mean?"

"You're a cheeky bastard, D.C. Curtis," Izzie said, mock seriously.

"I'd have given you fifty for an hour," Curtis joked and flinched as Drake slapped him across his right shoulder.

"Cheapskate!" she shouted at him and laughed. "You couldn't afford me, Tony."

The whole room exploded in laughter, Agostini included as the brief exchange allowed them all a release of the tension that had built up during McLennan's meeting with Lambert.

"Anyway, those legs of yours did the trick, Izzie. Lambert made you as a prossie right away and never gave you a second thought," said Ross.

"Oh, thank you sir," Drake said, "Easily forgotten eh, legs or no legs?"

"You know what I mean, Izzie," Ross grinned.

"You're forgiven, sir," she replied.

"Ahem," Agostini interrupted. "Sorry everyone, but we need to make sure we're all focussed on tonight. Have you made the necessary arrangements with the hospital, Andy?"

"I have sir, as you said, and the hospital authorities have been very cooperative. Our people will replace their staff before McLennan gives Lambert the room number. There are only four patients on that private wing at present and they're being moved to another floor temporarily until our operation concludes. Everything should go smoothly tonight."

"Excellent," Agostini said as the door to the squad room opened and much to everyone's surprise, Detective Chief Superintendant Sarah Hollingsworth walked in to the room, accompanied by her aide, Inspector Mark Bennings.

"Ma'am," Agostini acknowledged his immediate superior officer as she walked to the front of the gathered officers, Bennings by her side.

Ross and Drake exchanged surprised glances. It was rare for the Chief Super to make an unannounced appearance at an impromptu briefing like this, so rare in fact that Ross couldn't recall it having happened at all in his living memory. Whatever had caused Hollingsworth to appear like this had to be important.

"My apologies for barging in like this," she began, "but I've just received news that I think you'll want to hear. As D.C.I Agostini has no doubt informed you, I've been in touch with various friendly police forces across Europe in relation to your current case and have just received a phone call from Germany."

A ripple of murmurs circulated among the detectives present, quickly silenced as Hollingsworth held a hand up.

"I'm not great with German pronunciation so let's just say that Joseph Lenz is of an equivalent rank to myself. Herr Lenz is with the *Bundespolizei* who it appears, were alerted to our case by Stephan Jung, my contact at the *Bundeskriminalamt.*

I've just come from a very illuminating telephone conversation with Herr Lenz. I think you'll all be as surprised as I was to learn that Erich Ackermann is currently in a cell in the police station in Rostock. He was arrested at his home three hours ago."

Andy Ross stared at Hollingsworth. Another ripple of murmurs ran round the room, that quickly fell silent as the Chief Superintendent cleared her throat and carried on.

"It appears the German police have had their eyes on Herr Ackermann for some time, suspecting him of financial irregularities in his business dealings. In short, Joseph Lenz heads up a crack team that investigates serious fraud cases, not small run-of-the-mill everyday fraud, we're talking about cases where the amounts involved run into millions of *Deutschmarks,* or, since last year, 2002, the Euro of course and involve large scale movements of money across international borders. Like many such investigations, it can be a long and often frustrating maze for investigators to negotiate as we know only too well from the efforts of our own Serious Fraud Squad. However, as so often happen, it can be one small thing, maybe totally unrelated directly to the actual investigation in progress that leads to a positive resolution to the case.

Just such an instance has taken place in Germany today, thanks to you and your people, D.I. Ross."

"Really Ma'am?" Ross exclaimed in some surprise.

"Really," Hollingsworth replied. "Erich Ackermann has always sailed a little close to the wind in his business dealings apparently. Perhaps that's why he's been so successful, never being afraid to gamble, take a chance on speculative ventures, high risks for high profits, according to Lenz. A few years ago his various dealings saw his financial investment business take a massive hit, losses mounted, investors were becoming angry and deserting him in droves. Then apparently overnight all was well again. One of Ackermann's investors became suspicious when Ackermann began buying up large tracts of land and then making a fortune from subsequent developments. Where had all the new money come from? This investor knew it couldn't be from Ackermann's dealings on the financial markets as he spoke to a number of acquaintances, also clients of Erich Ackermann, all of whom reported their investments going down, not up.

The police listened to the investor, and instinct told their investigators that Ackermann was either involved with organised crime, money laundering was an obvious guess, or had become involved in other, illegal activities that were bringing in sudden large sums of money.

They quickly discovered that Erich Ackermann was also bankrolling a radical neo-Nazi political group calling itself *neue Morgendämmerung,* that's 'New Dawn' in English. That was enough to place him firmly in the sights of not only the Fraud Squad but the anti-terrorist police as well, which put him on the *Bundeskriminalamt's* radar too."

"Bloody hell, Ma'am," Ross couldn't help interrupting. "Sounds like this guy is a far bigger fish than we thought."

"Precisely, Detective Inspector Ross, which is why I'm so pleased that D.C.I. Agostini had the sense to alert me when this case of yours suddenly appeared to have far greater ramifications than the murder of young Aaron Decker first led us to believe. Anyway, the one thing the police needed was a thread to hang on Ackermann, something that would enable them to bring him in and sweat him, try to get him to crack a little and maybe open a floodgate. You've given them that thread. They knew about his connection to Aegis and once we told them what to look for, they were able to pinpoint every deal he'd set up with every bent official in various governments, Turkey, Greece, Italy etc.

Anyway, they picked him up from his own office, in front of his staff, and as soon as they got him into an interview room they went at him hard from the start.

"Ve haf vays of making you talk," Tony Curtis mimicked in a terrible German accent, with a Liverpudlian twang.

"Yes, thank you Constable Curtis," Hollingsworth said and Curtis turned red. She went on:

"Yes, well, it does seem like our German friends are allowed a little more latitude than we are when it comes to interviewing suspects and within a short time, they had him talking. Although they're sure he had nothing to do with the murders over here, apart from financing the whole operation, Lenz told him they'd got him lined up as an accessory to at least four murders in England and that they were quite prepared to ship him over here to stand trial. Lenz told him that English prisons are a hotbed of homosexual rape, with new prisoners subject to daily sodomy attacks by multiple hardened criminals and that he'd get at least ten years for his part in the conspiracy to murder, plenty of time for him to get used to it. Lenz told me he'd never seen the blood drain from a man's face so fast in his life. Ackermann is talking even as we speak. Ackermann, with his ingrained Nazi beliefs, is actually appalled by and terrified of homosexuality and Lenz knew it. So, it seems our man rose quickly in the Aegis hierarchy thanks to him bankrolling the purchase of the four submarines they use for their underwater survey work. He also negotiated crooked deals with certain officials once they'd located valuable historical sites. He siphoned off vast sums of plundered wealth into accounts Aegis knew nothing about in order to finance his search for the *U3000*."

Hollingsworth fell silent, as she allowed her last words to penetrate the minds of Ross and his team.

"This was all about the U-Boat, right from the start?" Ross said, incredulously.

"Indeed," the D.C.S. confirmed. "He knew exactly what the submarine was carrying, the gold and artworks of course, but more importantly he knew about the new technology she incorporated. He knew that if he could get his hands on it, and the final plans and drawings for the working prototype were supposed to be sealed in the U-Boat's safe, he knew the potential for profit was virtually limitless. Imagine a process that could literally revolutionise the worldwide shipping industry, removing the need for oil as a fuel source, with the only raw material necessary to operate even a massive supertanker being nothing more complicated then water. Ackermann thought it would make him the richest man in the world."

"So in the end it was still about money," Drake said with distaste. "All those people dead, and for what? A money making scheme that he didn't even know would work."

"Oh, but the thing is, he knew it does work," Sergeant. "Apparently he has the documents that show the Nazis tested the new system for over three months in the *U3000* before she was sent on her last fateful voyage. It was a mostly proven system and only the fact that Germany was by then almost defeated prevented Hitler having a fleet of those submarines and maybe even surface ships built that could have swung the war in his favour. Ackermann believed that any flaws in the original system could be ironed out and an improved design produced by Aegis's engineers. Anyway, that's by the bye, now. He's talking to Lenz who has promised to drop the conspiracy to murder charges if he tells all and names every crooked Aegis employee he's corrupted in his evil scheme."

"That's wonderful, Ma'am, so what do we do?"

"We go on as before," Inspector Ross. "We still have to nail those responsible for the crimes committed here in Liverpool and the UK in general. You have a sting operation in place for tonight, I understand from D.C.I. Agostini?"

"Yes, Ma'am," said Ross. "And if we can bring this man Lambert in and get him to talk, we may be able to pass on enough to the F.B.I to give them the information they need to prosecute the head of the American arm of the corrupt Aegis octopus."

"Ah yes, Mr. Kelly. Ackermann has mentioned him to Lenz, but hasn't given him any details that can be used to link him to the murders. It seems Mr. Kelly decided to take the murderous path towards their goal without consulting Ackermann, who wasn't interested in how Kelly got results, as long as he got them. Basically, he's a coward and a narcissist who really had developed a kind of Fuehrer complex. He actually thought he was going to be so damned rich he'd have a stranglehold on world commerce through what he saw as 'his' revolutionary propulsion process. So going back to Kelly, I know the father of the Decker boy has been helpful and I've spoken to the Supervisory Special Agent in Charge of the F.B.I. team who are investigating Kelly and they are willing to pick him up as soon as we can give them confirmation that this Finch chap will testify that Kelly gave the orders for the murders of Aaron Decker and T.J Knowles. I understand you used the threat of a Turkish prison on one of the men you already have in custody, D.I. Ross?"

"Erm, yes, I did, Ma'am. I know it's not…"

"Oh, don't apologise, Ross. I quite like the idea. Now I understand this Finch chappie wouldn't be very happy at the thought of returning to Iraq, for example?"

Ross smiled and then laughed out loud at the connotations of the D.C.S's words.

"No Ma'am, I don't suppose he would."

"Well then, we'll leave it at that shall we?"

"Yes, of course, Ma'am, thank you."

Hollingsworth had said what she'd come to say and nodded to her aide, who prepared to leave with her. Before she left the room she had one last thing to say.

"D.I. Ross, please wish your young detective constable, I believe his name is McLennan, the best of luck tonight. He's a very brave young man going up against an extremely dangerous killer. For his sake I hope all goes well for you all. I don't care what time you conclude this operation tonight, Oscar," she said to Agostini. "You call me and let me know the outcome, you hear me?"

"I hear you Ma'am," Agostini replied and with that, she was gone.

Chapter 38

Closing the net

"I knew I could count on you, Frankie," Paul Ferris exclaimed as his 'tame' computer geek and hacker Frankie Trout exultantly relayed the findings of his short but extremely productive foray into the innards of the computers owned by both Advance Transportation and Jeffrey Metcalfe.

"Yes, well, I did say it wouldn't take long didn't I?" said Frankie. "When have I ever let you down, eh, Mr. Ferris?"

"Never, Frankie, and that's why I come to you when I need a favour. Now, this is important. What you've just told me, there's no chance you've made any mistakes or misinterpreted any of the data you just relayed to me?"

"I'm sending you a copy of everything by email right now, Mr. Ferris, encrypted as usual of course.

Only you and I have the key to access it, so please, for my sake keep it that way okay?"

"No one will know you're helping me, Frankie, you have my word. This is just what we needed. You've done well, my friend."

"Yeah, looks like your target has been naughty in their dealings. Like I told you, Advance Transportation's confidential files show their lorries arriving at various European coastal locations on or around the same dates as Aegis Oceanographic registered ships arrived in the same ports. The next day, in each case, the lorries departed carrying freight for onward forwarding to an Aegis facility near the port of Brindisi in Southern Italy. Brindisi is a major centre for trade with the Middle East and Greece. By the time those lorries leave Brindisi their cargo has apparently been offloaded and new cargoes loaded, for transport back to the UK, so they're clean by the time they return. I've done some tracking via satellite records and soon after Metcalfe's lorries made their drop off at the Aegis facility an Aegis supply vessel left port, bound for Egypt, which is where the trail goes cold. I suspect that whatever is taken to Egypt is offloaded and later flown to the States or wherever your crooked guy at Aegis wants it in one of their fleet of private aircraft."

"You've done well, Frankie," Ferris said, satisfied he had enough for the team to move against Jeffrey Metcalfe.

"Oh, one last thing," Frankie went on. "The weights, Mr. Ferris. You do know that these big intercontinental trucks are sort of 'weighed in' and 'weighed out' at the beginning and end of each journey, right?"

"Yes, I knew that, Frankie."

"Well, the freight that those lorries was carrying on the trips to Brindisi was always far heavier than whatever they carried back to the UK. I don't know if that's significant, but thought I'd mention it."

"It could be Frankie. Thanks again. You've been really helpful."

"Yeah, well, I hope you catch the bad guys, Mr. Ferris."

"Me too, Frankie, me too."

Frankie hung up and Ferris saw the 'email received' icon flashing on is computer screen. He soon had Frankie's information printed and after checking it through and making notes that he could use to explain things clearly to D.I. Ross, he set off in search of his boss.

He found Ross, together with Drake and Agostini in the Headquarters Central Control Room, where they were making arrangements for extra officers to be drafted in to the area around the hospital during the time they expected the take-down of Randolph Lambert to occur. They were to be kept out of sight in surrounding streets, ready to add assistance if needed. No chances were being taken. Even traffic patrol cars were being diverted from their normal patrol areas to be on hand if needed in the vicinity of the Royal Liverpool University Hospital.

Ross saw Paul Ferris as soon as the D.C. walked into the control room and beckoned him across to join him.

"Your smile tells me you have some good news for me," Ross said, his eyes drawn to the folder Ferris held in his left hand.

"I do sir. It's mostly circumstantial, but I think we've got enough to bring Jeffrey Metcalfe in for questioning. These records are enough to link his fleet of lorries to the movements of Aegis ships arriving at a central point, in this case Brindisi, which is where I believe Kelly has set up his central clearing house for their plundered treasures. He moves them from there to Egypt, and then flies them out to either the States or wherever he wants them, maybe to illicit buyers, who knows?"

Ferris passed the folder to Ross who took a good look at the contents, passing it to Agostini in turn.

"Yes, it may be circumstantial but it's pretty damning," said Ross. "It's definitely enough to have him picked up and brought in. He's not a career criminal, so I doubt he'll hold up for long. If we hit him with some hard questioning he'll cave in, in no time."

"I agree," Agostini concurred. "Let's get a warrant issued for his arrest, send a couple of burly uniformed officers up to Lancaster to carry out the arrest and put the fear of God into him. Have him brought here, let him sweat for a while in an interview room and then threaten to charge him as an accessory to the murder of his daughter's boyfriend and I bet he'll crack and spill everything he knows."

"You're a hard man D.C.I Agostini," Ross smiled at his friend and his guvnor, who smiled back.

"We're two of a kind, Andy. Let's finish this and put this nest of bloody vipers behind bars for a bloody long time."

"Damn right, sir," Ross agreed, taking the folder back from the boss and passing it to Izzie Drake who quickly familiarized herself with the contents.

"Seems to me he's one cold and callous bastard," she commented as she placed the folder on a nearby desk. "Not to mention greedy and without any scruples whatsoever. What is his daughter going to think of her father, when she learns what he's done? Then there's his wife of course. Why do people do these things? There he was, nicely set up with a couple of companies making a decent living, certainly enough to keep his family in a small degree of luxury and then he gets involved in something like this."

"Money, Izzie," said Ross. "The root of all evil as they say. We can't say how much is involved yet, but it must run into millions of dollars at least."

Paul Ferris then added his own surprise, one which he knew might add weight to their case against Metcalfe.

"Oh, by the way, there's just one other point that I should mention. My source also did some digging and although Metcalfe is listed as sole owner of Advance Transportation, fifty percent of the company's equity is held by...any guesses anyone?"

"Aegis Oceanographic?" Drake proffered.

467

"Right," said Ferris. "I think that's enough, don't you sir?"

"Well done, Ferris," said Ross. "Yes, I think that proves Metcalfe is well in bed with Aegis, certainly enough to tie him in to their illegal cross-border activities."

Agostini, his mind working at almost computer-like speed had been listening carefully to all that was being said around him and now, bearing in mind the time, and that in a few hours Derek McLennan would be putting the final stage of their plan to snare Finch into operation, he made a decision to try to expedite things.

"Right, I want Metcalfe in this building ASAP, and there's only one way to get that done quickly. We don't have time to send someone up there to bring him back before we have to turn all out attention to matters at the hospital."

"You have an idea, sir?" Drake asked.

"Indeed I do, Sergeant Drake," the D.C.I. replied as he walked across to the nearest telephone, picked it up and asked the switchboard operator to connect him with Lancaster Police Headquarters on Thurnham Street in the university city. The others watched intently. Unlike his predecessor, D.C.I. Harry Porteous, Agostini certainly wasn't averse to getting directly involved in a hands-on manner with an investigation and was pouring all his efforts into an all-out effort to support his men and women in the field, rather leading from behind a desk.

Agostini was soon connected to Chief Inspector Mitch Wells, who at one time in the past had been his 'guvnor' when he was a uniformed sergeant. The two had remained in fairly close touch over the years and Agostini was confident Wells would accede to his urgent request.

"No problem, Oscar," was the immediate response from Wells. "I'll send Inspector Barry Houseman and Sergeant Pat Norman to pick him up and have him taken straight to you. Houseman is my best man, big and burly as you asked for, and can be very intimidating, so should put the fear of God into this Metcalfe character."

"Thanks, Mitch," Agostini replied. "And Norman?"

"Ah yes, Patricia Norman is a hell of a good copper. A black belt in three different martial art forms, and takes no crap from anyone. They'll have him wetting himself, believe me. He should be glad to get to Liverpool and ready to talk by the time he gets there if he's half the coward you think he is."

"Sounds good. I'd better go and let you get them on the road."

The two men said their goodbyes, and Agostini, smiling, turned to Ross and the others.

"Sorted," he said, firmly and with conviction, confident his old boss would have already dispatched Houseman and Norman to the address he'd provided to Wells, who'd whistled through his teeth as Agostini read it to him, well aware of the upmarket location of the Metcalfe home.

* * *

The arrest of Jeffrey Metcalfe couldn't have gone better as far as the police were concerned. His wife, Dorothy, had answered the loud knocking on the front door of their large, mansion sized residence on the outskirts of Lancaster, Houseman purposely using his fist on the door rather then using the polite approach of pressing the doorbell or using the ornate brass doorknocker in the shape of a stag's head.

"Police, Ma'am," Houseman announced in a loud voice, as though the uniform didn't tell the story. "We'd like to speak to your husband please. Is he at home?"

Dorothy Metcalfe could only nod in surprise at the sudden arrival of the police on her doorstep and quickly showed them into a large and beautifully furnished sitting room where her husband sat in a large, winged armchair, reading a newspaper. As luck would have it, Sally Metcalfe was seated on a nearby sofa, her legs curled beneath her, stroking a small tan-coloured dachshund that lazily opened a sleepy eye at the two interlopers to its domain and then promptly curled up and went back to its doggie dream world. Having been briefed by Wells, Houseman wondered if some of the antique statuary and paintings that adorned the room might be part of the man's ill-gotten gains from his crimes.

Looking up, Metcalfe's face registered first surprise and then a hint of apprehension as he took in the hard stares of the two police officers as they strode purposely into his inner sanctum, straight towards him, stopping just a few feet in front of his chair.

"Officers?" he said, trying to appear composed while his mind tried to work out why the police were in his home. "Is there something I can help you with?"

"Jeffrey Metcalfe," Houseman spoke without preamble. "My name is Inspector Barry Houseman, and this is Sergeant Norman, Lancaster Police. I'm arresting you on charges relating to the murder of Aaron Decker and of participation in the theft and international trafficking of stolen and contraband antiques, historical artifacts, and currency."

After completing the statutory warning relating to his right to silence and the possible use of his word being used against him in court, Houseman fell silent as he watched the colour drain from Metcalfe's face, his mouth opening and closing in shock, speechless at the Inspector's words. Behind the two officers, Dorothy Metcalfe stood stock still, frozen in place like one of the Roman style statues that stood either side of the interior of the sitting room door. On the sofa, Sally Metcalfe however, leapt up in shock, the poor dachshund sent scrabbling to the floor where it quickly ran and hid under the large oak sideboard that stood against one wall of the room.

"Daddy," she almost screamed. "What the hell are they talking about? What do they mean, by *charges relating to the murder of Aaron*? Please tell me they're making a mistake."

"Sally...I..." before he could say more, Sergeant Norman took hold of his elbow as he moved to lever himself from his chair and as he reached a standing position she swiftly pulled his arms behind his back and snapped a pair of handcuffs in place, closing tightly around his wrists, bringing an audible gasp from the man and equal gasps of shock from his wife and daughter."

"Are those really necessary?" his wife asked pleadingly, referring to the handcuffs.

"I'm afraid so," said Houseman. "Your husband faces serious charges, Mrs. Metcalfe. We're transporting him immediately to Merseyside Police Headquarters in Liverpool, where he'll be questioned by the detectives conducting the investigation."

"But Aaron was my boyfriend" said Sally. "My father couldn't possibly have had anything to do with his murder. I mean, even I was drugged at the time, and he wouldn't have..."

Sally stopped in mid sentence as doubt suddenly crept in. She'd wondered why, when Aaron was murdered, she'd only been knocked out for a few hours. Was it really possible her own father was involved in this nightmare?"

"I'm sorry Miss, we don't have time for this. They're waiting to speak to your father in Liverpool."

Houseman and Norman had then quickly and efficiently ushered the handcuffed figure of Jeffrey Metcalfe from his home, still in a state of apparent shock, leaving his wife and daughter in tears, clinging to each other on the steps of their grandiose home, which to both women suddenly seemed a cold and empty place as the reality of the situation took hold of the pair. Houseman and Norman maintained a planned, ominous silence during the journey to Liverpool increasing Metcalfe's agitation and trepidation as they steadfastly refused to respond to his attempts to illicit any information from them regarding his future. By the time Houseman delivered his prisoner into the custody of Merseyside Police, Metcalfe appeared on the verge of a panic attack. After ensuring he was fit enough to be questioned he was placed in interview room two, where he was left under the guard of a uniformed constable, to await the arrival of Ross and Drake who would be conducting his interview.

Ross and Drake had in the meantime greeted and thanked Houseman and Norman, who reported their own satisfaction with their own role in the affair, being pleased to have helped and as Houseman put it, "Glad to have helped bring a little bit of the soft criminal underbelly to the surface. I hope you now proceed to sink the bastard without trace."

The pair stayed long enough to also meet Oscar Agostini, who asked them to pass on his personal thanks to Chief Inspector Wells, after which, following a hot coffee in the cafeteria, the two uniformed officers took their leave of Liverpool, returning to Lancaster within an hour of their arrival in the big city.

Ross next sent the remaining members of the team home to get a couple of hours rest. They would all return later that night to take part in the operation supporting Derek McLennan. Last to leave was Paul Ferris, who was collected by his wife Kareen and young son, another Aaron. Ross, Drake and Agostini made a fuss of young Aaron, who had undergone painful sessions of kidney dialysis when younger, eventually receiving a kidney transplant at the tender age of six years. Now a well developed ten year-old, Aaron was something of a favourite among the members of the Murder Investigation Team, an unofficial mascot almost. Having only arrived quite recently Oscar Agostini didn't know the lad as well as the others but that didn't prevent him from ushering Aaron into his office, from where he emerged a few minutes later with a Merseyside Police wall shield, which Ross knew had been displayed on Agostini's office wall up until that time.

Ferris thanked the D.C.I. for his kindness and Agostini just winked at him as he patted Aaron on the shoulder, telling him he was almost a grown up now, and to look after his Mum while his Dad was busy at work. Young Aaron's chest swelled with pride at that, and Ferris and Kareen were both grateful to Agostini for giving Aaron that bit of self-importance and inner confidence.

With the Ferris family gone, the squad room took on an air of desertion, like a ship left without a crew, drifting at sea. Agostini followed Ross and Drake as they walked solemnly towards interview room two. He then entered the door to the viewing room where he would observe Metcalfe's interview through the

474

room's large one way mirror, listening in through the built-in intercom system.

Jeffrey Metcalfe almost jumped out of his skin when the door opened to admit Ross and Drake. After introducing himself and Sergeant Drake, and starting the tapes that would record the suspect's interview, Ross wasted no time in getting straight to the point.

"You're in some really deep shit, Mr. Metcalfe," he began. "I doubt poor Sally is going to forgive you when she hears how you conspired to kill her boyfriend, or how her job offer from the Aegis Institute came about through your own criminal connections with Francis Kelly and his bunch of thieves and cutthroats."

With those opening words, Ross had successfully peeled away the last veneer of Metcalfe's slim hopes of avoiding serious charges. To Metcalfe, that brief opening statement from Ross, and the use of Kelly's name had him believing the police knew everything there was to know about his activities. As had happened at the time of his arrest his mouth opened and closed but no words came out.

"Got nothing to say, Metcalfe?" Ross asked. "Well, let me fill in a couple of the blanks for you. It all probably began innocently enough with a genuine tender by your company to carry out a regular freight contract for Aegis's European Division. Then, somewhere along the way, you met Kelly, probably on one of his visits to the UK, and Kelly quickly saw you could be bought and manipulated into carrying out some of his less than legitimate business, am I right?"

Metcalfe nodded, and in a hushed voice, spoke at last. "It was a company golfing weekend, where we met. I told him about Sally. He said he could help her career, and things started from there."

"I thought so," Ross replied. "Now listen to me, you corrupt, greedy piece of shite; I hate killers and I hate people who hide behind killers almost as much. Unless you want to spend the rest of your natural life behind bars, I suggest you tell us everything about your involvement with Aegis from the time you met Francis Kelly. I want to know about the shipments, the false compartments built into the trucks of your subsidiary company and how the hell you let yourself be talked into setting up poor Aaron Decker and allowed your own daughter to be given a dangerous drug that might have killed her at the same time."

"You're not a man," Izzie Drake added as Ross drew breath. "You're the lowest form of animal life, Metcalfe. But the more you tell us, the easier the judge might be when we tell him you've cooperated fully with our investigation, got it?"

Metcalfe nodded, and after taking a deep breath, he talked. The tapes carried on turning, and Drake made copious notes as he revealed the full story of his involvement with Kelly and his plot to steal from and defraud not only those who'd employed his company, the innocent and legitimate wing of The Aegis Institute who had naïvely awarded him contracts on Kelly's recommendations, but governments who trusted Aegis to work for them, and how Kelly and his trusted security force would ruthlessly eliminate anyone perceived as being a threat to their activities, including Aaron Decker.

Andy Ross had dealt with men like Metcalfe in the past, ordinary men who allowed greed and avarice to completely overtake their sense of social responsibility. The temptation to turn a fast profit from what initially must have seemed a simple get rich quick scheme had ensnared many men before Metcalfe and would do so again in future. For now though, Ross and Drake were content that within an hour, Jeffrey Metcalfe, mostly inspired by fear of his now unknown future had provided them with enough to convict him of multiple offences and sufficient information the F.B.I. and C.I.A. would be able to use against Francis Kelly. The net was tightening, and now all they needed was success with their plan to bring Finch, a.k.a. Randolph Lambert into custody.

Chapter 39

A Hospital Operation

There was no doubt in the minds of Ross and Drake that the net was now firmly closing on those concerned with what had turned out to be a case with so many international ramifications.

"To think this started with the death of a young university cricket star, sir, and look where it's led us," Drake commented, as she and Ross sat in his office, doing their best to relax a little after finally handing Jeffrey Metcalfe over to the custody sergeant to be officially processed into the system. He'd be held overnight in the holding cells and brought up before the magistrates in the morning, when he'd be officially arraigned and transferred to prison to await his trial.

"True enough Izzie," Ross replied, his voice calm and quiet as he sipped from a mug of barely warm coffee. "But you know, it may have started for us with the death of Aaron Decker, but really it began on a cold night in Kiel, Germany back in 1945 when that submarine slipped its moorings and set to sea on Hitler's orders. Everything we've been involved with in this case all stems from that damned secret voyage."

"You're right, of course, sir," she agreed, "but we didn't know about any of that when we started out did we?"

"No, we didn't. And can those involved in this bloody catalogue of crime say it was worth it? With the number of years in prison they're going to serve, I doubt it, and don't forget how many people have lost their lives through the greed of people like Ackermann, Kelly and Metcalfe."

"Do you think we'll get enough on Kelly for the Americans to act against him?" Izzie asked.

"We will," Ross said firmly. "Derek McLennan will snare us this bloody Finch character tonight and we'll make him talk one way or another. He's the man who can link everything that's happened back to Kelly. I had a quick call from Jerome Decker earlier. Apparently Supervisory Special Agent David Lee and a special F.B.I Task Force is ready to move against Kelly. The F.B.I. has informed the Aegis senior executives of their suspicions regarding Kelly, and the board of directors is horrified and supportive of the Bureau's initiative. If we can send them a recording that implicates Kelly in murder, they will pick him up right away. Under U.S. laws, it appears Kelly is guilty of a number of serious financial offences already, so murder on top of that should wrap their case against him up nicely."

"Are you sure Derek will be okay?" Izzie said, switching back to the night's sting operation set up to entrap Finch/Lambert.

"I know what you're thinking," Ross said straight away. "Randolph Lambert is a dangerous man for sure, but Derek will be out of the way before the arrest goes down, and Lambert won't have a chance to get at him."

"I hope you're right, sir," Izzie said, worried for their colleague.

"He's a first class copper, Izzie. He knows what's at stake tonight and is professional enough to handle whatever happens."

"I know sir. He's come a long way since he first joined the team. Sometimes I forget he's all grown up now and isn't that wet behind the ears young D.C. any more. I'm sure he'll be fine."

"Listen, why don't you go home for a couple of hours? Peter must have forgotten what you look like. As long as we're all back here by midnight, there's no reason for you to hang around here."

Izzie stretched both arms upwards, suddenly realising how tense and weary she was.

"Well, I wouldn't mind having a quick shower and a change of clothes. As you say, Peter will be pleased to have me home for a little while. Hey, you never know, we might even be able to…"

"Enough, no more, too much information," Ross laughed, thinking of the newly-weds falling into bed together for a 'quickie' before Izzie reported back for work.

Izzie laughed too.

"I was going to say, we might be able to grab a quick meal together for the first time this week," the smile on her face growing broader as she spoke.

"Oh, right, yes of course you were," Ross replied, looking suitably chastised. "Just my dirty mind at work again."

"Yeah, don't I know it?" Izzie giggled.

"Go on, get off home," Ross smiled again. "I'll see you later."

"Okay, sir, you should go home too. Give Maria a treat."

"Izzie..." Ross warned playfully, throwing a crumpled-up piece of paper at his sergeant.

"Just saying," Izzie joked as she disappeared out of Ross's office, leaving him alone with his thoughts in the ensuing silence.

Ross spent a few minutes tidying a few pieces of paper of no great importance that littered his desk and then picked up the phone.

"Order us a Chinese, Darling," he said when his wife, Maria answered his call. "I'm coming home for couple of hours. Have to come back later; got a big op on tonight."

"It'll be here by the time you get home, Andy," Maria replied, glad her husband would be home soon, for however brief a time. She'd been married to a detective long enough to accept the unusual hours he had to work from time to time. "Drive carefully."

Ross turned the lights off as he left his office, and the silence in that small enclave within the headquarters building was instant as the overhead buzzing of the fluorescent tubes ceased instantly. He allowed himself a few moments of reflection in the squad room before leaving for home. A case that had begun with the death of a young man who appeared to have a great future ahead of him, an American, no less, who excelled at the very British game of cricket and whose record for bowling maiden overs had made him the darling of the university cricketing fraternity had turned into a case involving international conspiracy, multiple murder and a large helping of greed and avarice. Ross glanced at the large whiteboard at the far side of the room, now in semi-darkness and briefly contemplated each face placed there by Paul Ferris as the case had developed.

So many people, here in Liverpool and elsewhere had contributed to him being close to resolving the case. The Royal Navy, a German historian, the Devon and Cornwall Constabulary, even the C.I.A. and the F.B.I. for God's sake, not forgetting the most recent contribution from the police in Lancaster. Cross border cooperation? If ever a case had proved that crime prevention organisations around the world could work together to successfully crack such a wide-sweeping international conspiracy, this was it, he concluded. He knew Oscar Agostini would still be in his office on the upper floor of the building and pondered on calling in to see him before going home, but the thoughts of spending a couple of hard-earned hours with Maria overrode that option and he quickly made his way out of the building and was soon driving home.

Marie Ross was as good as her word. The Chinese takeaway had been delivered a few minutes before her husband's arrival at their neat detached home in Prescot. After enjoying a selection of dishes Marie had selected to tempt his palate, Ross made his way up stairs to take a shower and indulge in a change of clothes before heading back to work.

Andy Ross stepped from the en-suite bathroom with a towel around his waist, another in his hand, his hair still wet from the shower, to find Marie sitting on the bed, her legs crossed provocatively, her skirt having ridden up far enough to display a tempting glimpse of thigh.

"Feel better?" she asked as he used the hand towel to briskly rub his hair almost dry.

"Much better," he replied.

Marie patted the bed and beckoned him to come and sit beside her.

He'd given her a run down of the case as they'd eaten and she sensed he had a few reservations about the final stage of his plan.

"You're worried about Derek McLennan, aren't you?"

"Not so much worried as just a bit on-edge. Derek can take care of himself but the man we're after tonight has very little to lose at this stage and could be unpredictable. I just don't want Derek to get over confident and blow the whole plan as a result."

"Do you trust Derek?"

"Of course I do."

"So stop worrying and give him the credit he deserves, Andy. He's been with you a while now, so you should know whether he can do the job."

"Of course he can. It's just me being over-protective I suppose."

Marie smiled at her husband as she took his hand and placed it gently on her right knee.

"Well, well, Detective Inspector Andy Ross, the great mother hen. I can think of something to take your mind off your worries for a while. You did say you weren't going back to the office for a couple of hours, didn't you?"

"Yes, I did," said Ross as he caught the glint in Marie's eye as she slowly began to manipulate his hand further up her leg until he began to move independently and his hand found its way under the hem of her skirt. Clothes quickly discarded, the pair found themselves naked on the bed in no time and the next thirty minutes were spent in enjoying a brief interlude of intimacy that took Ross's mind far away from thoughts of death and conspiracy for a short time.

As they lay together in the warm afterglow of their lovemaking a large smile appeared on Andy Ross's face. Seeing his grin, Marie kissed him and then asked, "Are you going to tell me what's amusing you so much, just after you've made mad passionate love to your wife?"

"Oh, nothing really," Ross replied. "It's just that I suggested something similar to what we've just done to Izzie before sending her home and now…well, here we are, you know?"

"Andy!" Marie exclaimed. "You mean you actually told your sergeant to go home and get laid?"

"Well, sort of, I suppose."

"Yes, well, I know all about your 'sort of,' suggestions, poor girl. Anyway, I hope she took your advice," and the two of them laughed out loud together as Ross kissed her back and hopped off the bed, walking across to the wardrobe to select a suitable change of clothes for the late night operation at the hospital.

* * *

The office was buzzing with activity when Ross walked in shortly before midnight Almost everyone had beaten him to it, anticipating the operation that would take place in a few hours. Nick Dodds had arrived just before Ross. The detective constable had begged to be allowed to be part of the team that finally brought Finch in. Ross had agreed to him leaving Klaus Haller under the protection of his armed police guard at the safe house in St. Helens, after sending an extra uniformed officer to support them. As much as Dodds enjoyed Haller's company, he felt frustrated at being a glorified 'baby sitter' as he put it. Ross felt Haller would be safe enough as they knew precisely where Finch would be during the coming hours. Even Izzie Drake was there before him, grinning like a Cheshire cat at him as she sat on the corner of Paul Ferris's desk as the team's collator sat busily typing information into the computer.

"Something happen to hold you up, sir?" she grinned at him.

"I had a very enjoyable couple of hours at home, thank you, Sergeant Drake, Chinese takeaway in fact." Ross grinned back at her. "I take it you also took advantage of the short break to spend some quality time with Peter?"

"Oh yes, sir. As you suggested, we did enjoy spending some time together. Chinsese takeaway, eh? So that's what they're calling it nowadays is it?" Izzie replied, a red blush and a grin on her face as she spoke.

Ross merely winked at her and beckoned her to join him in his office, where Derek McLennan was already waiting for him, in company with D.C.I. Agostini. McLennan had handed the envelope containing the down payment from Finch, which would remain in Agostini's care for the time being.

"You alright, Derek?" Ross asked as Drake closed the door behind them as they entered the office.

"Fine thanks, sir," McLennan responded. The young detective constable had gone to a lot of trouble to look the part for this evening's operation. He wore a black leather jacket, faded blue jeans and heavy Dr. Martens boots. His hair was slicked back with gel and if anyone looked like a 'bent' copper, somehow Derek gave off just the right aura.

"You look…different," said Drake who, like Ross was used to seeing Derek in either his work suit or at worst, a casual jacket and trousers and open-necked shirt as opposed to the plain white t-shirt he currently wore under his jacket.

"Thought this look made me look a bit tougher," Derek replied with a sheepish grin.

"Oh, for God's sake Derek. You already met the man earlier. He knows just what you look like, and you haven't exactly grown much stubble in the last few hours," Drake added, a reference to his not having shaved.

"Oh, well, never mind," he said quietly.

"Leave him alone, Izzie," Ross said. "As long as Derek feels comfortable with his appearance, that'll do for me."

"Right sir. Sorry Derek," Izzie apologised.

"No problem, Sarge," Derek responded.

Back in the squad room a few minutes later with the whole team present, Ross quickly phoned Agostini who had asked to be present at the team briefing. Five minutes later, the D.C.I added his presence to that of the others in the room and Ross began his briefing as silence descended on the squad room.

"Okay everyone, you all know why we're here. I hope you all managed a meal, some rest and maybe a shower in the couple of hours you got to go home, and thank you all for volunteering to be part of tonight's operation."

A small ripple of polite laughter ran round the room. Nobody would have dared not to 'volunteer' of course and everyone did after all want to be there when Finch was brought to heel.

487

"You all know the essence of tonight's set up. We aim to take down the man known as Finch, real name Randolph Lambert. Lambert is the man, the only man as far as we know who can give us the intelligence we need to lay murder charges against this Francis Kelly character in the States. He's sort of like Kelly's first lieutenant, his enforcer, whatever you want to call it. As you know, Derek has laid the bait for Kelly, playing the role of a bent copper prepared to sell out the location of the two members of Lambert's so-called security force, in other words his hired killers that we currently hold in custody. It's obvious that Kelly wants no living witnesses that can tie him to this whole sorry business and it's our guess that Lambert, if given time, would probably see through our plan, but we're lucky that he's under pressure from Kelly, and it appears he believes that either Robin or Starling are willing to talk to us about their part in his schemes. Derek has already hinted that Robin, a.k.a Graham Young is the easiest target and has arranged to meet Lambert at the hospital and give him Young's location, at the same time as he disables the guards with drugged coffee. Of course, Graham Young has already been moved to a safe location, and our friend Lambert is due to receive something of a shock when he tries to do away with the patient in room 414.

You all know the roles assigned to each of you. Sam, you're the duty nurse, Nick and Tony, you're the two uniformed officers outside the room, drugged of course, and Paul Ferris and Sergeant Drake will be taking the part of the two uniformed officers inside the room. Make sure you all have your vests on. I don't think for one minute that Lambert will draw attention to himself by using a gun in the hospital when he feels sure he can achieve his aims with poison and a syringe, which seems to be one of the trademarks of his people's method of eliminating their enemies. It's quick, quiet and efficient. Seems Lambert picked up plenty of sneaky tricks during his time in the C.I.A. We're being supported by a dozen uniforms who will all be firearms trained and strategically placed at major exit points of the hospital and in the car park, just in case something goes wrong and Lambert evades us in the hospital. Derek will meet him as arranged, and in return for the information Lambert needs, he will hopefully keep to his side of the bargain and pay Derek his blood money before entering the building."

"Isn't it assuming a lot to think he's just going to hand over a wad of cash to Derek before checking that Robin is really where Derek says he is, sir?" Tony Curtis asked.

"That's a good question, Tony," Ross replied, "and ordinarily I'd agree with you, but as I said earlier, Lambert is under pressure, and will want to be in and out as quickly as possible. If he had any sense, yes, he'd check it out first, and he may still do that, just to keep Derek dangling. If he does, Derek, just protest for a minute that he's changing the arrangement you made with him, but then kind of grudgingly accept what he says and agree to wait in the car park or wherever Lambert suggests, okay?"

"Okay, sir. Don't worry; I'll be prepared for any eventuality."

"Good man, Derek."

At this point, D.C.I. Agostini reached across and placed a silencing hand on Ross's shoulder. The D.I. immediately gave way to the boss, who obviously had something to say.

"Sorry to butt in, D.I. Ross, but I just want to say something at this point. First of all, thank you for going ahead with this one, D.C. McLennan. I know you'll be well supported but still, you're the front man and thus the most exposed of us all. Your bravery won't go unnoticed, young man."

Derek McLennan actually blushed at the praise from the Chief Inspector.

"As for the rest of you, I know you'll all do your jobs as well as I know you can, but please let me stress that Randolph Lambert is a dangerous man. I learned earlier from Jerome Decker that before being recruited into the C.I.A. he was a member of one of the U.S. Army's crack fighting units, so he has plenty of experience in the art of killing, so I'm saying, be careful out there tonight."

There followed a general round of nods, and voices in agreement with Agostini's instructions.

"Mr. Decker also gave me more information on the prime target, Francis Kelly. Prior to joining Aegis, Kelly worked as a deputy director at USUMRA, the United States Underwater Marine Research Agency. He's a genuinely qualified marine biologist and salvage expert, but get this, before taking his degrees and as a younger man, Kelly was a member of the U.S. Navy Seals."

"I've heard of them, sir. They're a bunch of tough cookies, a bit like the SAS as far as I know," said Drake.

"Correct Sergeant, though a better comparison would be with the Royal Navy's Special Boat Service, the SBS, who are a direct equivalent of the Seals."

"So that probably explains why Kelly went for a man like Lambert to head up his private security force, and also why most of the men Lambert then recruited would also appear to be predominantly former Special Forces people and highly paid mercenaries," Ross concluded.

"Exactly," said Agostini, "so again, I stress that the watchword for tonight is 'extreme care', ladies and gents."

Ross had no desire to over-complicate things, so with everyone knowing what was expected of them in a few hours, he brought the briefing to a close. The team rose as one from their seats and most made their way to the coffee machine for a quick caffeine boost.

Ross and Drake spoke with Agostini and with Derek McLennan for a few minutes, finalising the plans and then McLennan became the first of the team to leave the building. Just in case Lambert had set up any kind of surveillance on him, they wanted McLennan well away from headquarters before any of the team made their own departures. He'd visit a couple of late night clubs looking for all the world like a regular punter, certainly not an on-duty police officer, before making his way to the hospital at the allotted time.

* * *

The early morning hours were usually the most peaceful in and around the Royal Liverpool University Hospital. As the clock ticked past two forty-five a.m. Derek McLennan made his way out of the hospital's main entrance, looking as though he was coming from inside the building. In fact, he'd entered by a rear exit some ten minutes earlier, met up with Ross and Drake and was now standing in the car park, looking up into a clear night sky. Myriad stars twinkled in that clear sky, McLennan was even able to recognise The Plough, one of the few constellations he knew by sight. Not a cloud showed, nothing at all to obscure the brightness of the moon which hung above him like a shimmering orb of light, a shining beacon in Space, watching over the Earth and its denizens as they slept, or, in some cases, worked.

Derek's daydream, or should it be night dream (?) was interrupted by the arrival of a car in the car park. Dazzled at first by its headlights, as soon as the driver killed the lights Derek saw it to be an almost new Ford Focus, exactly the car Lambert had told him to expect.

Derek walked confidently towards the parked car, even though the driver made no attempt to exit the vehicle. He knew Lambert, he must remember to call him Finch, would be sizing him up. Any sly glances behind him or hesitancy in his manner might be enough to blow his cover.

A quiet 'swish' was the only sound that heralded the opening of the driver's side window as Derek drew level with the Focus.

"'Well, well right on time, Mr. Raven. The punctuality of the British Bobby eh?"

Lambert flicked a cigarette out of the open window, its embers breaking up into tiny red flares as it hit the ground.

"Mr. Finch, good to see you," Derek responded.

"I hope our patient is well. I'm looking forward to seeing him very soon," Finch said without preamble.

"Everything's set up," said Derek. "Ten minutes from now, every member of the night staff in the side ward on the tenth floor will be fast asleep. All you have to do is walk in and walk out again. I'm presuming it won't take long?"

"You presume correctly, Raven."

"So, what about my money?" Derek asked quite brazenly.

"Not so fast there," the man in the car said as the door slowly opened and Derek stood back as Finch got out, closed the door and held a brown envelope in his hand. He was dressed in a convincing doctor's coat, had a stethoscope round his neck, and a name badge that read, of course, Finch.

"Here's your money, but it stays with me until the job's done."

"But, that's not how we agreed things," Derek protested, having been warned by Ross that this was likely to happen.

"Let's just call it a slight change of plan. You can wait here until I've eliminated my friend Robin, then when I come down here again you get half the contents of this envelope. Then you'll lead me to wherever they're holding Starling and then, and only then, will you receive the rest of your thirty pieces of silver."

Derek looked crestfallen, as he was supposed to. Ross had warned him to expect just such a move by Lambert. It was likely the man would try to evade paying McLennan a penny, the only danger being he'd try to eliminate the detective at the same time. McLennan was confident that Lambert would not be coming back down from the upper floor of the hospital, so his fears were minimal

"But that's not fair. You'll know I'm on the up and up as soon as you get up there," he gestured up at the hospital building.

"You'd better hope that's true, won't you? You get paid when I say so and not before."

Derek McLennan shrugged his shoulders in a show of resignation.

"I don't seem to have much choice, do I?"

"No, you don't, Mr. Raven. Now, where do I go to find Robin?"

Derek quickly gave the killer the directions to the side ward on the tenth floor where he could find Robin. He stressed that the staff and police guards would remain drugged for at least two hours, giving them plenty of time to move on to their next target, the fake Doctor Starling.

"You'd better be here when I get back," Finch ordered as he turned to walk towards the hospital entrance.

"I've nowhere else to go," Derek replied. "I'm putting my entire career on the line here, Mr. Finch. I'm relying on you as much as you're relying on me."

Lambert simply grunted and walked away. Randolph Lambert exited the lift on the tenth floor. All had gone well so far. No one had challenged him and he felt confident as soon as he saw the 'night nurse' slumped over her desk a few yards from the lift. He stepped confidently passed her, and rounded the corner that led onto the corridor holding Robin's room, so he believed. There, he saw two uniformed police officers, one asleep on a plastic hospital chair, the other spread-eagled on the corridor floor where he'd apparently slid from his chair as 'Raven's' drug had taken effect.

Without wanting to waste time, the killer stepped past the two policemen and quietly opened the door to the room they'd been guarding.

Randolph Lambert repressed a quiet chuckle as he found exactly what 'Raven' had told him to expect. Two more uniformed constables were slumped in their seats, one a female, their heads resting on their chests. The man was actually snoring! Just to be sure all was as it should be Lambert swung a kick at the right leg of the female officer, who made a convincing groaning sound and fell off the chair onto the floor.

In the bed, the patient lay sleeping, apparently, though Lambert couldn't be sure due to the swathe of bandages that covered his head. He was hooked to various machines, all of which he assumed to be recording various life signs or recording his bodily functions.

Lambert reached into the right hand pocket of his white coat and withdrew a pre-loaded hypodermic containing a lethal dose of ketamine as used to dispatch young Aaron Decker. Seeing the patient was hooked up to a saline drip, Lambert simply used the syringe to inject the lethal chemical into the drip, and then stood back to wait for the man in the bed to react. A few convulsions should be all that showed as Robin's system went into terminal shock with death following in seconds.

Instead, what happened next seemed to play out in slow motion in Randolph Lambert's mind as, like a zombie rising from the grave, the figure in the bed, far from going into convulsions, slowly sat up, it's right hand reaching up to the head, from where is slowly began to unwrap the swathe of bandages that covered the face.

As it did so, and as Lambert stood rooted to the spot in almost morbid fascination, the left hand, which had been under the bedcovers until that moment, suddenly appeared, holding a rather lethal looking handgun, which he instantly recognised as a Glock 26, used by many of Britain's police forces.

"Surprise, Randy boy," said the man in the bed as the final bandages fell away to reveal the smiling face of a stranger.

"Yeah, surprise, surprise" said a female voice from behind him and he turned his head enough to find himself facing two more Glocks, held by Izzie Drake and 'snoring' Paul Ferris.

"Very clever," said Lambert, knowing he'd been outmanoeuvred and well and truly conned. "I suppose this means Mr. Raven isn't as bent as he led me to believe," he added as Andy Ross stepped from the bed, demonstrating as he did so that the catheter that led from the drip wasn't actually fitted to his wrist but was merely taped in place. The lethal dose of ketamine was simply flowing into a plastic bag that was attached to the end of the feed line under the blankets, sufficient evidence to convict him of attempted murder.

"Oh no," Ross said. "Your Mr. Raven is one of mine, and straight as a die, Mr. Lambert, or should I say Finch?"

"My, my, you do know a lot, don't you, copper?"

"It's Detective Inspector Ross to you, Lambert, and yes, we know a lot more than you might imagine, seeing as Graham Young didn't take too kindly to you trying to kill him and has been talking to us as though his life depended on it."

Lambert's face fell as he realised the extent of the con that the police had pulled on him and inwardly cursed his own stupidity at not being more meticulous in checking out the credentials of the so-called 'bent' police officer who'd led him into this carefully laid police trap.

Before he knew it, Lambert's hands were roughly pulled behind his back by Paul Ferris, as Izzie Drake opened the door to summon the remaining 'sleeping' policemen into the room. As Dodds and Curtis made their entrance, Izzie Drake suddenly swung her leg and kicked Lambert firmly across his right shin.

"Ow, you bitch. Did you see that? She kicked me. That's assault, police fucking brutality," he complained to the others.

"Did she? I never saw a thing, did any of you see the sergeant assault this man?" said Ross, as he nodded at Izzie as she took her revenge for the kick Lambert had landed on her leg on entering the room.

Dodds and Curtis both shook their heads, and Lambert growled, "Bastards, fucking police bastards."

"Now, now, that's not very nice, is it, Mr. Lambert, especially as we've got a nice heated cell and maybe even a cup of weak tea waiting for you after you've been processed into our custody suite? I think it will be a long, long time before you see the light of day again, unless it's through a barred window," Ross added. "Though we might think of something that might mitigate the length of time you spend behind bars, Lambert."

"What are you talking about?"

"Later," said Ross. "Take the bastard away lads."

Dodds, Curtis and Ferris jointly hustled Lambert from the room, where they were joined by Sam

Gable, still dressed in her nurse's uniform, in the outer corridor.

"You too, eh?" Lambert said quietly as he realised the 'nurse' was yet another police officer.

"Yeah, me too. Life's a bitch, isn't it, Finch?" Sam said, grinning at the handcuffed killer. The small team of detectives were feeling pleased with themselves as they led Lambert away, leaving Izzie Drake to help Andy Ross to divest himself of the rest of his 'patient' disguise. Soon after, they followed the others after Ross first made a call to the hospital administrator, informing him the operation had gone smoothly and thanking him and his staff for their cooperation.

As Ross and Drake arrived in the car park, they caught up with the others just as Lambert was being forcibly loaded into the back seat of a police patrol car. Any hopes he'd harboured of attempting to break away from his police escort had disappeared when he arrived with them at the hospital exit to find a ring of armed uniformed officers waiting to ensure he was safely taken into custody.

As the car carrying their prisoner drove away at speed, escorted by two more cars and two police motorcyclists as outriders, Ross gathered his team around him.

"Well done everyone. I can't believe how smoothly that went. Anybody seen Derek? He should have been out here waiting for us."

They all looked around, each of them realising that they hadn't seen Derek since exiting the hos-

pital. A feeling of dread gripped them all as they realised Lambert could have done something to Derek
McLennan before entering the hospital. Ross called
the sergeant in charge of the extra uniformed officers
across but he confirmed that neither he nor any of
his men had seen Ross's undercover detective since
they'd taken up their positions.

"Sir, you don't think Lambert's done something to
Derek do you?" a worried Sam Gable asked, her face
betraying her feelings as she tried to envisage what
could have happened.

"I don't know, Sam," Ross replied as a sliver of trepidation ran down his spine. Had they congratulated
each other too soon?

"Search the car park," he ordered. "Look behind
and under every vehicle, every bush and tree in the
grounds. If Lambert did do something to McLennan,
he didn't have time to go far to dispose of him, so he
must be close by."

As the uniformed officers and the rest of the murder team, one dressed as a nurse, the others as uniformed officers themselves began to spread out to
search the car park with Ross resembling an escapee
from Doctor Frankenstein's laboratory in his hospital garb, with tubes and other paraphernalia dangling
from his arms and green hospital gown, Ross was
brought up in his tracks by a voice that came from
somewhere behind him.

"What's up, sir, someone lost something?"

Derek McLennan was striding towards him from
the direction of the hospital entrance.

"Derek, where the bloody hell have you been? We thought Lambert had topped you or something?" Ross virtually bellowed at him.

McLennan immediately adopted a sheepish grin as he admitted.

"Oh God, sorry sir, I was bloody desperate for the toilet."

Ross could only gape at him in disbelief, but Izzie Drake walked right up to the Detective Constable and without a second's hesitation, slapped him across the back of the head.

"You bloody dickhead," she bawled in his face. "Here we are thinking you're lying dead or injured somewhere and you're off having a bloody crap."

"Sorry Sarge, but I just had to go."

"Some bloody James Bond you are," Drake said with disdain as Derek stood looking crestfallen, until Izzie stepped closer and put her arms around him.

"Never mind, Derek," she said. "You're still the hero of the hour. We got the bastard, all according to plan."

"That's great," said McLennan. "Congratulations sir," he said, directing his words at Ross.

"Yes, well, it's congratulations to all of us," Ross replied. "Let's head back to headquarters. I want to see Lambert booked and behind bars before we go home. I want to interview him as early as possible in the morning, so it'll be a short night's sleep for us tonight, Izzie."

"No problem, sir," Drake answered.

"You go home, Derek, You've earned a good night's sleep, and Derek?"

"Sir?"

"Next time, put a bloody plug in it okay?"

"Okay sir," McLennan replied. "Sorry to cause all that trouble."

"Forget it, Derek. Really, it's forgotten. We were worried, that's all."

Within minutes the car park of the Royal Liverpool University Hospital stood deserted, the police presence gone as quickly as it had appeared, the moon and stars in silent vigil as always. Ross was looking forward to the morning, when hopefully, following his questioning of Randolph Lambert the final pieces of this convoluted and complicated case might just fall into place.

Chapter 40

The Morning after the Night Before

Andy Ross, Izzie Drake and the rest of the team were back in the office at seven thirty a.m. Most of them had managed no more than an hour or two of sleep after being sent home at three-thirty or thereabouts. Some, like Tony Curtis and Nick Dodds had simply returned to their homes, showered, changed and slumped in a chair for an hour or so, almost afraid to climb into bed in case sleep claimed them and refused to release them in time to return to headquarters. Both men placed their alarm clocks close to them as they slept fitfully in their uncomfortable positions. Sam Gable went home as ordered, showered, fell into bed totally naked, and woke an hour later, feeling cold as she'd been so tired she'd failed to pull the duvet over herself. Another hot shower revitalised her and she was soon dressed and ready to go back to work. Paul Ferris, as Ross and Drake had done the previous evening, enjoyed the pleasure of spending almost two hours in bed with Kareen, who woke instantly when she sensed his weight on the bed. If Kareen hadn't set their alarm clock for six thirty, post coital slumber would definitely have made Ferris late, but thankfully he just made it into the squad room before Ross's arrival.

Detective Chief Inspector Oscar Agostini was there, smiling with satisfaction at the results of the operation to apprehend Randolph Lambert. He also had an announcement to make, one he quickly shared in private with Ross before speaking directly to the team.

Ross raised a hand, and the team fell silent as they waited for the early morning briefing to begin. Ross couldn't help but notice a few yawns and stretches taking place but he knew it was simply fatigue and not boredom that was taking its toll on his people.

"Good morning everyone," Agostini addressed the small gathering.

Muttered but polite replies came from a few of the detectives.

"First of all, my congratulations to all of you on a successful completion of Operation Cuckoo last night," referring to the name he'd given the plan to apprehend Lambert at the last minute, "or should I say earlier this morning? Anyway, D.I. Ross has kindly allowed me to talk to you all this morning as I have some information to share with you with re- lation to the case."

That seemed to bring everyone to attention and their eyes and ears appeared to perk up as they waited to hear what the D.C.I had to say.

"As soon as Randolph Lambert was brought into custody, I informed Detective Chief Superintendant Hollingsworth. She in turn made contact with those agencies who share an interest in Lambert's activities. As a result of those calls, certain...erm...arrangements have been made that we will implement if D.I. Ross and Sergeant Drake are able to extract the information we want from Lambert."

Agostini certainly had the team's full attention now, though Ross's face was giving nothing away despite most of his team looking questioningly at him.

"I'm not going to go into all the details of what's been decided upon. That, as I'm sure you'll understand, doesn't really concern us, being a decision made at command level."

With those words, a few more whispers and mutterings could be heard as some of the team suspected they might not like what was coming. Agostini continued.

"As you all know, this case has morphed into something much bigger than we at first thought, and carries certain international ramifications that have had to be considered. The chief super has been in contact through the night with all those concerned and this is what has been decided.

If we can get a confession from Lambert that provides us with details of times and dates of crimes of violence, including murder, that directly implicates Francis Kelly, the U.S. authorities will immediately issue a warrant for Kelly's arrest. The F.B.I's serious crimes unit have already unearthed information relating to illegal financial activities perpetrated by Kelly, but the fear is that a team of clever and very expensive lawyers could find a way to secure bail for him if he was arrested on those charges, with the chance that might find a way to flee the country. A charge, or charges of multiple murder however could persuade a judge to deny bail and allow time for further inquiries to be made that will in all likelihood result in further charges being laid against him. Erich Ackermann in Germany is also incriminating Kelly in various illegal activities relating to Aegis Oceanographic's European operations, with the theft of antiquities and the pillaging of historical sites being at the top of the list. Kelly's biggest mistake in all this would seem to be allying himself with people who are not what we'd call career criminals. Most of them, like Ackermann for example are simply those who sought to exploit their knowledge and power to enrich their bank accounts. In other words, a bunch of greedy bastards."

That remark brought a round of laughter from the detectives, immediately followed by a question that came from Izzie Drake.

"Sir, I get the feeling this is leading up to something we might not like. Are you telling us that Lambert is going to be let off because he's being offered a deal of some sort by the Americans?"

Agostini smiled a knowing smile before replying to Drake's question.

"Very astute of you Sergeant Drake," he said, "and you're correct to an extent, though rest assured, Lambert is not getting away with anything."

"Then what, sir, if you don't mind me pressing you for an answer?"

"I don't mind at all, Sergeant. You and D.I. Ross will interview Lambert when we leave this room. Thanks to the efforts of Aaron Decker's father, the C.I.A. has been active in the last week and through their efforts, a number of countries including Greece, Turkey, Italy, Azerbaijan, Turkmenistan, and of all places, Japan, have all issued arrest warrants for Randolph Lambert and every member of his security force. You and D.I. Ross will at some point in the interview inform Lambert of the precarious nature of his situation. Although some of those nations probably have fairly modern and humane correctional institutions, I doubt Lambert will relish the possibility that he may end up incarcerated in a jail cell in Azerbaijan, for example , much less Turkmenistan or even Japan where he'd have a severe language problem for sure. If, on the other hand he is willing to tell us what we need to know, he will be tried in this country, and following sentencing, the United Sates will make an application for his extradition, which will of course be agreed to by the Home Office. Once on U.S. territory, Lambert will be charged with numerous offences but again, in return for his cooperation in the case against Francis Kelly he will be spared the death sentence for murder, and will receive a reduced sentence. At some point down the line, in consideration of his previous work for his country as a C.I.A. operative, he will be moved to a lower category prison from where he will eventually be released with a new identity, under close supervision by both the C.I.A. and the F.B.I."

It was Paul Ferris who was the first to fully comprehend the hidden agenda behind Agostini's words.

"What you're telling us, sir, is that the C.I.A. are going to put him back to work for them, isn't it?"

"I told you they'd soon catch on, sir," Ross smiled at his boss.

Agostini nodded, sagely, as he turned to face Paul Ferris.

"You, Detective Constable Ferris, are a very intelligent and perceptive officer, too good to remain a constable for much longer. Yes, you're quite correct in your assumption, but, let me reassure you all that if Lambert agrees to this deal, any operations he carries out in future for the C.I.A. will be extremely high risk 'black ops' with a very strong likelihood that he may not return in one piece, not that he'll be told that of course."

This time, the murmurs that sprang up around the room were of a more approving nature.

"So, any questions, ladies and gentlemen, or shall we allow D.I Ross and Sergeant Drake to go and talk to Mr. Lambert?"

"Just one question, sir, if I may?" asked Tony Curtis.

"Yes, D.C. Curtis, what is it?

"I was just wondering when D.C. McLennan will be receiving his licence to kill, sir."

The explosion of laughter that instantly filled the room in response to Curtis's remark instantly relieved any lingering tension that Agostinis's announcement might have caused.

Even Oscar Agostini couldn't help himself and joined in the amusement. As he stopped laughing, he managed to keep a straight face as he replied to Curtis's facetious remark.

"Good point, constable. I think we'll leave that one to 'M's' discretion."

The D.C.I was pleased to receive another round of laughter in return.

"Right, everyone, that's enough," Ross said, taking charge of the situation, "sorry, sir, but we'd best get on."

"Yes, of course, D.I. Ross," Agostini grinned at the fact that Ross had taken control after his slight lapse into levity. "Everyone better get back to work, plenty of reports to be written up after yesterday, I believe."

Oscar Agostini shook hands with Andy Ross before departing the room with another remark of thanks for a job well done.

"Okay then, Izzie, let's go talk to our prisoner," Ross said firmly as the pair made their way to interview room one."

* * *

Randolph Lambert looked calm and assured, seated at the metal table that stood in the middle of the interview room, a uniformed officer on guard at the door, as Ross and Drake made their entrance and seated themselves opposite him.

The two detectives had interviewed hundreds of prisoners in their time together and would follow their usual procedure this morning. Ross would lead and Drake would intervene as and when she felt it advantageous to do so. It wasn't a 'good cop, bad cop' routine but it had always worked well for them, with Drake's seemingly random interventions often proving a decisive tactic.

"Mr. Lambert, good morning," Ross said politely, as he took his seat. "I'm D.I. Ross and this is Sergeant Drake."

"Yeah, we met last night. You were dressed as The Mummy," Lambert replied.

"Indeed we did. I hope you're not going to be difficult this morning. We've already got enough on you to put you away for a long, long time."

"So, what's the point of all this, then?" Lambert replied, feeling confident that he, not the police was in control of the situation. All that changed when Drake opened the folder she'd carried into the room with her, looked at the first page she came to and suddenly said.

"Randolph Lambert, U.S. citizen, also known as Finch, leader of Francis Kelly's private security force and wanted for various crimes including murder in Greece, Turkey, Italy, Azerbaijan, Turkmenistan, and

Japan. Also caught red-handed attempting to murder a police inspector, namely D.I. Ross here, at approximately three oh-five this morning."

Lambert's face lost its composure for a few seconds before he replied.

"So, do you think I'm worried about it? I can bring in some real high powered lawyers to get me out of this."

"That's where you're wrong, Lambert," Ross said. "If you're thinking you can call on Kelly's lawyers, we should let you know that Francis Kelly is already in custody in the States," he lied, knowing the F.B.I. were waiting on the results of his interview with Lambert. "The F.B.I have been watching him for some time and I don't think he'll be wanting to even acknowledge your existence if it means he can cut a deal to save his own skin."

Lambert hesitated.

"Look," he said, "I don't understand where you're going with this. Fair enough, you got me on the attempted murder, but that's all. You can't prove anything else against me. I'm an American citizen and I want to speak to someone from my embassy."

"Funny you should say that," Ross smiled at him. "Someone from your embassy is very keen to speak to you, too. You might have heard of him. He's the deputy station chief for the C.I.A. in London at present, a certain Jerome Decker."

"Decker?"

"Yes, the man whose son you had killed, Lambert, the man you used to work for and the man who is

511

going to 'nail your ass to the wall,' to use his own words. It seems the United States is willing to waive it's right to apply for your extradition if any of the aforementioned countries apply to have you passed into their jurisdiction for trial and either imprisonment or execution. They do have the death penalty in Azerbaijan, don't they, Sergeant Drake?"

"Oh, yes they do, sir, and in Turkmenistan, I understand. They use the old fashioned way of hanging there I believe; slow strangulation hanging from a long rope, no nice neat scaffold like we used to have here. I looked it up this morning. It can take up to half an hour for a prisoner to die that way, dancing and dangling at the end of the rope, pissing themselves and losing bowel control whilst choking their guts out as they die horribly and slowly."

Lambert visibly paled.

"Hmm, Turkmenistan sounds favourite to me then. What about Azerbaijan?"

"Looked that up too, sir. Could be firing squad, could be hanging, it's up to the judge. Oh, yes, they like to do it in public too over there. Makes for good entertainment for the masses, helps to deter crime too."

Ross and Drake had hardly glanced at Lambert as they'd exchanged those few words, but Ross now looked him in the eye and could see the first hint of uncertainty in the man's demeanour.

"You guys wouldn't deport me to one of those places," he said.

"Why not?" Ross asked. "After all, you were quick to point out you're a U.S. citizen and Jerome Decker says they don't care what we do with you, so why don't we save the British taxpayer a fortune in keeping you locked up and fed in a nice soft British jail when we can accept the request of one of the other nations who want you and let them mete out some swift justice? Give me a good reason, Lambert, just one good reason why I should do anything that will save your miserable, murdering hide."

Ross knew they were winning. He and Drake had planted a seed in Lambert's mind and what came next would, as far as Lambert was concerned, be all his own idea. He glanced sideways at Izzie Drake, who gave him a sly smile in return. She knew, too.

"I can tell you stuff," Lambert suddenly blurted out. "Stuff that will help the Feds take Kelly down for far more than they probably know about. I can tell you enough to tear his organisation to pieces."

"Really? That's interesting, Mr. Lambert," Ross replied. "And what would you expect in return for this information?"

"A guarantee that I wouldn't be extradited to any of those places you mentioned. And immunity from prosecution over here and in the States."

Ross laughed out loud and Izzie joined in at Lambert's outrageous demand.

"You've got balls, Lambert, I'll give you that," said Ross. "You haven't a snowflake in hell's chance of getting off scot-free. We do, however, have an alternative proposal for you. I'd seriously suggest you give it some thought before replying."

"I'm listening," Lambert said, sitting back in the hard plastic chair and trying, unsuccessfully, to appear calm and unruffled.

Andy Ross spent the next few minutes outlining the C.I.A's proposal, stressing to Lambert that it had been ratified by the Home Office, and was thus officially sanctioned by the British government.

"If it was up to me, Lambert, I'd let you go to trial and be sentenced to life without parole," Ross snarled at the killer. "Sadly, I'm just a pawn of those in higher authority so I've been forced to make you an offer that I consider generous in the extreme."

Lambert looked pensive as he considered Ross's offer. Deep down, he knew it was the best, in fact the only offer he was likely to receive, and one that would enable him at some time, to taste freedom again, albeit under the control of his former paymasters at the C.I.A.

Finally, knowing he was out of options, Lambert nodded, almost imperceptibly, and Izzie Drake reached again into the folder she'd brought into the room with her and removed a two page document that she simply pushed across the desk towards Lambert, together with a ballpoint pen. Lambert cast no more then a cursory glance at the pages and then picked up the pen and signed in the appropriate place, pushing both document and pen back to her.

Inwardly, Ross sighed in satisfaction. It maybe wasn't the perfect result as far as he was concerned, but it would suffice and would certainly take a whole lot of criminals out of circulation once the various international law enforcement agencies made their moves. Most importantly, Lambert's testimony would now help to convict Francis Kelly of multiple murder, conspiracy to commit murder and more.

"We'll send someone to take your statement," Ross said as he and Izzie rose from their seats, leaving Lambert sitting under the watchful eye of P.C. Henderson.

Ross and Drake wasted no time in delivering Lambert's signed agreement to D.C.I Agostini.

"Well done Andy," said Agostini, who immediately phoned D.C.S Hollingsworth with the news. A minute later, after hanging up the phone, he turned to Ross and confirmed that Hollingsworth had already set in motion the international effort to bring down the whole of Francis Kelly's organisation. The board of directors at the Aegis Institute had given the American authorities *carte blanche* to enter any of their facilities in cooperation with the relevant local law enforcement agencies.

"What's happening with Lambert now?" Agostini asked.

"Paul Ferris and Sam Gable are with him. Ferris is the perfect man to take Lambert's statement, with his background in computers and knowledge of the business world, he'll make better sense of what Lambert's telling us, and Sam Gable will keep him on edge, make sure he doesn't try to keep us in the dark about any aspect of the case. She's good at that."

"Excellent," Agostini said. "As soon as Ferris gives us that statement, I want it copied and we can then send a copy to each of the police forces involved around the world."

"Sounds weird, that, sir."

"What? Around the world?"

"Yes. Who'd have thought it?"

"I agree, Andy, but it just goes to prove that the criminal fraternity has tendrils everywhere nowadays. It seems no section of the community is exempt from being infected by the desire to circumvent the law."

* * *

Lambert's statement took two hours to relate, after which, Paul Ferris and Sam Gable saw him being safely locked in a cell before heading back to the squad room. From there, as Agostini had requested, copies of that statement were sent to all the relevant forces involved in the investigation. Agostini and D.C.S. Hollingsworth both received a copy and at a meeting with Sarah Hollingsworth later that day, Oscar Agostini expressed his amazement at just how much information Randolph Lambert had given them.

"It looks as if Lambert always thought he might have to turn on his boss," he said to the Chief Superintendant. "He must have used his position of trust within Kelly's inner circle to gather and retain enough information to give himself a little insurance if ever he needed it."

"Well, he certainly needed it today," Hollingsworth agreed. "I spoke with the F.B.I. soon after you sent me a copy of the statement and they were ready to move against Kelly. I was assured they'd be taking action to arrest him within an hour of my call. I'm expecting to hear that he's in custody very soon. Ross was clever, telling Lambert that Kelly was already in custody. That gave him a sizable push to get his story in first, in case Kelly tried to put too much blame on his shoulders."

As Agostini nodded, Hollingsworth's phone rang and she looked at the instrument as though she could read its message just by doing so.

"This could be the call I've been expecting," she said as she lifted the receiver to her ear. After listening for a few seconds, she mouthed

"F.B.I." at Agostini, and then exchanged pleasantries, listened, and then Agostini sensed something wasn't right.

"He what?" Hollingsworth shouted into the phone. "But how? I thought your people had him under constant surveillance?"

Agostini felt a sinking feeling in his stomach, knowing very well what Hollingsworth was hearing on the phone. The Chief Superintendant continued talking for a minute or two before hanging up angrily.

"Kelly gave them the slip," she almost shouted at Oscar Agostini. "The bastard must have been tipped off."

"A leak?"

"Either in the F.B.I, or maybe someone on the Aegis board of directors perhaps. That was Special Agent-in-Charge Hal Morrow. He's bloody mad as hell, couldn't apologise enough. Seems Kelly left the building no more than twenty minutes before his agents arrived. Somehow, he made it to La Guardia airport where he boarded a private plane and was last seen heading in the direction of the Canadian border."

"Fucking hell, Ma'am, after all our work."

"I know, but Morrow says he hasn't given up yet. Kelly forgot in his panic to escape that his plane has a transponder and U.S. air traffic controllers are monitoring his flight. As long as he stays on his current heading, Morrow thinks he's heading for Alaska, where Aegis owns a massive deep water port facility and where their submarines are based when not at sea."

"Shall I tell Ross and his team?"

"Yes, do that, but make sure he knows the F.B.I. people are still tracking him."

Ross and Drake virtually mirrored Hollingsworth's and Agostini's reaction to the news, but refused to be downhearted. Andy Ross was certain that Kelly wouldn't get away, and his belief was vindicated soon afterwards when word came down from D.C.S. Hollingsworth that Kelly's short-lived bid for freedom had ended in his capture and arrest.

Agostini and Ross were soon seated in Hollingsworth's office, eagerly waiting for her to tell them more. She looked far more relaxed than she'd been during Agostini's earlier visit as she invited both men to help themselves to coffee from her rather plush and expensive percolator, both men availing themselves of this unheard of generosity.

"Well, gentlemen, it appears our Mr. Kelly was fast, but not fast, or clever enough. This is what I've just been told, much of which fits with what we talked about earlier, Oscar. The Americans were able to track his aircraft and with the cooperation of the Canadian Air Traffic Controllers, were soon able to plot his potential point of landing. His overflying of Canada was clever but it was soon evident he was heading for Alaska. As I explained, Aegis has its own private deep-water port facility there, not far from the settlement of Port Lions on Kodiac Island. They really can be predictably original in naming places, our American friends. The place was named after The Lions Club who helped pay for the building of the settlement apparently."

"Never heard of it, Ma'am," Ross observed.

"Neither had I until a few minutes ago," the D.C.S. replied. "But it appears Kodiac is a large island off the coast of Alaska, mostly visited by tourists who go there to see Brown Bears. The island is a bit bigger than Cyprus," she said as she turned her computer screen towards them, displaying a map of Kodiac she'd just found on the internet. "So anyway, Hal Morrow of the F.B.I's special task force told me that since obtaining permission from the CEO of Aegis, they'd already sent a team of agents to the inspirationally named, *Aegis Seaport* facility, as they have to every facility run by one of Kelly's salvage experts. It's been quite simple for them to target the Aegis installations run by Kelly's people; just look for the salvage people he'd infiltrated into the organisation. Oh, before I forget, they soon found the leak. One of Aegis's board of directors was conspicuous by his absence at a meeting last night and he was also picked up by the F.B.I. at Miami airport trying to board a connecting flight to the Bahamas with a case full of money, after being traced to a flight to Florida. He was sitting in the departure lounge, bold as brass, thinking he was on his way to a life of luxury in the sun, paid for by Kelly's dirty money. He'd tipped Kelly off about the F.B.I, being ready to move against him and then done a runner, the idiot. If he'd stayed put he may have been able to remain under our radar and got away in a few months, assuming Kelly didn't drop him in it once we got him. So, where was I? Oh, yes, Kelly was really stupid running as he did, with no thought about his flight being tracked. The pilot was an innocent in all this, just a regular company employee, used to flying executives anywhere they needed to go, often at short notice, so he wouldn't have thought to try and cover up their destination.

So, Kelly's plane landed at Aegis's small private airfield on Kodiac Island, from where he was picked up in car driven, unknown to him of course, by an F.B.I. agent who drove him straight to the base. From there, he walked to the Aegis base control centre, made sure the submarine that had been renamed *Aegis Explorer* was ready for sea, and gave orders that the base be placed on alert for a potential terrorist attack, with further orders to shoot to kill if any unauthorised people attempted to assault the base, crafty bastard. Of course, all the 'security' personnel at the base had already been detained and replaced by F.B.I agents. Kelly knew none of the local security operatives personally so the 'Feds' as the Americans call them weren't worried about him not recognising the security staff. He did know the head of security however who played his part in the deception with an F.B.I. gun at his back as he spoke to Kelly."

As she paused for breath, Agostini took the opportunity to speak.

"Sounds to me as though the F.B.I. ran a bloody good operation, all things considered, Ma'am."

"Yes," Ross agreed, "especially as they had to move fast once they knew he'd slipped through their fingers in New York."

"Very true, gents," Hollingsworth agreed, "though they were already on site of course, which none of Kelly's people, even the crooked director knew about. Anyway, here's the best bit, according to Morrow. Kelly walked through the Aegis facility as if he owned the place, and took the elevator that led to the lower levels where the submarine pens had been built. They could accommodate any two of their four modified subs there at any given time. In fact, the original modifications to the former military submarines had been carried out in Alaska, far from prying eyes, we now know.

Kelly was as confident as he could possibly be that he'd evaded capture according to the agents who observed his behaviour and body language as he marched along the underground dockside to the *Aegis Explorer*. He saw the gangplank waiting for him, leading straight to the door at the base of the 'sail' which I still think of as the conning tower, sounds better to me. Who thinks of a submarine having a bloody sail after all? So, he walked on board the submarine into the control room where he was met by the skipper of the sub, one of his trusted inner circle of cohorts, who was also being 'worked' by an F.B.I agent close behind him.

"Ready for sea?" Kelly asked.

"Aye, sir," the captain, a man named Ryan replied. "Do you have a destination for me yet?"

"Here you are," Kelly replied, handing Ryan a piece of paper. Ryan scrutinised it and then gave the agents spread around the control room a prearranged signal and they instantly encircled Kelly, identified themselves as Federal agents and took him into custody. His face was an absolute picture, according to Morrow, who described it as 'a perfect take-down.'

"You bastard, Ryan," was all Kelly could say as the captain of the sub handed the piece of paper to the senior agent in the control tower. It appears

Kelly was running to The Seychelles, where he probably has a nice little hideaway prepared, a bolt-hole ready for a time when he might have to disappear. They'll soon have it located now they have the sailing co-ordinates. It's possibly where all Kelly's private records are secreted away, as Ryan confirmed, after Kelly had been led away, that he'd taken his boss there on a couple of occasions in the past, always to different locations. There are over a hundred islands that go to make up The Seychelles, so it was important for them to get Kelly's own directions to his captain, to make sure the knew exactly where in the world he was headed."

"Brilliant," Agostini enthused. "You have to hand it to them. The F.B.I. has gone up a ton in my estimation."

"Mine too," said Ross. "Nothing like in the movies eh?" he smiled.

"They are a very efficient and dedicated force for law enforcement, gentlemen. I'm glad we had them with us on this one or Kelly might never have been brought to justice."

Detective Chief Superintendent Sarah Hollingsworth then took Andy Ross by surprise. Rising from her chair, she walked around her desk until she stood in front of the seated D.I. who promptly stood up to face her. Hollingsworth reached out her right hand and Ross automatically did the same as she proceeded to shake his hand vigorously.

"Well done, Detective Inspector," she said effusively. "You and your team have done a wonderful job on this case. How on earth you pulled all the threads together I have no idea, but I do know that D.C.I. Agostini has been singing your praises in my ear for days now."

"Really, Ma'am, I mean, thank you, Ma'am, you too, sir," Ross gabbled as he turned to Agostini who simply grinned at him.

"I know the two of you came up through the ranks together," Hollingsworth went on, "so I suggest the pair of you get together outside work hours of course, and enjoy a celebratory drink together. It might be nice to include the rest of your team, of course, D.I. Ross."

With that, Sarah Hollingsworth reached behind her to where her black leather bag stood on her desk. Reaching into it, she removed her purse and extracted a roll of ten pound notes, a hundred pounds in total, which she pressed into Ross's hand.

"A small token of appreciation for a job well done," she said. "I haven't lost my memories of the feelings that come from solving a big case you know. I stood where you are once, D.I. Ross. I wasn't always a Chief Super. Now go, you too, Mr. Agostini, and give my thanks to all your team on a job well done."

"Thanks a lot, Ma'am," said Agostini as he led an almost speechless Andy Ross from the room.

* * *

The lounge bar of the Fullers Arms reverberated to the sounds of raucous laughter and old but good jokes as Ross's team enjoyed a couple of hours of celebration after he'd returned to the squad room with the news of Kelly's eventual arrest. As is the case with close knit teams in many occupations, they had worked hard and now they felt they could play hard. The beers were flowing, at least in most cases, though Izzie Drake and Sam Gable were enjoying themselves with the fruits of Bacchus, red for Izzie, white for Sam.

"No one beats us, that's for sure," Tony Curtis slurred as his fourth pint began to take effect on his equilibrium.

"We're the best," Nick Dodds agreed.

"You two are drunk," Izzie Drake said to the two constables, accusingly.

"Not quite, Sarge, but we will be in a minute or two," Dodds said and another round of laughter filled the room.

"Hey, Derek," Curtis called out to Derek McLennan, who was threading his way back to the table from the direction of the gents.

"What's up, Tony?" McLennan called to him.

"Where you been, lad?"

"You know where I've been," Derek hiccupped.

"Oh yes, I forgot. Derek McLennan, Undercover Toilet Agent."

Derek blushed as everyone around the table, even Ross and Agostini joined in the laughter. Sam Gable sidled up to him and put a protective arm around his shoulder.

"You lot leave our Derek alone. He's my hero, he is, licensed to thrill is our Derek."

"Yeah, as long as there's a gents in the vicinity, just in case," Tony Curtis quipped, cueing more laughter.

Oscar Agostini stood up, banged his empty beer glass on the table and called for attention.

"Listen to me," he ordered. "You've all done a great job, but don't be late for work in the morning. You've still got lots and lots of reports to make out before we can officially close this case, so don't get too drunk, will you?"

As he was grinning like a Cheshire cat as he said it, his statement was greeted by boos and catcalls from the team.

As the general hubbub and air of celebration continued around them, Drake pulled Ross to one side.

"What's up, Izzie?" Ross asked.

"Just wondered if you'd phoned D.I. Jones in Falmouth, sir. He'd be pleased to know we got them all in the end."

"I phoned him before we left headquarters, Izzie, while you and Sam were adjusting your make up in the ladies loo."

"How was he? And Carole of course?"

"They're fine, Izzie. Brian was over the moon with the news. Sergeant St. Clair was out on a job when I called, but she'll be made up with the news too, no doubt. Now that we're on the cusp of cleaning out this nest of vipers, I asked D.I. Jones if he'd like to lead the team that hits the local Aegis facility down there. He'll have already spoken to his boss by now and they won't be wasting any time in moving in on the place. He can't wait to snap the cuffs on that Evans character who runs the Aegis operation, and his cronies."

"Surely not all the Aegis employees at the site are crooked, sir."

"No, they're not, but the first thing the local force down there will do is go in fast and hard, lock the place down and arrest Evans. Then they'll interview every employee and it shouldn't be difficult to weed out the good from the bad. Here's the best bit. I also phoned the Ministry of Defence, and it seems *H.M.S. Wyvern* is still on station as they call it, in the Channel and they're sending her to effect the arrest and impounding of Aegis's research and salvage vessel. Captain Howell will liaise with the Devon and Cornwall Constabulary to coordinate everything. Brian Jones is hoping they can hit the facility from land and sea at the same time in a joint assault, as he put it."

"Sounds as if he's looking forward to it, sir."

"He definitely is, Izzie. He reckons he owes Evans and his crew a bloody nose, figuratively speaking of course."

"Having met D.I. Jones and Sergeant St. Clair, I wouldn't be at all surprised if the bloody noses are more real than figurative when he and his people force their way into that place," Izzie smiled as she spoke.

"You know, Izzie, you could be right," Ross grinned back at her. "Now, let's go grab one last drink and then we'd better head for home. Marie will want to hear all about tonight from me and I'm sure Peter will want the same from you."

"Oh, I think that can wait, sir. Peter will have something else on his mind when I get home, I'm sure."

Ross groaned in mock indignation.

"Oh no, I really don't need to know that. I keep forgetting you newly wed types are all at it like rabbits for the first year or two."

"I'm hoping it will last a darn sight longer than that," Izzie laughed as she pushed off through the crowded bar, shouting "Same again sir?" as she went, a big grin on her face.

Ross laughed and nodded, unable to make himself heard above the general din in the Fullers Arms. His team were enjoying themselves, letting their hair down, and deserved to. Ross saw Izzie heading back in his direction, threading her way through the crush of bodies and thought, *Maybe Marie could be persuaded to wait for the full story until later...*

Chapter 41

Exeter Cathedral, Six Weeks Later

"A wonderful, moving service, I thought," said Captain Richard Prendergast, Royal Navy, (Retired), the Navy's archivist as he and the others gathered on the steps of Exeter Cathedral after the memorial service, jointly organised by the Royal Navy and the German Navy. A large congregation, including descendants of the crew members of *H.M.S. Norwich* and *U3000*, later known as *U966*, had attended the service of remembrance that took place on a warmer than usual late Autumn day.

"It was indeed," Oscar Agostini agreed, having travelled down from Liverpool with Ross and his team specifically to meet the rest of the people who'd been involved in one of the most difficult and complex cases he could personally remember during his long and varied career.

A number of the latter-day relatives, both British and German had sought out the group they knew to be responsible for finding their ancestors' last resting place, and there'd been much hand shaking, back slapping and a few tears as well as emotions ran high that day.

"I'd like to say a big thank you to Captain Howell and his crew and you too, George," Ross nodded in the direction of Coast Guard George Baldacre. You were all superb and worked so hard to assist us." The rest of Ross's team were there, all meeting the Royal Naval personnel, the Coast Guard, D.I. Brian Jones and Sergeant Carole St. Clair for the first time.

"Shall we walk a little, gentlemen, ladies?" Charles Howell asked, indicating the path that led through the grounds of the great cathedral, famous for possessing the longest unbroken Gothic ceiling in the world and so the little group did just that, breaking away from the immediate vicinity of the towering church structure to a slightly more peaceful, private part of the grounds.

A minute later, Howell stopped, and almost as one, the group seated themselves on the grass beside the path. Howell had signalled to one of his crew members as they'd walked away from the cathedral steps and the rating had proceeded to thoughtfully place a thick tartan design throw on the grass for Izzie, Sam and Carole to sit on and avoid getting grass stains on the outfits they'd worn for the occasion.

"I thought it might be nice, as it's probably the last time we'll all be together, if we could sit here and let Detective Inspector Ross enthral us with the final details of the case as I'm sure some of us haven't as yet heard the full story."

"Good idea, Charles," Prendergast agreed, "if you don't mind of course, Andy?"

"Not at all," Ross replied and in the space of the next fifteen minutes he tried to give the others as much detail as he could of those final days and more importantly, the final hours of the operation to bring Francis Kelly and his cohorts to justice.

"I have to say, we wouldn't have achieved anything at all in the end if it hadn't been for the help and perceptions of our special guest here today." Ross indicated the diminutive figure of Klaus Haller, who'd been invited along as a gesture of thanks. He had, after all, been instrumental in identifying much of the Hydra-like formation at the head of the Aegis operation to murder, steal and defraud on an international scale hitherto unknown to Ross and his team.

Haller rose to his feet and bowed, saying only, "I thank you, Inspector Ross, for allowing me to help you and your excellent officers. It was an honour."

Haller blushed as the others gave him a brief round of polite applause. Captain Howell wasn't finished however. "We found so much more, as you now know, when we completed our examination of the remains of *U3000*. In one of the as yet undisturbed packing cases, instead of gold, we found a number of art treasures, sadly damaged by water seepage over the years, that may have been worth a small fortune back in 1945, and which were probably intended to help pay for the development of the new, revolutionary hydrodynamic drive."

"I thought that was the purpose of the gold," Brian Jones commented.

"So did we at first, Detective Inspector, but when we raised the safe from Max Ritter's cabin, which remained watertight through the years, we found a copy of his sealed orders. Apparently the gold was intended to be one of four similar shipments being made to a secret location in Argentina where the Nazis hoped to regroup and raise a new political party and a new army, with the stated intention of continuing Hitler's policies and eventually giving birth to a 'Fourth Reich' as stated in the orders."

"Four shipments?" Oscar Agostini asked. "So what happened to the other three?"

"A very good question, Detective Chief Inspector," Howell replied. He and Agostini had got on from the moment they'd met before the service. "We can only guess at present. Maybe all or some of those shipments reached their destination, maybe they ended up on the bottom of the sea. We were kind of hoping that a very clever and well respected naval historian might be willing to work with a joint committee from the Royal Naval Archives Branch and their German counterparts in trying to trace just what did happen to those shipments."

He looked directly at Klaus Haller who, realising that Howell was referring to him, clasped his hands together in excitement and exclaimed,

"I would be honoured, highly honoured, thank you."

"No, it is we who thank you, Herr Haller."

"So the hydrodynamic engine never saw operational service?" Ross asked the captain.

"No Andy, not during the war at any rate. The experimental engine fitted to *U3000* had undergone sea trials with limited success and Ritter might have been able to evade the entire British and American navies if it had been operational when he made his Channel dash, but he'd been forbidden from using it. The risks were too great of it malfunctioning at great depth and causing the loss of the U-Boat. It's rather ironic when you think how things turned out for Max Ritter and his crew.

So, anyway, what happens next to the bad guys you've now got safely in custody?"

"Oh, the law will take its course," Ross said. "Kelly will be tried in his own country of course and I believe when the United States hand out life sentences, they tend to mean life, so I don't think he'll be seeing the light of day again, and that's if he manages to escape a death sentence."

"And the men you arrested in Liverpool?"

"Ah well, Graham Young, a.k.a. Robin is singing like a canary, forgive the pun, and the one known as Starling, real name Billy Figgis, is being all big and brave, and a real hard case and won't talk, but we don't need his testimony, what with all we've learned from Young and of course, the big cheese, Randolph Lambert, known to his minions as Finch. Lambert is doing all he can to push as much blame onto Kelly as he can in an effort to lessen his sentence and avoid being extradited to some nasty country that might not be too humane in their treatment of prisoners."

This precipitated a round of laughter from the others.

"And what about Jeffrey Metcalfe?" Captain Howell asked. "D.I. Jones really surprised me when he told me of his involvement."

"Well, he won't be seeing freedom for some time either," Ross said, his face suddenly adopting a look of disgust at the mention of the man's name. "He's probably one of the most black-hearted, cold and calculating bastards I've ever encountered. When we questioned him, he cracked completely and told us everything. It seems he was more involved in Aaron Decker's murder than we thought. When Sally Metcalfe was offered the job with Aegis, Aaron was intrigued and he did everything we already knew about, but there was something else. While he was down in Falmouth, he happened to see a number of Advance Transportation's lorries coming and going from the Aegis facility. At that time, Aaron of course suspected that Aegis were up to no good, and innocently, he became concerned that his girlfriend's father might have been unwittingly dragged into their plot, by them using his trucks for nefarious purposes. Not believing Sally's father could be part of the criminal activities, Aaron went to him with his suspicions. He might as well have signed his own death warrant, because there was no way Jeffrey Metcalfe was going to risk losing the vast sums of money he was making through his involvement with Francis Kelly. Metcalfe reported straight to Kelly, and Lambert was tasked with ensuring that Aaron Decker was 'taken care of' as Metcalfe coldly put it."

"What a bastard," said Prendergast, then, "do excuse my language, ladies."

Izzie and the other women smiled. They were used to much worse in their day to day work with the police. Izzie completed that part of the story while Ross took a breather.

"We all thought Aaron was targeted because he'd found out what they were up to and tried to blackmail those responsible, but in fact, when he'd said he thought he could make some money out of his discovery, it was because, in his own way, he probably thought he could make a few pounds from the story of the discovery of the two previously unknown World War Two shipwrecks. Aegis went as far as trying to buy him off, paying him to go away, but that only made him more suspicious apparently. Of course, once he found out what was really going on, his sole motive was to protect his girlfriend, Sally, from what he thought were unscrupulous people who might have conned her father. He paid a high price for his naïve attempt at chivalry."

Everyone fell silent for a few seconds. Thoughts of a young man imbued with old-fashioned standards of 'doing the right thing' filling most of their minds.

"Where is Aaron's father by the way, Inspector?" George Baldacre asked. "I thought he and his family would be here today."

"He very much wanted to be here," Ross replied, "but Jerome Decker was recently appointed as head of a new C.I.A. international task force, set up to trace every last vestige of the crimes perpetrated by Kelly and his people. He and his family left London two weeks ago and I really don't know where they are now. Knowing Mr. Decker, he'll never rest until every last minion of Kelly's, down to the most insignificant customs official or museum employee around the world is brought to justice. The U.S. embassy was represented here today though, and I'm wondering where he is, as a matter of fact. Last I saw, he was chatting to one of the Members of Parliament who showed up today."

Right on cue a loud voice could be heard calling, "Andy, Andy Ross," and they all turned to see a tall, immaculately dressed man striding along the path towards them. Ross stood up to greet the newcomer.

"Ethan, it's good to see you," he said as he shook hands with his old friend. "Everyone, please say hello to Ethan Tiffen. Ethan works for the U.S. Immigration Service and was here to represent the Decker family and the embassy today. Ethan and I have known each other since he helped me out on a case a few years ago."

"Sorry I couldn't get away sooner, Andy," Tiffen apologised "Those M.P.s of your sure can talk. Anyway, good to meet you all. Jerome Decker sends his good wishes and apologies but our government decided he was needed somewhere else and fast. As he said, they've already buried Aaron and held his funeral service and memorial service so this was really more for the families of those boys who were lost at sea all those years ago. He hopes you all understand."

"Of course we do, Ethan. If you ever talk to him in the future, tell him we all wish him well, his family too, and thank him for the help he gave us in our investigation, okay?"

"You got it, Andy, no problem."

"So you don't know where Mr. Decker is?" Agostini asked the question.

"I don't, I'm afraid, and even if I did I'm afraid that information would be regarded as highly confidential."

"I won't say another word," Agostini said, as Ethan Tiffen reached into the inside pocket of his jacket, pulled something from it and passed it to Andy Ross.

Ross looked at the postcard Tiffen had given him and saw a picture of the Great Pyramid of Giza. Turning it over, Ross saw nothing had been written on the card, leaving nothing but a blank space. His brow furrowed for a second until he saw Tiffen wink at him. Ross nodded back, so imperceptibly no one else would have noticed. Jerome Decker was in Egypt, he was certain, taking up the chase for the missing antiquities and treasure that he knew had been passed through Cairo on their way to various dealers and collectors. Ross almost felt sorry for those who were about to be hunted down by Decker and his fellow

C.I.A. operatives. He'd heard a few stories about the ways in which the C.I.A. worked within foreign borders, and the methods they sometimes employed and he had no doubt that more than a few lives would never be the same again once Jerome and his team tracked them down.

"So, that just about wraps everything up, I suppose," Charles Howell said. "I can only say that it's been something of a privilege working with you all. Seeing the way in which you gradually pieced the case together has been, well, educational to say the least."

"Whoa there, Charles," Ross said forcefully. "Let's get this straight. Without the initial help of Captain Prendergast, followed by the wonderful cooperation from the Navy, and you and your crew and those on the *Whitehaven Castle*, all that technology, the submersibles and so on we'd never have solved a thing. All of us are grateful to you and everyone else who helped us."

"We are quite the mutual admiration society today, are we not?" Klaus Haller smiled as he spoke.

"And you all deserve to be, Herr Haller," Oscar Agostini told the little German historian. "I've been a policeman for more years than I care to remember and I can honestly say I've never seen such wonderful inter-agency and international cooperation and determination to succeed as I have in this case. My boss, Detective Chief Superintendant Sarah Hollingsworth has authorised me to invite you all to lunch before we go our separate ways, courtesy of the Merseyside Police."

A round of spontaneous applause broke out among the little group seated there on the grass in the shadow of Exeter's beautiful Gothic cathedral.

"Wow," said Brian Jones. "I wish our Chief Super would be so generous once in a while."

"Ha, not much chance of that," Sergeant St. Clair added.

Three hours later, after a superb meal in one of Exeter's finest restaurants, the group finally began to break up, with the Royal Naval Captain, Charles Howell the first to depart, needing to return to his ship before evening, followed soon after by Captain Prendergast, who had a long journey to London ahead of him. Promises were made to keep in touch in future, such were the bonds that had been formed during the case, perhaps none as strong as those between Ross and Drake and their Cornish counterparts, Jones and St. Clair.

Relieved the case was over, and pleased to have put the perpetrators of so many crimes behind bars, it was nonetheless with a sense of some regret that Andy Ross and Izzie Drake finally drove away from Exeter later that day, followed by McLennan, Dodds, and Curtis in one car, and Oscar Agostini in another, driven by Sam Gable.

For now, their time on the south coast was over. As Izzie put it,

"Let's try not to have to take too many sea cruises in future, eh sir?"

"Feet on dry land, Izzie, that's a promise."
He couldn't have been more wrong.

Epilogue

Liverpool a month later.

"I can't see her, sir, can you?" Izzie Drake asked as she and Ross walked along the waterfront. Behind them, the world famous Royal Liver Building, The Cunard Building and the Port of Liverpool Building, collectively known as the Three Graces dominated the skyline, as they have done for over a century. Their brickwork glistened in the autumn sunshine, the three buildings providing a majestic vista for those arriving by sea at the port of Liverpool.

"Not yet, Izzie, but she asked us to meet her here. Maybe she's been delayed."

The two detectives walked slowly, the path lined by young trees planted to add a touch of natural beauty to the overall effect of Liverpool's already impressive waterfront. The phone call Ross had received earlier had taken him by surprise but he felt a sense of obligation to answer the plea from Sally

Metcalfe to meet her right where they now sought her.

"Look sir, is that her, over there?" Izzie pointed to where a young woman, dressed all in black, sat on the wall close to the water's edge a hundred yards away, seemingly staring out over the water.

The detectives quickened their pace and sure enough, as they drew closer, they both recognised the hunched figure as being that of Sally Metcalfe.

"Sally?" said Ross quietly, not wanting to startle the young woman, who slowly turned to face them. Ross could see she'd been crying, and was even now fighting hard to control her emotions. "Is everything alright?"

"Inspector Ross. Sergeant Drake, thank you for coming," Sally replied, ignoring Ross's direct question.

"You look upset, Sally," Drake said quietly. "What can we do for you?"

Sally hopped down from the wall, and began to walk along, towards the pier head. Ross and Drake looked at one another and followed, quickly catching her up and walking with her, one to her left the other on her right. After they'd walked for about ten seconds in a silence that seemed like a lifetime to the detectives, Sally at last began to speak.

"I'm leaving Liverpool for good, Inspector, the university, everything. None of it means anything any more. I wanted you to know that."

"I see," Ross replied. "You're going home to Lancaster, I presume?"

"No, I can't go back there either. The shame of knowing what my Dad did is just too great. My Mum's a broken woman, Inspector. All those years she loved him, lived with him, even worked with him and never knew what a black-hearted villain he really was, it's proved too much for her. She's moved out of the house, has filed for divorce and is staying with her sister in Leyland until she figures out what she intends to do"

"I see," Ross said, a little confused, "so you ...?"

"I'm staying with a friend in New Brighton until I begin my new job."

"A new job? But your post-grad studies, the offer from Aegis?" Izzie asked.

"I could never work for the Aegis Institute after what my father did, Sergeant Drake. Oh, I know the actual Institute is genuine and legal, but it's still Aegis isn't it? My father had poor Aaron killed when all he tried to do was protect me, didn't he, Inspector Ross?"

Ross nodded, unable to deny the truth of Sally's words.

"I'm afraid so, Sally," was his short reply.

"So, what job are you talking about, Sally?" Drake asked.

"I've managed to secure a post with the British Antarctic Survey," Sally replied. "I'll be sailing on the *Ocean Venturer* in six weeks. I'm qualified to fill a number of scientific study posts and they're glad to have me. The pay isn't fantastic but the experience will be terrific for me and help with my future."

"Well, we can only wish you well, Sally, and I really mean that," said Ross.

Sally Metcalfe halted in her stride, looking out over the water for a few seconds. Ross could sense she wanted to say more and knew that silence was often the best way to get a witness to talk, just give them time to pull their thoughts together. Sure enough, Sally turned to face him and asked the question that must have been burning into her brain since she first found out the truth behind Aaron Decker's murder.

"Why did they use Tim and Martin, Inspector Ross? What on earth could have turned Aaron's friends, well, I thought they were his friends, into killers?"

Ross looked at Sally with a sadness in his eyes that he couldn't hide. He really felt for this girl who had unwittingly been a pawn in the deadly game that had been played out across continents, but that had come home to roost directly in her own back yard, figuratively speaking.

"Money, Sally, one of the oldest motivators in the book, allied in Tim's case with a large slice of jealousy."

"Tim was jealous of me?"

"Well, of you being with Aaron, yes."

"I thought that was all over, that he knew it was never going to happen between us."

"The thing is, Sally, his mind never actually accepted that you didn't 'fancy' him. He thought that if you hadn't met Aaron he'd have still had a chance with you. Then of course, there was the cricket."

"You're not seriously telling me that boring old cricket formed part of his motive for murder?"

"I'm afraid it did," Ross said, shaking his head as he spoke. "When Aaron came along, Tim lost what he thought was his place as the pin-up boy of the university cricket team. All of a sudden, along came this American who could play cricket better than a native, and as Aaron racked up more and more playing records, so Tim's inner resentment grew. Aaron quickly established a record for bowling the most maiden overs in a season, followed by the best batting returns anyone could remember for a long time, and when you combined those statistics with Tim's latent and irrational thoughts about his relationship with you, it added up to a motive for murder, which a man called Randolph Lambert, who worked for Francis Kelly, the man behind the illegal activities being conducted under the Aegis name was quick to exploit."

"But how did he know all this about Tim? And what about Martin? Why did he get involved?"

"Let me explain, Sally," Izzie Drake said, giving Ross a break. "When your father passed all the information relating to Aaron to Francis Kelly, it was passed on to Lambert, head of Kelly's internal security force. Usually Lambert would have sent one of his hired killers to do the job, but he saw a way to get the job done without involving his people, using Tim and Martin, who was up to his neck in debt to some not very understanding people and this was his chance to clear that debt and get a fresh start. Lambert's people are clever and resourceful. He simply sent a couple of his men along to find out the easiest way to eliminate Aaron."

Sally physically flinched at Izzie's words.

"Sorry, Sally but there's no way to sugar coat what took place. They must have spent time on campus, learning all they could about Aaron, probably even befriended him, bought him a few drinks, same with his two housemates, which is how they probably learned of Tim Knight's feelings for you and his resentment of Aaron. They probably came here intending to do the job themselves but when they identified the possibility of using a couple of outside dupes to do their dirty work it was too good an opportunity to pass up. We later found out that your father was the source of the ketamine used in the murder, through a pharmaceutical company he'd done work for."

By now, Sally Metcalfe was in tears, understandably, and Ross gave Izzie a look that said he thought they'd told the young woman enough.

Izzie dutifully fell silent and instead took a pace towards Sally, wrapping a comforting arm around her shoulder until the girl managed to stop crying and with a heave of her shoulders, composed herself once again.

"Thank you for telling me everything," she said eventually, at the same time withdrawing an envelope from her handbag, which she passed to Ross.

"I really asked you to meet me today because I wanted you to have these, Inspector Ross," she said as Ross slowly opened the unsealed flap of the envelope and removed the contents.

The first of the two photographs Ross extracted showed Aaron Decker in his wet suit, his head bare, seated on a quayside he recognised from his visit to Falmouth. Aaron was smiling and giving a thumbs-up sign to the camera. The second photo showed an equally happy and smiling T.J. Knowles, dressed in t-shirt and brightly coloured floral patterned knee-length shorts, looking for all the world like an eager surfer, ready to ride the waves. Ross smiled at the sight of the two young men, and wondered why Sally wanted Sally wanted him to have them.

"You never met or knew Aaron, Inspector," she explained. "You worked so hard to solve his murder, and I just wanted you to see him when he was alive, happy and with his whole life ahead of him, so you won't just think of him as a dead body in future when you recall any thoughts you may have of him. The same goes for the other man. I never knew him either, but it's obvious they became good friends and it's better to remember him like this than as a floating body, shackled to a sunken ship, don't you think?"

Ross understood and felt privileged that Sally Metcalfe had chosen to share these memories of Aaron Decker and T.J. Knowles with him, but still had a question for her.

"I really appreciate these, Sally, thank you, and I know exactly what you're telling me by giving them to me, but where did they come from? They might have proved useful earlier in the investigation. And, don't you want to keep these yourself?"

"I only received them a few days ago," Sally replied. "One of Aaron's tutors found them tucked in between the pages of a book Aaron had been using for some research matter, and he'd not looked at it for some time. He picked it up and they fell out and he thought I might like to have them. The ones I've given you are copies, I still have the originals."

"Well, thank you again, Sally," Ross said. "They certainly will help me in remembering Aaron and T.J. in the proper manner. I never forget the victims in any investigation I carry out, but these photos will serve to remind me of the humanity of those who I seek justice for."

Ross couldn't think of anything else to say, and just placed the photos back in the envelope and transferred it to the inside pocket of his jacket. Izzie Drake gave Sally a hug, and added her thanks to those of her boss.

"I doubt we'll meet again, Inspector," Sally said as she prepared to take her leave of the detectives. "I've no desire to stay in England any longer than I have to and I've certainly no wish to return in a hurry once I've left all this pain and heartbreak behind."

Ross understood the young woman's feelings, but knew he had to say something to remind her there were still certain realities she'd have to face in the future.

"I know how you must feel, Sally, but there's still the matter of your father's trial. You may be needed as a witness."

"Oh, I hadn't thought of that," Sally said with a hurt look on her face.

"Well, there's a chance you won't have to give evidence," he replied, giving her a straw to clutch at. "Your father has admitted everything in his statements to us and if he pleads guilty to all charges when his trial opens, the judge might sentence him without need for you to give evidence."

"Oh, I do hope so," Sally said, hope appearing in her expression as she spoke. "We haven't been informed of a trial date yet, but as far as I'm concerned he can rot on remand for ever until it's time. He used to be a decent man, Inspector. If there's a shred of decency left in him, he'll do the right thing and save me and my poor Mum from having to testify against him."

"I hope he will, too Sally. It certainly won't do his case any good for a jury to see and hear his own wife and daughter testifying against him on such serious charges."

With that, Sally Metcalfe took Andy Ross completely by surprise as she stepped in front of him, stood on tiptoe, threw her arms around his neck and planted a kiss on his cheek before pulling away, saying a quiet "Thank you," and standing in front of him again smiling up at him.

"Wow," said Ross. "What did I do to deserve that?"

"You just gave me hope," Sally replied. "If I do have to come back, perhaps the British Antarctic Survey

People will be able to get me home, given enough notice. They have planes as well as ships, so we'll cross that bridge if and when we come to it."

"I had to tell you about the trial, Sally, you understand that don't you?"

"Yes, but I don't think my father will want either me or my mother testifying against him in court, so it's likely he'll plead guilty, I think. He wasn't always a bad man, so maybe he still has a spark of decency in him, somewhere."

"Let's hope so, eh, Sally?"

Izzie reached out and gave Sally a quick girlie hug and whispered, "good luck," in her ear, and then stood back.

Sally Metcalfe looked as if she was about to speak again, but instead she simply flashed a big smile at the two detectives, and took a step backwards.

"Well, better be off then," she suddenly said and turned on her heel before anyone could say another word and with that, Sally Metcalfe walked away from the two detectives, who watched as her diminutive figure grew ever smaller as she drew further away from them until she eventually disappeared into a small crowd of people walking in the same direction she was.

"Well, that was unusual," Ross said to Izzie Drake, who smiled at him.

"What, the photos or the kiss?" she grinned.

"Well, both, I suppose," Ross replied. "I feel sorry for that young woman. She's lost her boyfriend, her family's effectively been destroyed, her father's facing trial and facing life imprisonment and her career's destroyed before it had even begun, and yet she still has more humanity and depth of feeling in her than many people twice her age. I think I'll always remember Sally Metcalfe as The Mersey Maiden, in honour of the case and its cricketing connections."

"You're just an old softy at heart, sir, you know that don't you?"

"Hey, I'm just a well worn old copper, Izzie, one who's been round the block a few too many times, but can still be surprised now and then."

"Yeah, sure, I'll believe you," Drake smiled at her boss.

"She's going to need a lot of mental strength to get through the next couple of years, that's for sure,"

"I have a feeling she'll make it alright, sir."

Andy Ross nodded in response to Izzie's words. There seemed little he could add.

Ross and Drake took a slow walk back to headquarters, for the most part both being content with a companionable silence, each lost in their own private thoughts on the immensely complex and at times emotionally upsetting case they finally felt was drawing to a close. They still had information to glean from Lambert and Young, and maybe even Starling if and when he cracked, and the Americans would doubtless learn much from Francis Kelly, but until the trials, their involvement was almost over.

* * *

Later, alone in his office, Andy Ross sat at his desk looking at the two photographs Sally Metcalfe had presented him with. He opened the top drawer of his desk, and removed two drawing pins from a small container. Rising, he walked across to where a cork-board hung on the wall opposite his desk and carefully pinned the photos in place directly in the centre, amidst duty rosters, various flyers and notices pertaining to routine police business. Returning to his desk, he sat down, opened the bottom drawer of his desk and removed a bottle of Glenmorangie and a small whisky glass, placing them on the desk in front of him. He kept the whisky for special occasions, and it had been quite a while since the bottle last saw the light of day. After wiping the whisky tumbler out with a tissue, he poured himself a small measure, stood up and looked across his office at the photographs of Aaron Decker and T.J. Knowles.

Ross held the glass up in front of his face for a second, surveying the amber liquid within, then gestured with the glass towards the cork board on the opposite wall.

"I won't forget you lads, or your Mersey Maiden, Aaron, that's a promise," Ross said, and then gulped the fiery Scotch down in one in a final toast to the two young men.

He'd just returned the bottle to the drawer, leaving the glass on his desk to rinse later when Izzie Drake knocked and entered his office, balancing two coffees on a plastic tray.

"Thought you might want one," she said and Ross motioned for her to come in and sit down.

"Aha, caught you," she smiled, seeing the whisky glass and easily being able to smell the lingering fumes of Glenmorangie.

"Guilty pleasures, Izzie," he smiled in return. "Want one?"

"No thanks," she declined his offer. You know I'm not big on spirits. Got any red wine in that drawer?"

"Sorry," he apologised.

"Oh well, maybe another time. Suppose the coffee will have to do for now."

Ross was about to speak when the phone on his desk rang. Ross lifted the receiver, then recognised the voice at the other end of the line and gestured to Izzie, who pressed the button on the base unit of the phone that switched on the speakerphone facility. He obviously wanted her to hear this conversation.

"Mr. Decker," Ross said in surprise. "Good to hear from you. Where are you calling from?"

"I can't tell you that, Inspector, but please, call me Jerome. I think we've worked together long enough for you to use my given name. Did you get my message from Ethan by the way?"

"I did, thanks," Ross acknowledged, knowing that Decker was in Cairo though he wouldn't say so on an open telephone line. "And call me Andy, please."

"Okay Andy, that's great. How's that beautiful, sexy little sergeant of yours?"

"I'm fine, thank you Mr. Decker," Izzie said, knowing Decker was unaware they were on speakerphone.

"Ouch, you got me, Sergeant Drake," Decker half laughed.

"Don't worry," Izzie replied. "I might have been offended if you'd said *'How's that fat ugly little sergeant of yours?'* but beautiful and sexy I can live with, thanks."

"Okay," Decker laughed again.

"So, Jerome, what can I do for you today?" Ross asked, intrigued to be hearing from the C.I.A. man.

"Oh, it's kind of more what I can do for you, Andy. I have some information you might find useful in putting the case to bed."

"Really? Please go on, you have my full attention."

"Right, well, I suppose you'd call this more of a postscript to the case really. It's just that it has such a twist to it that I just knew you'd want to hear about it."

"Okay, you've baited the hook and now you've got me dangling, Sergeant Drake too, so please tell me what you've got."

"Ah, well, it wouldn't do to keep a beautiful, sexy lady waiting would it?"

Izzie Drake visibly blushed this time. Decker continued.

"So, here goes. As you know, I'm in charge of certain matters pertaining to our friend in New York," an obvious reference to Francis Kelly. "Among other things, it was a priority to locate and impound those submarines. Kelly tried to escape in the *Aegis Explorer* and thanks to the cooperation of the Aegis Institute's CEO, we soon located and had orders sent to

554

the *Aegis Wanderer,* and *Aegis Seascape* to return to port where their crews were arrested and the vessels impounded."

Decker paused long enough for Ross to realise there was a 'but' coming. Ross again took the bait.

"That's only three subs accounted for, Jerome. You're going to tell me there was a problem with number four."

"You got it, Andy. The final submarine, one of the Kilo class vessels renamed the *Aegis Seaquest* received identical orders to the others but failed to respond at first. That's when the Aegis executives launched their own inquiry and found out that the *Aegis Seaquest* had undergone an extensive overhaul and engine modification when she last docked in Alaska."

"What kind of engine modification, Jerome?"

"Aha, you're quick, Andy, I'll give you that. It seems that Erich Ackermann possessed what he thought was a duplicate set of plans for the hydrodynamic propulsion system as installed on *U3000* or whatever goddamn number you want to give it. His mother either appropriated the plans or was given them to look after by the admirals at Kiel when the war looked lost. Somehow they survived and were eventually passed to Ackermann. Of course, they wanted to get their hands on the actual engine, which is partly why they tried to get their hands on *U3000*, but Kelly also ordered the engineers at the Kodiac Island facility to use the plans Ackermann gave him to retrofit the *Seaquest* with an updated version of the system, adding a few modern refinements."

"Kelly told you all this?"

"No, Andy. The engineers at the Kodiac base carried out the work in innocence, after Kelly told the Aegis board that his own research scientists and engineers had developed a potentially environmentally friendly means of ship and submarine propulsion. With no reason to disbelieve him, the board sanctioned the development costs and the project went ahead. The system was only installed on the *Aegis Seaquest* three months ago and was still undergoing extensive sea trials. The problem is, we believe the plans Ackermann's mother possessed were either incomplete or just a draft copy, one that was later modified before being fitted into Max Ritter's submarine. When he was told the submarine was missing, Kelly clammed up and wouldn't talk so the F.B.I. called the Germans who must have threatened Ackermann with God knows what if he didn't talk because he told them all he knew. He said he thought Kelly would use the plans in conjunction with the actual engines when they salvaged them, to create an improved version of the original. He never thought Kelly would try and build a system based on the draft plans alone.

Anyway, returning to the *Aegis Seaquest*, it transpired that after a day's silence from the sub following the recall order the Aegis Seaport facility received a short but frantic transmission from *Seaquest* which read, and I quote, *'Hydrodynamic system failure, unable to disengage. Nose down attitude, no con-*

trol. *Diesel override inoperative. Stuck on seabed, depth 200 fathoms.'* This was followed by her position. Two hundred fathoms is one thousand, two hundred feet, Andy."

"My God, this sounds reminiscent of the *U3000's* predicament," Ross said quietly. The look on Izzie Drake's face mirrored his own. "Don't mind me asking, Jerome, but just when did this take place?"

There was a silence at the other end of the line, just a few seconds before Decker replied, but enough for Ross to guess the answer wasn't going to be a positive one. Finally, Decker spoke again.

"A week ago."

"A week? And what's been done to find the submarine since then?"

"The Aegis board, by now fully aware of Kelly's crimes remember, contacted the F.B.I. and the U.S. Coastguard immediately. The biggest problem was that the submarine's last reported position placed her four hundred miles from land, west of Santiago in a relatively shallow section of the Pacific Ocean, off the coast of Chile. The Chilean government were made aware of the situation but possessed no ships capable of helping and the submarine was after all in international waters, so the U.S. Navy sent two destroyers and two of their best deep sea salvage vessels to the sub's last reported position."

"I have a feeling you wouldn't be telling me this unless there's some bad news involved, Jerome." Ross felt he had to comment.

"Yeah, you're right," Decker said, a hint of sadness in his voice. "I know you and the sergeant there will know what the salvage guys went through after your own recent experiences, you know, sending submersibles down and so on. To cut a long story short, by the time they reached the submarine it was too late. The *Seaquest* had literally nosedived into the seabed and become embedded in the mud and silt at the bottom of the ocean. Their air had run out Andy. Thirty men suffocated to death."

Decker fell silent.

"Tragic," Izzie Drake said as she and Ross assimilated the information.

"Even more deaths that, morally at least, can be laid at Kelly's door," Ross said eventually.

"Yes," Decker agreed. "It could have been more if she'd been fully crewed. The Russians originally used a crew of fifty-two on the Kilos, but of course, in civilian use, no weapons technicians and other specialists were needed."

"So that's it then?" Ross asked. "A bitter end to Kelly's plans."

"Well, yes, apart from another tragic little twist you'll be interested in," Decker replied. "You see, back in 1945, it seems the skipper of *U3000* or *U966*, whatever, slept with a young whore named Claudia Rheinhardt in a Kiel brothel just before sailing. She was young and inexperienced and part of a programme known as 'Whores for Hitler' where young women volunteered or in some cases were sent by their parents to work in up-market brothels, servicing German officers and high ranking civilian officials."

"That's sick," Drake shouted.

"True, Sergeant Drake, but they really believed they were helping the war effort, helping the Fuehrer by keeping his elite troops supplied with good sex."

"Yuk."

"So, anyway, soon after Ritter sailed Claudia Rheinhardt found herself pregnant. Even in the Nazi's organised brothels, birth control could be a hit-and-miss affair. Under normal circumstances the baby would have been born and sent into the Lebensborn programme, brought up in an orphanage, or adopted and raised by an approved couple to be part of Hitler's future master race. The war ended before that could happen and so the child was eventually born and raised by his mother who told the young growing boy many made-up stories of his war hero father. He was brought up bearing his mother's name and was in quite a lot of trouble as an adolescent; fights, petty crime and so on. He finally changed his name and joined the German Navy when he was eighteen, virtually disowned by Claudia, who died two years ago and left under a cloud years later after striking a senior officer. He was a submariner though, and was later recruited by Ackermann to command one of the submarines he'd paid for on behalf of the Aegis Institute. This was the man who was in command of the *Aegis Seaquest*. When he changed his name, he took the name of the man his mother told him was his father. Andy the captain of the *Aegis Seaquest* was Max Ritter."

"Bloody hell," said Ross.

"Oh my God," Drake exclaimed as she threw a hand over her mouth in shock.

"That's unbelievable," Ross added.

"I know, Andy, I know," said Decker. "He was nearly fifty eight years old and was Kelly's most trusted captain. He must have been told about his father's last mission by Ackermann and would probably have relished the opportunity to use the propulsion system his father first trialled at sea all those years ago."

"And he met an identical death to his father," Drake said softly.

"And in a similar way, he was working for an evil and unscrupulous leader," Ross added. "Thanks for telling us, Jerome. I suppose it's fitting that the case ends with a submarine disaster, after all that's taken place from the war through to today."

"Yes, I thought you'd think that way," Decker said. "Now, I'd better go back to work. I still have lots of people to see, places to go, you know what I mean?"

"I do, and I wish you luck, Jerome Decker the third," Ross said with great gravitas in his voice.

"And the same to you, Detective Inspector Ross, Sergeant Drake," Decker said and then, before they knew it, the line went dead. Decker was gone.

"Typical Yank," said Ross. "Always in a hurry."

"Nice of him to call though, eh sir?"

"Yes, it was Izzie. I suppose that really is the end of the case for us now, until the trials."

"I wonder…"

"What?" Ross asked.

"If the child born to Claudia Rheinhardt really was Max Ritter's? I mean, she was a whore after all. She must have slept with hundreds of men while working in that brothel. How could she be sure Ritter was the father?"

"We'll never know, Izzie, will we? Max Ritter was a hero at the time though, with his Knight's Cross and Oak Leaves. Maybe she thought it romantic to assume the father of her child was a famous U-Boat commander rather than one of the many run-of-the-mill officers she had to sleep with during her time in the brothel."

"I can understand that," Drake said softly. "She was little more than a kid herself when young Max was born. She probably wanted him to have a father figure to be proud of, rather than telling him he was the result of her copulating with dozens of unknown men in a seedy Nazi brothel. I wonder if he ever found out the truth about his birth?"

"That's just one more unanswerable question, Izzie, something nobody can answer. With her being dead and the younger Max too, it really does feel like the real end of the case, thank God."

"I can't say I'll miss it," Drake sighed, "even if we did meet some interesting people along the way. It's weird to think that it really started and ended with a man named Max Ritter. If you don't mind, I'll call

Carole St. Clair later and give her and Brian the news about the submarine and the younger Max Ritter. I'd like to think we might work with her and D.I. Jones again one day."

"Same here, and yes, by all means give her a call, say hello to her and Brian from me," said Ross, as he rose from his chair. "Come on Izzie, let's go tell the others about Decker's news. Better not forget the D.C.I. too."

"He's okay to work for, Mr. Agostini, isn't he, sir?"

"He's a good bloke, yes. We worked together in our younger days, you know that of course?"

"Yes, heard all about it. You two got up to some real tricks back in the day, so I hear."

"Right, well, enough of that," Ross laughed. "Let's go talk to the team, and you know what, Izzie?"

"What, sir?"

"I'm going to give everyone the rest of the day off, including me and you."

"But what about D.C.I. Agostini, sir?"

"Oh alright, he can have the rest of the day off too."

Drake's laughter was so loud, so infectious that Ross couldn't stop himself from joining in. It was good to laugh again.

Little did they know however, that at that moment, on the continent that the original Max Ritter had been heading for many years earlier, the seeds of their next case had already been sown...

Dear reader,

We hope you enjoyed reading *A Mersey Maiden*. Please take a moment to leave a review, even if it's a short one. Your opinion is important to us.

The story continues in *A Mersey Mariner*.

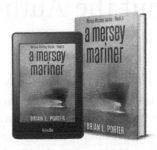

To read the first chapter for free, please head to: https://www.nextchapter.pub/books/a-mersey-mariner

Discover more books by Brian L. Porter at https://www.nextchapter.pub/authors/brian-porter-mystery-author-liverpool-united-kingdom

Want to know when one of our books is free or discounted? Join the newsletter at http://eepurl.com/bqqB3H

Best regards,

Brian L. Porter and the Next Chapter Team

About the Author

Brian L Porter is an award-winning author, whose books have also regularly topped the Amazon Best Selling charts. Writing as Brian, he has won a Best Author Award, and his thrillers have picked up Best Thriller and Best Mystery Awards. His short story collection *After Armageddon* recently achieved Amazon Bestseller status and his moving collection of remembrance poetry, *Lest We Forget*, is also an Amazon best seller

Writing as Harry Porter his children's books have achieved three bestselling rankings on Amazon in the USA and UK.

In addition, his third incarnation as romantic poet Juan Pablo Jalisco has brought international recognition with his collected works, *Of Aztecs and Conquistadors* topping the bestselling charts in the USA, UK and Canada.

Brian lives with his wife, children and a wonderful pack of ten rescued dogs. On the subject of dogs, please take a look at Brian's latest release, *SASHA, A very Special Dog Tale of a very special Epi-Dog* published by Next Chapter, which tells the remarkable real-life story of Sasha, Brian's very own 'miracle dog' whose story will both entertain and inspire readers as you read her incredible tale of survival and happiness against all odds!

He is also the in-house screenwriter for Thunder-Ball Films, (L.A.), for whom he is also a co-producer on a number of their current movie projects.

A Mersey Killing has already been optioned for movie adaptation, in addition to his other novels, all of which have been signed by ThunderBall Films in a movie franchise deal.

A Mersey Mariner

The *Alexandra Rose* sailed into the Mersey Estuary accompanied by an all enveloping fog. The doleful tone of the ship's foghorn announced her presence to any ships in the close vicinity. A slow passage of just over three weeks had brought the ageing cargo liner, its crew and small complement of passengers on a slow voyage across the Atlantic from Rio and the ship itself appeared tired and weary from the journey. Captain George Gideon rang the telegraph, signalling 'All Stop' and the *Alexandra Rose's* diesels ceased their rhythmic throbbing as the ship slowly came to a halt and Gideon awaited the arrival of the Mersey Pilot Boat to escort the ship into port.

Gideon dispatched his second officer, Robert Gray to inform the passengers of the short delay in entering port. Soon afterwards Gray returned to the bridge to inform the captain that one of their passengers lay dead in his cabin.

With no readily visible signs of violence on the body and the ship's doctor suspecting foul play, Gideon informed the port authorities who in turn notified Merseyside Police.

So begins one of Detective Andy Ross's most baffling cases, as the dead man was travelling alone and appeared to have no connections to any of the other passengers or crew of the *Alexandra Rose*. When a second body, a crew member from the unfortunate *Alexandra Rose* is discovered in similar circumstances a week later in a local hotel, Ross and his assistant, Sergeant Clarissa (Izzie) Drake must deploy all their investigative talents in an effort to untangle the web of mystery surrounding the two deaths.

A Mersey Mariner is the fourth book in the Mersey Mystery series, featuring Detective Inspector Andy Ross Ross, Sergeant Izzie Drake and their specialist murder investigation team.

A Mersey Maiden
ISBN: 978-4-86747-027-5 (Mass Market)

Published by
Next Chapter
1-60-20 Minami-Otsuka
170-0005 Toshima-Ku, Tokyo
+818035793528
17th May 2021

Lightning Source UK Ltd.
Milton Keynes UK
UKHW040705260521
384404UK00001B/55

9 784867 470275